HARM'S WAY

A Novel

by

Clarke Wallace

© Copyright 2019 Clarke Wallace

All rights reserved.

No portion of this book may be reproduced in whole or in part, by any means whatsoever, except for passages excerpted for the purposes of review, without the prior written permission of the publisher.

For information, or to order additional copies, please contact:

Beacon Publishing Group
P.O. Box 41573 Charleston, S.C. 29423
800.817.8480| beaconpublishinggroup.com

Publisher's catalog available by request.

ISBN-13: 978-1-949472-78-3

ISBN-10: 1-949472-78-7

Published in 2019. New York, NY 10001.

First Edition. Printed in the USA.

Mind-altering chemicals will make a conventional war of the future, potentially as dangerous as nuclear warfare.

Richard A. Gabriel
Former Pentagon intelligence officer & author
'No More Heroes': Madness and Psychiatry in War

PRINCIPAL CHARACTERS

WASHINGTON

Edward W. Grosvenor—Head of Special Projects, CIA (operations)
Gerry Smith—his Assistant
Nicole Hagen—CIAID, CIA (research)
Nathan Edgars—Federal Dept. of Science & Technology

MOSCOW

Vladimir Alexandrovich Lyubimov—Federal Security Service (FSB)
Olga Tuseva—assistant to Lyubimov
Leopold Sergeevich Baranov—Russian Academy of Science
Col. Yury Nikolayev Petrovich—Military Intelligence (GRU)
Boris Fyodorovich Yevtushenko—Russian scientist

CREW TSS CASIMIR III (Gydnia)

Captain Stanislaw Jablonski
Chief Engineer Henryk Niski

Lt. Filip Sotek—Entertainment Officer
Junior Officer Jerzy Olecki
Chief Officer Pawel Klimek
Dr. Ludwik Dudek
Dr. Helena Witka

PASSENGERS

Harmon C. Page
Leszek Poplawski
Thomas E. Slater
Hugh & Gweneth Ashcroft
Kim & Angus Stockwell
Victor Petrie
Peter Lount

CHAPTER ONE
Saturday, October 1, 9:12 PM

On a brisk Saturday evening, Boris Fyodorovich Yevtushenko and his wife Anna Karlovna arrived at their favorite Moscow restaurant. They enjoyed the Café Troika with its cozy elegance of brass lamps, stained glass windows, and colorful carpets hanging on the walls.

The maitre d' guided them to the smaller, intimate dining room. Boris shook hands and exchanged easy banter, as was his habit, with those familiar faces at nearby tables.

At seventy-five, he had lost none of his lust for life. His booming voice alone was a tribute to this raucous, mountain of a man who, belying his seemingly good health, was kept alive by a pacemaker embedded in his chest.

Boris paused by a lone patron poking at a small electronic notebook between sips of what the elderly Russian took for *dovta*, a sour milk soup. Despite the man's small, black moustache, he looked familiar. Especially the eyes. Unable to place him, Boris walked on.

The couple was well into a *narkurma* of fresh lamb when he felt the first jolt of an errant heartbeat. Watchful of her husband's well-being, Anna asked if anything was wrong. He assured her it was nothing, when jagged heartbeats tore at his insides.

Boris staggered to his feet, deafened by the sound of his own blood pounding in his ears. Wallops from the pacemaker jarred him as his outstretched fingers grabbed at the table. Unable to hang on, he toppled backward, taking the tablecloth and everything on it with him.

Anna Karlovna dropped to her knees amid the clutter of dishes and broken glass to gather her husband in her arms.

The trembling stopped with Boris Fyodorovich's dead, gray eyes staring up at her.

On an empty stretch of Shore Road hugging the ocean water north of York Harbor, Maine, a stereo-thumping muscle car with dark tinted windows cranked in behind a lone Toyota. Its driver, taking the occupants for teens raising hell on a Saturday night, waved them on to have the large, black vehicle hug his rear bumper.

It wasn't until they reached the Bald Cliff cut-off when the Chrysler swung into the oncoming lane and slammed broadside into the smaller car. The driver hit the gas to be battered headlong into the guardrails strung with the rusting steel cables.

The Toyota shot out into the empty void, dragging with it a maze of tangled wire and snapping posts as it dropped to the ocean below.

Its airbags exploded on impact. The car bobbed on the surface before sinking nose-first. Water poured in through the battered door and from under the dashboard.

The dazed driver, impeded by the seatbelt and cumbersome airbag, fumbled in the dark for the window switches to discover the car had lost its electric power.

A sudden jarring shook the vehicle. He felt it tip to one side then the other, coming to a grinding halt upright among what to him were boulders on the ocean floor. Unable to release the jammed seatbelt clip, he pulled on the lever to recline his seat.

The water was neck-high as he worked himself out from under the lap portion of the belt. He kicked off his loafers and wriggled free of his jacket. Forcing himself to keep moving, he struck the driver's door with his shoulder. Getting nowhere he tried the passenger side with no better luck.

Aware boulders were jamming both doors, he worked himself into the back seat, pulling it down to escape through the trunk.

With his lungs on fire, he moved his lips along the roof's soft under-padding. Finding a small pocket of air, he sucked in what he could, knowing it might be his last breath.

He ducked down again, the sting of salt water trickling into his nostrils. He shoved his arms through the round opening, wedged his feet against the passenger seat and drove his body forward, feeling the sharp edge of the steel plate tearing at his shirt.

Once inside the cramped space taken up mostly by his over-sized golf bag, he snagged the trunk's lid release as the trickle of salt water in his nostrils became a flood.

He felt himself floating free, his mind separating from his physical self as the burning sensation in his chest was replaced by a euphoria of giving up the struggle.

It was then an innate sense of survival took over, forcing his leaden arms and legs to drive him up toward the surface.

A light flashed through the water above him. With it came a blast of cool night air as sputum mixed with salt water erupted from his mouth and nose. He opened his eyes to a fuzzy outline of light bouncing along the high embankment. His shout for help surprised him, coming as an eerie, high-pitched squeak.

The beam jumped back along the uneven cribbing of large broken boulders and swung out over the water.

A startled voice broke the stillness. "Good Lord!"

The driver squinted at the bright light, his body wracked by spasms of coughing.

"Are you…the sonofabitch…who ran me off the road?"

"No, son. I'm a priest. I noticed the broken guardrails—"

"Bless you, Father," said the driver, coughing up more ocean.

CHAPTER TWO
Monday, October 3, 10:15 AM

Thin-haired Ira Neddick, senior officer of the Maine state police in Kittery, was well into a breakfast of assorted donuts, when Constable Johnson appeared in his office doorway.

"He's here," said the younger man, nodding back over his shoulder.

"Let 'em wait," said Ira, picking out his favorite, a chocolate dip.

Word had reached the detachment in the early hours of Sunday morning. Ira was told a car had smashed through guardrails on the Bald Cliff cut-off ending up in the ocean. The driver was in bad shape when dropped off at the York County Hospital's emergency entrance, according to his two-man night staff.

Ira recognized the name: Harmon C. Page. The same dude who'd bought the old rambling, clapboard house out on Moody Point, near Ogunquit. Prospective buyers had shown little interest until this hotshot from Washington, D.C. had scooped up the property for a song.

Why anyone would squirrel himself away in the middle of nowhere to live in a drafty pile of timber, was beyond Ira. Unless, he decided, he had something to hide.

"What was he driving?" he asked, pushing himself away from the desk. "A submersible?"

Johnson grinned. "No. An ordinary red Toyota two-door."

"You told him it's still parked where he left it?"

"I thought you might tell him, chief. He's pissed off because you haven't given a green light on having it hauled out of the ocean."

Ira polished off one of two remaining chocolate dips. "What's the rush?"

"Don't ask me. The ER docs told him he was lucky to be alive. Having been diagnosed with symptoms of hypothermia. More tests were needed, for possible internal injuries. Page ignored them by signing himself out of the hospital."

"Sounds like he was operating a motor vehicle while under the influence." Ira came over to the door, holding out the carton of donuts. "We'd have nailed his ass to the wall, had our night crew not screwed up the breathalyzer."

"Don't blame them." Johnson helped himself to a glazed donut. "It was too late by the time they got the call." He pointed to the blue folder over on his superior's cluttered desk. "It's all there, with Page claiming he was run off the road."

Ira looked Page over. He was lean and younger than he had imagined. Late thirties, early forties, a shade over six feet. Brownish hair, sideburns touched with gray. Nor did he expect a scientist of his reputation to parade around in faded jeans, an open denim shirt, and a leather jacket.

Tight mouth, erect shoulders assured him this guy would be one big pain in the ass.

Ira started across the room. "Always insist on a breathalyzer, Johnson," he said aloud. "It'll save you one hell of a lotta grief."

The policeman plunked the donuts down on the counter.

"G'morning, Mister Page. I'm Sergeant Neddick."

Harm nailed him with hostile blue eyes.

"I'm damn near killed, and your biggest worry is a botched breathalyzer test?"

"Only because you admitted to my night crew you'd been drinking. A 'breather would've confirmed it."

"Confirmed what? That I had two glasses of white wine with my *seafood linguine*?"

"Could be enough." Ira looked among the donuts for the last chocolate dip. "It's not commonly known that the human liver takes an hour to metabolize one third of an ounce of alcohol. Besides, you insisted a second vehicle forced you off the road. Which is inconsistent with what my crew found at the scene."

Ira waited for a response. None came. "Our preliminary report of your impact with the guardrail indicates excessive speed. A single set of skid marks was found on the gravel shoulder, back from where you sailed out over the water…"

"Because the bastard driving the muscle car had no reason to brake." Harm eyed the donuts. "I told your guys as much. I also suggested they look for a late-model Chrysler. Black. A damaged right front fender with obvious traces of red paint from my Toyota. Nor did they show any interest when I mentioned the Washington D.C. plates."

Ira eased the donuts across the counter. "A description of the driver would help."

"If you read the incident report, you'd know I couldn't *see* him through the tinted windows. But then, you've already decided I was pissed."

"It crossed my mind."

"And you've yet to sign off having my Toyota pulling out of the ocean. My insurance rep has been asking you to do it. The key is still in the ignition. To say nothing of what the salt water will do to my cell phone. Or golf clubs."

"Shrink them?" Ira mused. "What are they? *Callaways?*"

"*Wilsons*. I was taking them to Los Angeles later today. But thanks to you—"

"For how long?"

"A few days."

"Back to Saturday night. Where did you have your seafood linguine? And who with?"

"It's in the report."

"I want to hear it from you."

Saying nothing, Harm pulled out a BlackBerry to check for messages.

"You told me you left your cell in the vehicle?"

"This is a loner from my *helpful* insurance agent." Harm shoved it back in his jeans. "What bothers him is why you haven't authorized having it hauled ashore."

"Priorities, Mister Page. Tell me more about where you were before driving home?"

"Having a late dinner in Kittery."

"Accompanied by—?"

Harm picked the lone chocolate dip, and headed for the entrance. "That's my business."

"I have more questions, Mister Page—" Ira called out, bothered by him taking the last chocolate dip.

"We'll talk," said Harm over his shoulder. "Once you've fished my car out of the ocean."

CHAPTER THREE
Monday, October 3, 11:32 AM (Moscow)

Vladimir Alexandrovic Lyubimov, in a worsted gray suit and tan cashmere coat, trudged along the park's cinder path, his face reflecting the stubborn look of someone far from enjoying himself. He blamed his mood on a friend who couldn't get it through his thick skull that meeting in the middle of nowhere was *no* guarantee of privacy.

Vladimir's rule of thumb: *Never discuss in private what can best be said in public.* Shout outrageous trade or state secrets at the Kalinina Prospekt during rush hour or lunch at a noisy café in Utilsa Arbat, and no one would be the wiser.

Yet his good friend, Leopold Sergeevich Baranov, would settle for nothing less than meeting here in Gorky Park.

He and Leopold had been close since childhood. As kids, they had fished for carp on this very bank of the greenish-brown Moscow River, or paddled a popular collapsible canoe. In winter, they'd skate along the Park's zigzag of frozen pathways, flirting outrageously with pretty girls.

They were inseparable, until Vladimir took off for university in Leningrad and on to Stavropol province as a Komsomol leader within the Communist Youth League. He had been invited back to Moscow to join the KGB, since renamed the FSB, the Federal Security Service.

Not so politically minded, Leopold had enrolled in the sciences at the State University of Moscow, eventually the youngest since its founding in 1755 to head the Department of Biology. He was also credited with putting its Institute of the Brain on the international map. This garnered him an invitation to join the prestigious Russian Academy of Sciences.

Leopold stood motionless in the clearing, arms folded across his slight frame. He wore slacks, a tweed sports coat over a thick wool sweater, and a scarf wrapped several times round his neck. His tongue moved back and forth across his lips, affirming his penchant for being constantly perplexed.

Vladimir appeared at the far end of the clearing, the familiar large head topped with thick, curly hair, giving the scientist a fleeting uplift.

"You've come," Leopold called out, believing he might not have shown up.

Vladimir crossed the open space, exchanged the usual Russian hug, and lowered himself onto a wood-slatted concrete bench. He stretched out his legs to bring immediate relief to a right foot plagued with a recurring bout of gout.

"I'm here, no thanks to you, Leopold Sergeevich," he grumbled. "After what you've put me through." He breathed in the pungent scent of wet pine and decaying leaves. "I can only hope the walk is worth my while."

Leopold sat beside him, his narrow face dissolving into small, anxious lines. "Without question, Vlad."

Vladimir tugged a gold flask from his coat pocket, unscrewed the cap, and passed it over. Leopold took a sip, coughing at the sharpness of the single malt whiskey.

"Is it a personal matter?"

"No," he wheezed. "We... have a problem."

"*We?*"

Leopold handed back the flask. "The Academy. You might have heard about us losing a valued colleague. He died over the past weekend."

"Boris Yevtushenko. Resulting from a faulty—"

"It was nothing short of murder, Vlad."

Vladimir's thick, dark eyebrows rose in unison. "You have proof?"

"How could it be otherwise? He was strong as a Siberian sled dog. His recent physical examination befitted someone half his age."

"We're talking *mechanics*, not health. The autopsy proved what everyone expected. Your colleague died from a faulty pacemaker. And don't ask *me* for a second opinion, because it's not possible." Vladimir took a drink. "Let it go, Leo. For everyone's sake."

"We will, Vlad, on one condition. Give us a second opinion on what caused the pacemaker to break down."

"You're asking for something well outside my jurisdiction." Vladimir screwed the lid on the flask, leaving enough for the long trek out of the park. "Besides, I don't have the authority I once had."

How well Vladimir Lyubimov understood this singular admission. With the Soviet Union's collapse in the early nineties, heads had rolled. Especially in the departments of counter-intelligence and communications. Close friends and associates lost their jobs. Yet, today, he could name a dozen of the old KGB regime still at Lubyanka Square under the new Federal Security Service.

"You're surely not without some influence," Leopold was saying. "To be honest, we have no one else to turn to."

Vladimir appreciated the candid reply from someone seldom so forthright.

"Give me a *shred* of evidence—"

"I've admitted we have nothing, isn't that enough? We will abide by your findings." Leopold drew in a deep breath. "Should our suspicions prove correct, however, I fear another scientist's life might be compromised."

"Whose?"

"Doctor Leszek Poplawski."

"Winner of the Nobel Prize?" said Vladimir. "Interesting. Some years ago, Leo, we in the department searched for a better understanding of why people do what they do. Say what they say. We wanted a viewpoint distinct from the psychologists' usual rhetoric."

"You chose Leszek Poplawski. An excellent choice."

"I remember him as a man full of passion, with a unique insight into the human psyche. To say nothing of his dry wit. He spoke Polish, his mother tongue, Russian, and a smattering of English. He was with us on several occasions, such informal evenings ended drinking late in a local bistro." Vladimir smiled at the thought of it. "He must be getting on."

"Well into his late eighties, though you'd never know it. He's healthy as can be."

"You said the same of Boris. What's his early background?"

"He was a young researcher at the Jaqiellonian University in Krakow when Germany invaded Poland.

13

September, 'thirty-nine, Hitler turned the country over to his close friend, Hans Frank, as governor."

"With devastating consequences."

"True. Hans Frank rounded up every Polish scientist, shipping them off to concentration camps. All because he couldn't trust them to follow orders. Many died, including brilliant minds such as Stanislaw Estereicher and Kazimierz Kostanechki."

"What happened to Doctor Poplawski?"

"Russian troops found him more dead than alive, Vlad, at war's end. They shipped him off to Moscow. No one thought he'd recover. Then again, they didn't know his fighting spirit."

Vladimir's legs began to twitch, a sure sign time here was up. "Now you're saying his life is in danger once more."

"*Might* be. Boris Yevtushenko was Leszek's assistant and close friend. We think their research into the *neurotrop* has something to do with Boris' death."

"A neurotrop?"

It's a specialized cell, a neuron, capable of transferring information rapidly from one part of the brain to another."

"Simple enough," Vladimir quipped. "Where would I find the good Doctor Poplawski?"

"In America, visiting his daughter, Hanna Bajda. Our phone calls have received nothing more than a disembodied voice. 'Leave your name, phone number, and a brief message'…"

"That's very American. Is she married?"

"Divorced. She arrived in the United States as an infant after the war. An orphan. Her mother had died in a bombing raid. She believed her father had perished along with the other Polish scientists. When Ms. Bajda discovered he was still alive, she tracked him down to Moscow."

"And what do you expect from me?"

"Find Doctor Poplawski, Vlad. Warn him of the possible danger. Protect him, if necessary."

Vladimir pocketed the flask. "Finding him is one thing, Leo," he said, easing himself to his feet. "Checking into the pacemaker without raising curiosity is another."

With a firm handshake, Vladimir Lyubimov lumbered back along the cinder path.

"Do your best," Leopold called out.

State Patrol's Ira Neddick was halfway into the Page incident report when the foreman of a marine construction company called. He told Ira of hiring local SCUBA divers, as agreed, to find the red Toyota. They discovered it in forty feet of water.

For his company to bring it ashore, it would take four, five hours. He quoted a price. Ira approved it, hoping he'd be on hand for the retrieval. If not, the vehicle was to be left in the secured area behind the state police building.

Satisfied, Ira picked the report, unsure where he'd left off.

Vladimir Lyubimov took thirty agonizing minutes to walk back to the Garden Ring Road on Gorky Park's northern boundary. His knees felt like rubber, leaving him to pray they'd hold up until he reached his limo and driver parked across the street.

While waiting for the traffic to ease, he scolded himself for caving in to his friend's wishes. Finding the old scientist in America would be difficult enough; retrieving Boris' pacemaker, should it still be intact, was even more complex.

He reached the parking area at the church of St. John the Warrior to find his car had disappeared. In its place was a hand-tooled Russian *ZIL,* one of few left in service.

From it emerged a robust, late-forties officer in the black uniform of the Russian Navy. Rows of colorful military patches were on display below his left shoulder.

"Vladimir Alexandrovich." shouted Colonel Yury Nikolayev Petrovich, his voice rumbling across the empty lot. "You are indeed a sorry sight."

"Don't *Vladimir* me, you Georgian ruffian," he scolded him. "What have you done with my limousine, my driver?"

"I dismissed them." He reached Vladimir to give him a good-natured hug before stepping back. "I took the liberty of reserving us a late lunch at the Samovar. Their specialty today is *kotlety po Kievski*—"

"I've been enjoying their chicken Kiev long before you were filling your first diaper," mumbled Vladimir, lumbering on towards the *ZIL*. "Besides what gives Military Intelligence the authority to spy on me?"

"And what makes you think we'd do such a thing?"

"I'm under no illusion you were tuning in on your state-of-the art satellite communications. And everything else that goes with it these days."

Yury grinned. "You FSB types do the same to us. Though it's unlike you to arrange a meeting out in Gorky Park so not to be spied on..."

A loud buzz erupted from the officer's tunic pocket. He removed a cell phone and turned aside. "They fucked up?" he barked. "I'll fix it when I get there."

Vladimir eased himself onto the limo's back seat to sink into its soft tan leather.

"I'm here solely to give you counsel," said Yury, slipping in beside him. "It concerns our mutual friend, Leopold Baranov. You should know it's unwise dealing with him and his band of scientific *wunderkinds*."

"You people have a nasty habit," said Vladimir, "of blowing things out of proportion."

"Perhaps you are unaware, Leo dropped by my office several days ago. He pleaded with me on behalf of the Academy to track down an old scientist believed to be visiting America."

Vladimir looked away to hide any hint of surprise. "Why should it interest me?"

"Because our friend has this absurd notion Boris Yevtushenko did not die from a faulty pacemaker. I failed to convince him our tests showed his death was directly attributable to a short circuit. Our findings were verified by a laboratory in the private sector, to prove no bias."

"Should both of you be wrong—"

"You understand Leopold places the Academy's interests above everything, everyone. Friendship not excluded. We turn him down and what does he do? He comes to you."

Vladimir sank deeper into the leather seat. That Leo would choose to talk to Military Intelligence *first*, was nothing short of distressing.

CHAPTER FOUR
Monday, October 3, 10:32 AM

The air conditioning at Central Intelligence Agency headquarters in Langley, Virginia, had broken down. What wasn't anticipated was the extreme heat and humidity this late in the year.

Edward 'Ted' Grosvenor of Special Projects (Ops), at his desktop computer in shirtsleeves, was drying himself off by wiping the back of his neck with a damp handkerchief. He was a big man with keen dark eyes, salt-and-pepper hair, and a broad forehead dotted with youthful freckles.

The office suited Ted's tastes, with its antique oak desk and pine bookshelves. Of the many framed photos on the office wall, taken on numerous vacations, were three of his favorites: A lone schooner at anchor in Nassau's Goodman Bay, a lush vineyard in the Bordeaux region of France. And, best of all, Québec's Mont Tremblant with snow-laden pine trees guarding the steep ski runs.

Taking up space on the same wall was a mirror in an antique pine frame. A large leather golf bag nearby was crammed with PINGS, the titanium drivers nestled in furry brown covers.

A section of the office had been set aside with leather chairs and a matching sofa. A glass-topped coffee table held a tray with a large coffee thermos, china cups, a pitcher of fresh cream and a sugar bowl.

A low buzz from the intercom broke the silence. Ted reached over to push a button.

"Yes, Margaret."

"A call from Moscow, Mister Grosvenor," came her voice from the outer office. "Line three. The connection isn't very good. And it doesn't come through our usual links."

"Not from our Moscow station?" he asked, certain the call had been misdirected.

"No. It's from Mister Ly…u…bim…ov. If I'm pronouncing it correctly."

"*Lyubimov*?" Ted couldn't count how many times the Russian sonofabitch had outwitted 'The Company' during the Cold War. In one distasteful way or another.

Ted pushed the intercom to hear a pleasant 'how-do-you-do' from a female voice. She spoke English, he discovered, with an accent thick enough to cut with a knife.

Margaret was listening in when the door from the corridor burst opened. Special Project's Gerry Smith, a boyish thirty-something in a cotton sports jacket and no tie, strode in as if he owned the place. She blushed and hit the intercom's mute button.

"'Morning, Ms. Jennings." He nodded toward his superior's office. "What's he up to? Having trouble sinking a putt?"

Margaret patted her short, graying hair. "No. Conferencing with Moscow."

Gerry reached across her desk to release the same mute button, only to have her slap his hand aside.

He grinned. "Who from Moscow?"

"Mister Lyubimov."

"Vladimir Lyubimov!" he said, turning toward inner office.

"Wait," she burst out too late as he disappeared inside.

Ted Grosvenor aimed a stop-where-you-are forefinger at his assistant.

"I'll get back to you, Ms. Tuseva. Email a recent photo and have a good day." He glanced up. "Does it ever cross your mind to wait until Miss Jennings sends you in?"

"I thought she had, boss." Gerry headed for the coffee table. "In case you missed it, she prefers *Ms.* Jennings. Makes her feel younger." He picked up the thermos. "What's up?"

Ted joined him. "A call from Vladimir Lyubimov, of all people."

"He's 'way before my time." Gerry poured two coffees. "Didn't you try whacking him in Greece during the Cold War? 'Terminate with extreme prejudice'. That sort of stuff."

"Naples." Ted came over to take the proffered cup, adding generous amounts of cream and sugar. "The freelancer who picked up our contract was found floating face down in the crystal-clear waters of Capri's Blue Grotto."

"Great spot to visit," said Gerry. "Not so great to die."

Ted carried his coffee back to his desk. "Neck so badly twisted, the head was facing his back side. One of a dozen contracts we put out on Lyubimov." He loosened the striped tie with his free hand. "What's with our A/C?"

"The refrigeration overheated. Something about a screwed-up switch. It's being repaired as we speak."

"Not soon enough. I spoke to Lyubimov's assistant who *almost* speaks English. I could hear him in the background muttering what sounded like Russian curses. We've never met, though I'd recognize the sonofabitch from thousands of the goddamn clandestine photos we took of him."

"What's he after? A free pass to settle in the good old U.S. of A.?"

"No, he wants us to find a Polish-born Russian scientist wandering loose around America. Leszek Poplawski. Nobel prize winner. According to Ms. Tuseva, the Russians found him close to death in a German internment camp during World War II. They took him to Moscow and brought him back to life."

"And you told Vladimir to bugger off."

"I told him I had a lazy-assed assistant who'd be happy to find the old gent." Ted sipped his coffee. "You're aware The Company is encouraging us to make friendly gestures toward our Russian counterparts. Despite we're not always on the same page. Prep Lyubimov's background while I have Nathan Edgars at S&T shed some light on our missing scientist."

Gerry nodded. "I'm to remind you to tell Edgars to change the tee time a week from Thursday. Back to 7:30 AM. Lots-a warning, knowing how antsy he is." Having finished his coffee, Gerry came over to Ted's desk. "Have you anything specific on Poplawski?"

"He has a daughter, Hanna Bajda, in Connecticut." Ted waved a slip of paper. "Ms. Tuseva gave us a phone number and promised to email us a recent photo of both father and daughter, ASAP."

Gerry glanced at the ten digits. "Area code eight-zero-six. Your Ms. T. got that right." He shoved the slip in a pocket. "Has anyone thought to phone Hanna Bajda?"

"Yes, with no luck. Ms. Tuseva suggested they're on to a whirlwind tour of America."

Gerry pulled stapled sheets from inside his suit jacket and dropped them on the desk.

"Accounts is querying my expenses for the Toronto trip. Could you put those cretins straight?" He headed for the door. "Trips to Canada ain't that cheap, despite a fluctuating buck."

Ted nodded, and punched a button on the intercom.

"Margaret, get me Nathan Edgars at S&T." He sat back as cool air swept through the room. "Thank God," he muttered, feeling the sweat already drying on the back of his neck.

Ted was finishing off a nasty email to Accounts, advising them to quit pestering his assistant over his travel expenses, when the intercom buzzed.

"Mister Edgars, sir," came Margaret's pleasant voice. "Line three."

The head of Special Ops talked while pecking at the keyboard. "Nathan. I want to—"

"You're canceling our foursome a week Thursday."

"I'm changing the tee times back to the original 7:30 AM."

"You're aware rearranging tee times means big trouble. Irwin won't like it. He's flying in from Israel late the previous evening, and you know how lack of sleep screws up his game."

"He takes his golf too seriously as it is."

It was a given Ted would share a golf cart with Secretary of the Interior, Irwin Rasky, at the Pines Golf & Country Club across the Potomac. Nathan Edgars would bring another golfer from Science & Technology to make up a foursome.

"Tell me, Nathan, does the name Leszek Poplawski ring a bell?"

"*Ring a bell*? He won the Nobel Prize for chemistry back in 'fifty-six. He shared it with Nikolai Semenov, a Russian, and Cyril Hinshelwood, an Englishman. He was half their age. During World War II, Russian troops found him dying in a German concentration camp. They brought him to Moscow, saved his life."

"Anything else?"

"He is also a good reason why we Americans are light years behind the Russians in research of the brain." A pause came over the line. "Why?"

"Because he's here in America."

"He can't be!"

"Which begs the question: why didn't you labor-intensive types know about it?"

A groan broke over the line, "I'll be right over."

CHAPTER FIVE
Monday, October 3. 11:05 AM

Nathan Edgars, stripped to his shirtsleeves, paced Ted Grosvenor's office on the fourth floor of the CIA complex. He was a thin, articulate bureaucrat with an unsmiling face, made even less appealing by a weak chin.

His tie was always held firm by a small, plain gold clip, pants too neatly creased and his black Italian leather shoes polished to a high gloss.

With Nathan Edgars, nothing was ever out of place. Except this morning.

His white shirt was stained dark with sweat under his arms and V-shaped down his back from shoulders to his belt.

"I'm dumbfound," he moaned.

"You should be."

"How could Doctor Poplawski be here without us knowing?"

"How about an unofficial visit with his daughter living in Connecticut?"

"You're kidding me. Where are they now?"

"Sightseeing most likely. Disneyland, the Everglades, Alaska. Who knows?" Ted waited for a response. "Cat got your tongue?"

"I'm in shock."

"All he needed was a visa."

Nathan stopped pacing. "Chickens…"

"Not the sort of response I was expecting."

"Coming home to roost. Eight months ago, Ted, we axed a project specializing in a particular aspect of brain research." Nathan lowered himself on the arm of the leather couch. "The scientist working the independent program—we have our fingers in a lot of things—showed up one morning knowing nothing of a decision made the night before. He was told his funding had been cut, his contract terminated."

"And you frog-marched him out of wherever he was."

"It took four security team to do it. No one wants a disgruntled contract employee smuggling out important material."

"Humiliate him, even better. Was he incompetent? A boozer? Wrong for the job?"

Nathan shook his head. "Members of the advisory committee agreed he was steering an important project in the wrong direction. Apart from taking us away over budget."

"You broke his contract, repossessed his cell phone. Separated him from his notes, his lab and research material. I can see why he'd be pissed off." Ted checked the time, already late for a meeting several levels below. "I'm curious about your chickens coming home to roost."

Nathan fidgeted with the loose knot in his tie. "There were rumors Doctor Poplawski and his team in Moscow had hit pay dirt. Their research carried little credibility until—"

"Let me guess," Ted interrupted. "It was the *same* new direction your own project head had taken his research when you threw him under the bus."

"We had no idea," said Nathan, coming close to a whine, "that the Russian work on the *neurotrop* was so advanced."

"What's your ex-head's name?"

"Harmon C. Page. A bright guy. If not someone who insisted on doing things *his* way."

"That's easily fixed. Give him back his lab. His team. Double his grant. Triple it."

"The poor bastard's wife had already filed for divorce and taken their only kid west to live in Los Angeles. Then we pull the rug out from under him."

"Nice move."

"As it is, he cut his connection to Georgetown University and extensive research at the Vets' Hospital here in Washington. He sold the home in Foggy Bottom and traded in his late model BMW soft top for a far less expensive Toyota."

"Where is he now?"

"Up the coast. Hunkered down in a forlorn old clapboard home on the water between Kittery and Ogunquit."

Ted didn't need a GPS to know where this was going.

"Realizing you idiots had screwed up, you went to see him. Pleaded with him to return to work."

Nathan turned to stare out the window. "Yes. I assured him we'd double the funding. He could rehire his entire staff, plus anyone else he wanted on his team."

"And?"

"He told me to fuck off."

"Not that you didn't deserve it."

Nathan reddened, "Worse, we were afraid the Russians would've heard by then that we'd cut Harm loose. On top of that, you're telling me Leszek is here. In the States, on the pretense of visiting his daughter."

"Whoa. Pretense? For what other reason? Unless, you're worried the Russia's *real* motivation was to connect with the hotshot you cut loose."

Nathan was pacing again. "What's stopping them from offering him work in Moscow? Setting him up with his own research lab? Page and Poplawski working together on neurotrop research. What a total goddamn insult that would be to our reputation."

Ted glanced at his watch again. "Bring me up to speed. In a language plain enough for me understand."

"Neurotrops simply regulate traffic on the pathways of the brain. The transmission of nerve impulses which activate muscle mechanisms. We call it *neurophysiology*—the study of how nerve cells receive and transmit information."

"You call that *plain* enough?" Ted mused. "Have Page and Poplawski ever met?"

"The first time at a conference in Paris. They got on well, despite the language barrier. Both men, by the way, are nothing short of brilliant in their specialty."

"Suppose there's no conspiracy, Nathan? If Poplawski's sole purpose for coming here was to enjoy quality time with his daughter."

"How do we know? The US government would be most upset if Harmon Page's knowledge and expertise is passed on to a foreign power." Nathan picked up his suit jacket from a nearby chair and pulled it on. "I'd feel much better knowing where either of them is at any given moment. Or God forbid if they've already contacted each other."

Ted walked Nathan to the door agreeing, despite his better judgment, to track down the errant Poplawski and his daughter.

"One condition," he said. "We keep this *off the record*."

Nathan paused, nodded, and stepped out the door.

He had no sooner left than Ted had second thoughts. Hadn't he learned the hard way that promising anything *off the record* seldom, if ever, paid off?

What troubled him was Edgars of S & T and Lyubimov of the FSB both worrying over the whereabouts of the old scientist.

For totally different reasons.

Vladimir was at his desk with the phone pressed against his ear. While waiting for someone to answer, he glanced around at his modest office with its venerable mahogany desk and old glass-front bookcase. He brought these treasures with him whenever he was repositioned, as he liked to put it, for one reason or another.

He took special pride in a framed photograph showing him shoulder to shoulder with former Soviet leader Mikhail Gorbachev. They were raising their fluted glasses at a retreat one summer in the Urals. He'd forgotten the occasion...

"May I help you?" purred a voice in his ear.

"Someone asked the same thing five minutes ago, Vladimir growled into the receiver. Put me back on hold and and I'll—"

"Doctor Baranov speaking."

"Must I remind you, Leopold, of the irreparable damage you've caused our friendship?"

"Vladimir! I take it Yury Nikolayev Petrovich couldn't keep it to himself."

"Don't blame him. You persuaded me to review Boris' death only *after* he turned you down."

"I thought—"

"Get it through your thick skull that a faulty mechanism in the pacemaker ended Boris Yevtushenko's life—"

"And you believed him."

"—Meaning the death was accidental. End of story."

"Is finding our Russian colleague in America in jeopardy as well…?"

Vladimir hung up, struggling with his conscience. It prompted him to reach a friend of long standing.

Konstantin Shchusev was the chief pathologist with the Militia, the police arm of MVD. Vladimir phoned him at the forensic lab, wondering if the autopsy of Boris Yevtushenko's body had been handled by his department.

The reply was no, the chief pathologist admitting it puzzled him that it had gone to an independent lab to 'ensure no biased results'. The body and the pacemaker, packed separately, had both ended up in Konstantin's department, waiting further instructions.

Vladimir asked if his own department might check out the unit, if only for curiosity's sake.

Though an odd request, Konstantin saw no harm in it. Provided, he cautioned, both kept it between themselves. Vladimir was to return at a moment's notice.

A delighted Vladimir was hanging up when his personal assistant appeared in the doorway.

Olga Elana Tuseva was a striking woman with shoulder-length auburn hair, eyes as dark as coal dust, and lips a bright red. She wore a leather outfit accentuating her slim figure.

"Slip down to our lab," Vladimir said, "and let Misha know a package will arrive needing his attention. I will catch up with him—"

"You and I have already discussed it," Olga cut in.

"Well before we knew Ms. Tuseva, that the pathologist would cooperate."

"I knew what you'd do, sir, being someone who never lets anyone down. Our chief technician is on notice a package will be delivered this afternoon. He is to examine it for a possible malfunction, your words, and report to us in the morning."

"You gave him no other details?"

"None." Olga stepped back into her adjoining office, leaving his door open, as usual.

Vladimir shook his large, shaggy head, mystified how Ms. Tuseva always managed to keep a step ahead of him.

CHAPTER SIX
Tuesday, October 4. 8:40 AM. (Moscow time)

Vladimir Lyubimov arrived later than usual at the gray stone building. Misha Mikhail Kodenko, his chief technician, was waiting for him in the corridor outside his second-floor office.

He was a tall, bespectacled, younger man in jeans and a wrinkled, plain blue shirt under an off-white lab coat.

"It's time you showed up," Misha grumbled. "I'm here about the package delivered to me late yesterday afternoon."

Vladimir waved him into a chair, only to have him remain standing in the doorway.

"It lacked the proper forms. ID, among other things. And you, Vladimir, a stickler for detail. In it was a pacemaker registered to Boris Yevtushenko buried, until a few days ago, in the scientist's chest."

"Why would you think it belonged to him?"

"We checked the serial number against the manufacturer's listed data."

Vladimir shrugged it off. "I only wanted nothing to prejudice your initial findings."

"Meaning you had no trust in my team handling something so highly classified."

"That's far from the truth, Misha."

"I know you better than that. My team and I stayed up all night stripping it down, reassembling it. Testing. Re-testing it—"

"And nothing more…"

"…And we found the unit suffered no physical damage. No exposed wiring. No charred or blackened pieces due to extreme heat. We discovered, instead, an excessive build-up of energy sending out electrical charges measured in nanoseconds."

"Which caused—"

"…Which caused the pacemaker to ramp up out of control." Misha paused, letting it sink in. "There is no question that Boris Fyodorovich Yevtushenko was murdered."

Vladimir sat back stunned with Leopold Baranov's plea from Gorky Park ringing in his ears. *We think the pacemaker might have been tampered with.*

"Despite reliable, independent sources confirming his death due a manufacturer's defect," said Vladimir, "you and your team insist it's not so?"

Misha jammed his hands in his lab coat pockets. "What do we think? They delivered a verdict everyone expected. He died from a faulty pacemaker."

"You're telling me they lied, yet you give me no explanation how it happened."

"We're working on it," his chief technician snapped back.

Vladimir shuffled through loose papers on his desk. "I can't see you proving what has already been disproved."

Taking this remark as mean-spirited, Misha Kodenko stormed out of the room.

CHAPTER SEVEN
Tuesday, October 4. 7:45 AM.

Ted Grosvenor arrived early at Langley to find his secretary already at her computer.

"Good morning, Margaret," he said. "Send for Gerry—"

"He's in your office, sir," she replied, her thin face warming to a smile.

Ted opened the door as his assistant's head poked up above the back of the leather sofa.

His eyes were half-open, the wrinkled shirt unbuttoned at the collar.

"We found your elusive scientist and his daughter," he said, having pulled an all-nighter. "They were discovering the awesome beauty of the Grand Canyon."

Ted poured them both a fresh coffee. "Where in the Canyon?"

"Hopi Point. Eighty-nine years young, and the old fart rides a mule down seven thousand feet into the valley over the weekend. And back up. It's so goddamn steep, boss, *mules* carrying tourists have been known to lose their footing. So hot you carry your own supply of water."

"Something to avoid. Where are they now?"

"They've moved on to Vegas and the *Bellagio*." Gerry stood up, stretched, and took the proffered black coffee. "The hotel with the dancing waters. The old guy even won some good old American greenbacks at the slots last night."

"Where are they going next?" Ted asked, carrying the coffee over to his desk.

"United Airlines has them booked on a morning flight to Chicago. Then on to Buffalo, picking up an Avis rental on the Canadian side. In Ms. Bajda's name. It's our guess they'll take in the sights of Niagara Falls, then on to Toronto. Air Canada has them flying to Montréal in the morning."

"No one has contacted with them?"

Gerry sipped his coffee. "No, per your orders."

"Have we anyone in the Buffalo area?"

"Closest are Ladly and Locke. They're working the Burns file out of Boston."

"Have them head to the Falls. We'll pass on a recent photo of Poplawski that Lyubimov is sending us."

"I'll forward it to Ladly's cell," Gerry said, "so they'll know who to look for."

"Have the pair stick with them. Any idea where they'll go after Montréal?"

"No scheduled flights under Poplawski, boss. Or Bajda. Nor are they registered at any Montréal hotel."

"Meaning they're on the move. Check Amtrak. VIA Rail. How did you find them?"

"We were tracking hotel and plane reservations when I had several of our guys ferret out Harmon C. Page. He'd moved from Washington—"

"To Maine."

"We tried his home outside Ogunquit. The answering machine came on with him saying he'd be gone a few days. Our techs recorded his incoming messages, and what d'you know? Several were from Poplawski asking Page of his whereabouts."

"Did he say anything else?"

"Just that the old guy was most distressed to leave without saying hello or goodbye. The latest message coming from Hopi Point."

Gerry picked up his jacket. "Several messages were from your golfing buddy, Nathan Edgars, pleading with Page to get in touch, wherever he is."

Ted remembered Nathan telling him Page's ex-wife had moved out west taking their daughter with her. "Try the airlines, car rentals, and limo services in Los Angeles. And have our techs screw up his message machine so it's out of order. I don't want Page and Poplawski contacting each other."

"We tried tracing Page's cell. No luck."

"Fair enough. Montréal's a port city. Check shipping schedules for Poplawski and his daughter. Day cruises. Overnights. And get back to me."

A beaming Gerry Smith returned within the hour. "You're a genius, boss. According to Montréal shipping agent McNeil/Rossman, Poplawski is booked aboard *TSS Casimir III*. A passenger liner with Polish registry. I'm waiting for details, like date and Departure. The ship once made Montréal a regular port of call."

"No longer?"

"Nope. This transatlantic crossing is more of a final farewell gesture before she's dry-docked. Scrapped."

"When did the ship arrive?"

"Ten days ago. The *Casimir III* is a vessel that never sleeps. It's been taking locals, and those staying aboard, on a side trip down the St. Lawrence. On to Boston, Bar Harbor Maine. Prince Edward Island and back to Montréal. It's no luxury liner, yet packed with ardent devotees among its transatlantic aficionados, marking its final trip back to Europe. To anywhere."

"Any good news?"

"We've found Page."

"Tell me he's not with Poplawski."

"He's in Los Angeles. His name popped up on an airline computer. He returns to Boston late tonight. American Airlines. His flight lands at Logan. Around midnight…"

Margaret's voice cut in over the intercom. "Excuse me, Mister Grosvenor. Mister McNeil of McNeil/Rossman is sending Gerry an email confirming the TSS *Casimir III's* schedule. With stops at London/Tilbury, Rotterdam, and the Polish port of Gdynia."

"When does it sail, Ms. Jennings?"

"Wednesday. October 5th. 4 PM."

"*Tomorrow?*" Ted scowled at Gerry who was fumbling with his cell phone.

"I've got it," said Gerry. "It just came in."

Ted put his secretary on hold. "Have Ladly and Locke concentrate solely on Poplawski and his daughter. Cover their arrival in Niagara Falls, and shadow them wherever they go."

Gerry nodded, pocketed his cell and left the office.

Ted hummed as he hit the intercom. "Margaret, phone Nathan Edgars. Tell his secretary to have him drop everything and get his butt over here."

Ted stood in his office doorway several hours later as Margaret look up from her typing. She removed her headphone.

"No word from Edgars?" he asked.

"He's on his way, sir."

"Have Gerry meet him in reception. Then get Vladimir Lyubimov on the line." Ted was hardly seated at his desk when the call came through.

The voice belonged to the Russian woman.

"Ms. Tuseva," he said, happily remembering her name. "Mister Lyubimov is with you, I trust."

"He is next to me and sends his warmest…hmm…regards. He is eager to learn what success you are having in locating our beloved Doctor Poplawski."

"We found him, Ms. Tuseva. He's safe and sound."

"And where is it that you found him, please?"

"Traipsing around the Grand Canyon with his daughter."

"… *Traipsing*? *Grand Canyon*? I am not quite understanding of these words."

"It's our big ditch. Somewhat like to your Upper Volga." The line crackled and came back to life. "Doctor Poplawski arrives in Montréal for a return trip home aboard the Polish liner *TSS Casimir III*. You understand what I am saying?" He repeated it adding, "The ship sails tomorrow on its return to Gdynia."

Ted waited for what seemed a settling of a Russian difference of opinion.

"Anything wrong, Ms. Tuseva?"

"It is only in my…translation. Mister Lyubimov is hoping you will not be unduly perplexed if we ask another favor. To place someone of reliability on board the *Casimir III.*"

"Why so?"

"To watch over Doctor Poplawski, who is troubled with ill health. A shortness of breath. A voyage on open water could be…hmm…"

"Difficult."

"Yes. Difficult. It would be to London only, Mister Grosvenor. Where we would handle the…remainder of the voyage."

A pause came over the line. "…There is no opportunity, we are thinking, for ourselves to be making such arrangements from here on a shortage of notice."

"In plain English, Ms. Tuseva, what's the problem?"

Ted listened to another lively exchange before Olga came back on the line.

"Do not overly concern yourself. We are… hmm… anxious, because Doctor Poplawski tends to… to lack balance on his feet. His forgetfulness is not uncommon, for someone of his age. He is so deeply respected here. You are understanding me?"

"Of course. And let Mister Lyubimov know we will do our best." Ted didn't have to convince himself that Ms. Tuseva was winging it as she went along. "In the spirit of cooperation between our two nations, of course."

A joyful burst of Russian and mangled English ended with her saying they would remain at the office for Mister Grosvenor's decision.

Ted had no sooner rung off than the intercom buzzed again. Margaret told him his assistant was on his way up with Nathan Edgars.

"Change of plans, Margaret. Tell Gerry to dump him in an unoccupied office down the hall. And come here alone."

"No rest for the wicked," Ted sighed when his assistant joined him moments later.

"Albeit a rough translation," said Gerry, sitting on an arm of the leather couch. It's 'no *peace* for the wicked.' Old Testament. Isaiah 48:22."

Ted could seldom tell when his assistant was screwing around. Or not

"Where did you learn that?"

"Sunday School 101. Remember next time, and it will get you a free candy bar."

"I'll take your word for it. Now, our friend Vladimir is imploring us to have an operative on board the *Casimir*. Solely to keep tabs on the old man."

"Why?"

"God only knows. We've already committed ourselves, meaning we'll need a cabin as far as London/Tilbury. Let's hope the goddamn vessel is booked solid, and that'll be the end of it."

"If not? Who goes on such short notice?"

"Preferably someone from our department. Who's fluent in Polish."

"From our department? That's a tall order, boss. What clearance?"

"Minimal. We're only doing the Russians a favor."

Gerry got up, stopping halfway to the door. "What's their game?"

"According to Ms. Tuseva, poor old Poplawski has creeping senility."

Gerry sighed. "Are we're talking about the *same* old geezer who rides a donkey down into the Grand Canyon and back? Who spends the night gambling in Vegas? And wins."

"Time was running out for them to keep an eye on him."

"If it was that simple, why would Moscow's Federal Security Service be involved?"

Ted wished he had an answer.

A scowling Nathan Edgars stood with his back to Ted's large office window.

"Why, in heaven's name would the Russian authorities want the CIA to have someone on board the *Casimir*? And why oblige them by supplying someone?"

"It was a simple request, Nathan. Surely you over-achievers from the scientific community can come up with some reason why."

Nathan thought for a moment. "We've heard rumors of a Russian scientist dying from a faulty pacemaker. He was in a Moscow restaurant when his lights went out."

"I'm aware of that. What's his name?"

"Boris Yevtushenko. Y-e-v-t-u-s-h-e-n-k-o. B—"

"I can spell *Boris*." Ted scrawled it on a small pad, adding to it: *update—death caused by a faulty pacemaker in Moscow restaurant.* "It happened a few days ago."

Nathan came away from the window to help himself to a coffee.

"On the weekend. Someone at work read about it in a Reuters news clip. I met Boris at several international conventions. I remember seeing him in the hotel bar, never at the working sessions. Big, boisterous guy. Drank us all under the table."

Ted could easily imagine *anyone* drinking Nathan under the table…

Gerry arrived and read the note. "Our surveillance team is back," he said. "The place is old and rural enough to have its own mailbox out by the road. Where ditches replace sidewalks—"

"You're talking about Harm Page's house?" Nathan cut in. "Tell me he hasn't been in touch with Doctor Poplawski!"

"It's doubtful." Ted nodded at Gerry.

"The answering machine is an old Panasonic Easaphone. It comes with a little hand-held gizmo you beep into a phone. It replays your messages from wherever. Modern phones use predetermined coded digits. Our boys wiped it clean."

A worried glance from Nathan Edgars, and Gerry's explanation trailed off.

Ted motioned for him to go on.

"To ensure it won't replay messages. They also poked through a filing cabinet, looking for anything between

Page and Poplawski, like correspondence. They let it go because they weren't briefed on what to look for."

"I *knew* it." Nathan groaned.

"Drop surveillance on Poplawski, Gerry. Have Ladly and Locke pick up Page at Logan. American Airlines. At 12:15. Tonight. If he causes trouble, charge him and 'cuff him."

"Charge him with what?" Gerry asked.

"Let's say supplying secrets to a foreign power."

"That's treason!" Nathan burst out. "You have no proof. The correspondence could be nothing more than personal emails."

"And if they're not?"

"Let *me* handle," Nathan pleaded. "He'll be worn out when his flight arrives at Logan. I'll reserve two suites at an airport, meet him there, talk him into staying overnight."

"He's right, boss," Gerry cut in. "By the time we nailed down a warrant…"

Ted said to Nathan. "We'll do it your way. Just don't snivel and whine when you pitch Page a contract and turns you down. Again. He has reason enough to be pissed off."

He turned to Gerry. "Have Ladly and Locke shadow Poplawski and his daughter as far as Toronto. Then catch an early morning flight to Boston. That will give them time to check out Page's place in Ogunquit and clear out before he arrives home."

He glanced at Nathan. "It's your call. Let me know when you've settled in. Our operatives will be on standby, should you screw up."

Nathan Edgars tried not to take the off-handed remark personally.

CHAPTER EIGHT
Wednesday, October 5. 12:13 AM.

The American Airlines flight from Los Angeles touched down at Boston's Logan Airport, Terminal B earlier than its scheduled midnight arrival.

Worried he might have missed him, Nathan doubled back to spot Harm, in the familiar jeans and leather jacket, leaving the Avis counter. He caught up to him short of the exit to the parking lot.

"Not even a friendly hello?" Nathan asked, walking beside him.

Harm went on through the revolving doors. "Whatever you're peddling, I'm not interested." He glanced across the parking area at the long row of rentals. "I won't ask how you knew I'd be here."

"Be as it may, you've had a long flight. Now comes the tiring drive up to Ogunquit." Nathan forced himself to sound casual. "Because of that, I took the liberty of booking us suites at the Hyatt Harborside nearby, thinking—"

"Enjoy yourself." Harm pressed the ignition key's remote to hear the click of a lock and the parking lights flash from a Camry parked nearby. He tossed his luggage in the back seat and climbed in behind the wheel.

"Get in," he said, stepping on the brake and pressing the ignition button. "I'll drop you off at your hotel."

Nathan slipped in beside him to fumble with the seatbelt. "The research project wasn't supposed to end this way, Harm."

"You guys didn't like the direction I was taking, despite what the Russians were already doing. Not having the balls to fire me yourself, you sent some smart-ass flunky to do your dirty work."

"I'm sorry," Nathan said, worried how the conversation was taking a wrong turn.

"We want you back."

"It won't happen. And don't give me your 'it's a cross I'll have to bear' routine. It's the way you rationalize every goddamn thing when you're caught with your pants round your ankles."

Nathan groaned inwardly. "At least listen to our last offer. Should you turn us down, it will be the end of it. No hassles."

"And who'll speak for those whackos back at S&T?"

"They'll have no choice but to drop it." Nathan pushed on. "Stay over. I'll explain at an early breakfast what we have in mind."

Harm stifled a yawn. "You won't come unhinged in the morning when I tell you to go screw yourself?"

"No. Scout's honor." Nathan relaxed back against the seat. "How come you're not driving that sporty little red car of yours?"

"Because it's parked in forty feet of ocean."

The remark was enough to kill any conversation.

Harm's suite at the Hyatt Harborside Hotel & Conference Center was comfortable enough, with an uncluttered view of Boston's brightly-illuminated suspension bridge reflected on the still waters of the harbor.

He looked for the small coffee maker to set it up for the morning, when there was a knock and he opened the door. A young bellhop smiled as he balanced two short-stemmed snifters on a small silver tray.

"Compliments of the guest in Suite 212, sir," he said, handing over a Courvoisier. "I'm to remind you of an eight o'clock breakfast meeting at the Harborside Grille."

Harm nodded, dropping loose change on the tray. He was closing the door when it struck him that staying overnight was a waste of time. Following an unsettling few days in Los Angeles, he wanted nothing more than to wake up at home, tucked under his goose down duvet. Birds chirping at the feeder; breathing in the aroma of fresh-brewed coffee.

Deciding to tell Nathan in person that he'd changed his mind, Harm stepped into the corridor as the bellhop came out of Suite 212.

He held the door open for Harm before disappearing into an elevator.

Noticing Nathan was on his cell facing the picture window, his back to the room, Harm leaned against the open door sipping his cognac, when he heard Nathan mention his name.

"I talked Page into staying overnight, Ted. We're meeting for breakfast. Is the *Casimir* sailing on schedule?"

Curious, Harm waited for what came next.

"Good. I'm pitching one last effort to bring him back onside. He won't listen, we know as much. It will delay him long enough to keep from interfering with your agenda."

Harm stepped back into the corridor. *Delay me from interfering?* With what? Nathan Edgars, he decided, was up to his old tricks: playing both ends against the middle.

CHAPTER NINE
Wednesday, October 5. 8:45 AM. (Moscow)

Shouts coming from the outer office had Vladimir Alexandrovich Lyubimov shaking his head. Olga Tuseva appeared in the doorway, hands pressed against her hips.

"Misha Kodenko is here to pester you. No appointment. As if anyone can just barge in."

Misha's flushed face showed no higher than Olga's shoulder. She nailed him with a hip as he tried stepping round her.

"Let him be, Ms. Tuseva."

Olga moved aside, giving the chief lab technician a poke in the ribs before leaving the door ajar.

"Don't let her get to you," said Vladimir, giving him a fatherly smile. "She only picks on those she likes. Now, I hope you've come with good news."

It depends, Vladimir. We found what triggered the pacemaker to react as it did. It came from an external force manipulated by someone we're convinced was in the same room at the time."

The casual remark caught Vladimir by surprise. "Can you prove it?"

"Not until we find what mechanism locked onto the pacemaker."

Vladimir leaned forward, his thick eyebrows knitting together. "Surely whoever did this, would have been noticed."

"Not if he drew little attention to himself by using, say, an electronic tablet or cell phone. Most people use them in public. Even in restaurants."

Vladimir's legs began to cramp, and he stretched them out under the desk.

"You said there was no evidence it had been tampered with. Now, you're telling me…"

He watched his chief technician remove a battery-powered toy car from his lab coat pocket. Protruding from its side was a metal armature. Misha produced a small, hand-held remote unit with a modified numeric keypad. He handed it to Vladimir and placed the car on the desk.

"Depress the numbers on the keyboard as I give them to you. Six, nine, three, four, seven."

Vladimir did so, scowling when nothing happened.

Misha suggested the reverse order.

On reaching 'three', the armature sprang to life, clanging and spinning around the desk scattering folders and loose papers in every direction.

"That's enough!" Vladimir shouted over the racket.

Misha shut it off, explaining how the pacemaker might have been programmed to race out of control.

"And you plan to prove it by using a mere *toy*? When we're dealing with a sophisticated piece of equipment, Misha, that ended a man's life?"

The tech jammed the gadgets back in his lab coat. "My team will drop any further work. I hope it satisfies you."

"Without question," Vladimir exploded. "And send the pacemaker directly back to the chief coroner. It's long overdue."

Misha Rodenko stormed from the room with Olga Tuseva appearing seconds later in the doorway.

"Misha Rodenko was only trying to show you what his team has accomplished, sir. And you, treating him with such little respect."

Vladimir's face reddened as he cleaned up the mess on his desk.

"You cannot use a child's toy, Ms. Tuseva, to prove so serious a matter."

He looked up to find Olga had already gone.

"Have the maitre d' send a list of those dining in the small room that Saturday evening," he called out. "The night Boris Yevtushenko died," he added with a murmured 'please' at the end.

If Olga heard him, she didn't answer.

Early morning light filtered down through the clouds, enveloping the dome of the Capitol building in a rosy wash. It moved across the open spaces to bathe the Washington Monument and Lincoln Memorial in the same glow.

Such autumn splendor was wasted on Nicole Hagen, who was stalled in rush hour traffic on a bridge from Alexandria to Washington D.C.

She was a woman in her mid-thirties, wearing a high-collared white blouse and a tailored brown corduroy vest with matching slacks. Her dark hair hung loose on her shoulders with a late summer tan accentuating her natural features.

If something was striking about her, it might have been her skin stretched over high cheekbones, the pale blue eyes, the full mouth. She was a woman who turned heads, of both genders, though seldom aware of it.

The sun had slipped out from behind a marshmallow cloud, forcing Nicole to dig sunglasses from her purse. While pulling them on, she noticed the driver ahead was taking his own sweet time. She honked, knowing it would do no good.

Nicole arrived at an unassuming building on K Street, swiped her ID and followed her usual routine of forsaking the elevator to walk up seven floors to her office.

She was not amused to find a note pinned on the door telling her to report at once to Gerald Smith at the Central Intelligence Agency at Langley.

It annoyed her, having to battle her way back over to the Potomac and out onto the crowded George Washington Memorial Parkway—as if she didn't already have enough on her mind.

Nicole sneaked glances at her iPad as she drove along, to learn Smith was an assistant to Edward W. Grosvenor, Special Projects, CIAOD. Big deal.

Needing a distraction, she turned on the stereo of her late model BMW.

"... and seven-forty," intoned the cheery voice. "Good morning, Washington. Traffic is already heavy at this hour. Inbound on I-66, an accident beyond Highway 28. Shirley, northbound, is slow heading toward the 14th Street Bridge..."

Clad in a bulky terrycloth robe, Harm Page poured himself a coffee.

He was pleased for having left Boston. The California trip had been a disaster, prompted by an earlier call from his twelve-year-old daughter, Samantha. She pleaded with him to bring her back east to live. He had caught a flight to Los Angeles soon after.

He had arrived to face an ex-wife accusing him of putting Sam up to this charade. Nancy's lawyers filed a restraining order, keeping Harm away from Sam on the probability he'd spirit her back east.

On the strength of this, the judge restricted any contact with his daughter, setting a date for a subsequent hearing. Harm had little choice but to return home.

Reaching his study, Harm sipped his steaming coffee while pushing the rewind button on his Easa-phone to check for messages. It whirled and stopped. He pressed playback. Nothing happened.

He tried again, reminding himself to buy a more updated version. He picked up the cordless phone to dial Mrs. Sonin, his closest neighbor a mile up the road. He relied on her dropping by to collect the mail and water the plants when he was away.

She answered on the first ring, her voice laced with an old New England country sternness. Having been asked if there had been any messages, she told Harm of hearing the familiar voice of her nephew, Ira Neddick of the state police, asking him to call as soon as possible.

"And someone else with an accent so thick, Mister Page, I could hardly understand him."

"He left his name...?" Harm's voice trailed off as he glanced out the study window to see a blue car pull up at the end of his driveway. Two men had climbed out and were taking mail from his battered, rural mailbox.

Telling her he'd call back, Harm dropped the phone and charged out the front door.

He hop-scotched barefoot down the gravel driveway, reaching them as the heavier of the two tossed the bundled mail football-style to his companion.

Harm leaped up and snagged it in mid-air, mumbling aloud how stealing from the U.S. Postal Service was a criminal offence.

"Oh yeah?" said the husky-voiced big guy with a black moustache and flattened nose of an ex-boxer.

"Don't sweat it," cut in the smaller, balding one. "Our buddy lives around here. We figured this might be his place, what with no name on the mailbox."

"What his name?" Harm asked, balancing himself as he removed gravel jammed between his toes.

"Doherty," said Moustache.

"Don't know him," Harm replied, turning back toward the house.

Once inside, he looked out the window to see the car had disappeared.

What bothered him, they were looking for a *guy* called Doherty, when the only one Harm knew hereabouts was old widow Doherty, known for knitting eye-catching wool sweaters she donated to the local church bazaar.

Ted Grosvenor had barely removed his jacket when his assistant bounded into the office.

"You remind me of *Tigger*," Ted said, sitting at his desk. "Forever bouncing all over the goddamn place."

"A quote from *Winnie the Pooh*. Top made of rubber, tail made of springs." Gerry headed for a coffee. "I preferred gloomy old Eeyore when I was a kid. He oozed character."

"Forget Eeyore. The *Casimir* pulls up anchor sometime this afternoon. What's up?"

"Our Foreign Office pressured the Canadian Feds into jumping all over the *Casimir III's* shipping agent in supplying a cabin. I kept us out of it."

"We're throwing a *Hail Mary* here, Gerry."

"No sweat. They came up with a pricey one. They're waiting for an answer."

"*Pricey* means an outside stateroom. Go for it."

Gerry hauled out his cell phone, working the little keys with both thumbs. "Done. We'll have to settle for a researcher not from our department who speaks fluent Polish." He handed over a slip of paper.

Ted typed the coordinates into his computer with one finger. "Researchers," he said. "The unsung heroes of this godforsaken business. That's how L. B. J. enshrined them." He hit ENTER and watched names fill the screen.

Gerry pointed at one midway down. "There. Research Division. ID Section Nine, Department Seventeen."

Ted looked closer. "She's a *woman*, for Christ's sake."

"So is half the population of America, boss." Gerry leaned in to hit a key. "Nicole Hagen. Second generation Polish-American. Maiden name, Brynczka. Her mother, French Canadian. Hagen started in Support, Logistics Section, then into Plans. The powers that be must've thought highly of her because they pulled her out, shipping her off to Camp Peary. The Farm. Then on to Italy as a Non-Official Cover Operative."

"A NOC," Ted mumbled, reading on. "No immunity. No backup. That's tough stuff."

"Then to London before coming home to marry some guy in Communications."

Ted looked up. "Not *Josh* Hagen!"

"The same, boss."

"What a dull bastard. Never boozed, never smoked. Never made a fool of himself at office parties. What good did it do him? He croaked at his desk from a massive coronary."

Ted scanned down through the woman's stats. "I'd have thought more of him had he been humping his secretary on her desk when he bought it."

Margaret's voice came over the intercom. "Mister Ladly calling from Ogunquit. Line 2. He is wondering why the subject showed up without someone warning them."

Ted jabbed the flashing button. "Ted here, Eric. How in hell did that happen?"

"Don't ask me. Page charged out of the house while we were poking through his mail. Surprised the hell out of us after Gerry promised we'd be long gone before he showed up."

Ted shot Gerry a scowl. "Anything in the mail?"

"Not much. A Lands' End catalogue folded around a local weekly and the usual bills. Hydro, phone. And a postcard."

"Who from?"

"We only had time to see the photo side before Page grabbed the bundle."

"A photo of what, Eric?"

"A sunset."

"Over Vegas?"

"More like over the Grand Canyon."

"How did Page react when he caught you rifling his mailbox?"

"Pissed off. We'd covered ourselves earlier by picking a name off another rural mailbox."

"And he believed you?"

"It… seems so."

Ladly's reply lacked confidence. Ted let it go.

The intercom buzzed again. "Mister Edgars on the other line, sir. From Boston."

"Tell him to take a number, Margaret." Ted went on with Ladly. "Should Page leave the house, Eric, tail the bastard." He hung up and glanced at his assistant. "A postcard from the Grand Canyon. No doubt from Poplawski. How'd we screw up?"

"Ask your good buddy, Edgars. He should've warned us Page was on the loose."

"What else on Ms. Hagen?"

"She returned to London after her husband died, putting in a transfer to come back stateside two years ago."

"And?"

"I'd say a bad career move, because they stuck her away in Research to handle both Polish and French material reading technical journals and newspapers, monitoring foreign social media—that sort of thing."

"What about her initial training at The Farm?"

"She did fine. Y'know, how to run agents, surveillance techniques and unarmed combat, among other things. She aced handling 9 mm automatics, pissing off those macho types in her class, I'm sure."

"We're looking for a babysitter, Gerry, not a marksman." Ted glanced back at the screen. "A Master's *cum laude* from Harvard—my old alma mater—in institutional psychology."

"Then you two have something in common. She speaks several other languages besides Polish—Spanish, Italian, gets by in German. She was seconded to the September 9/11 team probing into the disaster at New York City's World Trade Center."

"Her personal life?"

"From what I've learned on such short notice, she's been much of a loner since her husband died. She teaches computer tech at a local community college several evenings a week to fill in the time, several friends told me. She'll need clearance. An upgrade."

"Time's running out, Gerry. Bring her in. If she screws up, it's your balls in the wringer. Keep the briefing to a minimum. Impress upon her that it's no big deal. Use Compdata as her cover. She'll need recent photos of Poplawski, those Ladly and Locke took at Niagara Falls."

"Fine, except—"

"Remind her to *watch* the old gent, not hold his hand."

"She's here now, boss—"

Ted stared at him. "Where's here?"

"In the Bubble. I left her there, not knowing how else to calm her down. Besides, she told us to stuff the assignment, whatever we had in mind."

"A widow who figures it's her right to be pigheaded when it suits her? Bring her up. I'm in the mood to kick ass."

CHAPTER TEN
Wednesday, October 5. 8:25 AM

Harm removed an elastic around the Lands' End catalogue. Tucked in the fold was the usual utilities and phone bill, and something Harm didn't expect: a postcard of the Grand Canyon. He flipped it over:
My dear friend Harmon,
Hanna, who writes this, and I are here at Hopi Point in your Grand Canyon. Las Vegas next, then Niagara Falls.
I am sailing home from Montréal on the TSS Casimir III on Wednesday, 5 October. 3 PM departure.
I am greatly disheartened to have missed you, after we left messages on your answering machine.
Do widzenia. Leszek.

The name *TSS Casimir III* struck Harm as familiar. Hadn't Nathan Edgars mentioned the ship while on the phone back at the airport hotel? He'd asked someone called 'Ted' if the *Casimir* was leaving on schedule.

He glanced back at the Leszek's message. The *same* ship was leaving Wednesday. The fifth. 3 PM. *Today*! It wasn't yet 9 AM, meaning he had time to drive to Montréal, or, better, fly there and spend what time was left with his old friend before the ship sailed.

Harm used the borrowed cell phone to reach the Montréal Harbor Authority and was passed on to the ship's purser's office. He asked them if he could speak to Leszek

Poplawski. The passenger couldn't be reached, he was told. But with the ship's departure delayed from 3 to 5 PM, there was time enough to call back later.

Harm couldn't believe it when he heard himself ask for any last-minute cancellations aboard.

Was he kidding himself? Why not? He had only to pack enough for what, a five, six-day transatlantic crossing? And catch a direct return flight from wherever to Los Angeles in time for Sam's custody hearing? That would give him plenty of time with Leszek Poplawski, a dear old friend…

"You're in luck, sir. You must understand, Mister…?"

"Page." Harm grinned. "Harmon Page."

"You must understand, Mister Page, we've had two cancellations, with one already taken. The second is also a stateroom on the Boat Deck. Upgrades are snatched up the moment—"

"I'll take it," Harm said, shaking his head in disbelief.

"Very good, sir. There are three ports of call. London/Tilbury, Rotterdam or Gdynia—"

Harm took a breath. "London/Tilbury."

"For your interest, there are formal evenings on board, though none compulsory. You have a choice of first or second sitting."

"Second is fine."

"We are reserving a stateroom for you, Mister Harmon Page, on the Boat Deck level. We hope you will find it to your liking."

Harm gave him his credit card information and hung up to collapse on the sofa with a broad grin plastered across his face.

"You can't *refuse* an assignment, Ms. Hagen," Ted told her while lining up a putt.

Nicole, seated in a leather chair, crossed her legs in an unconscious reaction to his less-than-friendly attitude.

"Why not? The request didn't come through the proper channels."

Gerry, aware a battle of wits was about to erupt, turned away to talk on the cordless phone.

"Who should know it better than you, Mister Grosvenor? Sticking a note on my office door, ordering me out here to a department I'm unfamiliar with, by someone I wouldn't know from Adam."

Gerry glanced over his shoulder. "From Gerry."

Nicole shot him a frosty look. "All for an assignment that is fuzzy at best."

Ted leaned on the putter. "Precisely why we've submitted it through your superior."

"Which means it has yet to reach him."

"This happens to be an emergency, Ms. Hagen."

"An emergency needing me to be nursemaid to an old buzzard on a transatlantic voyage." Nicole walked over to stare at the old pine-framed mirror on the wall. "As your assistant clearly put it."

Gerry sighed. "Locke on the line again. Harmon Page is still giving them trouble."

"Tell Eric to throw him in the car's trunk. And bring the sonofabitch back alive."

She pressed a thumb against the mirror and turned away.

"Now that you've dealt with whoever this beleaguered *Harmon Page* might be, cut to the chase, Mister Grosvenor."

"There's no chase, Ms. Hagen, which raises the question why someone of your caliber and education ends up doing little more than clerical work. From a NOC to reading transcripts, journals, books…social media."

"That's my business."

"Then why am I left with the impression someone's got it in for you? Either that, or you've simply lost the spark it takes to make things happen."

"I lost a husband, damn it. And you ask me that?"

"Records show he died more than two years ago. The saddest of moments, to be sure. But it's time for the grieving to end and you to get on with your life."

Gerry cut in again, if only to stave off open warfare, "I can't reach her superior…"

Nicole took Ted's putter from him and eased him aside. "You can't reach him because it's Wednesday." She studied the distance from the ball to the overturned coffee cup, mostly facing away from her.

"You might catch him in Paris or Medicine Hat." She struck the ball while still talking. "Honolulu or Come-By-Chance. He travels a lot."

It careened across the carpet, ricocheting off the wall and disappeared into the cup.

Ted swore he was seeing things. "Who taught you that?"

Nicole looked unsmiling at the special projects chief. "My father, who lives on the family ranch in Colorado. He taught me how to ride, how to shoot straight, how to play golf, and how *not* to be intimidated at moments like this."

Ted took the putter, slipping it back in the golf bag. "You're free to go, Mrs. Hagen."

Gerry groaned. "You said it yourself, boss. Time's running out…"

"Then contact the White House, Gerry. Tell Willy Novak we've run into a snag. Ms. Hagen won't cooperate. It's up to him to work it out."

Nicole bristled. "Who the hell is Willy Novak?"

"The president's chief liaison officer."

Nicole's blue eyes were on fire. "I'm in, damn it, but I'll throw up after every meal."

Ted walked her to the door. "We'll load you up with a boatload of Dramamine. Wait with my receptionist."

He closed it, blocking Gerry from following her.

"What's the latest on Page?"

"Eric says he boarded a fishing boat. They're following him up the coast by car."

"And the rental?"

"Parked by the Cape Porpoise pier. He could only be heading for Montréal, boss, to meet Poplawski before the ship sails."

"No question. Our immediate problem is Hagen. I don't want her pulling any shit like this at the last minute. Stick with her, making sure she packs cocktail outfits along with everything else. I'm sure that won't be a big stretch for her."

"Check."

"And contact the ship's Purser's Office to confirm her accommodation. No goddamn glitches. I'll arrange to fly her out of Dulles."

Gerry said, "I'm curious why she pressed her thumb against your mirror. Then backed off?"

"A bright move," Ted admitted. "No space between the thumb and its reflected image meant she'd be staring into a two-way mirror. A space between thumb and reflected image meant she had nothing to worry about."

"I like her already," Gerry said with a smile. "As for Willy Novak, God only knows what we'd ever do without him."

"True enough." Ted Grosvenor went back to his desk to see a light flashing on his phone. He picked it up to hear Nathan Edgars' voice burst over the line.

"Page, the sonofabitch, checked out of the hotel last night, Ted. After promising to meet me this morning for breakfast."

"He's back in Ogunquit, Nathan. No thanks to you."

"It's not my fault, God damn it. I *trusted* him."

"He obviously didn't trust you. Anything else?"

"He told me some weird story about being run off the road up the New England coast over the weekend. The car ended up in the ocean. With him in it. Is it true?"

"Could be." Ted hung up, wondering what Harmon C. Page would do next.

Harm dialed the international jetport at Portland, booking a flight to Montréal. Another call went to Mrs. Sonin, asking if she could keep an eye on the house for the next ten days.

Packed and anxious to go, he was leaving in the rental, when he noticed the same blue car parked back up the road. It followed him when he pulled out of his driveway.

Having no idea why, he phoned an old friend…

"The target is on the move, Mister Grosvenor," Ladly's voice broke over the static. "Heading north from Ogunquit."

"Stick with him, Eric," Ted said, hanging up as his assistant came in. "Page told Nathan some cockamamie story, Gerry, about his car ending up in the Atlantic. With him in it."

"I'll check with the local state police—"

Margaret's voice filled the room. "Eric Ladly again, sir."

"God damn sonofabitch, Mister Grosvenor. Page's driving all over the map."

"Where are you now, Eric?"

"Cape Porpoise. He parked his rental to talk to an old geezer at a fishing shack." The line crackled and cleared. "They're walking along the wood pier. Shit. They're climbing aboard an old fishing boat."

"Nab him. Charge him with resisting arrest." The connection popped and hissed again. "I'm losing you…" The line went dead.

Cap'n Perry watched the men charge along the pier toward them. The taller was waving a badge that glinted in the sunlight.

"Are those the pair you were talkin' about, son?" the old man shouted from the fishing boat's covered wheelhouse.

Harm looked up from loosening the boat's bow line.

"Appears so, Cap'n," he yelled over the roar of the diesel engine. Jumping aboard, he grabbed the wheelhouse railing as the ancient craft swung out toward the open water of the bay.

A breathless Eric Ladly stopped to watch it bob past the reefs.

Locke caught up. "What now?"

Ladly jammed the leather badge holder back into his suit pocket.

"What Grosvenor expects of us. We don't let that cunning bastard out of our sight."

Ladly and Locke followed the fishing boat's progress while driving along the paved road close to the water. It had disappeared several times behind juts of land before heading back the way it had come.

They were pacing up and down the Cape Porpoise pier when the little craft docked. Cap'n Perry tossed them a mooring line. Locke caught it while Ladly jumped aboard flashing his ID.

"Where's your passenger?" he yelled over the noise from the engine.

The skipper shut it off and lowered his butt on the gunwale.

"Dropped him off up the coast." The captain took a pouch of Bull Durham tobacco and cigarette paper from his scruffy denim jacket. "Like he asked."

"Where up the coast?"

"A spell beyond the mouth of the Kennebunk River. Past Spoutin' Rock." Cap'n Perry drew a line of tobacco along the paper he was holding between two stained fingers.

Ladly peered down into the tiny, dimly-lit galley, making out the sink full of dirty dishes and an unmade bunk. There was a toilet and makeshift shower where the bulkhead narrowed.

"Where did he get off exactly?"

The skipper licked the sticky side of the paper, rolled it over the tobacco and squeezed it closed before answering.

"Parson's Beach. Soaked his pants right up to his arse while wadin' ashore."

"You knew Page?"

"We fish together."

"How often?"

"When the weather cooperates. He'd bring along a case of Moosehead and his young daughter, before she went west to live with her mother. A pretty girl who loved fishin'. And his dad."

Ladly climbed back on the pier. "You could be in deep shit, old man. It's a federal offence to harbor a fugitive."

He watched them step off the pier and head for the parking lot.

"Best you bring a warrant with you next time, y'hear?" he called out.

He waited as they peered inside the rental car, rattled the door handles, and got back into their own vehicle. They drove off, leaving a rising cloud of dust behind.

Only then did Cap'n Perry tap a foot on the uneven floorboards.

A section of the weathered planking creaked open. Harm brushed off the dust and cobwebs as he climbed out from a cramped place next to the diesel engine.

"How was it, son?" the old captain said with a grin.

"A tad noisy," Harm said, lowering the hatch into place. "Any idea who the Hardy Boys were?"

The skipper shifted the unlit cigarette between his dry lips. "The one with the moustache and busted beak stuck a badge in my face. It had an eagle's head on it."

"Central Intelligence." Harm couldn't imagine why the CIA would be after him. He thrust bills into the old man's hand, refusing to take them back.

"I wouldn't trust those shifty bastards," said the old man. "Nor should you, son."

"Aye, aye, Cap'n," Harm said, climbing up onto the pier.

Olga Tuseva stuck her head in her boss's office, all smiles.

"Guess who?"

His personal assistant's guessing games were not one of Vladimir's favorite pastimes.

"No clue," he replied, with little enthusiasm.

"According to the Café Troika's maitre d', a stranger ate alone in the small dining room last Saturday night. No server recognized him." Olga leaned against the door frame, arms folded. "The *same* person was texting *while eating*. Very *un*-Russian, yes?"

Vladimir stared at her in disbelief. "*Texting?*"

"On a cell phone. I was having the maitre d' email us the list of those dining in the smaller dining room. Then I decided to pick it up myself, giving me the chance to talk to the staff."

"His *name,* Ms. Tuseva."

"Alexey Gritsenko. They tagged him as a run-of-the-mill government employee."

Vladimir made it a practice never to underestimate a servers' uncanny ability at judging people. He told Olga as much. If they agreed among themselves that this individual seemed to be a government employee, she should take their word for it.

"Find this Alexey Gritsenko for me, Ms. Tuseva."

"That should be easy," she chided him. "Among the thousands of government employees in Moscow alone."

"First, have Misha here at once. From his lab. From an extended breakfast, from a smoking. From wherever…"

A disheveled Misha Kodenko slumped into the spare chair by Vladimir's desk.

"This is about the pacemaker," He blushed through his scrawny beard. "Because you know we still have it."

Vladimir stared at his tech. "You didn't return it?"

"I should have told you. We hadn't finished running a test with an ordinary cell phone. We thought we might have found…"

"I have only now learned, Misha, someone at the Troika café used a cell during dinner last Saturday night. Seconds later, the scientist was dead."

The chief lab technician straightened, relieved yet trying not to show it.

"You must continue, Misha Rodenko. Understand?"

"What bothers me," said the chef tech, "is once we prove Doctor Yevtushenko was murdered, what's to stop the killers from coming after us?"

"You have connections. Find a similar pacemaker. Old, new, it doesn't matter. We will return it to the coroner at the Militia forensic laboratory, admitting we have come to the same conclusion as everyone else: it was a faulty pacemaker that killed him."

"Someone is sure to check the serial number of the bogus pacemaker, putting us under suspicion."

"When those behind the murder want to destroy it with no one the wiser? We must be patient. We have the evidence, the original pacemaker. We will wait for those behind the killing to make a wrong move. And they will."

Misha nodded, feeling better. "I will put a bogus pacemaker in the same packaging as the original and return it to the coroner."

Vladimir, coming from behind his desk, put an arm around his chief technician's shoulders as they walked to the door.

"We are a team, you and me, Misha Mikhail," he said. "Never doubt it."

Olga Tuseva swept into Vladimir's office moments later, her saucy smile saying it all.

"You've found Alexey Gritsenko!" Vladimir exclaimed.

"He's one of many accountants buried in the Department of Statistics."

"A hitman in Statistics. What better cover? How did you find him?"

"By taking your advice and using my computer. I started with the Central Registry. As cooperation there is a joke, I brought up the individual departments."

"A major task," said Vladimir, "considering we're the largest single employer in all Russia."

"There he was, an accountant of the lowest order, sir. He covers himself by sending email applications to other departments to improve his lot. And getting nowhere. I reached him by phone, inviting him to a late lunch at the same café."

"When?"

"Today."

"Cancel it. I won't put your life in danger."

"Not *my* life, sir," she said. "Your's."

That Vladimir would be back in the saddle, pleased him. He told her it was unlikely Alexey Gritsenko would return to where he committed murder and their connection to Russian Intelligence.

"I lied to him, saying the first name that popped into my head. I told him you were with the Dairy Board." She hid a blush the best she could. "We needed a positive ID."

Vladimir's face lit up. "Excellent. We'll tell him we're looking for an accountant to put the Board back on its feet."

Olga tongued her red lips, an unconscious habit when she was excited. "I'll have the maitre d' arrange for the servers from Saturday night to be assigned to work the lunch."

"With our crew as backup." Vladimir glanced at her. "We do good work together, Ms. Tuseva."

"We always have, sir," she replied to the unexpected compliment.

"Page can't vanish into thin air," Ted muttered from behind his desk.

Gerry waved his cell as he stepped away from the window.

"I was confirming Hagen's booking with the purser's office when it struck me. Surely Page wouldn't have the balls to book himself aboard the *Casimir III*."

"You'd never know..."

"And what did he do? He picked up a last-minute cancellation."

"The conniving bastard will have to reach Montréal. We'll cut him off. Have our team check local airports. Flights to Montréal. Flag one-way airfares."

"There's always the Homeland Security option, or the Canadian equivalent—"

"Get either of those involved," Ted growled, "and we're up to our crotches in trouble. They know nothing about keeping something low-key."

"Which leaves Ladly and Locke handling it."

"Good. We'll add extra backup, if needed." For Ted, this screw-up had turned personal.

Harm parked the rental at the Portland jetport and walked to a lone vehicle parked at the nearby taxi stand. He tossed his luggage in the back seat, telling the cabbie he'd be a minute.

Picking up his ticket, he tore it into pieces and dropped it in the recycling bin on the way out.

He had no sooner settled in the cab's passenger seat when the familiar blue car braked in front of the entrance. He saw Moustache and his partner pile out and bolt for the entrance.

"Where to?" the cabbie asked, his eyes barely visible under the wide peak of his Boston Red Sox baseball cap.

"A quick flight to Montréal would work for me," Harm said. "The office screwed up. I was expected there hours ago. I'm thinking of a small plane."

"That rules out Trudeau International. Most independent pilots round here don't have the instrumentation or permission."

"Any ideas?"

"We got small airports scattered all over. Bangor, Biddeford. My brother-in-law operates a Cessna out of a strip near North Berwick. He could use the business. He also has a friend with a small airfield over the border near St. Hubert." The cabbie grinned. "Mind, he's rough 'round the edges. He'd take you, as long as you're not a fugitive from justice…"

"Not that I'm aware of," said Harm, settling back against the seat.

Vladimir Lyubimov mulled over the menu, not knowing what to expect. Seated opposite him was Alexey Gritsenko in a loose-fitting, pin-striped gray suit and plain striped tie.

From what Gritsenko had gleaned from the Dairy Board's recent financial statement, he told his host improvements could bring the over-bloated board back to its senses.

It amazed Vladimir, the thoroughness Gritsenko had shown in so short a time. He had to remind himself what this nondescript, bespectacled killer did in his spare time.

The small dining room was filled with members of his team passing themselves off as regular patrons. Each was primed for that moment when the target would grasp why he'd been invited for lunch.

Vladimir was suggesting the *golubsty,* a café specialty, when he was called to the foyer. Waiting for him was an anxious maître d' and a dispirited Olga Tuseva.

"I am deeply sorry," the maître d' explained, "the individual seated with you shows no resemblance to the patron from last Saturday evening."

"You have no doubt?" Vladimir asked.

"None. My servers agree this gentleman is short and chubby, lacking the broad shoulders of the previous patron. More important, he displays none of the *presence* of the other man."

Vladimir apologized at once and steered Olga to a quiet corner.

"It is beyond me, sir," she said, "how it could turn out so terribly wrong."

"As the Americans say, Ms. Tuseva, you cannot win them all. Tell Mister Gritsenko urgent business forces me back to the office. He may choose whatever he wishes from the menu at no cost to him."

"And our team?"

"Let them finish lunch. You, Ms. Tuseva, will choose where you and I will eat before returning to the office."

It would take Olga no time to decide.

The Café Margarita was on a tree-lined square overlooking the picturesque Patriarch's Pond. It was named after a popular fictional heroine in Mikhail Bulgakov's popular novel. It was also one of Vladimir's favorite places to dine.

He and Olga shared a table by a window with its brooding dark wood paneling. They began with shots of *zubrowka*, an herb-flavored vodka. Olga could think of nothing better, after being so discouraged.

"It confuses me, sir" she said, "why the killer used a *real* name as an alias."

"A brilliant move," Vladimir replied with obvious delight. "He's adding his own brand of authenticity. First, ask yourself, who is Alexey Gritsenko? An anonymous little fellow buried in a remote government office. Should his name crop up for whatever reason, those checking would know he exists."

"How would that help?"

"It gives the assassin time to fulfill his contract. He'd work from a variety of aliases, you understand, dropping those when they've served his purpose. He replaces them with equally obscure ones."

"We must track him down, then," said Olga. "Before this 'Alexey Gritsenko' disappears."

"We will also caution our friends at the Central Intelligence Agency how this contract killer operates: using aliases of real people."

In the silence that followed, Olga Tuseva promised herself to find this elusive bastard, if for no other reason than he made her look like an amateur.

With his head buried in the Cessna's engine, the overweight pilot cursed on whacking his thumb with the wrench. Having someone with him broke his concentration.

"Fly someone I don't know across the border? Are you nuts?" he said to Harm. "At least not before Homeland Security shows up to check you out. That, or fuck off."

"How long will it take him to get here?" Harm asked, knowing time was short.

The pilot took another swipe at the stubborn bolt. "Christ only knows."

The Aeroflot flight from Moscow to Montreal's Pierre Elliott Trudeau International Airport, via New York, landed on schedule. The passengers were ushered to the baggage area and on to Canada Customs. Among them was a businessman in a tailored gray pin-striped suit. He was the first in line at the Canadian Customs booths.

The officer compared the passport photo with the passenger standing before him, stamped it and handed it back.

"Enjoy your stay, Mister Gritsenko," he said, waving over the next in line.

CHAPTER ELEVEN
Wednesday, October 5 11:10 AM

Thomas E. Slater slumped forward, hitting his head on something solid. "What the hell...?" he muttered, pushing himself up on his elbows.

A face appeared over the back of the seat, the cabbie's dark eyes amused.

"You are perhaps wondering where you are, m'sieu," he said in his French-Canadian accent. "You are presently kneeling on the floor of my taxicab. 'Appily, we are close removed from the 'arbor."

Thomas hauled himself back onto the seat. He was a big man with a mass of light brown hair, broad shoulders, and a pleasant round face. "The harbor?"

"The 'arbor of Old Montréal."

The traffic light turned green. The cabbie stepped on the gas. "We arrive here directly from your *adieu* party in Ottawa. Which, I am told, ended at nine o'clock this morning."

Thomas pulled his unbuttoned raincoat around him. His mouth was dry, his tongue thick and pasty. He remembered some of the debauchery, prompted by his good buddy MacLeod. Drinks at the National Press Club, gathering steam in the lounge at the American Embassy, and on to the rowdy bar in the Chateau Laurier. Lap dancers over in Gatineau came vaguely to mind.

"*Vos amis* placed you into my taxi," the cabbie said, over his shoulder. "I kept you company while they marched up to your apartment to pack for you. Et voilà," he announced, driving through the wrought iron gates of the Old Port without slowing down. "Nous sommes arrivés. We are 'ere."

Thomas stared at the top half of a ship protruding above Pier 3. Emblazoned on the smokestack was the red crest of the Polish Shipping Lines.

The driver, handing over a passport, along with the MCNEIL/ROSSMAN travel folder, stepped out of the cab. Thomas did the same as he fumbled for his wallet.

"Do not trouble yourself, m'sieu," he said, removing Thomas' baggage from the trunk. "Your friends were kind enough to have taken care of everything."

Thomas slipped him several large bills anyway and watched the taxi pull away. He could only wonder what those misfits back in Ottawa had packed for this trip.

The noise of tractors, front-end loaders, shouts, and low-pitched whine of the loading cranes filled the air around the ribbon of concrete pier between the warehouse and the towering black hull of the *TSS Casimir III*.

From high on the starboard flying Bridge was the vessel's master, Captain Stanislaw Jablonski, an impressive figure with in a mane of thick gray hair. He wore a starched white uniform with four braided gold bars on the sleeves.

He was watching longshoremen struggle with the slings operated by the stern crane. They were rigging up a Mercedes-Benz van to hoist it aboard. He could see its wheelbase was too wide for the sling's stirrups. As if there wasn't delay enough on leaving port.

Directly opposite him were the second-floor warehouse windows serving as the embarkation area. Here, the *Casimir's* seven hundred passengers would be caught up in the tedious procedure of passport control, ticket checks, first and second sitting assignments in the dining room.

A lone figure, standing motionless on the rooftop parking opposite, caught the captain's attention. The eyes were shaded by a baseball cap, and he wore a heavy-knit seaman's sweater.

"You damn fool," Stanislaw muttered in Polish.

"Friend of yours?" came a voice behind him.

"Not that I know of, Henryk," the senior officer replied. "And you showing up here before departure means only one thing."

Chief engineer, Henryk Niski, leaned on the railing beside him. Dressed in white, he was a short, thick-chested Pole with a leathery face.

"The spare parts for the hydraulics," he mumbled, "were to be air-freighted here before we left port. They failed to appear on the manifest."

"The package was never shipped, Henryk. Those land-locked idiots at head office decided it wasn't worth it."

The chief engineer stomped back to the bridge, "Should anything go wrong in mid-Atlantic, you and I will know who to blame…"

"Have someone remind those *cretins* below," Stanislaw called after him, "that the Mercedes would fit on the slings from the for'ard hold."

Henryk gave a perfunctory wave over his shoulder.

Thomas eased through the doors of the embarkation area to face baggage littering the floor and endless queues of passengers standing shoulder to shoulder.

The racket brought on a fresh wave of nausea. He walked to the nearest, shortest line, dropped his luggage beside him, and took a long, deep breath.

"Some party," he heard the woman say next to him.

Thomas concentrated on keeping her in focus. She had dark hair and long legs poured into slim, expensive jeans. Her blue V-neck sweater, he noticed, complimented the blue eyes. He tried hard to recognize her and gave up.

"I'm sorry," he said. "I didn't realize you were there."

Her smile was genuine. "I wasn't. But what you're wearing gives it away."

Thomas glanced at his tuxedo showing beneath the raincoat, and the slightly off-kilter tartan cummerbund around his waist. His black bow tie hung loose around his neck.

"I thought you looked familiar," she said, putting out a hand. "But then again maybe not. I'm Nicole Hagen 'From Washington'."

"And I'm Thomas Slater." he said, shaking it. "From Ottawa."

Midway down the same line, a tall, dignified Englishman sucked in air between his clenched teeth. The long wait was catching up with him. Not that he would admit it.

The stoic looks on her husband's face Gweneth Ashcroft knew, meant impending trouble. The fixed stare at nothing, a constant wiping of his forehead, settled it.

"For goodness sake, Hugh, do sit down," Gwen whispered. "Somewhere. Anywhere. I will handle this. Besides, we seniors have rights." She paused for dramatic effect. "I'll have Isobel Cornish-Smith sign us up with the local chapter of Gray Power the moment we return."

Hugh Ashcroft's brown eyes came alive. "Over my dead body," he muttered, holding himself together by concentrating on a dark-haired woman ahead of them.

Nicole saw the older man giving her a pleasant glance. She returned it with a smile. "Your name was *Slater?*" she said to Thomas.

The mere nod of his head brought on a feeling of light-headedness.

"Then I've bad news for you. You're in line A to J. You want R to Z."

"If anyone complains," he murmured, "I'm Thomas Edward. My middle name."

Thank God, Nicole mused to herself, someone on board had a sense of humor. She felt better already, despite what lay ahead. Seasickness being high on the list.

Leszek Poplawski eased from his daughter's tight embrace. He was somewhat shorter, with his broad shoulders built on a sturdy frame. His thin hair was in sharp contrast to a thick, healthy beard.

"I must go," he whispered in Polish, kissing her damp cheeks.

The moon-faced Hanna Bajda sniffed. "There is still time to change your mind, papa."

"America is *your* home, my child. There will be other times. Other visits." He hugged her once more and drew back. "Go, please, before you miss your flight home."

Leszek, finding the moment too painful, turned away to step through the sliding doors.

"I love you, papa," he heard her cry out as the door closed behind him.

"Where are you going?" announced a squat, uniformed security guard blocking his way.

Leszek hesitated. "I am being... on board already." Having arrived earlier, he and Hanna had been welcomed aboard for the buffet lunch.

"Your embarkation card," said the weary guard.

Leszek fumbled in his pockets, removing what he hoped was it.

"Zielony," he said, holding it out. "Green." The guard waved him on.

Leszek circled the packed room to stop short of the glass-covered gangway. He glanced at the ship's black hull marked with the large white letters proclaiming it to be the legendary *TSS Casimir III*. This view of the vessel brought Leszek to tears.

"Next, please," Entertainment Officer Filip Sotek called out over the bedlam. A tall, affable man in his late thirties, Filip shared one of the many embarkation tables with his assistant, Junior Officer Jerzy Olecki.

"Have your tickets, passports, and husbands ready," he dead panned, delivering the same message in several other languages.

His assistant nudged him. "Mister *Clean*," said Jerzy, nodding across the vast, noisy room.

Filip noticed the ship's first staff officer standing at the entrance to the covered gangway. Pawel Klimek wore a tailored navy-blue uniform with its cluster of gold braids. He was often mistaken for the ship's master, a confusion, Filip knew, Pawel enjoyed if not embraced.

"I'll bet my last zloty he's looking for you," said Jerzy.

Filip eased the passenger list and passports over to his assistant.

"Let's hope he sees things our way for a change."

"That's what I like about you," said Jerzy. "Your misguided sense of optimism."

Pawel Klimek fidgeted with the cuff of his jacket. As the ship's second in command, he found it intolerable to watch embarkation procedures lag far behind schedule. The original 1600 hrs. departure was already pushed forward, making it five o'clock.

Filip reached Officer Klimek, knowing, from experience, anyone in his line of fire was in for a rough ride.

"You're looking for me?" said Filip in English.

"Explain to me why, Mister Sotek," Pawel replied in Polish, "the long lines of passengers are still waiting to be processed."

"Canadian customs showing up late to handle the departure. Add to it the Montréal Port Authority's confusion over which terminal would be free when we returned from the side trip to the Maritimes."

Getting no reaction, Filip went on. "Taking your frustration out on me is pointless. I'm not in charge of embarkation."

"I am not here to argue," Pawel snapped at him. "I'm to pass on Captain Jablonski's decision. You will find a replacement from among the crew."

"With due respect—"

"With due respect, Mister Sotek?"

"*With due respect*, our passengers pay good money for this voyage—"

"Good money is what one expects from Cunard."

"At least consider an alternative. I've reached the Montréal musicians' union who've agreed—"

"On whose authorization?"

"Mine."

"It falls within *my* jurisdiction."

"A replacement would be with us as far as London/Tilbury. We'd throw in a bonus and the expected flight back to Montréal."

Pawel's face turned red. "Why can I *never* give you an order without you questioning me? The order stands." Pawel turned away to stomp back across the gangway.

"Let me guess," Jerzy Olecki said as Filip plunked down beside him. "A decision Mister *Clean* failed to run by the captain."

"I should've listened to you," Filip dropped his voice. "Without making it obvious, Jerzy, check out an older couple halfway down A to J."

Jerzy looked them over. "The husband, tall with a paisley scarf? The wife, slightly younger with a Tweed skirt and matching jacket. English, for sure."

"He looks as if he'll keel over at any moment. Go over, Jerzy, making any excuse to bring them here. Being mindful—"

Jerzy pushed away from the table. "Being mindful the Brits are a stubborn lot."

Gwen Ashcroft couldn't believe it. The young officer coming along the line had stopped beside them. One glance at their tickets, and she watched him roll his eyes.

"Ah, Mister and Mrs. Ashcroft. Sorry, you are booked in a stateroom. Meaning you are in the wrong queue. Come with me, please."

"It is our lucky day," Gwen murmured as they followed him.

"Horse muffins," growled Hugh. "It's called preferential treatment, because we're old."

"Had we been left much longer, Hugh, dear, they would be wheeling you aboard on a stretcher. Or to a hospital on shore."

In line K to S, a blonde-haired Kimberly Stockwell, her trim figure poured into brown slacks and sleeveless top, poked her husband with her elbow. "Did you see that?"

"See what?" said Angus, killing time with his nose stuck in the *Wall Street Journal*.

"The old couple pulled from the line and taken directly to an embarkation table."

"Maybe they're in the wrong—" He glanced up to see his wife purring over the two ship's officers at the same table. He felt his wife's thigh push up against his leg. She was at it again...

CHAPTER TWELVE
Wednesday, October 5, 5:13 PM

The *Casimir III*'s cargo holds had been closed fore and aft by late Wednesday afternoon, the two cranes secure and the gangway rolled away.

In his outside cabin on A Deck, Leszek Poplawski stood tip-toe, peering out the small, round porthole. The view was nothing more than thick, blackened logs forming the outer portion of the pier. Haunted by leaving his daughter in tears, he returned to unpack.

From the folds of a sweater, he removed a photograph. It was his favorite from many taken of Hanna aboard the *Maid of the Mist* as the little vessel bobbed in the swirling, pounding water of Niagara Falls.

They had been among a hundred-odd other 'adventurers' wrapped in disposable plastic blue ponchos. Hanna was laughing as he snapped it, her deep-set hazel eyes cast against a face lashed with spray.

Having time to spare before departure, they had visited the Old Port of Montréal where they dropped by a drugstore to have the digital photos made into prints. Hanna had given her father one set, keeping a second for herself. She had had this photo enlarged and mounted in a plain wood frame as a going away present.

Placing it on the bedside table, Leszek looked with warmth at the round, happy face, when he felt a shuddering underfoot.

The old man's joy changed to sudden pain, remembering how he had insisted Hanna not wait for the ship to sail. He had worried she would miss her flight back to Connecticut.

Would she have gone? No. *She was stubborn, like her mother.*

Leszek bolted from the cabin.

A pair of black and red, snub-nosed tugs nudged the ocean liner away from the pier. From both ship and shore came the raucous sounds of frantic good-byes. The passengers, packed deep along the vessel's starboard open decks, were tossing the traditional spirals of colorful streamers toward the well-wishers lining the pier below.

Many of those on shore, affording a better view, appeared on the building's open upper parking area and observation platform.

The blown kisses and clicking cameras were captured by a Canadian Broadcasting Corporation television crew on board.

Nicole Hagen, among those crowding the Boat Deck rail, was having second thoughts. The unexpected drive to Langley was bad enough without a bewildering, short briefing by what's-his-name? Gerry... Smith. Yes.

A harried packing left no time for her to delegate someone to water the house plants. Then came a flight to Montréal with her, the sole passenger in a well-appointed government jet.

Nor did Nicole appreciate being bullied into accepting the assignment, having always had a sense of control. On graduating from Harvard with honors, she was flattered by an invitation to join the Central Intelligence Agency, a challenge she couldn't refuse.

What followed was a steady progress up through the ranks. Her marriage to Josh Hagen. Shaken by his sudden death, she had settled into a lesser routine. Now this, with no hint of what lay ahead. Other than watching over an old Pole with one foot in the grave.

When she and Thomas had reached the terminal's embarkation table, the easy banter between them had been misconstrued that they were traveling together.

Nicole was assigned to one of a handful of staterooms on the Boat Deck; Thomas to an inside cabin on A Deck. Both had asked for second sitting. Eating together seemed a good idea.

Her spirits lifted on seeing him holding two frosted glasses aloft as he shouldered his way toward her through the crowd.

"What on earth are those?" Nicole shouted over the commotion.

"Whiskey sours," he said, handing her one.

"Surely there's an international regulation forbidding shipboard bars from opening before clearing port—"

The sound of a plaintive, haunting cry of "Papa!" caught Nicole's attention. It came from the terminal building's roof observation platform.

She recognized the woman, her hair pulled severely back in a bun, the flat broad face from the photos given to her of Poplawski and his daughter. Nicole looked back to see a tearful Leszek Poplawski struggling through the crowd making little headway.

"The woman over there," she shouted to Thomas, "is trying to attract the old man's attention. He's behind us. Can you bring him to the railing?"

Thomas looked back, thrust his drink at her and turned away.

A tearful Leszek had given up, when a big man shouted something he missed. He felt the stranger take his arm and guide him through the crowd.

On the pier below, Harm, having reached Montréal too late, scowled at the widening gap between ship and shore. He was aware of the CIA agents not far off. Moustache was smiling as he aimed his cell phone in Harm's direction, then turned to disappear in the crowd.

Frustrated by missing the ship, he hauled out his borrowed cell, choosing a number from the short list of outgoing calls.

Nothing ventured, he decided, nothing gained.

Gerry stepped into his boss's office as the intercom came alive.

"Agent Ladly for you, Mister Grosvenor. Line one."

Ted put the call on speaker phone. "I'm counting on nothing but good news, Eric."

"You got it. I'm sending you a photo attachment on my cell taken moments ago. You'll see Page on the crowded pier. Tugs in the background guiding the *Casimir III* out into the basin. He didn't make it. If there's anything else—"

Ted turned to ask Gerry for the first port of call. It was London/Tilbury.

"Pack up, come home, Eric." Ted clicked off the connection. "On your way out, tell Miss Jennings to connect me with Vladimir Lyubimov. STAT."

Gerry grinned, pleased with the results. "And it's still *Ms*. Jennings, boss."

The three-man crew from the Canadian Broadcasting Corporation had come on board in Montréal. They would tape interviews expressly for noonday television news. The field producer, Jeremy Watts, had heard whispers about seven of the *Casimir's* crew, an officer included, who had jumped ship on arrival in port. It had been hushed up, Jeremy was certain, by the Canadian Government.

Knowing there was no such thing as a *small* cover-up, he had only to corner the liner's captain about these antics and watch him squirm on camera. The producer, counting on the exclusive story behind it, would find a slot on the CBC TV's prestigious *The National*.

With cameraman André Lessard picking up fill-in shots of the ship's general activity, Jeremy and script assistant, Yvette Charbonneau, had settled in the Grand Lounge to look over her list of possible interviews from among the passengers.

"Celebs," said Jeremy, wearing baggy cords and T-shirt. "That's our ticket."

Yvette suggested he should've used his charm to get them on the *Royal Caribbean* or *Cunard*, if he wanted to interview celebrities.

"That's all I need. A smart-ass script assistant. So, who's who?"

Yvette mentioned a woman from Pennsylvania making her thirtieth trip aboard the *Casimir III*; a 93-year-old who first crossed the Atlantic under sail. A Polish ambassador returning from duties in Peru.

Jeremy insisted she'd better turn up something better to work with.

She suggested a novelist with a book on the *New York Times'* bestseller list a few years back. When she mentioned his name, Jeremy crossed him off, having never heard of him.

"He obviously hadn't heard of you either," she said. "He turned us down."

A dozen others included a Polish scientist, who the Russians refer to as the 'Father of Brain Research'. "My contact tells me he's a Nobel—"

"A Polish Nobel whatever, who's sure to speak lousy English," Jeremy cut in. "*Boring…*"

Yvette had made the arrangements through McNeil/Rossman with meals and overnight accommodation. They would leave the ship in the morning at Sept Iles.

"André will tape our approach to Québec around midnight. Officer Sotek tells me it's worth it, with the reflection of the city's colored lights on the water…"

"Who's Sotek?"

"Our contact on board. The entertainment officer. And don't screw up, Jeremy. He's gone overboard helping arrange everything for us."

"Overboard? Very funny. He's probably angling to get into your tight little jeans. Not to forget free booze. You promised me something else."

"I didn't *promise* you anything. Captain Jablonski has already refused an interview."

"First an asshole author, and now some prick of a sea captain."

"I'll see what I can do. Don't expect a miracle."

Jeremy leaned in close, drawing her perfume into his lungs. "Without a miracle, Yvette, we're royally fucked."

Olga Tuseva poked her head in Vladimir's office.

"Our friend, the American, is on the line with good news. If I am interpreting him favorably, he wishes to speak direct to you."

Vladimir, embarrassed by his poor English, hesitated before picking up the phone.

Passenger Victor Petrie, in flannels, a blazer and an open-necked shirt, leaned on the railing of the Sport Deck. He was drinking a dirty martini while listening to a conversation drifting up from the deck below.

"Your friends packed for you," the woman was saying, "and you're telling me you don't know what they sent along for you to wear?"

"No. They might have packed 'Thing', for all I know."

"Who's *Thing*?"

"My dog. Short for *Everything*. A little terrier, a little sheepdog, a spaniel's floppy ears..."

The woman's deep-throated laugh made Victor smile.

"Stop, before I embarrass myself. Let's go inside."

"You told me you enjoyed fresh air."

"Not this fresh."

"Let's see what's in store for me. Maybe *Thing is* munching on my deodorant stick."

"You're impossible," the woman said, her voice fading.

Victor raised his glass. "To you, Ms. Hagen. Have an eventful trip."

Blonde Kimberly Stockwell sat yoga-fashion on the cabin floor. She was practicing *the cobra* in a lacy bra and bikini panties, when the door handle rattled. "It's unlocked."

Her husband, Angus, came in and took one look at her. "Damn it, Kimberly, what if I'd been the cabin steward?"

"I'd tell him to take a number," she teased.

Angus closed the door and sat on the lower bunk, cluttered with his wife's clothes. He disliked this kind of talk, even in fun.

"How did it go?" she asked, flexing her thigh muscles.

"There was a cancellation for one of the staterooms," he said, distracted by his wife raising her buttocks off the floor. "I was telling the chief purser we'll take it, when another officer whispered in his ear—"

"I'm counting on a happy ending, Gus."

"I was told the stateroom was no longer available."

"Fuck it."

"We were offered a slightly larger *inside* cabin on B Deck. I turned it down."

"So how will we entertain in this shitty little hole-in-the-wall?"

Angus stepped over his wife to reach the porthole. "One guest at a time?"

"Gus-Gus," she purred, pulling herself up beside him, "all this exercise makes me horny."

He felt her foot rubbing the inside of his thigh. "It's almost eight, honey. Second sitting begins—"

"It's been delayed due to our late departure." She tongued his ear and pressed her body against him. "But you go, and I'll ring for that cute little cabin steward."

Angus sighed and began removing his tie, unbuttoning his shirt.

Captain Stanislaw Jablonski studied the young woman before him; the unblinking brown eyes, the slight aggressive arch of her back.

"I made it perfectly clear, Mademoiselle—"

"Charbonneau."

"Mademoiselle Charbonneau, I do not give interviews. Nor am I accustomed to having my orders questioned."

"We have been invited on board the *Casimir III*, Captain," said Yvette, stretching up to her full height of somewhere under five feet, "to tape material for television. We were assured an interview with you, however brief, would be no problem."

"Who authorized it?"

"Your head office. In Gdynia."

"Who at head office?"

"You do not believe me..."

A smile replaced the frown on the captain's tanned face.

"Mademoiselle, you will have your interview, after second sitting. There are conditions. No political or abrasive questions. This is a nostalgic last trip for the *TSS Casimir III*, for guests, crew, and me."

Yvette restrained herself from giving him a big hug.

In the time since the *Casimir* left the Port of Montréal, passengers had been quick to form a bond to one or other of its many bars.

The Poles favored the Polish Bar & Hunter's Room; the Brits had transformed the American Bar into an English pub, if in spirit only. Both were across the Promenade Deck's foyer from the Grand Lounge. As for the Americans and Canadians, they could be found wherever the mood suited them.

The Disco, sandwiched in the stern between decks, was a no-man's land of eclectic tastes, attracting anyone who enjoyed hard rock, sweat, and very late nights.

The ship's forward Boat Deck Bar attracted a veritable United Nations of insomniacs, talkers, listeners, and the odd social butterfly. Spouses of either gender found solace here, and poker players were drawn to the adjacent card room.

The Bar was a picture of tradition, much to Nicole Hagen's delight, with its polished mahogany panels, a leather-trimmed zinc countertop, and shiny brass foot rail.

She and Thomas Slater were among those dropping by for after-dinner drinks. Though formal wear was encouraged, few dressed up on this first evening. Nicole wore in a light cotton dress with a cardigan over her shoulders. Thomas was in slacks, a turtleneck, and a blazer. She teased him about what good taste his friends had into packing for him.

He was promising to pass her remark on to his friends, when he noticed Peter Lount, their tablemate and the ship's guest lecturer, surveying the crowded room from the doorway.

"D'you want to hear more, Thomas asked, "about ancient ships buffeted or sunk by Atlantic storms?" He nodded toward the entrance, "If so, I'll wave Peter over. Personally, I heard enough at dinner."

"True, he can be little boring," Nicole replied, "but I can't remember anyone ever pulling my chair out for me at dinner."

"That's because, Ms. Hagen, most women pull out their own chairs, pump their own gas."

Nicole laughed. "I'm old-fashioned. I'll prove it. I'm buying. What's your pleasure?"

"Cockburn's Special Reserve," he said, as they squeezed in beside the English couple.

Hugh Ashcroft recognized her, and his face lit up. "Hello. We were in the same line before boarding."

"And you were put off," said Nicole, "when given what you described as 'preferential treatment' by the young officer."

Hugh's eyes twinkled. "Are you always this observant, may I ask?"

"How could she not be," chided Gwen, "when you made such a fuss."

Nicole would astound Thomas by ordering their drinks in fluent Polish.

Jeremy Watts had put the captain at ease during the interview held in the comfort of officer's mess. He asked about his background, of changes in sailing technology. Yvette, pleased how it had gone, checked her clipboard, giving him a subtle nod to wrap up. She glanced at André, the cameraman, to make sure he was ready.

"From what I hear, Captain Jablonski," Jeremy was saying, "you have an important passenger on board who the Russians consider one of their own."

"Indeed, Mister Watts. It is Doctor Leszek Poplawski, a highly-respected Nobel Prize winner."

"If so, why would he not have been given a stateroom? It would seem more suitable."

"Doctor Poplawski insisted on what he likes best, having a cabin close to the water."

"I've also heard rumors," Jeremy pressed on, "that, by today's standards, the *Casimir III* is not fit to face a transatlantic crossing."

The room had gone quiet.

"Merde," Yvette murmured.

"I assure you it is not so," the Captain replied. "We have a Magnavox MX 1105 Satellite Navigator and Sperry U.G.P. autopilot. Not to mention a Loran C navigation system and two Krupp radar plotting aids. Denny Brown stabilizers—"

"In comparison to today's liners, it would still seem somewhat old-fashioned—"

"You are obviously unaware, Mister Watts, of a new trend. The *Stella Solaris*, built in 1953, was refurbished some years ago and returned to its original elegance. It serves a growing number of travelers of *all* ages, wanting genuine, unpretentious comfort."

"That may be—"

"As for yourself, you would undoubtedly be attracted to those behemoth 'floating hotels' where pampering has no limit. Rock climbing, surfing..."

What sounded much like 'bravo' erupted from among the officers.

"That maybe so, Captain Jablonski, but it's a sad ending for a ship due not to be refurbished but scrapped on reaching its home port."

"A sorry note for me, yes. It would be remiss of me not to mention the reception last evening, by the Polish consul-general, marking a rich connection in the past between Canada and Poland which—"

"A reception," Jeremy interrupted, "where you'd hardly arrived when summoned back to the *Casimir III*. It seems members of your own crew had jumped ship. An officer among them."

"Pure fiction, *Mister* Watts."

"You say it didn't happen?"

"Precisely." Removing the small metallic mic clipped to his lapel, Stanislaw dropped it on the hardwood floor, crushing it beneath his black leather shoe.

"Get these ingrates off my ship, Mister Sotek," he said, in leaving the room. "Québec City will not come soon enough."

CHAPTER THIRTEEN
Wednesday, October 5, 11:59 PM

It was almost midnight when the watch on the bridge of the *TSS Casimir III* picked up the lights from the old City of Québec. They formed a matrix of clear white dots along the darkened waters of the St. Lawrence.

As the vessel drew near, these same lights fused into a solid glow against the cloudless sky. Announcement of such a spectacle broke from the ship's loudspeakers, with passengers streaming from the bars and nightclubs and onto the ship's open decks.

From his vantage point on the portside flying bridge, Captain Jablonski felt the fresh wind of the clear autumn night cut across the ship's bow and move upward along her superstructure. He wore a light jacket over his white uniform as he studied the revelers crowding the railings below.

Having so many passengers roaming about the ship at midnight, on their first night aboard, was a good omen. Yet with it came a pang of loneliness.

Nothing seemed the same since his wife died. Hildy had been his buffer, his safe haven. Since her death, the *Casimir* had become his home.

The door to the bridge grated on its hinges. Chief Engineer Niski stepped out and stopped to take a deep breath.

"Too much fresh air isn't good for you," Stanislaw called out. "Not when your system is accustomed to diesel fumes."

"Tell me that during the next Atlantic storm," said Henryk, moving in beside him, "when you're out here freezing your gonads off." He paused. "I'm truly disappointed your interview didn't go well. Still, we have more important matters to discuss. And I can only hope you haven't cheated on me—"

"Me? Spoil a taste of victory?" Stanislaw grinned. "Not on your life."

The game they played began once the ship had passed beneath the westerly Pierre Laporte Bridge and its neighbor, the historic Pont de Québec.

Whoever spotted the pilot tender coming from the harbor first, was declared the winner. They concentrated now on finding the tender, a task made difficult by the glimmer from the city lights on the dark water.

"There!" Stanislaw burst out. "Ten o'clock. Bouncing like a cork."

The close friends, sharing wide grins, shook hands before the chief engineer went back to work.

Yvette sat on a large metal case in the Main Deck's foyer as André packed away the last of his camera equipment.

"It is not fair," she said pouting, something she seldom ever did.

André shrugged. "What can you expect from a shit like Watts?"

"I'd still like to know how the *cochon* learned of the defections."

"He's known for his contacts." André sat down beside her. "He can't get off the ship fast enough to file it to *The National*. Too bad…"

Yvette stared at him. "*Comment?*"

"I figured Watts was up to no good, commenting on those jumping ship. The deal was: nothing controversial. I stopped the tape. He'll find nothing—"

Yvette let out a shriek of delight, throwing her arms around André's neck. She let go when a ship's officer came along with several seamen. He asked about the third member of their party.

Yvette squeezed André's hand against her thigh. "He'll be here."

The officer nodded. "The tender will arrive soon to take you ashore…"

A jarring metal on metal sound cut him off as the seamen wrenched a hinged section of the bulkhead open. Beyond shone the lights of Quebec City flickering on the St. Lawrence River below.

"Ah, m'sieu," Yvette said, "how is one expected to reach the tender from here?"

"You climb down a ladder, mademoiselle."

"Oh, mon Dieu," Yvette whispered. "C'est pas possible…"

The river pilot, who would guide the *Casimir III* downriver to Sept Isles, stood ramrod still on the tender's deck as it pitched and swayed in the open water. He was taking the last few puffs from a *Gauloise,* when the skipper stepped from the wheelhouse.

"Remind the ship's duty officer, Louis," he said, "we have a passenger coming aboard." He turned, shouting toward the wheelhouse, "We are ready for you, m'sieu."

Harmon Page stepped out, a bulky yellow life vest fastened over his leather jacket. He hesitated, compensating for the rolling deck, before joining them.

"Climbing the rope ladder, M'sieu Page, is a task you might find awkward. We therefore attach a rope around you, should you somehow lose your footing."

"That's encouraging," said Harm. "And my luggage?"

"It follows, once we have you safe on board." He motioned to his wheelsman. "Ease 'er in close, Henri," he shouted, "and open the bell light."

The spotlight's intense beam burst across the waves and climbed to encircle an opening high in the ship's hull. There was a rattling noise as the Jacob's ladder clattered down the ship's side, a few rungs disappearing in the choppy water.

The tender struck the steel hull as the safety rope was dropped from above. The pilot tossed away the cigarette. After several swipes, he caught the rope, snugged the loop portion over his head and under his arms before scrambling upward.

An aluminum case marked *Property of the Canadian Broadcasting Corp.* was lowered first. Harm and the skipper swung it aboard and manhandled it off to one side.

The relieved pilot reached the tender, followed by producer Watts' slow, shaky descent. Once on deck, he scrambled for the safety of the wheelhouse.

André, the cameraman, came next, making every step count.

"Where's the producer?" he yelled as he removed the safety rope.

Harm, nodding toward the wheelhouse, looked up.

"Who's she?" he asked, as the seamen cinch the rope around a young woman and easing her onto the ladder.

"Yvette. Our scared-shitless script assistant," said André.

They watched her take a few awkward steps, stop to look down, and freeze.

"*Merde*," murmured the skipper, charging back into the wheelhouse.

An officer appeared in the opening above them in shirt sleeves. With no life vest or safety harness, he started down.

Both Harm and André saw him try to persuade Yvette to keep moving.

"You'll have to deal with her from there!" the officer yelled at them.

They glanced back at the wheelhouse where the skipper was on the phone.

"You first," André mumbled. "I've been that route already."

Having little choice, Harm hauled himself up on the railing with André's help. He was grabbing the rope ladder when the tender suddenly bumped against the steel hull and bounced away, dragging him with it.

Harm felt his body drop as water surged up around his thighs. He struggled to snare a submerged rung with his foot. He caught one and began climbing upward, oblivious of passengers crowding the railings watching his every move.

    Harm squeezed in beside the frightened young woman.

    "Yvette, isn't it?" he asked, holding onto to her. "I'm Harm, here to help you down."

    She pressed her trembling face against his shoulder. "I... I can't," she whispered.

    "Nor can we hang around here all night. Take a deep breath and move a foot down onto the next rung."

    Yvette opened her eyes. "You'll stay with me?"

    "I've nowhere else to go."

    They took the first step together, followed by several more, when a movement of the vessel forced the ladder to swing away from the hull. Harm held her close as it swung back.

    Assuring her it was nothing, they were on the move again

    Hands reached up for her. Harm gave Yvette a one-arm hug before the skipper and André eased her onto the tender's shifting deck.

    He started up, slowed by numbed fingers and a cold wind biting through his wet clothes. He had lost track how he was doing, when crewmen were hauling him off the ladder.

    They held him upright on wobbly legs, until he was standing on his own.

    Filip Sotek, in a crumpled white shirt, wrapped a heavy deck blanket around Harm's shoulders.

"I was the officer shouting at you," Filip said, introducing himself. "I mistook you for the tender's crew, not a passenger."

"Not to worry," said Harm, pulling the blanket tighter to ward off the shivering.

"An unwarranted welcome, nevertheless, Mister Page. As for the ship changing course, we were in danger of drifting out of the channel."

Hugh and Gwen Ashcroft were heading back to their stateroom moments later when they took in a curious scene of a passenger draped in a blanket. He was locked in a hand shake with a ship's officer as a photographer captured it live.

Gwen bumped her husband with her elbow and stopped. "He's the one who rescued the young woman a moment ago."

"His intentions were misplaced," Hugh mumbled, walking on. "He should have left the heroics to those trained for the job."

"Don't tell me you wouldn't have done the same," Gwen tut-tutted him, "when you were a few years younger."

"You think you know me that well?" Hugh said, waiting for her to catch up.

"...On behalf of the Master and crew of the *TSS Casimir III*," intoned chief purser Rysard Marzel, "I commend you, Mister Harmon C. Page, for your courage and fortitude. On a personal note—"

Officer Filip Sotek interrupted. "In Mister Page's best interest, Mister Marzel, he should be taken directly to his stateroom before he catches pneumonia."

Rysard Marzel's podgy cheeks puffed out. "You...have a point, Mister Sotek."

Filip guided Harm across the foyer. "Despite his long-windedness, the purser has good intentions. By the way, you saved us from one hell of an ugly situation. Captain Jablonski will insist on thanking you personally. If there is anything else…"

"I could do with a hot shower," said Harm, still gripped by the shivers. "Followed by something warm to drink. Like a hot rum toddy."

"The Boat Deck Bar is down past your cabin," Filip said, pleased at how this American had handled himself. "If we could meet within the hour, I'd settle for one myself."

CHAPTER FOURTEEN
Thursday, October 6, 6 AM

Victor Petrie had pulled on sweats for an early morning jog around the Boat Deck. From there, he dropped by the computer room set aside for passengers.

It took him less than a minute to finish what he'd come to do, before heading to the fitness center on C Deck.

Kimberly Stockwell lay on the lower bunk bed, staring up at the ventilation duct in the ceiling. Angus, stretched out on top of her, began to ejaculate. She heard the familiar groan from deep inside his chest, followed by a gradual stiffening of his entire body.

Raising her buttocks, Kim forced herself up into his groin. She felt the searing pain of his fingernails digging into the bare flesh of her shoulder. She stifled a cry as his thrusts slammed her down again and again into the flimsy mattress. Kim held on, knowing it would soon be over.

With perspiration making their bodies glisten, Angus slipped onto his back, eyes closed.

Kim was getting out of bed when a voice echoed through the cabin from the corridor.

"Good morning, ladies and gentlemen. Seven o'clock. Thursday, the sixth of October. Today will be mostly sunny with a high of sixteen degrees Celsius, sixty-one Fahrenheit..."

"That's noise abuse," said Kim, looking around for her exercise outfit.

"It's a wake-up call for those at first sitting," Angus said.

"... the wind out of the northeast at twenty knots..."

Stanislaw Jablonski stared into the bathroom mirror, ignoring the same disembodied voice as he studied the lines around his mouth. They seemed more pronounced this morning. He noticed his eyes reflected a deep sadness. Deeper and fresher. Yet not without good reason.

Several days before the *Casimir* departure from Gdynia, he had been called to the shipping line's head office on Boulevard Dluga. His appearance before The Company's advisory committee had seemed routine.

He had been assured, *unofficially*, he would take over sea trials of the new liner replacing the *Casimir III*. A commission as the ship's first master would follow.

What happened that sunny day was nothing Stanislaw could have imagined.

The sparse equipment in the ship's fitness center amused Victor Petrie. Abdominal, leg extension. A bench press. Lifecycle. Curl and triceps bars, scattered mats, and skipping ropes hanging from a hook on the wall.

He began with stretching exercises, sit-ups, knee-bends, and push-ups until he had worked up a sweat. Lying on the angled bench, he lifted the barbell off its retainers and lowered it slowly to his chest. He took a breath and pushed it up at arm's length.

He was lost in the workout when the door opened, breaking his concentration. He pushed the barbell up to lock it in place, to realize he couldn't see the retainers for sweat running into his eyes.

"Higher," said a voice. Soft hands touched his, guiding the bar onto the slots.

A slender woman came into focus. She was walking round the gym in her black yoga tights and tank top of shocking pink.

"This is nothing like what I saw in your ship's brochure."

Victor sat up, certain she had taken him for the ship's fitness instructor.

"Life isn't always what it seems, Miss—"

"*Mrs*. Stockwell." Kim planted herself in front of him, legs apart. "Off your butt. And for God's sake, don't go easy on me."

Harm was sleeping the sleep of the dead when the voice woke him.

"…the relative humidity is sixty-five per cent, the barometer reading—"

"Stuff it," he said, burying his head under the pillow.

Two doors along the Boat Deck corridor, Hugh Ashcroft was checking his new binoculars, having already showered and pulled on flannel pants, an Oxford shirt, and a wool cardigan.

"…and, along with the day's activities, a Polish language class will be followed by horse racing in the Little Lounge…"

Gwen emerged from the bathroom, her damp hair wrapped in a towel.

"What is that atrocious racket?" she asked, using another towel to dry herself.

"A subtle warning to those attending first sitting," said Hugh, removing the lens caps.

"...and a reminder of tonight's welcoming dance in the Grand Lounge. Formal attire isn't necessary, but it's appreciated. The clocks go ahead one hour at midnight."

"Subtle, my eye." Gwen stared at the binoculars. "Where in heaven's name did those come from?"

"Abercrombie & Fitch. New York. They're Bausch & Lomb. And jolly expensive."

Gwen cocked her head to one side. "I don't remember shopping there."

"We didn't. I was with Sir Oliver what's-his-name, when you trotted off to ogle modern art at the Guggenheim."

"Sir Oliver *Turnbull*, Hugh. I can only hope you remembered his full name. Then again, I expect you muddled through."

She met her husband and Sir Oliver, who had been classmates at Oxford, after graduation, when the two were invited to join British Intelligence. Both would later transfer from the SAS to liaison initially with the Central Intelligence Agency in Washington. Sir Oliver would retire there to live comfortably on Long Island.

She and Hugh were to visit New York this time after he suggested returning by ship instead of flying home; something they hadn't managed in years. Gwen was overjoyed, especially when he took upon himself to make the arrangements.

Hugh was sorry, he told her, when the eastbound *Queen Mary 2* was booked solid. Never one to give up, he landed a last-minute cancellation on the *TSS Casimir III*. Its first port-of-call would bring them home to dock at London/Tilbury.

"Ollie bought me these," he said, holding the binoculars up to his eyes.

"Whatever for?"

"Bird watching."

"My dear Hugh, you *loathe* the very idea of bird watching."

"Most decent of him, nevertheless."

"If not misplaced."

"Not so." Hugh lowered them. "I've learned a great deal about our feathered friends."

"Name one *single* species, Hugh W. Ashcroft, that you will spot during our crossing, and I'll—"

"You'll what?"

"I will never again allude to your total aversion of the sport."

"The *rissa triactla*," Hugh replied. "Known as the black-legged kittiwake. White head and body, grey wings, yellow bill…"

Gwen's eyes went wide. "I do declare."

The knock at the captain's quarters came while Stanislaw was having difficulty buttoning his white shirt. Despite having reminded laundry personnel time and again to use less starch.

"Enter," he said, passing from the bedroom into the main room.

"*Dzien dobry, Kapitan*," said Chief Purser Marzel, in a gesture of rigid formality.

"*Dobry*," said Stanislaw, tucking in his shirt.

Marzel held out a neatly-typed report he had put together on such short notice.

"It concerns the incident last evening. The rescue…"

Stanislaw glanced around for his black tie. "Tell me in your own words."

For the chief purser, a verbal report was akin to being whipping in a public square.

"We received…a message yesterday, captain, from our Montréal shipping agent…that a passenger had missed the ship. He was advised to fly to Québec City and catch the tender delivering the relief pilot to us."

He paused to collect his thoughts. "A problem arose…with the unscheduled disembarking of a member of the television crew—"

"I want a short explanation, Mister Marzel, the rescue of the young woman was carried out by a *passenger* and not by our trained personnel."

"Officer Sotek—"

"Mister Sotek, yes. Who set a fine example of our safety protocol. No safety rope, no life jacket. Thankfully, we didn't lose him overboard. Or anyone else."

"Thankfully yes, Captain."

"I take it the passenger's clothing he was wearing is being cleaned and pressed and returned to him as soon as possible." Stanislaw found his black bow tie draped over the back of the sofa. "Send a bottle of wine along to his cabin with our compliments."

"He happens to occupy one of our staterooms, sir."

Stanislaw looped one end of his tie over the other. "Then make it a bottle from my private stock. Champagne.

And arrange a reception in his honor. In my quarters."

He looked for his shoes. "Work it into my schedule." He spotted them under his desk.

"Don't expect much from him, captain. He's a grumpy sort. Should he show up at all."

"I've handled *grumpy* sorts in my time, Mister Marzel. Our Good Samaritan's name?"

"Harmon C. Page, sir. An American."

"I will thank him personally tonight at the welcoming dance." Stanislaw bent down to retrieve his shoes. "That's all."

The chief purser made an awkward salute, forgetting he was clutching the written report in the same hand.

Ted Grosvenor reached his office to find his assistant pouring himself a coffee.

"What's up?"

"Plenty, boss. Lyubimov of the FSB called fifteen minutes ago. I figured he must be desperate, asking for you but settling for me. Ms. Tuseva did the talking. She mentioned the dead scientist who deep-sixed it in a Moscow restaurant…"

"Yevtushenko." Ted poured himself a coffee. "I heard. Done in by a screwed-up pacemaker."

"She wanted us to know her boss thinks the unit might have been tampered with."

"*Might* have been?"

"A *possibility*. She's asking us to take extra good care of Doctor Poplawski during the trip. When I wanted to know why, she lost her flow of English."

"If Vladimir had warned us in the first goddamn place, we'd have been much more supportive." Ted reached his desk and sat down. "If anything screws up, you know who will get crapped on. Us."

"Then again, what Ms. Tuseva said seemed genuine enough. Being subtle isn't easy, when you're stumbling through a foreign language."

"So?"

"Granted, he hasn't been entirely candid, but I'm convinced he had no idea the situation would turn to rat shit."

"Had we known, we'd have supplied Agent Hagen with some sort of protection." Ted caught his assistant's wry smile. "You supplied her with a handgun and didn't tell me?"

"Slipped my mind."

"More like you thought I wouldn't go for it."

"Let's just say, she wasn't overjoyed carrying a handgun—possibly because we played down the importance of the assignment."

"Standard issue?" Ted asked.

"She insisted on a Walther over our Glock. The PPK is lighter, she says, with a less bulky grip. It's easier changing magazines, especially when you're between a rock and a hard place. We lazy ones like the Glock, counting on it needs little servicing."

"To say nothing of it being a damn good handgun."

"Not one you prefer," said Gerry. "I arranged with the Mounties to supply her with a Walther before escorting her to the ship. To avoid any bureaucratic screw-ups."

"Now, if you don't mind—"

"There's more, boss. I reached Ira Neddick of state police to ask about the Toyota registered to Page. He had hired a Kennebunkport construction company with equipment needed to haul it out of the deep, once a local SCUBA club had located it."

"When did he hear about the Toyota?"

Gerry wandered over to sit on a corner of the desk. "Late Saturday night. A priest noticed missing guardrails. He helped Page ashore and dropped him off at a local hospital. According to Ira, he shouldn't be alive."

"Page's lucky day."

"That's for sure. Ira will email us a preliminary report. Then he called back moments ago. The Toyota had just been dropped off in his secured parking area."

"And?"

"He noticed the Camry had serious damage to the left front fender and driver's door. What happened, he said, was no accident. He found black paint from a second car that must have forced Page off the road. Ira scraped bits of the black paint off the Toyota. He did the same with the vehicle's original red paint."

Ted punched in his password into his PC as he sipped his coffee. "It raises a lot of questions, Gerry."

"It being the *same* Saturday night the Russian scientist was murdered. Both scientists in the same line of work. A coincidence?"

"Unlikely. Do we know where Page is now?"

"Not since Ladly and Locke left him stranded on the pier in Montréal."

"Have Neddick send someone to Page's at Ogunquit. Having missed Poplawski, maybe he came home to lick his wounds."

Peter Lount had been up early organizing lecture notes and illustrations on his laptop. He arrived for breakfast at nine o'clock sharp. The menu, in Polish, English and German, included a selection of soups.

He was still pouring over it when Thomas Slater joined him.

"G'morning, Pete," he said, pulling out a chair on the opposite side of the table.

"Hi," he replied, without looking up. "And it's *Peter*. Poles sure take their breakfasts seriously."

"It's an ungodly hour to eat anything. Correction: It's an ungodly hour to get out of bed. Since I am, prunes first."

"You sound like my mother."

"Perish the thought."

The server, a pleasant man in his mid-thirties, appeared beside Thomas to pour coffee from a china carafe.

"You mentioned prunes, sir," he said, after placing a jug of thick fresh cream on the table.

"Prosze," Thomas replied. "I bliny z syropem. Z boczek wedzony smazony."

Peeved at arriving first but served last, Peter ordered bacon, scrambled eggs, tea, and dry whole wheat toast. He asked Thomas what he'd just ordered.

"Pancakes with syrup. Smoked bacon…" He smiled.

"Ah."

Nicole appeared in jeans and a green sweatshirt.

"Good morning all," she said, sitting next to Thomas.

"Wait 'til you see what's for breakfast," Peter said, disappointed she didn't sit beside him. "Soup, of all things."

"It's what the Poles enjoy," said Thomas. "Nicole will vouch for that."

"A Polish tradition," said Nicole. "I might even try…" She found herself staring at Leszek Poplawski eating breakfast alone at a table near the windows. "Where was I?"

"Deciding what's for breakfast," her tablemates said in unison.

Breakfast for the second sitting passengers was long over when Harm reached the Grand Lounge in search of a coffee. He found the ship's house band in rehearsal.

He remained in the entrance, taking in the room's elegant hand-carved oak panels alternating with smoked mirrors, the hardwood dance floor, and the hanging lamps. Scattered around were tables mixed with comfortable upholstered chairs and sofas.

He found the old-fashioned style added warmth to its surroundings. He could also imagine the live music, couples dancing—

"Mister Page…"

Noticing Officer Sotek waving from across the room, Harm was joining him when an argument erupted among the band members.

"Trouble in music land?" said Harm, shaking Filip's hand before sitting down.

"I'm auditioning an assistant fry chef to replace the missing drummer."

"A fry chef moonlighting as a drummer? He's several beats behind."

"You're right, and it's a long story. Now you, having the lean and hungry look of someone who missed breakfast." Filip waved over a steward on coffee duty.

Harm suggested croissant and coffee.

"Live a little, Mister Page. How do you like your eggs?"

Harm couldn't resist. "Over easy, please."

"And the steak?"

"Medium rare," Harm said, unable to recall when he'd had a steak for breakfast.

Filip added fresh orange juice, hash browns, croissants and a Thermos of hot coffee.

"Sorry I can't stay," he said. "I have a Polish language class for passengers, should anyone show up. Anything I can do, let me know."

"I'd like to find Leszek Poplawski."

"You know him, then?"

"Let's just say we're in the same line of work."

"You're in very good company. He's a wonderful old man. You'll find him on A Deck. Cabin 323. The captain offered him a stateroom for the trip over, but he insisted on a small cabin close to the water." Filip stood up and straightened his tie. "If he's not there, try the Polish Bar or the horse races in the Little Lounge." Filip winked, "Drop by, and I'll give you a hot tip."

The entertainment office had no sooner left than the steward appeared with his breakfast. The band had started up again, Harm finding the drummer still off-beat.

Harm soon discovered everything below deck turned into a rabbit warren of long, endless corridors. Suspecting he'd gone too far, he was doubling back when he bumped into a young woman in uniform coming down a nearby stairway.

Harm glanced at the white blouse, bereft of insignias, and matching skirt. The outfit gave her tanned face a healthy, warm look.

"You look lost," she said.

"I'd like to know where you're hiding A Deck," Harm said with a grin.

Her smile sprouted small dimples. "Carry on and you'll end up in the ship's laundry. A Deck is one flight up. Odd numbers on your right, if you're heading toward the back end of the ship."

"'Back end of the ship' doesn't sound nautical, for someone in uniform."

She blushed. "It's my first assignment on board, Mister…"

"Harm Page. And you?"

"Helena Witka," she said. "Pick up a mini map from the purser's office; It will help you get your bearings. And I speak from experience. No offense, Mister Page, you seem like someone who'd take pleasure in *not* following directions."

This observation amused him, watching her continue down the corridor.

He arrived at A Deck and cabin 323. With no one answering his knock, Harm went on looking for the horseracing venue.

Harm hesitated outside the Little Lounge. He hadn't seen Leszek for the past several years. Eager to meet him again, he stepped in to face a room packed with noisy racing fans.

He noticed Filip and a younger officer seated at a table with a large rotating wire basket. Inside were two oversized dice. Spread out on the polished floor was a long green plastic sheet marked off at intervals and divided into lanes.

He counted six large wooden horses lined up at the starting gate with numbers painted on their flanks. Cut-out 'jockeys' wore what Harm took for authentic racing colors. Two seamen stood by who, he decided, would move the horses corresponding to the roll of the dice.

"Pick a favorite, go home rich," Filip's voice broke over the loudspeaker.

"For today's final race," the young officer called out, "the winner will be the *last* horse past the post."

The crowd booed loud and clear.

"They're off," he barked, imitating the flat, nasal twang of American racetrack announcers and giving the wire basket a hefty spin.

Harm watched the young officer lean forward as the basket slowed to a stop, the seamen were poised to move the horses.

"Number Two, Royal Flush, moves ahead one square." Another spin. "Number Five, Willy Nilly, gallops into an easy lead by four lengths."

"Slow down, Willy," shouted a passenger, to the delight of everyone in the lounge.

"Royal Flush rests along the rail," the officer's voice broke in. "Heart's Aflutter holding firm as Willy Nilly strides for home."

Several more rolls of the dice brought a roar from the crowd. Royal Flush had pulled off a stunning victory by coming in dead last.

"A grand total of twenty-five American dollars," Filip announced, "goes to each of our lucky Royal Flush winners. Winners of previous races, come to claim your prizes."

They hurried from every corner, a joyful group jostling each other in good fun as they surged toward the table. A blonde side-swiped Harm as he joined the crowd, grabbing him to keep her balance.

"I'm very sorry," said Kimberly Stockwell, still holding on to him when Filip joined them.

"You missed all the fun, Mister Page," he said. "Mrs. Stockwell here broke the bank, along with several others."

Gwen Ashcroft joined them, waving her winnings. Filip introduced Harm to both.

Gwen eyed him. "Tell me I'm wrong, Mister Page, but wasn't it you in the foyer last night? Soaking wet and shivering under a blanket. A hero of sorts…"

Filip, not wanting Harm dogging such notoriety during the trip, made an excuse to ease him aside.

"Care to wager, Kimberly?" Gwen said a moment later as they squeezed onto a table's padded bench opposite Nicole.

"Ten U.S. dollars says you're wrong."

Nicole sipped her chilled white wine. "Wrong about what?"

Gwen replied, "Remember last night when we were on deck admiring the lights from Québec City, and this man—"

"Rescued a woman," Kim broke in, "trapped down the side of the ship."

"Hugh and I saw him later," Gwen said, "soaking wet and wrapped in a blanket…"

Kim took over. "Gwen swears that Officer Sotek introduced him to us a moment ago, but I say she's dead wrong. The one doing the rescuing wasn't as tall or as good looking as this guy."

"You were so star struck meeting him," Gwen quipped, "that I'll wager an extra ten English pounds you didn't catch his name."

Kim looked Gwen in the eyes. "Page."

"His *full* name."

Nicole stared from one to the other. "Not *Harmon* Page?"

Kim's mouth drooped at the corners. "You know him already."

"No…not really." Nicole remembered Ted Grosvenor referring to Page during their meeting as 'the sonofabitch who was giving them trouble'.

"There!" Kim squealed. "The gorgeous hunk stooping over the old guy in a chair."

Nicole put him down as hardly a hunk. What surprised her: the old guy was Leszek Poplawski who had bounded to his feet with both men hugging each other.

"Ah, he has a sensitive side," Kim murmured. "Imagine getting him between the sheets."

"Never tell a book by its cover," Nicole said, pouring more wine in their empty glasses.

"What cover did you give Hagen?" Ted Grosvenor asked, seated at his desk. "And don't tell me *B & J*." He was referring, with humor, to *Brewster & Jenkins*, an old clunker the Company had once used when needing a fictitious firm.

Gerry sat near the coffee table, his open laptop on his knees.

"I made her a VP consultant with Compdata International, per your orders."

"Shouldn't we have heard from her by now?"

Gerry put the laptop aside. "And what? Tell us the old guy hasn't fallen overboard yet? Besides, we told Hagen the assignment was no big deal."

"Is her communication with us secure?"

"She has only to hook up through the ship's SEACOM M II satellite. Her laptop comes with the usual built-in scrambler and sophisticated electronics system that totally baffles me."

The console buzzed as his secretary's voice filled the room. "A message from Agent Hagen, Mister Grosvenor."

Gerry joined him as the blank screen settled down with a single line of type. It was ID'd by Nicole Hagen's code.

Met up with Poplawski. Much more alive than you made me believe. Did I overhear you and Smith discuss someone called Harmon Page, in terms less than flattering? 'Cuff the sonofabitch. Throw him in the trunk. Bring him back alive'? Something like that.

Ted typed with two fingers. *Grosvenor here, Agent Hagen. Why mention him?*

Page is here, on board.

"Jesus," Ted muttered.

I did not connect him to Poplawski until witnessing their affectionate hugs moments ago.

Ted typed. *How did he get on board?*

On the pilot's tender, late last night out from Québec City. It is clear you didn't want him here for whatever reason. How do I handle him?

He is not to be trusted.

Have Gerry warn me of any further surprises.

The transmission ended.

"The pilot tender, for Christ sake," Ted grumbled.

"Don't be so hard on yourself, boss. We saw the photo of Page on Ladly's cell. The ship is well away from the pier. I told you the next stop is London/Tilbury. That clinched it."

"The sonofabitch outsmarted us."

Gerry went to pour himself a fresh coffee. "Agent Hagen should be told how concerned the Russians are about Poplawski's safety. She's there solely because of him."

"Hold off for now. Send her Page's background. It'll give her some idea who she's dealing with. Fired by S&T. Meanwhile, have the team check Page's background. Gambling problems. Drinking habits."

Ted sat back. "Credit rating. Have IRS cooperate. You know the routine. Where his money's sitting? Offshore accounts? Everything, right down to his last fucking parking ticket."

"What I can't find out," said Gerry, "I'll have Edgars at S&T fill in the blanks."

Ted reached for the phone. "Leave him to me."

Nathan Edgars found Ted nursing a beer at the bar of the Old Ebbitt Grill on 15th Street.

"I would've preferred meeting in your office or mine," Nathan shouted over the noisy noonday crowd. "I can hardly hear myself think."

Ted nodded at the empty stool he'd been saving for him.

"This will cost you a gin and tonic." Nathan sat down. "Gordon's. On the rocks. And be brief. I'm up to my neck in work."

"Tell me about Yevtushenko," Ted said, after ordering the gin and tonic. "The dead Russian scientist."

"What about him?"

"It wasn't a faulty pacemaker that killed him. More likely, he was murdered."

"*Murdered*?" Nathan replied, wide-eyed.

"It's not yet confirmed, but it seems so. You mentioned to me about Page's car ending up in the ocean…"

"I didn't believe him."

"You should've. His Toyota was forced off the road, with him in it. Whoever pulled it off didn't expect him to survive." Ted sipped his beer. "Two scientists in brain research. Your line of work. One American, one Russian. Both on a hit list over the weekend. From what I hear, Doctor Poplawski could be next."

"You're not saying it's for sure," said Nathan.

"Tell that to my Russian counterpart with Moscow's FSB. He's worried enough to have us babysit Doctor Poplawski while the *Casimir III* crosses the Atlantic."

"We're not involved," said Nathan, as the bartender set his gin and tonic down in front of him.

"I'm sure you're not. Still, the White House will take a jaundiced view of any fuckup. Should it happen, we'll piss all over you for not coming clean. It's called non-disclosure of information."

Nathan groaned. "You can't do that!"

"While you sit on your ass, hoping things will work out on their own? I sure can."

Nathan turned the glass around in circles, not lifting it off the table.

"I'll find out what's going on."

"Page is on board the *Casimir III*. The meeting between him and Poplawski proved *very* touching. Hugs all round."

Nathan squirmed in his seat, saying nothing.

"Which leaves me wondering, Nathan, why Page would bust his ass to get on board in the first place? When he didn't even know the old man was in America."

"Our worst fear in letting Harm go." Nathan lifted his glass to his lips, "And how the Russians would react when hearing about it."

Ted finished his beer. "Like what?'

"Like offering him a job."

Ted eased himself off the stool. "If you guys have convinced yourselves of that, we're too fucking late to do anything." He left Nathan with the bill.

CHAPTER FIFTEEN
Thursday, October 6, 11:25 AM

Nicole Hagen sat cross-legged on the bed, the laptop on her knees. She wanted nothing more than a quick response from Ops. If those idiots in Langley—

The screen came alive with a confusion of letters and numbers that gave way to a request for verification from Gerry. Nicole typed in her code and waited for his response.

Can you confirm Harmon C. Page officially on board?

She typed: *According to the purser's office, he is registered as a resident of Ogunquit, Maine. Tell me the connection between him and Poplawski.*

Both specialize in research of the brain.

How does Page fit in?

It is complicated. He could be more trouble than we anticipated. Don't trust him.

And you, assuring me nothing but a peaceful transatlantic crossing.

My apologies. I will email Page's bio. He is likely to have a hidden agenda where old man Poplawski is concerned. A word to the wise: keep your Walther out of sight but handy. Bye for now.

Nicole slipped off the bed to open the middle dresser drawer. *A word to the wise?* This didn't make her feel any better. She dug down among the folded wool sweaters and cotton turtlenecks and pulled out the Walther PPK plus two extra magazine clips with .32 caliber rounds.

Freeing the weapon from its waistband holster, she eased the clip from the butt end, checked it, and slapped it back into place.

It felt like second nature, handling a firearm again. It brought back memories of joining the CIA, the intense training at The Farm. It was her father who taught her, at a young age, to handle a variety of handguns and rifles. Shooting at everything—pop cans, targets, wolves on the prowl for livestock—neighbors back in Colorado called her a modern *Annie Oakley.*

Nicole went into the bathroom, returning with her large, open canvas catch-all bag. Inside was the usual a dizzying array of beauty aids; an electric curler and hair dryer, facial creams and moisturizers for every occasion. Packets of eye shadow, combs and sanitary napkins.

She was burying the pistol and extra clips deep inside the bag when a knock at the door interrupted her.

"Who is it?" she called out.

"It's me, Thomas. We're almost where the Saguenay flows into St. Lawrence. Whale watching at its best."

"Hold on," she said, leaving the canvas catch-all open on the dresser.

Vladimir Lyubimov was hanging up the phone when Olga Tuseva appeared in the doorway. "Any luck with the Yevtushenko murder?" she asked, turning over a handful of files.

"I've reached the few trusted contacts I have at Military Intelligence," he said, "wondering why the possible cover up. No one would say anything, even off the record. Which means, Ms. Tuseva, we're definitely on to something."

"What about Colonel Petrovich at Military Intelligence?"

"He's, at best, a younger fair-weather friend," said Vladimir. "Taking me to lunch when it's convenient, yet seldom returning my calls—a discourtesy I find typical of the military."

"Then perhaps Aliosha can help us," she said, hoping it sounded like an afterthought.

Vladimir recalled all too well, Olga's fiery, short-lived affair with Aliosha Kazakov of Military Intelligence. He had seen no harm in it, trusting Olga's discretion, while others had taken the opposite view. Which included Yury Petrovich, who abruptly ended their relationship.

"Must I remind you, Ms. Tuseva, that Aliosha is married now?"

Olga took the bait. "Married, sir, and already bored."

"And should Military Intelligence receive the slightest hint you are fantasizing about one another, Officer Kazakov's career would be over."

She promised to keep the encounter beyond discreet.

Vladimir added this to his mental collection of *bad moves.*

Harm and Leszek were among a dozen others stretched out on deck chairs, soaking up the sun following the mid-morning ritual of coffee, tea, and sandwiches.

"I had just flown back from Los Angeles," Harm was saying, "when I arrived home to find your postcard from the

Grand Canyon. I had no idea you were in America, Leszek. I phoned through to the ship, hoping at least to say goodbye—"

"*Whales!*" came loud cries from those crowding the railing.

Passengers materialized from nowhere, armed with cameras, cell phones, iPads, and binoculars.

Harm and Leszek had abandoned their deck chairs to reach the railing, when a voice called out.

"Dzien dobry, Doktor Poplawski."

Both noticed a dark-haired woman not far off motioning to him. Leszek explained how she and her friend helped him wave goodbye to his daughter on the dock.

With Leszek's insistence, they joined her and her friends, exchanging introductions between sporadic sightings of the whales.

Harm decided to remember these passengers by their first names, it being a long voyage. The delightful English couple, Hugh and Gwen. The striking blonde, Kimberly, and her soft-spoken husband, Angus. The affable Thomas, the big guy who Harm thought looked familiar but couldn't place him.

And then there was Nicole, who seemed to ignore him. Yet she interrupted with her fluent Polish while he was explaining to Leszek about the whales.

Harm picked out Peter as the self-appointed tour guide, with cameras hanging round his neck and firing off a barrage of commentary about the beloved creatures while snapping photos of them.

"What you see are *Delphinapterus leicus*, better known as belugas or whites." *Snap, snap.* "They have teeth lining both upper and lower jaws, while sperm whales have teeth only in the lower portion." *Snap, snap.*

Harm saw a large, flattened 'fluke' rising high in the air before it disappeared. The water went still, sending a collective sigh among the crowd.

With the spectacle over as unexpectedly as it had begun, someone in their group suggested they squeeze in drinks at the Boat Deck Bar before second sitting.

Harm and Thomas watched Nicole steering Leszek away with the others. They saw the old man glance back, embarrassed. Harm gave him an assuring nod not to worry.

"You've been unceremoniously ditched," said Thomas.

"I'll scratch her off my dance card. I'm Harm Page, by the way…"

Thomas stuck out his hand. "You're obviously a good friend of Leszek Poplawski. A Nobel Prize winner, no less. And I'm Thomas Slater."

Harm's eyes lit up. "*Thomas Slater*? The author behind *Vietnam*? You, yes. Your photo is on the back cover of the book. On the *New York Times'* bestseller list for how many weeks? Fiction based on fact."

Thomas gave him a modest grin.

"You treated both north and south Vietnamese, as human beings," Harm went on. "I've googled you, looking for your other books."

"None so popular. I write mostly travel pieces, like the Casimir's last voyage, and ghost the odd memoir of dignitaries who insist on coming off the page looking far better than they should." Thomas leaned on the railing.

"According to Nicole Hagen, you were the *idiot* dangling down the side of the ship last night."

"That's how Ms. Congeniality put it?"

"A little too harsh, in my opinion. I could see you had no choice. Yet Nicole's reaction surprised me. It's as if she'd taken an instant dislike to you."

"Never met the lady. And don't let me hold you back from joining the others."

"I'm happy where I am," said Thomas. "Not everyone has the guts to dangle down the side of a ship to rescue a damsel in distress. I'm curious: I'd like to hear your initial reaction, facing such a challenge." Thomas paused. "That's the writer in me."

"Five pounds," said Gwen. "Or the equivalent in euros. Cash."

All eyes at the Ashcroft/Stockwell table fastened on Thomas and Harm talking with the dining room steward. Gwen wagered Harmon Page would end up at their table.

Angus Stockwell asked how much five pounds was worth in American currency.

"Too much," said Hugh Ashcroft, turning to his wife. "Think about it, Gweneth. The steward could place him in a half-dozen empty spots. Those are terrific odds *not* in your favor."

"Then you accept?"

"How can I lose?" he said.

Thomas Slater had move on, leaving the steward flipping through pages on a clipboard.

"Any more takers?" Gwen asked.

The others shook their heads.

They watched with growing interest as Harm trailed behind the steward, who had stopped to talk to the sommelier, before changing direction and coming directly toward their table.

"Cash only, gentlemen," said Gwen Ashcroft with a smile.

Leszek was looking over the luncheon menu, alone at a table by a window. He was under the scrutiny of Nicole, Thomas and Peter dining not far off.

"I doubt if he enjoys eating by himself," said Nicole.

"Maybe he prefers it," Peter said. "With his old shipboard buddies from the trip signing up for first sitting. Imagine a real, live Nobel Prize winner eating with us."

"We'll invite him over," said Thomas. "He can only say no."

It suited Nicole. "Who wants to ask him?"

"It's a group decision," Thomas said. "We all go over."

Stanislaw Jablonski, finishing off a yeast cake with jam in his captain's quarters, looked up at his stern-faced chief engineer standing erect by the door.

"You're implying Chief Officer Klimek is on a witch-hunt, Henryk?"

"Pawel feels compelled to get to the bottom of the defections in Montréal. As crew liaison, he should've known his 'informers' let him down."

Stanislaw worked the last piece of cake onto his fork. "He's taken on the defections as a personal matter, when he should have nothing more than hurt pride. If what you say is true, Henryk, I will not stand idly by while he whittles away all morale."

"He twists everything around to suit his own purpose. Like his late father, the most uncompromising, pig-headed captain in the fleet. God knows how you ever landed the son as your chief officer."

"Pawel is my problem, my friend. *Your* problem is showing up for the welcoming dance tonight."

It was a command, Henryk knew, not a suggestion.

Harm and Leszek had come out on deck after lunch, taking in the sun and fresh air.

"Can you imagine, Harmon," the old man said, "my daughter insisting on exploring all of America in ten days?"

"I'm sure you both made the most of it."

"I have many photographs in my cabin to keep the memory alive." Leszek paused. "She had them printed from her cell phone Come, we will look at them and…hmm…celebrate with something special for our meeting together: Vodka with pieprz."

"Vodka with… what? Pepper?"

"*Pieprzowka, y*es," he said, taking Harm by the arm.

Leszek poured generous amounts of *Pieprzowka* into their glasses.

"Na zdrowie," he said, downing his in one gulp.

Harm replied *na zdrowie* as best he could and swallowed it.

Leszek's wrinkled face broke into an impish grin. "You like?"

Harm nodded, dealing with the fire reaching down to his toes.

"You have talked to my daughter on the telephone, Harmon." He picked up the framed photo of Hanna on the bedside table and handed it over. "When you were exchanging our correspondence that she translated for me. Yet she tells me you have never met. The photograph you hold was taken at Niagara Falls. We were sailing almost under the torrent of water on the little boat."

"*The Maid of the Mist*," Harm replied, looking at Hanna's round, smiling face, the large, bright eyes and pointed nose. Her dark hair was soaked, despite the protective plastic hood.

Leszek removed a thick envelope from the bedside table, eager to show him more photos. Washington, D.C., the Grand Canyon, and Las Vegas was among them.

"How old was Hanna when she came to America?" he asked.

"Szesc... six. She was arriving as a refugee. To a Polish-American family knowing little of her. She is a teacher now, Harmon. Ten years ago, she came to Europe seeking her mother's grave. She found it in Jaslo. She searched for a father she had taken for dead and traced me to Moscow."

Those of the Falls brought back memories for Harm, being there with his own daughter, Samantha, at age ten. The *Maid of the Mist* had been the highlight of their three-day stay. The haunted house also rated up there with it.

Leszek showed him photos taken of each other, wet faces in the crowd of blue ponchos.

Harm looked at someone behind Hanna, partially obscured by the flimsy hood. A familiar face? Harm poked through other photographs from a different angle. He found one and held it up.

"Do you remember him?"

The old man smiled. "He was watching my daughter, making me amused. I am thinking he might be trying to…how do you say it in English?"

When 'making a pass' didn't register, Harm settled for 'getting to know her'.

"*Get to know her,* yes. We were all very much…hmm…crowded together. He took photos of Hanna and me together."

"Did you see him again?"

"We saw many faces from the boat everywhere, Harmon. We were taking lunch in a café, when I saw him and his friend. And during our walk around the garden of flowers." Leszek refilled their glasses. "I have feelings I noticed him in Montréal, when I was looking down on the pier from the deck of this ship before we sailed."

"But you're not sure."

"I have told myself it could not be. Why would he be there?"

Harm held onto the photo. "May I keep it?"

"Of course. It is a good likeness of my daughter."

Harm glanced again at the face behind her. The moustache. The broken nose. A coincidence? He doubted it.

Senior Officer Pawel Klimek's narrow face reflected unease as he stood inside the captain's quarters.

"I find it distressing, Captain, at your lack of interest in what lies behind those who jumped ship in Montréal. With your cooperation, I had hoped—"

Stanislaw cut him off with a wave of a hand. "It is a diplomatic matter now, Pawel. Besides, you are making too much of it."

"With due respect, sir, those who left the ship did so to make some sort of protest, which leaves me to believe others will attempt the same tactic at London/Tilbury."

"You have proof?"

"These rumors persist."

"I trust your judgment. But there is to be no overzealous intimidation of the crew. Is that understood?"

The officer's face remained impassive as he saluted and left the room.

A single long blast from the ship's whistle ended the obligatory afternoon boat drill, sending passengers happily inside.

Harm was adding his cumbersome orange lifejacket to the pile by the Boat Deck Bar, when Angus and Kim Stockwell showed up. Angus suggested Harm join them for a drink.

The adjacent card room was an oasis of quiet concentration, a sharp contrast to voices and laughter coming from the bar. They were no sooner in the door than Angus was asked to make up a fourth at poker.

"Bring me a scotch like a good girl," he said, patting his wife on the fanny.

"What's the matter with the American male?" grumbled Kim, walking on with Harm. "*Like a good girl* as if they don't want their women to grow up. As it is, Mister Page, married to a poker-playing stockbroker can be the shits."

"It's Harm," he said, as they stepped into the crowded bar.

"I'm Kimberly. Better still, Kim. What cabin are you stuck with?"

"One down the hall."

Kim's eyes widened. "A stateroom? We almost had one at a last minute, but someone snagged it first. You're in good company. The Ashcrofts are there, if I'm right. Nicole Hagen as well. You must be near them."

Harm eased Kim through the crowd to an empty space at the bar. "What's your pleasure?"

She smiled a smile that covered her face. "A chocolate vodka martini."

"A martini for you, a scotch for me, and the same for your husband."

"Leave him out of it. He orders one while playing poker, yet never touches it."

"To make other players think he's a drinker," said Harm, ordering their drinks. "It works best, I can only imagine, when playing with those who don't know you."

"That's what Angus says. Mind, we all come on board pretty much as strangers." Kim leaned back against the bar. "What better time to put inhibitions on hold? Women especially. Like our classy lady over there by the window."

Harm glanced over his shoulder. "You mean what's-her-name…"

"Nicole Hagen. If she'd relax, she'd be quite sexy. Long legs. Shapely tush tucked into those designer jeans. What more could you ask?"

"A little warmth," Harm said. The drinks arrived, and they clinked glasses. "And a sense of fun, which she seems to lack."

Kim sipped her martini. "Tell me, is she divorced? Widowed? Or unmarried?"

"Unattached is the best I can do. She's someone with an obvious cool exterior."

"A sea voyage could easily fix that," said Kim, studying her. "It brings out the insatiable sexy yearning in most women, no matter how prim and proper they seem."

Harm grinned. "Is that so?"

Kim licked the flaky bits of chocolate off the rim of her glass. "Out here, there are no rules, Harm. No regrets. You, you're single, divorced, or whatever. Why not take a run at her?"

He gave it some thought, to come up with, "She's not my type."

"Push the right buttons, and 'Miss Cool' will be crawling all over you. Top to bottom." Kim moved closer to him. "She's watching us."

"She's watching everyone."

"Which makes me wonder if she's ever made it with a woman. Good thighs, ample boobs. Full, sexy mouth." Kim sighed. "Probably not."

Harm was enjoying this woman, her banter, her perspective on life and love. "Are you always this candid with a stranger?"

"You're no stranger, but the rarest of males who make a woman feel good. Besides, you're sexy."

"And you're beautiful..."

"...And married."

"You should take a run at her," said Harm. "Set her inhibitions free."

Kim pouted, resting her head against his shoulder. "I'm not good at rejection."

Thomas arrived, looking around the crowded room before spotting Nicole by the window.

"Sorry I'm late," he said, reaching her. "Leszek and I ended up in the wrong station for the boat drill."

"No to worry," she said. "I enjoy watching others."

"Do you always scowl when you people-watch?"

"Only when I'm hungry."

"It's not that kind of scowl," he said, following her gaze to the other side of the room.

"You've got Harm and Kimberly Stockwell in your sights."

"Maybe. Do you find her attractive?"

"As kids, we'd say she's cool. Today, they'd call her a MILF."

"And who's putting the make on who over there?"

"What if they're just enjoying each other's company? Harm, by the way, is the same guy you treated shabbily while whale watching. One-upping him with your perfect Polish doesn't win you any brownie points. And then slipping Leszek Poplawski away to the Boat Deck Bar, as if you had something against him." Getting no response, he asked what she'd like to drink.

She settled for a *Rusty Nail*.

Nicole knew she had no reason treating Page as she did, put off by Ted Grosvenor's warning to stay away from him. She had thumbed through Page's confidential, personal, and professional background Gerry had emailed to her. Reading it raised more questions than answers.

Why shouldn't he be trusted? Why was there no reason given for his dismissal from S&T? Why did he turn down a generous offer to return there? The broken marriage, and a daughter wanting to return east to live with her father, yet couldn't?

Harmon C. Page avoiding a handful of Grosvenor's field agents to climb on board the ship. Why? With no authorization to stop him? And no order keeping him under surveillance…?

Victor Petrie appeared beside her.

"I'm heading to the bar," he said. "You look as though you could use a drink."

She told him Thomas is looking after it.

Victor stepped closer. "On a serious note, Ms. Hagen, we both know this transatlantic crossing isn't all fun and games. Not for you and I."

Nicole stiffened.

"Think about it," he said, walking off.

"You're still scowling," said Thomas, handing over the icy *Rusty Nail*. "Don't tell me Petrie put you in a bad mood."

"Why would he?" she snapped at him, only to regret it.

CHAPTER SIXTEEN
Thursday, October 6, 8:45 PM

The welcoming dinners for the two sittings were held on the first full day aboard. Chief Officer Klimek and Entertainment Officer Sotek had represented the Ship's Master at the first sitting. It left Captain Jablonski and other senior staff to bring the traditional pomp and circumstance to the second sitting.

Amid the hubbub of passenger chatter, the ship's quartet broke into a *Sousa* march.

With it appeared the Master of the *Casimir III*, followed by his officers in white uniforms emboldened with gold braid. They arranged themselves around the captain's table.

Suspended above them was a large replica of the *TSS Casimir III* with its miniature lights flickering from the portholes and windows.

It was at a time like this that Stanislaw missed Filip Sotek's presence. The younger officer added a sense of levity to every event. Despite his absence, the mood was more jovial than usual, thanks to an unexpected source.

Chief Engineer Henryk Niski, the quiet one, regaled his fellow officers with tales from times past; when stokers with the coal-driven steam engines never saw the light of day during long, tedious voyages.

"It took them forever to wash off the dirt," Henryk reminisced.

"Had I been there," cut in Ludwik Dudek, Chief Surgeon, whose florid cheeks spoke of his affinity for the bottle, "I'd have found something to clean them from the inside out."

Stanislaw turned to his junior surgeon directly across the table.

"What would you have recommended, Doctor Witka?"

"A solution of *Stilincia*, Captain," said Helena, who was in her slim, white uniform. "A remedy my great grandmother claimed cleansed the skin of unsightly blotches. Would it have worked on Mister Niski? It's anyone's guess."

The remark was greeted with applause.

"Try topping that," said Stanislaw. Turning to Marzel Rysard, he asked him to point out the passenger involved in rescuing the young woman at Québec.

The chief purser's throat went dry. The odds of finding Page in this crowded dining room were not in his favor. Luck was with him as he spotted Page at a table directly down from the main entrance.

"At three o'clock, Captain. A table of five. Mister Page is to the right of the English lady. Mrs. Ashcroft, if I'm correct."

Stanislaw, expecting a stern-faced, grumpy sort, found someone who appeared open, relaxed, and sharing a laugh with the older woman.

"He's quite the opposite from your description, Mister Rysard. Have Mister Sotek set aside a permanent reserved seating for him in the Grand Lounge. Add anyone he might suggest."

"I've seen him with Doctor Poplawski, and the author, Thomas Slater. Both gentlemen you'll find sharing a table off to your left, toward the windows."

Stanislaw picked them out, though his attention focused on the passenger next to the old man.

"The woman beside Doctor Poplawski," he said. "I recall the face, but not the name."

To fellow officers around the table, the '*I recall the face, not the name*' was the captain's way of learning who a woman was behind the pretty face. This, they knew, helped him decide on a partner to share the opening dance with at the welcoming night festivities. Whatever transpired afterward, was anyone's guess.

"Her *name*, Mister Rysard?"

Marzel Rysard studied the beautiful woman's light summer tan, her easy manner. Doubtless, an American. Dark hair piled up behind her head, knotted with a colorful ribbon. The dress, an expensive white strapless sheath, scooped low enough to expose an intriguing portion of cleavage. A gold chain hung around her neck, what the officer decided was a diamond broach. A stateroom, surely. Leaving…

"Nicole Hagen, Captain," he said, hoping he was right, "who travels alone."

Stanislaw glanced around the table. "Stop gawking, gentlemen," he said. "To you, Doctor Witka, I apologize for their rudeness."

"None needed, Captain," she replied, enjoying this game of cat and mouse.

Stanislaw would not have caught Nicole Hagen in such a happy frame of mind some time later. She had returned to her stateroom, having done so earlier to reach the Agency, but was put on hold. Having had enough, she called a number Smith had given her as a last resort.

"Don't hang up," came Gerry's uplifting tone. "At the sound of the beep, leave your name, phone or cell number, the time of your call, and a brief message."

"Screw you," Nicole murmured. If Langley wasn't taking this assignment seriously, why the hell should she?

There was a knock at the door. She opened it, and Victor was there with his hands in his pockets.

"It's time we talk," he said. "It won't take long."

"Good," she replied.

"I know who you work for, why you're here. Then again, maybe they didn't tell you."

"Tell me what?"

"I work for them too."

Nicole forced herself to keep her cool. "I've never heard your name mentioned at Compdata. Not that it matters."

"I'm talking about your *real* job. On assignment with the Agency. Your boss, Ted Grosvenor, must've figured you couldn't hack it on your own. Whatever, I'm your backup, which we'll discuss later. I'll let you know where, when."

"*I* make the decisions, Victor," Nicole shot back. "Until I've been told otherwise."

"I'm merely the messenger," he said. "My cabin? Yours?"

"The Grand Lounge."

"I'm tied up until midnight."

Nicole closed the door and leaned against it. How, she wondered, could a simple transatlantic crossing turn into something so screwed up?

The entertainment officer, cordless mic in hand and backed by the house band, greeted those filling the Grand Lounge.

"Welcome, ladies and gentlemen, to this the first official function in the final transatlantic crossing of the *TSS Casimir III*. My name is Filip Sotek, and I'm paid to keep you entertained. Should you have complaints, direct them to my assistant, Officer Olecki. He's the one working the sound system. Compliments to me, complaints to him."

Laughter rippled through the room as Filip paused to watch the woman in the white dress only now join those at the reserved table.

"You're late, Madame," he said. "Luckily, you've missed nothing but free champagne."

Nicole, blushing not unhappily, sat down between Thomas Slater and Hugh Ashcroft.

"Now that that's taken care of," Filip went on, "we have, for your added enjoyment, brought, at great expense by the Polish Shipping Lines, a guest lecturer of exceptional promise. Our man about Washington D.C."

Filip shaded his eyes to look over the crowd. "Stand up. Don't be shy."

Peter, at the reserved area with the others, was barely on his feet when Filip motioned him to sit down. "No time for a long monologue, Pete. Those interested in your informative lectures, can catch you three times during the voyage…"

Filip caught a seaman in the doorway nodding in his direction.

"... Enlightening us with a history of our very own *Casimir III*. Included will be the facts behind the sinking of the Titanic, and tales of other sailing ships of the past—"

The entertainment officer broke off to translate it into several other languages.

"And now, on behalf of Captain Stanislaw Jablonski, the ship's officers and crew, it gives me great pleasure to welcome you all aboard—"

The musicians burst into a lively rendition of the *polonaise* as the ship's officers appeared amid an explosion of spontaneous clapping. They took their places in a special section away from the dance floor.

Filip raised his hands and the applause died away, the music becoming a gentle version of the same tune.

"The ship's master," Filip continued, "will now carry on the tradition decades old of symbolically welcoming each of you by randomly selecting a dance partner. Ladies and gentlemen, I give you Captain Stanislaw Jablonski."

Stanislaw swept into the lounge, trim and erect, his thick gray hair framing a tanned beardless face. The four rows of braided gold on the sleeve and his short-cut white jacket added to his singular presence. A showman in his own right, he reached the dance floor acknowledging a few of the more familiar faces with a nod. Passing the bandstand, he murmured to the musicians, "Strauss."

Nicole and Hugh were sharing a whispered conversation when a hush fell around them. She glanced up to see the captain watching her with amusement.

"Madame Hagen," he said in English, "would you do me the honor of the first dance?"

"I'd be delighted, Captain," she replied in Polish.

While waiting for her to join him, Stanislaw acknowledged Harm with a smile.

"It's you, Mister Page, who saved us much embarrassment at Québec."

Harm stood up to shake the officer's outstretched hand, "I had help—"

"I wasn't proud of a crew who are *paid* to handle such emergencies. I will make up for not having thanked you personally sooner, I assure you."

Nicole had reached Stanislaw's side. He kissed her hand and, with a friendly nod to the others, guided her out onto the dance floor.

The band broke into a rendition of the Blue Danube waltz.

For the Chief Engineer Henryk Niski, the late evening came to an abrupt, painful end when partnered with a lively matron during a polka, her knee caught him in the groin.

He had excused himself and retreated to the safety of the officers' table.

You're setting a bad example," he grumbled as the puffing captain sank down onto the chair next to him. "Dancing with the same woman most of the evening, when insisting we rally around to keep our female passengers on the dance floor."

Stanislaw wiped perspiration from his face. "The Hagen woman, Henryk, is a breath of fresh air. I felt myself physically aroused. Can you believe it? I don't recall when this happened last."

"Two trips ago. The blonde with the wiggle."

Stanislaw shoved the handkerchief into his lapel pocket. "You remember too much."

Several numbers later, Filip announced Ladies' Choice, prompting Nicole to return the captain's favor. The music soon stopped, and another round of new partners began. Harm, having danced with Kim, looked around for another partner when Nicole appeared in front of him.

"I owe you an apology, Mister Page. Thomas Slater told me I might have been somewhat rude during the whale watch this morning."

"No need to apologize, Ms. Hagen. I don't speak Polish. You obviously do."

The music started again, a slow number. With little choice, she put an arm on his shoulder. "It seems you and Doctor Poplawski are close friends."

"We've known each other for some time," he said, finding little room to brighten the conversation.

"I was hoping to dance with him, but he seems to have disappeared. Do you have any idea where he might be?"

Harm dug deep for an exit line. "He's probably whooping it up in his favorite watering hole. I should find him before he toddles off to bed."

"I'll come with you," she said, unwilling to be abandoned there on the dance floor.

They found Leszek where Harm thought he'd be, in the Polish Bar with fellow passengers from the initial trip, along with Thomas Slater.

No one missed Nicole raising her sheath dress high enough to swing a leg at a time over the bench, then the other, to sit beside Thomas. Harm squeezed in next to Leszek, who introduced him as an old friend; Nicole as a new one.

"We're drinking *Winiak Luxusowys*," Thomas said to Harm, "Try it. It will blow your—"

Heads turned as the captain appeared at their table.

"I thought you might change your mind, Doctor Poplawski, and remain longer with your daughter. You are here and we are delighted. And to you, Mister Page, I'm organizing a reception in your honor, and please don't let me down."

He turned next to Nicole. "Having had the pleasure of dancing with you earlier, Madame Hagen, I was hoping we might continue where we left off."

"The pleasure is mine, captain," she said, easing herself away from the table.

A late-night snack of caviar, marinated herring, oysters and Polish lobster, among other delicacies, signaled an end of the evening for a weary Leszek. Thomas was ready to leave too, and both set off together for A Deck.

Nicole sat in the Grand Lounge with an empty martini glass. Victor was to meet her at midnight. It was well after one o'clock. She noticed Peter Lount drinking with Kim Stockwell who, she noticed, had changed into a slinky black number, cut low with a large zipper open from the bottom showing a good portion of thigh. Nicole decided the outfit showed too much boob, but who was she to say?

As for Petrie, the waiting was over.

Kim and Peter had ordered more drinks when the band picked up with a slow oldie. Peter steeled himself to ask her for another dance, when duty officer Jerzy Olecki beat him to it.

"Dobry wieczor, Pane Stockwell. Prosze, moje nazwisko Jerzy Olecki. Czy moge prosic o ten taniec?"

"What's he saying?" Kim asked Peter.

"How should I know?"

"I am asking you, Madam," Jerzy said in English, "for the pleasure of this dance."

"And how do I say `*thank you'* in Polish?"

"*Tak* will do, Ma'am."

Peter watched her glide into the young officer's arms, their bodies meshed together. Something he'd not yet managed to do.

With the song ending, they returned with Jerzy wishing her pleasant dreams, in Polish.

Kim lowered herself on the arm of Peter's chair, her cheeks flushed.

"All that sterile, white uniform topside," she purred, "and a blasting furnace below." She hiccupped. "Cocky little bastard. I could feel him harden right through his pants."

Peter blushed as she trailed her fingers along the hairline at the back of his neck.

"Why don't you and I get it on, Peter? Your cabin." She dropped her hand to his thigh, moving it painfully slow toward his crotch. "I'll show you a *coupling,* Petie, you've only fantasized about."

Peter eased her hand away. "I'll catch up with you. Cabin number—"

"And that's it, Mister Lilywhite?" she hissed in his ear. "Worried others will see the ship's perfect little lecturer slink off to fuck a brazen, sexy married woman?"

Peter squirmed as Kim brought her face down close to his.

"You can't imagine what you're missing." She reached down to massage his crotch. "My hands, my tongue all over you." Kim squeezed hard and let go.

Picking up her small beaded purse with the long strap, Kim left the Grand Lounge ready to find excitement somewhere aboard the ship.

Angus Stockwell, a study in concentration, was into yet another game of seven-card stud. He glanced at Victor Petrie and set down two kings and a pair of aces.

"Jesus Christ," growled another player, "you must have horseshoes up your butt."

A few more good hands, and Angus knew this transatlantic gig would soon be fully paid.

"I know when to quit," Victor said, dropping his cards on the table. He had no sooner left the room than he saw Nicole step out of the small elevator.

"We were to meet hours ago," she snapped at him.

"It slipped my mind," he said, offering no apology.

"You're playing games with me, Victor. I'll listen to you, and that's the end it."

"Your cabin or mine?"

"Outside, where we won't be interrupted, or distracted."

"I suggest the stern. A little more sheltered from the wind."

"In twenty minutes."

"Count on me, Ms. Hagen," he said, continuing along the corridor.

Not ready to return to her cabin, Kim discovered the all-night Disco tucked away between decks. It was accessible by a circular wrought-iron staircase from the level above.

The room was hot, loud and crass, its young-minded clientele packing the small dance floor; the music a mixture of American heavy metal and hardcore rock.

No one missed Kimberly's slow descent down the stairs, her black outfit showing the long-tapered legs, the soft, white creaminess of her breasts overflowing the lacy bodice. The blonde hair caught in the flashing blue strobe lights.

Discos were her passion. Loud, raunchy, the open flaunting of sexuality. Couples, singles. Bodies out of control, wet with perspiration.

In the glass booth slightly elevated above the dance floor, was the DJ in an outrageous baggy striped pants and matching top. A large headset was clamped over his ears as he boogied away.

Kim was swaying seductively to the music when someone bumped her. He was young, wearing a white sweat-soaked T-shirt and jeans. Tall and muscular, his uneven grin showed off white teeth behind a wide mouth. He brought his face inches from hers and pushed her playfully with his hips, then his groin.

She felt his breath warm on her face, her nostrils filling with the almost acrid smell of his body sweat. Heat spread up from her crotch, setting nerve endings on fire.

"You good, very good," he murmured as a second body touched her from behind.

He was short with broad shoulders, a bullish neck, Kim took them for seamen, having somehow slipped into the disco and losing themselves in the crowd.

The pair danced around her in the flashing lights, sandwiched her tightly between them, rubbing their crotches against her, only to pull back and touch her hips with their rough hands.

They were soon playing with her large front zipper, up and down, up and down, then lowered it to expose the upper fullness of her braless breasts.

"We go," the taller whispered in her ear.

Something in those brown eyes, a hardness masked by the smiling face, warned her off, but she gave in, kissing him on the open mouth. "You, alone."

He grinned. "You..." He searched for the words in English, "...leave after I gone. Come to stern. I am meeting you there."

She was dancing on her own again, fighting with her conscience. She could still taste the seaman's sweat on her lips. And she needed more.

Kimberly crossed the Promenade Deck, shivering in the coolness of the night. Reaching the mesh-covered pool, she started down the steps nearby.

The area below was small and dimly lit by beacons mounted at intervals along the open railing. The vibrations and noise from the ship's propellers was warning enough that being here was the wrong place at the wrong time.

She was shifting the purse strap higher up her shoulder when she heard muffled footsteps from yet another lower level. A chain linked to a CREW ONLY sign blocked the way.

She made out the head and shoulders of the same tall man on the other side of the chain, in an open wool pea coat and T-shirt. He lifted her over it and carried her down the steps.

On the deck above, a breeze tugged at the yellow wool scarf keeping Nicole's hair back from her face.

She paused in the shelter of a small alcove, tying the scarf tighter when Victor found her. He pointed beyond the net-covered swimming pool to steps leading downward.

The cramped space wasn't what Kim had hoped for. Dull yellow lights embedded in the low ceiling showed the floor piled with garbage bags. What little space remained was taken up by a
large steel capstan and coils of heavy rope.

The sweeping lines of the vessel narrowed with a section of the steel hull, cut away at chest height. It gave Kim an eerie feeling of being too close to the dark, undulating vastness of ocean. The constant *thump, thump* of the ship's propellers added to her growing uneasiness.

She had no sooner reached the bottom step than the seaman pulled her against him, forcing her lips apart with his thick tongue.

"Not so goddamn fast," she whispered, hearing shoes rattle on the steel steps above her. An impatient woman's voice burst out.

"The Company shouldn't have sent you without telling me."

"Ted Grosvenor had his reasons."

Kim dragged herself up a step and looked back over her shoulder. She caught a glimpse of Nicole Hagen seated in jeans and heavy sweater on the top step near the pool, and Victor on the steps below her.

"Langley didn't want Page anywhere near Poplawski," Kim heard him say as a callused hand fumble with the zipper of her dress. She ignored it, forcing herself to catch what more was said.

"...The Russians are worried about the old man Poplawski's safety."

The seaman's mate suddenly appeared beside her. Kim closed her eyes, straining to hear.

"We'll keep a low profile, Victor. No obvious connection between us."

Kim, feeling fingers moving lower down her body, drove a knee up into his groin.

Nicole and Victor heard a muffled grunt and scuffle from below. Waving Nicole to stay, he removed a handgun from inside his jacket, and continued down to the lower level.

Victor stopped by the chain supporting the CREW ONLY sign. He peered down into the flat light, making out a woman pinned back against the steel capstan her anguished face partially covered with long, blonde hair.

"Never flirt with sailors, Kimberly," Victor murmured to himself. "Especially when at sea."

Tucking the handgun away, he rejoined Nicole to guide her back across the deck.

"What was it?" she asked, put off by his silence.

"Nothing more than innocent fun," he replied.

CHAPTER SEVENTEEN
Friday, October 7, 2:10 AM

Harm felt water moving up past his chin. He was taking a deep breath, when he heard a voice calling him. He grabbed for something to keep him afloat, when the voice came again.

Harm struggled to sit up, clutching a pillow tight to his chest, his naked body drenched in sweat. He looked around the room, at the dresser, the TV, and his clothes left on a chair.

His cabin!

There was a thump at the door. He tossed the pillow aside, shook his head to brush away the cobwebs, and grabbed his bath robe from the foot of the bed. He pulled it on and opened the door.

Kimberly swayed against him, her wet blonde hair in tangles. She was clutching the front of the black dress where he noticed the zipper no longer held it together. One of her high-heel shoes was missing.

"I didn't know...where else to go...," she whispered.

Harm gathered her up in his arms, kicked the door shut and stretched her out on a twin bed. He noticed the left eye was swollen and discolored, as were both cheeks. Welts covered her upper arms and thighs.

He untangled the long purse strap coiled around her neck and eased off the remaining shoe.

"I'll call Sick Bay—"

"No. Please..." she whispered through bruised, swollen lips.

"We'll clean you up, then decide." He moved the damp hair away from her face. "Is this your husband's handiwork?"

"*Angus*? God, no."

"It looks as if more than one bastard caused this much damage," he grunted, disappearing into the bathroom.

Kim heard water running as she struggled to her feet, painfully slipping the spaghetti straps off her shoulders.

Harm returned, wrapping her in a towel as the cocktail dress dropped to the floor.

Kissing him on the cheek, she stepped into the bathroom.

It wasn't long when he heard the groans.

"The water's *freezing*, you masochist."

"What did you expect?" Harm pulled on his jeans and sweat shirt. "It's Mother Nature's way of reducing the swelling. And the pain."

"If you're that brave, come in with me."

"I've got other things to do," he said, picking up the dress.

There were smudges of grease along with small rips in the fabric. The metal toggle had been torn free from one side of the zipper itself.

The bathroom door opened. Kim came out, drying her hair.

"You're a miracle worker, Harmon Page."

He glanced up and looked away.

"What's the matter?" she teased him. "Never seen a naked female before?"

"Maybe not one quite so beautiful," he replied, snapping the toggle back into place.

Kim wrapped herself in the towel, it barely covering her thighs, and sat down beside him.

"If you ask me what happened, save your breath."

"Bottling it up won't help."

"When I'm as much to blame?"

"No one has the right to use force, Kim." Harm stood up, poured her a good shot of whisky from a bottle on the dresser. He handed it over and sat down. "Not without a willing partner. You obviously weren't one of those."

"Tell anyone what happened," she said, drinking the Scotch, "and I'll deny it."

"How will Angus deal with it?"

"He'll sulk, for a while."

"You either know him that well, or it's wishful thinking."

Kim stood up, handed him the glass, and dropped the towel.

"A bit of both," she said.

Harm helped ease the dress over the bruises, guiding the spaghetti straps onto her shoulders.

"Tell me," she said, "are you not in some kind of trouble?"

"Should I be?"

"You've made some people on board very nervous." She removed a makeup brush and two small compact travel pouches from her purse. "Put it this way," she said, opening one with a bluish cream. "Our sweet, sexy *Widow* Hagen isn't who she pretends to be." Using a little brush, she spread the cream on her puffy eyelids. "Nicole told us she's a computer analyst, when Ms. Goody Two-Shoes really calls Langley home."

Harm grinned. "She's not with the CIA, if that's what you think."

"I heard her say it, in so many words, Harm." Kim dabbed the brush into the second pouch. "Victor too. She was pissed off because they'd sent him on board without telling her." Kim worked cream into the discoloration on her arms and legs. "Victor told Kim how 'Langley' tried to keep you away from Doctor Poplawski, and here you are, stirring up a hornet's nest."

It seemed too far-fetched for Harm to accept. Yet it fit. Moustache and his sidekick were CIA, and they almost succeeded in cutting him off from reaching the ship.

"Nicole was sitting on the steps near the swimming pool, while I was below defending my virtue. I heard Victor telling her some guy he referred to, 'Ted Grosvenor', must have his reasons for sending him."

Harm recalled Nathan Edgar mentioning a 'Ted' back in his hotel room. The same guy?

Kim looked to see what bruises she had missed. "Nicole said the Russians were worried for Doctor Poplawski's safety. She told Victor not to make any obvious connection between the two of them."

"They didn't realize you were listening?"

Kim put the compacts away in her purse. "No, I would've known it."

"Which brings us to the pair who raped you."

"I...was dancing with them in the Disco. One of them suggested we get together. At the stern. Two levels down from where the pool is. I made it clear only one show up, when the other bastard joined in."

Harm wrapped his arms around her and held on.

"I'd better go," she whispered, squeezing him before stepping back.

He handed over the shoe and walked her into the corridor. Loud voices drifted down the hall from Boat Deck Bar, and he eased Kim back inside the cabin. The voices faded.

"How will you explain the cuts and bruises to Angus?" he asked as they stepped back into the corridor, "when the makeup wears off?"

"I'll tell him I got loaded and fell down a stairway."

"Good luck with that. Whatever you heard, Kim, keep it to yourself."

She gave him a warm hug and walked on, swinging the single shoe by its strap.

Harm returned to his cabin, pulled on his runners and leather jacket, and went back into the corridor. Once outside, he crossed the Promenade Deck's stern to the pool tucked under a heavy rope mesh and dropped down to the next level.

He climbed over the CREW ONLY sign with the noise from the ship's engines echoing in his ears.

Aided by what little light penetrated the small area, he found Kim's other shoe. He spotted torn black bikini panties and tossed it overboard.

Nicole Hagen, wrapped in a wet bath towel, dug a jar of moisturizer from the large canvas makeup bag on the dresser. She was scooping out a blob of white goop, spreading it on her face, when there was a knock at the door.

Thinking it was Victor, she crossed the room barefoot and yanked it open.

Harm pushed past her. "What the hell are you up to, Hagen?"

Nicole pulled the towel tight around her. "You're *drunk*. Screw off."

"Not drunk. Pissed off."

She disappeared into the bathroom. "Tell me why," she called out, "then screw off."

Harm sat down on the corner of the dresser. In doing so, his elbow hit the canvas carryall knocking it onto the floor.

He bent down picking up what had fallen out. "You've convinced everyone," he said aloud, "that you're a computer analyst."

Nicole appeared in the doorway, wiping the cream off her face to see him on his knees.

"What the hell are you doing?"

"I accidentally bumped your bag onto the floor." Harm held up what looked to him like an instrument of torture. "What's this?"

She grabbed the electrical eyelash curler and plunked the large bag back on the dresser.

"You, here at this ungodly hour, asking what I do for a living? I'm with Compdata Corporation. Satisfied?"

"That's bullshit," he said, getting up off his knees.

"Take it or leave it," she shot back. "I'm going to bed."

"You obviously need your beauty sleep." He stopped at the door. "By the way, the same yahoos who chased me to Montréal, had shown up earlier on the *Maid of the Mist* in Niagara Falls. Is it a coincidence that Leszek and his daughter were there at the same time?"

Nicole yanked back the duvet. "I don't know what you're talking about."

"You're a CIA operative, Hagen." He stepped out the door, closing it behind him.

Nicole stripped off the towel and climbed into bed, wondering how in hell he knew that much about her?

CHAPTER EIGHTEEN
Friday, October 7, 6:15 AM (Moscow)

A rumpled, pajama-clad Vladimir sat on the edge of the bed staring at the big right toe. It looked purplish-red and swollen. He'd seen it before, coming and going unexpectedly.

His physician had diagnosed it as *gout*, caused by excessive accumulation of uric acid. Heredity played a major role, Vladimir was told, though blaming one's dead relatives for such an affliction did not sit well with him. He was even less inclined to accept the advice that exercise and diet would help keep the problem at bay.

Too early to get up, yet aware the pain would keep him awake, he was easing his legs back into bed when he heard the loud jangle of the doorbell echo through the old apartment. He limped over to the window, eased the heavy brocaded curtains aside, and looked out.

Olga Tuseva was on the concrete porch two floors below. She was bundled in a canvas coat, with its high collar turned up. She was waving at him.

Aware she had the number code to the foyer door, he hobbled down the corridor, left his apartment door ajar, and moved on to the kitchen.

He had the coffee brewing and a saucepan of milk on the stove warming before she would make it up two flights of stairs. It gave him time to retrieve his dressing gown from the bedroom.

"Good morning, sir," Olga called out from the hallway.

She tossed her coat and purse on a straight-backed chair and walked into the kitchen.

"The delightful aroma of coffee," she exclaimed, removing two mugs from a cupboard and turning the flame down under the milk.

Vladimir appeared in the doorway. Judging from her short leather skirt, net stockings and a bright, woolly turtleneck, he knew his assistant had been up all night.

"How was your evening?"

"Wonderful in every respect," she replied, her eyes flashing through the bright blue liner.

"And Aliosha Kazakov. Still married, is he?"

"After last night," she said, smiling, "it's uncertain."

Waiting for the coffee to finish brewing, she told him how the evening began with cocktails at a variety of clubs and lounges, before they arrived at Café Pushkin for a late dinner.

So much, Vladimir decided, for an evening away from inquisitive eyes. Yet the Pushkin appealed to him, with its French windows, high ceilings and shelves filled with ancient books. Where servers once wore imposing sideburns.

"You couldn't believe it," she said, reliving the moment. "Aliosha knew all these weird and wonderful places."

She told him how they had dropped by Lubyanka Square where musicians and customers sang folk songs together, drank and toasted one another other. Then on to eating cedar nuts, marinated moose with cabbage, grilled reindeer tongue with cowberry sauce.

"We got lost down little lanes that were crowded on either side with old, low stucco houses. We ended up at a café next to the ancient Mayakovsky theater. It was full of writers, journalists, and actors. Good fun. No pretensions."

She slipped into the hall to return with her leather purse.

"You'll know how much we enjoyed ourselves," Olga professed, removing a crumpled paper from her purse, "when you get the bill."

"All for a good cause, I hope," Vladimir said, guiding his assistant down the hallway.

They reached the broad, wood-framed glass doors and stepped into the darkened study.

Olga enjoyed how the room reflecting the past, with its ornate wrought iron fireplace, the mahogany paneled walls lined with bookshelves. The high, wing-back armchair and a tall floor lamp, its sand-colored shade still, it seemed to her, bearing its original tassels.

Vladimir turned on the lamp, retrieving his reading glasses from his rolltop desk.

Olga handed him a sheet of paper with a hand-written list of names. He asked if she had read it.

"Only a glance," Olga said, looking over his shoulder. "I promised Aliosha the list would not leave this apartment. He admitted not being able to guarantee these were the only aliases used by someone he referred to as Tobias."

"Tobias? I thought he was long gone." Vladimir smothered a yawn. "It bothers me, Ms. Tuseva, why Aliosha

Kazakov would put his career at risk by giving you these names."

"I'd like to think he was doing me a favor. Truthfully, he's never forgiven those within Military Intelligence who opposed our relationship. Your friend, Colonel Yury Petrovich, considered his rise through the ranks being far too fast."

"What do you think?"

"Aliosha did so on his own initiative. A small thing, but he is a man of principle."

Vladimir studied each name before moving on to the next. "Military Intelligence could easily have leaked these to us, and turn out to be false."

"Then you haven't read *all* of the names," she said, pointing close to the bottom of the page.

Vladimir glanced down and gave out a short, sharp grunt.

"Alexey Gritsenko."

"Yes, a Tobias alias for sure."

"Proving he murdered Boris Yevtushenko, Ms. Tuseva. And us having the Gritsenko name before it disappears from the list is perfect timing."

Olga sat on the arm of the old armchair feeling good about herself.

"Aliosha believes Tobias might be on the *Casimir* already, sir."

Vladimir leaned against the back of the wing-back chair, his face reflecting a new concern.

With Boris Yevtushenko's murder, as his friend Leopold Baranov had warned him, Leszek Poplawski's life was in danger.

Olga was saying, "If he is on board, we might find one of these aliases appearing on the ship's passenger list."

"Good thought. Now, we will burn Aliosha's list, as agreed, after you and I each memorize all the names, separately."

With it done, Vladimir removed a match from a small box on the mantle, lit the sheet of paper and tossed it into the fireplace.

"When you reach the office, Ms. Tuseva," he said, "send Mister Grosvenor a message through the Canadian Embassy in Warsaw. Warn him that Boris Yevtushenko was indeed murdered, and that his killer is likely on board the *Casimir lll*."

Olga frowned. "Aliosha insisted he only *might* be."

Vladimir removed his reading glasses, cleaning them with a corner of his silk robe.

"Military Intelligence does nothing in half measures. We will include the actual codename in a second dispatch."

"Will Mister Grosvenor know the man?"

"Yes. If only the codename." Vladimir was ready to face another day. "Come, we'll have our coffee," he said, stepping into the hallway. I'll get ready and meet you at the office."

Olga caught up to him. "I'll wait for you, because I'm taking you somewhere special for breakfast."

Vladimir smiled "You have something in mind?"

"McDonald's."

"Home of the Egg McMuffin," he said, bemused by his own English pronunciation. "Does it come with a chocolate milkshake, Olga?"

"It can be arranged, sir," she said, delighted he used her given name.

Ted Grosvenor arrived at the office to find his assistant already into a coffee.

"Margaret told me about some call," he said, heading for his desk.

"From Ira Neddick, boss. He'd talked to the Biddeford police chief, asking about any vehicle with a bashed right fender reported in his area—" Gerry put down his cup and fixed one for Ted.

"And?"

"It turned out, a deputy pulled over one last Saturday night with a busted headlight and crumpled fender. It sped off, lost control, hit a tree, and ended up in a ditch. The driver and passenger disappeared"

"A black Chrysler muscle car?"

"You got it. The VIN was filed off. Strange enough, it carried Washington D.C. plates. He had the vehicle hauled into their parking lot and contacted the District of Columbia license bureau, or whatever it's called." He brought the coffee and put it down on the desk. "They turned out to be authentic plates, never issued."

"How could that happen?"

"The police chief couldn't figure it out. The more he pushed for an answer, the less he learned."

"And the Chrysler?"

"Suits turned up at the Biddeford cop shop not long after flashing some pretty heavy authorization. With zilch explanation, they wrapped Mister Muscle in a canvas tarp, cranked it up on a flatbed, and hauled it away."

"Who were these guys?"

"No one knows, but we do owe a debt of gratitude to the Biddeford chief. He had the smarts earlier to have scraped flakes of red paint off the black car's bashed fender, and he filed them away for safekeeping."

"Have him courier a sample over to Neddick, Gerry, to compare them with Page's Toyota."

"Done already, boss. We'll have the results within the hour."

"Good. It's crucial we ID whoever might have carted off the Chrysler off, starting with the usual suspects. I'll tackle my source at the Pentagon and you—"

Margaret's voice broke from the intercom. "There's an email marked urgent for Mister Smith, sir. From Agent Hagen."

Ted gave up the chair to his assistant, who sat down to hit a series of keys.

Out of it came Nicole Hagen's key code and message.

Trying to reach you since late yesterday. You guys are supposed to be available 24/7. Isn't that the idea behind this charade?

Gerry typed, *What's up?*

Springing Victor Petrie on me was not very professional.

"Christalmighty," Ted muttered.

Clarify pls.

Petrie is under the impression I could not handle the assignment. And you guys sent him along as backup, or to take over.

Update what you discussed.

He told me Grosvenor had personally assigned him here. He is pushy. Arrogant. And you thought Page as a pain in the ass.

Ted, leaning over his assistant's shoulder, typed with the usual two fingers.

Grosvenor here. Victor is messing with you, Mrs. Hagen. Surely you had doubts when he mentioned backup.

You tell me I had reason to doubt it? When you gave me the lowest classification? Petrie knows who I am, why I'm here. My Compdata cover.

Ted worked the keys again. *He is passing himself off as what?*

An academic. Eastern European studies. Also connected to a conservative think tank up in Toronto. When I mentioned Doctor Poplawski might be in trouble, he said you had already told him the Russians felt the same. What gives?

Ted said, "Tell her Petrie only floats for us on occasion, Gerry. We'll get back to her. And to keep a lid on it."

"Leaving Hagen in the dark…"

"That's the way we'll handle it, until we find out how Petrie's involved."

Gerry signed off and vacated the chair. "Eastern studies seemed a great cover when he worked for us. He also floats for the FBI."

"And the Pentagon. I'll pull in a few favors from them first."

"Payback time for good old Charlie?"

Ted grinned. "The prick owes us as much."

Nicole remembered her promise to meet Leszek on the sun deck for a mid-morning coffee. Unable to find lip gloss among those she kept on the dresser, she brought the canvas bag from the bathroom and dumped the contents on the bed.

She found it and began putting everything back, when she realized her Walther PPK was missing. So, too, the magazine clips that went with it.

"That sonofabitch." she muttered.

Ted studied the fresh fish basking on trays of crushed ice. The Custis & Brown was one of several barges moored at the Washington Marina's floating seafood market.

"Nice stuff," came a voice behind him. "Provided you like seafood."

"You're late, Charlie," Ted said without looking.

The newcomer wore a non-descript cotton windbreaker and baggy pants. He was inches shorter than Ted and wider around the mid-section.

Charlie shifted his deep tinted sunglasses down his nose and glanced around him. Outings like this gave him heartburn.

The only activity was a big woman serving a customer at the far end of the barge.

"No one's watching us," Ted muttered, "if that's what's bothering you."

"Easy for you to say." Charlie replied, popping a couple of *Tums* in his mouth while trying to look as if he was talking to himself, with no connection to Ted.

"Should the Pentagon get wind of our *tête-à-tête*, I'm truly fucked."

"I appreciate your quandary."

"Bullshit. I'm the one putting my ass on the line."

"Tell me about Petrie."

"He's contracted to us…"

Ted hid his delight. "Tell me something we don't know."

Charlie scratched absently at the back of his neck. "Like what?"

"Like how he's so tuned into what we're doing."

Charlie moved a few feet away to inspect a briny tank of live lobsters. He tapped on the glass, annoyed when the creatures ignored him.

"I can only say it involves a Polish scientist."

The woman was coming toward them, wiping her hands on her apron.

"Leaks mostly originated with the dudes at S&T. At their recent annual golf tournament…"

"Can I help either of you?" she asked, dashing Charlie's hope she'd think they weren't together.

Ted asked for a pound of the soft-shelled clams.

She moved to a stall halfway down the barge.

"Those assholes at S&T," Charlie went on, "never know when to shut the fuck up."

"There's more to it than that."

"You wanted to know if Petrie's under contract to the Pentagon. You got your answer."

"Listen, dickhead, your latest promotion came from material we slipped to you."

"Bullshit. It was a joint operation."

"Joint operation, my ass. What's Petrie up to?"

Charlie scratched the back of his neck again. "I can only say he's making a fucking bundle out of whatever it is."

"There's a muscle car missing its VIN registration. Black with…"

"There you go, always pushing me."

"…*unused* Washington D.C. plates."

"All I know is some asshole lost control during a car chase up in Maine. It ended up bouncing off a tree and ending in a ditch."

"*After* ramming a Toyota into the ocean. The driver wasn't supposed to come out of it alive."

Charlie rolled his eyes and turned away. "What more d'you want from me! *Blood*?"

"I appreciate this," Ted called out, wishing he'd come down harder on the little prick.

Paying for the clams, he phoned his wife and suggested lunch at their favorite Georgetown restaurant. A second call went to his assistant for an update.

"The flakes of red paint, boss, that the Biddeford police chief couriered to Ira Neddick? They matched Page's Camry parked in the state cop's back lot. How's Charlie? Whining as usual?"

"You got it. Ellie and I are having lunch in town. I'll fill you in when I get back to the office."

Ted packed away his cell, pleased the morning had gone better than he expected.

Nicole Hagen's intention of joining Leszek on the sun deck hit a snag. Page was with him, both bundled under blankets. Not prepared to confront him over the missing handgun, she wandered about the ship, despite a fog and chill in the air, ending up on the open Sport Deck to work on her sea legs.

Since the *Casimir III* had reached the Gulf of St. Lawrence, she noticed a slight motion that left her somewhat queasy. She dismissed it with a resolve not to let it get the best of her.

Hugh Ashcroft joined her at the railing, binoculars in hand, looking to Nicole very British in flannels, a tweed jacket, and an ascot tucked into an open shirt.

"I hope I'm not interrupting, Ms. Hagen."

"It's Nicole," she said, welcoming the distraction. "What catches your attention this morning?"

"Sea birds," he replied. "And it's Hugh. We'll be opposite the coast of Labrador soon. If not already." He handed her the binoculars. "A little too foggy to see much of its rugged, barren features. *The Land God Gave to Cain.*"

"That could only be the title of a book," she said, looking through the field glasses.

"Indeed. By Hammond Innes who set the fictional story right over there in Labrador. It seems the author spent six months in some exotic place, like Labrador over there, taking notes and the next six months writing a topnotch thriller about it."

Nicole felt the vessel shift even more, bringing on a tightness in the pit of her stomach.

"And by the by," Hugh added, "optimism is the only way to handle that awful notion of being seasick for the rest of the crossing."

Nicole looked at him over the top of the binoculars. "Am I that transparent?"

"It isn't easy to hide it. Then again, you don't appear to be someone who'd give up so easily. On a first sign of feeling 'green around the gills', come up here to an open deck, as you've done. Positive thinking is still the best cure."

"Aye, aye, captain," she said, peering at nothing but fog.

Hugh enjoyed this playful side of this woman. "You're probably looking at the Québec community of Baie-des-Moutons."

He swung her around to face starboard. "In the other direction, the Newfoundland communities of Parson's Cove and Cow Head. What a country, with its rocky, jagged shoreline. How the English Devon coast looked some thousands of years ago."

"Made the more beautiful," she added, "by its isolation."

Hugh smiled. "A wonderful turn of phrase, Nicole. How refreshing."

"I'll take it as a compliment," she said, handing back the binoculars. "Do you have any idea when we'll reach the Atlantic?"

"We have yet to pass through the Strait of Belle Isle later today, and into the Atlantic by dinnertime." Hugh fine-tuned the binoculars' focus. "Ah, a kittiwake."

Nicole saw nothing.

"Directly above you, white head and body, grey wings, yellow bill—"

"Dzien dobry, Pani Hagen," came a voice from below them. "Can you spare us a moment, prosze?"

She glanced down to see Leszek and Page on the deck chairs.

"You go," Hugh said. "My birdwatching has just begun."

"The Boat Deck Bar for drinks, then," she said. "Around one o'clock?"

"Splendid," he replied, waiting until she had gone before shifting the binoculars to the two men below.

"Hi," Harm said pleasantly, shifting his legs on his deck chair to make room for her.

Nicole took this to mean the spat last night was forgotten. Not so for her. She sat down beside Leszek, speaking to him in rapid Polish.

"Excuse me," Harm cut in, "We didn't ask you down here to—"

"To do what?" she said, cutting him off.

"We hoped you might volunteer in helping us when we get into a pickle over language."

"Your point is?"

"It's my obvious lack of putting the technical stuff across to Leszek. Like now—trying to explain about neurobiologist Peter Huttenlocher using an electron microscope to count the connections between brain cells."

"I have no idea how I'd fit in."

"By translating what I've said into Polish."

"You expect me to understand such technical jargon?"

"I expect you to try."

"And if I'm not interested?"

"I'll go over your head."

"And how would you manage that?"

"By contacting your boss, Ted what's-his-name, at Langley."

Behind her blue eyes came a frostiness that even Leszek needed no translation to understand.

CHAPTER NINETEEN
Friday, October 7, 1:59 PM

Ted Grosvenor gunned his late model Lexus down the narrow roadway toward the CIA complex.

Gerry Smith's call a half hour earlier urged him back here ASAP. It had interrupted a relaxed, lunch of *scallops Newburg* with his wife, Ellie.

Reaching the grass quadrangle, he braked in front of the main building.

Ted walked into the outer office to find Margaret's chair empty. He opened his own door as his assistant turned away from the window.

"Your allotted spot down there is still empty, boss," Gerry mumbled. "Meaning you abandoned your car in the tow-away zone out front. Again."

"All because you made it sound as if all hell had broken loose. You'd better have a good excuse."

"The Russians may already have someone on the *Casimir.*"

Ted stopped in mid-stride. "Where did that come from?"

"Our guys in Budapest got it through the Canadian embassy. It seems a passenger on board has executive status, *extreme prejudice*—or whatever the Russians call it."

"Orders to kill. FSB's Department Five."

"Whoever sent it thought it *might* have originated with Vladimir Lyubimov."

"How would they know that?"

"They wouldn't say. Why would Vladimir send us info anonymously?

"Maybe he feels his line of communication has been compromised."

"When we've been dealing directly with him?"

Ted stopped by the coffee table to pour himself a glass of ice water.

"Russia's Federal Security isn't always on side with its Military Intelligence. Look no further than our relations with the Pentagon. It's pathetic, at times. Each protecting its own turf."

"What now?"

"If it originated with Vladimir, he'll get back to us to confirm it one way or the other."

"I'll alert Budapest."

"Don't bother. It'll come from another source."

"Which means Hagen is caught up in some pretty shady stuff."

"Once we hear from Vladimir..."

A 'ding' came from Ted's computer brought Gerry walked over to glance at the screen.

"Something's being routed through the British embassy in Qatar."

"Tell me it's good news."

"It IDs the Russian on board the *Casimir III* with only a codename."

"What is it?"

"Tobias."

"*Tobias?*" Ted put down his water glass and joined his assistant. "No wonder Vladimir leaked it to us. The sonofabitch is a virtual killing machine."

"If good old Vlad's given us that much," said Gerry, "why not throw in his name?"

"My guess? He doesn't know it. You can bet he'll work his ass off trying to find out." Ted sat on the edge of his desk. "Men like Tobias are still needed, still employed. Still killing for hire."

"What's it with the scientific community," Gerry asked, "that attracts a hired killer?"

Ted reached for the phone. "We'll soon find out."

Nathan Edgar's executive assistant answered on the third ring, saying he wasn't available.

"Where is he?"

"Stopping by the fish market on his way home, Mister Grosvenor."

"The floating market at the marina?"

"Yes, sir."

"What's he driving?"

"His new Mercedes."

"Patch me through to his cell, Miss Arbuckle."

"Mister Edgars complains such calls distract him while driving."

"Good. *Do it.*"

Nathan's voice snarled over a crackling line. "Who is it?"

"Look at the little window on your cell phone, for Christ sake, and you'd know."

"Ted! Why does everyone call when I'm behind the wheel?"

"Because you have a nasty habit of sneaking out of work early. Where are you?"

"On Pennsylvania, driving past the FBI building."

"Good. Meet me in the Elephant & Castle. Across from the Old Post Office."

"Can't do it. We're having guests for dinner. This salmon is already smelling up my new car."

"The *pub*, Nathan, or I'll crash your goddam dinner party. And you know how unpleasant I can be, even *off* the golf course."

"I can't stay long…"

The Elephant & Castle was packed with the usual Friday pre-rush hour crowd. Ted was at the bar ordering a Moosehead, when Nathan squeezed in beside him.

"Why do we always meet in such noisy places?" Nathan grumbled.

"Because I can get more out of you when you're rattled. I've been waiting for you to shed some light on your international scientific community."

Nathan ordered a Perrier water from the barman. "I'm working on it."

"*Working on it.* The mantra of every public civil servant. Listen, and don't interrupt."

Ted began with July '85 when Vitaly Yurchenko, a high-ranking Moscow-based KGB operative, defected to Rome.

"While being transferred to Washington under tight security Yurchenko was almost murdered by a Russian disguised as an airline employee."

Nathan glanced at his watch. "What's that to do with me?"

"That same year, a senior KGB officer defected in London. He wasn't so lucky... Are you listening? Or are you fixated on the salmon stinking up your new Mercedes?"

"I'm worried, yes."

"Too bad. A deputy director of ours stationed in Athens was killed not long after unification of the two Germanys. A good friend of mine stationed in Paris, was blown up by a bomb rigged to the ignition of his Audi. Witnessed by his wife and their two kids, Nathan, ages three and five. We were convinced, and still are, he had identified the assassin."

"I don't get the connection—"

"The *same* hit man is likely living it up on board the *TSS Casimir III*."

Color spread across Nathan's cheeks. "Good Lord!"

"We're certain he whacked the Russian scientist, Boris Yevtushenko, in a Moscow restaurant. Meaning Leszek Poplawski could be next on his hit list. That's why we need to know more about these hits connected to you bunch. Here and abroad."

"What more can I do?" Nathan shot back. "We've put out feelers."

"*Feelers*? And what next? Committee meetings, followed by what your in-house legal team advises? Mostly the wrong advice. With all the media hype about your exciting new joint projects, surely you realize something's fucked up."

Nathan sipped his Perrier water. "You're being a little hard on us," he mumbled.

"Oh yeah? There are lives at stake. Harmon Page, your *former* researcher. And *my* field operative. Apart from

Leszek Poplawski, and anyone else who gets in the line of fire." Another matter. What do you know about Victor Petrie?"

Nathan Edgars brightened. "Nice fellow. *Bon vivant.* Excellent golfer—a four handicap."

"When did you see him last?"

"At the annual S&T golf tournament. The same invitation you turned down. He flew in from God-knows-where. He regaled us with the latest, dirtiest jokes and donated a full set of Callaways."

"Which he'll overcharge directly to the Pentagon, He only *floats* for us, on occasion. Lots of the usual tongue-wagging on inside gossip. Stuff so crucial it never should have left the building. With Petrie soaking it up like a thirsty sponge."

Nathan frowned. "Like what?"

"Like Page being canned. Prize giving. Wink, wink, nod, nod."

"He didn't seem out of place."

"He wouldn't." Ted finished off his beer. "Find out what's going on…"

"The problem is—"

"…Before it's too late," he said, walking off.

Nicole showed up at Leszek's cabin on A Deck, hoping he wouldn't be deep into an afternoon nap. She found him pouring over an old, worn ledger.

"I'm here to apologize," she said in Polish, "for not being more helpful with…Harmon Page."

Leszek waved her into the cabin's only chair. "An apology is not needed, Madame Hagen. Though I am aware you and Harmon have no time for one another."

"They call it 'rubbing each other the wrong way'," she said, translating it into Polish.

The old man smiled as he filled the two small glasses from the bottle of *Pieprzowka*.

"I would be happy to translate for you, should you need me." Nicole raised her glass. "*Na zdrowie*, Doktor."

"*Na zdrowie*, Madame."

Nicole glanced around, disappointed at the cabin's lack of amenities. "Your work on the brain must be fascinating."

"It is, Madame, when you consider how the brain in humans is a mass of pinkish-grey matter that weighs some three pounds. To say nothing of some ten billion linked nerve cells."

"I know so little about it, apart from our genes representing a unit of heredity."

"Genes. The chemical blueprint of life," Leszek replied, pleased with her response. "The brain not only controls all human emotions, love, hate, fear, anger and sadness, it selects and interprets countless messages received from all parts of the body." He refilled their glasses, enjoying this unexpected visit.

"There is something that disturbs me," he went on. "It was quite unjust for my good friend Harmon to talk to you as he did this morning. I will speak to him."

"No, please. He was just being childish."

"It is not for him to contact your superior, in order to receive your cooperation."

Nicole nodded. *I'll strangle him.*

Returning to Langley, Ted stepped off the elevator to bump into his assistant munching on a sticky bun.

"Margaret told me I was to wait for you," Gerry said between bites.

"Where is she?"

"At her usual Friday hair appointment. How's our pal, Nathan Edgars?"

"He either knows one hell of a lot, or sweet bugger all." Ted pushed his office door open. "We have a ship with a nasty killer on board, Gerry. I want the sonofabitch Tobias ID'd, a list of his aliases, photos. We can't wait for Vladimir to come up with it."

"I'll keep the team on it." Gerry followed him. "We've yet to find a positive link between the muscle car and the Pentagon, other than taking Charlie's word for it."

Ted assured him he wasn't bluffing. "Charlie has this quirky habit of rubbing the back of his neck when he's telling the truth. Scratches his balls when he isn't."

Ted watched his assistant shove the last of the bun into his mouth.

"How you can eat that sweet shit," he said, "is beyond me."

Angus Stockwell studied his wife's face. "The bruise here still shows."

Kim felt his fingers prod the discolored skin below her left eye. He added more blush.

It had become obvious early in their marriage, how Kim relished physical contact beyond what Angus could offer her. Whenever she strayed, her response was always the same. What went on, she would say, was nothing like he imagined.

Nothing like he imagined? When someone last night had obviously beaten her up? He caught a glimpse of her and Page slipping back into his stateroom. He saw the telltale bruises later.

Worse, she had come back to their cabin saying nothing.

Kim, in a skimpy bra and bikini briefs, watched him tying the black bow tie. He had bought a clip-on before leaving New York, but she had replaced it with a tie-it-yourself version.

"No one would realize the other was a clip-on," he said, making the loops. A few pulls here and there, and it took shape.

"*I* would," she said, zipping herself into an off-the-shoulder number with silver sequins.

He pulled on his tuxedo jacket. "I'll go on ahead. See you at dinner." He kissed her on the nose and slipped out into the corridor.

Kim knew where to find him: playing poker.

She was tidying up, mostly her own clothes scattered about the little cabin, when there was a knock at the door. She opened it and let out a squeal.

"You've come to swap cabins!"

"Not on your life," Harm said with a grin. In jeans, a denim shirt and runners, he held out her missing high-heel shoe. "No use having one without the other."

"Come in."

"As you see, I have to change for dinner."

"You didn't have to look for my shoe," she said, tossing it onto the lower bunk. "Unless you didn't believe me."

"I believed you. I wanted to check out the area for myself. It worried me that Victor might've seen or heard you last night."

Kim picked up her purse. "Not a chance; it was gloomy down there. Besides, he was too involved arguing with Nicole. I must admit, their conversation intrigued me."

"Don't let it."

Kim gave him a kiss on the cheek, asking him to save a dance for her tonight.

A trio played music from a small dais set up in the dining room during second sitting, encouraging passengers to dance between courses.

The friendly talk, good food, and flowing wine had much to do with the high spirits at the Ashcroft table. Adding to this were the women in their finery and the men in their tuxedos. Harm was seated on Gwen's right, Angus on her left. Hugh and Kimberly sat opposite them.

The lively conversation swung between Kim, who supporting the legalization of marijuana to her husband, and Angus, thumping for the fluctuating popularity of gold stocks.

Hugh decried how North Americans butchered the English language.

"When someone is driving an automobile in America," he said, "how can you say, *'go ahead, back up'* in the same breath?" much to the delight of the others.

Harm enjoyed the friendly banter, the light-hearted laughter. Victor had come by asking Gwen to dance. He wondered how she'd take it, if she knew she was dancing with a CIA operative. Throw Hagen into the mix…

Kim came around the table to drag Harm onto the dance floor.

"You're light on your feet," she said, a moment before he stepped on her toes.

Leszek caught up to Harm in the busy Promenade foyer after second sitting. He was enthused how he had spent much of the afternoon with Nicole.

"We practiced on my English," he said, steering him into the Polish Bar. "Madame Hagen was full of wonder when I told her of the workings of the brain."

"I can only imagine it," Harm said as they sat at an empty table.

"I sense in both of you certain, hmm…"

Harm filled in the blank, "Hostility."

"It is why I am asking you here to the Polish Bar, Harmon."

Nicole appeared in the doorway with a smile that instantly faded.

"You see?" said Leszek. "She is looking forward to joining us."

She came toward them in a short red dress with matching high heels, her makeup at a minimum. The simple design of the round, gold earrings gave her tanned face a warm glow.

Harm wished she didn't look so damned good.

Leszek hurried off, a bold excuse Harm guessed, to let them settle their differences.

"Our old friend thinks you and I don't get along," he said when she sat down opposite him. "Let's drop the charade, work together. Keep Leszek from whatever ugliness is going on."

Nicole glanced at him with indifference.

"I've put you off, for some reason. Right from the start."

"Why would you think that," she asked, "when we've never met?"

He leaned forward. "You tell me."

"Because Compdata wouldn't sanction any cooperation between us."

"You're with the CIA. Leszek's in danger of some kind—"

"Mind your own business."

Harm pushed himself to his feet, his hands pressed down on the wood table.

"Whatever's going on, Hagen, it's too big for you to handle by yourself."

Nicole sat motionless, watching him disappear out the door.

Why do men fixate on the obvious? She'd said *Compdata*, yes, hoping the idiot might realize she couldn't admit being with the CIA. Meaning Page was blind in one eye and couldn't see out of the other.

Reaching the foyer, Harm bumped into Thomas coming from the Grand Lounge.

"If you're looking for fun," said Thomas, "you won't find it in there. The Ashcrofts called it a night. The Stockwells are arguing over Angus' obsession with poker.

Peter Lount has had a little too much to drink, and God knows where Nicole has gone."

Harm nodded back toward the Polish Bar. "She's jabbering away in there with Leszek."

"Nicole's put you off. Not that you two hit it off from the start."

"I told her so. Go in there, Thomas. Put her in a better mood."

"Not me, thanks. I'm off to catch up on my notes and turn in early."

Harm looked at his watch. Early? It was already well after midnight. He reached his cabin, distracted over his confrontation with Nicole while fumbling for his key card.

He had to admit, there might be another side to it. What if she had been implying it wasn't Compdata, but Central Intelligence who wouldn't sanction them cooperating?

It made sense. He slipped the card into place and pushed the door open...

Hands grabbed him by the shoulders, yanked him inside and slammed him up against the wall. Pinned there, he felt thumbs digging deep into the soft flesh at the base of his neck.

The intruder's s face, caught in the dim light from the window, appeared grotesque with the nose and lips twisted oddly out of shape, the hair flattened against the skull.

Harm felt his strength draining away, his body unresponsive as he sank to the floor. He was being dragged helpless into the unlit bathroom, lifted and dumped in a bath of cold water. Nor could he stop a plastic bag from being pulled down over his head, bunched and knotted tight behind it.

Harm heard the bathroom door close. He tore at the plastic, whose smooth surface made ripping it impossible. Unable to see for the plastic covering his face, he felt for the outer edge of the tub, worked his arms up over it, and splashed down onto the tile floor.

He took a breath before dragging himself across to the wall and easing his back against it. Another breath, and Harm inched slowly, painfully upward until he was standing on wobbly legs. Pressing himself against the wall, he shifted sideways toward the bathroom door, one agonizing step after another.

Breathing had become difficult for him when he reached it, each breath drawing the plastic closer to his nose, his mouth. Forcing himself not to panic, he grasped the door handle in both hands and found he didn't have the physical strength to turn it.

Harm slumped against the door, one breath short of dying. Staying alive, he knew, depended on finding something as simple as…

It came to him! As simple as the metal clothes hook on the bathroom door.

Harm grabbed the plastic bunched behind his head, stretching it up to snag it on the hook. He missed it. With it came a crushing weariness of his body shutting down.

He was trying once more, when his legs gave out from under him.

He lay motionless, his eyes closed.

If I'm dead, he asked himself, *why am I gulping air into my lungs?*

Harm opened his eyes and looked up to see shreds of plastic dangling loose from the metal hook.

With a flood of tears blurring his vision, Harmon C. Page knew he had cheated death not once, but for a second time.

CHAPTER TWENTY
Saturday, October 7, 1:46 AM

Thomas Slater sat on the narrow bunk, his bulky shape wrapped in loose gray sweats. He was staring at a blank screen, when there was a knock at the door. Curious, he put the laptop aside, stretched, and opened the door.

A bedraggled Harm Page leaned barefoot and bleary-eyed against the wall, his shirt and tuxedo dripping wet.

"Good God," Thomas said, helping him into the cabin. "What the hell have you been up to?"

"Ask the other guy," Harm wheezed.

"A hot shower comes first," he said, tossing him a striped bathrobe. "Down here, the *inside* cabins don't have showers. They're along the hall. Get out of your wet tux and everything else. Go on ahead. I'll catch up."

Thomas shoved a scotch through the flimsy cotton curtain with steam fanning out along the white tile ceiling from the only shower in use.

"I gave your tux and what needed laundering to my night steward," he said. "They'll return everything to your cabin by noon."

The water stopped. Harm stepped out, swapping the empty glass for the proffered towel.

"Whoever it was, he wore what I took for a nylon stocking pulled down over his face."

"Good facial distortion without losing all around visibility. One guy?"

"One tough sonofabitch. He jammed me up against the wall, burying his thumbs deep in either side of my neck."

Thomas looked at the identical bruises. "He worked his thumbs under your collarbone to compress the carotid arteries. Cutting off the blood flow. Applied hard enough, brings on temporary paralysis and mental disorientation."

"You got that right." Harm tossed him the towel and pulled on the bath robe. "You're a walking, talking Wikipedia of torture and mayhem."

"Having an insatiable curiosity helps. I came across the technique while researching material on self-defense. William J. Underwood wrote the book. A feisty old Brit who applied the body's pressure points to overcome adversaries twice his size. Twice his weight. Twice his age." They stepped into the corridor. "Then what happened?"

"He physically dumped me in the bathtub, pulled a plastic bag down over my head and taped it tight at the back of my head. Or neck, whatever. Not that it's the first time I've been whacked."

"Recently?" said Thomas.

"A week ago. A Saturday night. I was run off a highway up in Maine. The state police decided I was pissed."

"Any connection between it and what happened here?"

"I doubt it. I had no intention of coming on board, until I scooped up a last-minute cancellation."

They stopped at Thomas' cabin. "I don't want to upset you, but it seems this guy had no intention of you leaving the ship, alive. My guess? He was planning to come back, remove the plastic and strip off your tux, making it look as if you drowned in the bath on accident."

"Meaning he'll be pissed off when he finds I'm still breathing."

"That's the downside. Being who Nicole is, she should be told about this."

Harm walked on, "Knowing her, she'd put it down to a bad dream."

Where are you going?" Thomas called out.

"Back to my cabin."

Thomas caught up to him.

"I'll go with you, making sure there's no ugly bastard hiding under your bed."

After what happened tonight, Harm thought it was a good idea.

CHAPTER TWENTY-ONE
Saturday, October 8, 9:15 AM

The room service steward had cleared away the breakfast dishes in Harm Page's cabin, leaving a carafe of coffee, cups, cream, and sugar.

Though still bothered by last night's encounter, and wary of his surroundings, Harm had looked forward to this scheduled breakfast with Leszek.

He was helping himself to another coffee, when Leszek, in a flannel shirt, baggy pants and slippers, emerged from the bathroom. He sat down asking where he had left off.

"We touched on Weisel and Hubel," Harm said, "and sensory deprivation."

"I am remembering now."

"Visual stimulation." Harm let it go. "More coffee?"

He shook his head. "I am worried you are keeping something from me, Harmon. Perhaps you are feeling our progress is too slow?"

"Not at all, Leszek. It's more like: I hear your Russian colleagues are worried about you."

"There is no reason to worry."

"They're concerned enough to ask the United States Central Intelligence Agency for help. The CIA has someone on board to make sure you're comfortable during the crossing."

"I have done nothing to fear, Harmon. Nor do I wish a stranger keeping eyes on me."

"Not to worry. Your 'guardian Angel' is someone you care about. It's Nicole Hagen."

Leszek's eyes widened. "It is not possible to believe."

"She is the last person I'd have thought of," said Harm, "given her sharp tongue and abrasive personality."

"You dislike her, Harmon, even though she is here to guide my safe passage?"

"I confronted her about her CIA connection, and she denied it."

"Putting your nose, how do you say…?"

"Out of joint."

"Like *my* nose when you did not reply to my messages left on your telephone."

"Only because the same bunch Hagen works for must've tampered with my phone. Had it not been for your postcard, I never would've known you were in America. As it is, those bandits tried to stop me from reaching you."

"It is true, Harmon?"

Yes, Leszek. When you sent me the postcard about sailing home, I was lucky enough to pick up a last-minute cancellation. And here I am."

Leszek broke into a smile. "It warms me to have you here. But why would this Central Intelligence not want you on board? I have dreamed many times of you and I sharing our research, beyond our letters and brief discussions at conferences."

For Harm, the CIA's involvement meant the stakes were high, but why?

"There is yet another reason, Harmon, why a miracle brought you on board. It is that I am plagued by the constant fear of old age stripping me of my memory. I have already moments of experiencing forgetfulness."

Harm was struck by his old friend's honesty. "You and I know how our brains thrive on being stimulated. Once we talk about our work over the next few days, believe me, what you fear is lost will come back to you."

"I am only hoping so. We must still make a permanent record of what passes between us."

"I'll take notes. Your daughter translates it and—"

"You make excuses," Leszek interrupted, "not valuing who we have on board. Madame Hagen has expressed great willingness to help, even to make notes in your language while translating them into Polish for me."

What bothered Harm was having Nicole Hagen that close to them, with no idea of their work.

"Go to her, Harmon," Leszek whispered. "Make peace."

Harm helped himself to another coffee, knowing he owed his old friend that much.

Thomas was curious, not by what Harm Page had told him, but what he hadn't told him. It prompted the author to visit the ship's library, searching for the Polish equivalent of Funk & Wagnalls.

"You are lost, perhaps?" asked the bespectacled librarian loaded down with an armful of books.

"I'm looking for information on a Polish man of letters," said Thomas, reaching out to steady the pile until it was set down on the librarian's desk.

"You speak the language, then."

"The odd phrase."

The librarian warmed to this honesty. "His name?"

"Leszek Poplawski."

The librarian glanced at Thomas over the half-moon rim of his reading glasses.

"You are aware he is a passenger on board this ship. A very private person. We strive to keep it that way."

"I appreciate it, if I wasn't sharing the dining table with him." Thomas grinned. "God forbid should I appear ill-informed of his accomplishments."

The librarian accepted this with a curt nod. "Then you must also understand the Russians claim him as their own. Give me a moment to find what you are looking for."

While waiting, Thomas thumbed through several current weekly magazines on a table by the entrance. An item in *Maclean's* capsule news section caught his attention. It noted a Russian scientist had died from a faulty pacemaker in a Moscow restaurant...

Harm knocked on Nicole's door, feeling the sway of the ship beneath his feet.

She appeared, ashen-faced.

Harm noticed the rumpled bed behind her.

"Lying down won't help curb seasickness," he said. "You need fresh air."

She winced as the vessel swayed again. "I'm fine."

"Is that so? Try those little patches from Sick Bay. Or Dramamine. Taken now and—"

"Are you finished?" she said, irritated more by how lousy she really felt.

"No. Leszek and I are having a problem with language. Technical stuff."

Nicole pushed loose strands of damp hair away from her face. "Where is he?"

"In my cabin. Leave it for now. Take a pill *before* the vessel really begins to…"

Nicole put both hand over her mouth and bumped the door shut.

She was removing an unopened package of sea pills a moment later, compliments of Grosvenor's secretary, when the laptop buzzed. Washing two Dramamines down with a glass of water, she sat on the bed and picked up the laptop.

She typed, *Working Saturdays, are we, Gerry? Those periodic weekend public tours?*

Not quite. We have ID'd Victor's employer.

You insisted he worked for us.

We figured he might be floating for another dept. But no.

There you go. Playing games.

No games. He's tied in with the Pentagon. Freelance contract.

What's he doing on board?

No idea. We are working on it. Any news on your end?

Page and Poplawski are thick as thieves. They want me to help translate when language is a problem. A break for our side. Any idea how Page knew my CIA connect?

No. Page is a wily bastard. Ted Grosvenor doubly puzzled over Petrie/Pentagon. Could you pry it loose from Petrie?

Short of what?

Your call. How are the sea legs?

Have taken two Dramamine before rough weather hits us. Nicole considered confessing about her stolen handgun. She decided against it. *Reaching Atlantic shortly or maybe there already. Bye for now.*

Nicole had joined Leszek and Page, feeling better. After listening to the two men chatter about their work, she knew their discussion was far over her head. She was relieved when they gave her a break after lunch, while they mapped out what to tackle over the coming days.

She used the spare time to explore parts of the ship she had yet to visit. The health club, not that impressive; the room set aside for chess, a game she hadn't played for years. The library came next with its fine collection of Polish works.

As for the odd heaving of the ship, Dramamine had been a wise choice.

Having finished her self-directed tour by mid-afternoon, Nicole dropped by the Boat Deck Bar where Feliks, the bartender, was polishing glasses.

After exchanging pleasantries in Polish, he told her, if she was looking for her friends, they were playing a round robin shuffleboard tournament on the Sport Deck.

The black disk careened down the deck's weathered oak planking, smacked into her opponent's red disk, driving it out of play.

"Well done, partner," Hugh shouted to his wife at the other end.

Gwen acknowledged this stunning win with a nod to her husband and free advice to the team of Harm and Peter Lount.

"You are short on strategy," she said, having knocked them out of the competition, "yet worthy opponents."

Harm grinned. "Until next time," he said, turning to Thomas whose partner, Kimberly, at the opposite end, would take on Gwen and Hugh. "Watch these Brits," he warned them aloud. "These English play as if they invented the game."

"I'll have you know, you upstart Yank," Hugh called out, "shuffleboard was outlawed by King Henry VIII. He called it a devilish sport upon discovering his soldiers were playing it rather than practicing archery."

"Was it before or after he cut off Anne Boleyn's head?" Thomas quipped.

"Afterward," said Harm, finishing his beer. He decided to go back to his cabin to read over notes from the earlier session with Leszek. He suggested Thomas drop by after the game.

Harm had taken his key card from his pocket, when he noticed the door ajar, the curtains pulled. Hearing a curious scraping sound from the bathroom.

He took it whoever was poking around wasn't waiting for him. Looking for what, then? Curious, Harm came in, closed the door, and squeezed between the wall and the far side of the dresser.

The scraping stopped. The bathroom door opened A shadowy figure, smaller he judged than the last intruder, had slipped over to the closet, pulling open its louvered doors.

A small beam of light was flashed around inside. What followed was his clothes flung into the room, along with what he took for his luggage.

The intruder was on the hunt for something, he decided, and the dresser drawers beside him would be next.

Harm struck first, tackling him from behind. Both landed on the nearest twin bed. He dragged the intruder to his feet, aimed a fist where he hoped a jaw might be, and let it fly.

He heard loud thump, and silence.

Harm switched the light. At first, the room seemed empty, until a moan came from the space between the beds.

A head appeared, the eyes glazed, the dark hair ruffled.

"Well, well," said Harm. "How thoughtful of you to drop in."

Nicole pushed the hair out of her eyes. "You know why I'm here."

"To pick up whatever's worth stealing?" Harm, noticing the cut lip and the swollen cheek, disappeared into the bathroom. He returned with a warm, damp washcloth.

"Cash, credit cards, travelers' checks—"

"I'm looking for my handgun, goddam it. The Walther PPK .32mm you stole from me."

He leaned across the narrow bed. "What would I do with such a nasty piece of hardware?" he asked, handing her the washcloth.

She pushed his hand away. "Shoot people."

Harm sat on the bed, finding her surprisingly attractive in the form-fitting dark jeans, black hoodie and bare feet with bright pink toenails.

"Burgling has its drawbacks," he said. "By rights, I, Harmon C. Page, should make a citizen's arrest. Charging you with breaking and entering, assault and battery...foul language. Under the authority vested in the ship's captain, I would be obliged to—"

"And I'll hit *you* with assault," she fired back, snatching the washcloth. "And battery. Obstructing a federal agent. Theft of a dangerous weapon to say nothing of —" She stopped in mid-sentence. "Why are you grinning?"

"You, admitting being a federal agent."

Struggling to stand up, she lost her balance and flopped back down, angering her even more.

"I did not."

"You did."

"I didn't. Give the handgun back, and we'll forget what happened."

"I would, if I had it." Harm slipped off the bed, poured her a scotch, and handed it over. "Tell me about the scraping noise when you were in the bathroom."

"You should know." She winced as the scotch touched her cut lip. "Thieves like you wrap a weapon in plastic and hide it in the toilet's reservoir. "

"I'll remember that. When was I supposed to have stolen it?"

"When you knocked my makeup bag onto the floor the other night." She wiped her face with the washcloth. "It's a good thing I'm a little rusty at protecting myself, or you'd sitting here in far worse shape than me."

"A CIA-trained spook. You're that good—?"

"Hello," came a familiar voice from the hallway.

"The door's unlocked," Harm called out.

Thomas came in to stare at Nicole who was crouched barefoot between the beds. She was pressing a washcloth against her cheek with one hand, holding the glass in the other.

"Then again," he murmured, "I'll drop by another time."

Pushing herself slowly to her feet, she nailed Thomas with a *don't you dare ask,* polished off the whisky, handed him the glass, and walked out the door.

Thomas glanced at the empty closet and cluttered beds and floor.

"There's a rumor," he said, watching Harm cleaning up the mess, "you and Kim were seen ducking back into your cabin the other night. She was later sporting some nasty bruises. Now I find Nicole with you and—"

"Leaving you to wonder if I beat up women on a regular basis?"

"That would about cover it."

"I came back from shuffleboard to find someone had broken in here."

"Luckily it wasn't the same guy who almost killed you."

"I struck first. It turned out to be Nicole."

"What was she up to?"

Harm stopped to pour two scotches. "She was looking for her handgun."

Thomas grinned. "Our Nicky brandishes a *handgun?*"

"A Walther PPK.32mm."

"No firm like Compdata would arm its personnel with handguns."

"That's because she's not with Compdata."

"Who then?"

"She's an agent with the Central Intelligence Agency."

Thomas lowered himself down on a twin bed. "You're kidding me. The CIA. A genuine *spook?*"

"Full-fledged."

"The PPK?" asked Thomas, drinking his scotch.

"It's missing. She's convinced I stole it and sneaked in here to find it."

"Which takes us back to Kimberly and her obvious bruises."

"With Angus playing poker, she took off for the all-night Disco, picking up two seamen who shouldn't have been there. She agreed to meet one of them below deck. Both showed up."

Thomas's face clouded over. "She reported it?"

"No. If I do, she says she'll deny it."

"Why is it when women are raped, they feel it's their fault? That's what the bastards are counting on. How do you fit in?"

"I was wrestling with a nasty nightmare, when she appeared at my door, looking as if she'd been hit by a train."

"And she came to you. Not her husband."

"For whatever reason."

"Because there's a healthy camaraderie between you."

"I persuaded her to take a cold bath to reduce the swelling."

"And the bruises?"

"She used makeup to cover up the worst of them. I was walking her to the elevator when we heard voices coming from the Boat Deck Bar. We ducked back inside my cabin."

"Someone saw you both and that's when the rumor started." Thomas felt better. "Tell me more about the CIA's Agent Hagen," he said, smiling. "That's a lot of info to handle all at once."

"She's a field operative, assigned to keep tabs on Leszek. It seems he's a security risk. Petrie's involved as well. Same outfit."

"You'd best tell Nicole how you were almost bumped off while on board."

Harm glanced at the scuffed knuckles of his punching hand. "I'll keep it in mind."

"You won't, and that's what pisses me off." Thomas finished off his drink. "See you after dinner."

"No pre-dinner libation in Boat Deck Bar?"

"I have reading to catch up on," said Thomas, stepping into the corridor.

CHAPTER TWENTY-TWO
Saturday, October 8, 11:15 PM

A formal Saturday evening in the Grand Lounge had been, as Kimberly Stockwell put it, one round of dancing, drinking, socializing, and just plain fun. Along with Leszek dancing with Gwen, and Nicole swept off her feet by the captain.

Harm was dancing with Kim, with her taking advantage of an old slow number by resting her cheek against his.

"I hope you noticed I'm behaving," she whispered in his ear.

"A model of decorum," he replied. "Especially with the captain."

"A sweet man." Kim eased herself closer to him. "He went on about his favorite composer, Gustav Mahler. How his 'dissolution of tonality' influenced Benjamin Britten. All the while thrusting his crotch into me."

"It didn't bother you?"

"He was just testing me." Her arms circled around his neck. "You're a very good man, Harmon C. Page. A little square—sadly, you don't take advantage of a woman who throws herself at you. But then, that's part of your charm."

"Flattery will get you anywhere," he said, not unaware of their bodies pressed together.

"I'm married, and my husband is on board." She blew lightly in his ear. "Maybe I'll have that little chat with Victor."

"Don't even think of it," he said. "These types don't play games."

Kim tightened her arms around him, only to have Peter Lount claim her next.

"Peter cut you off," Thomas said, with Harm dropping into a chair beside him. "Just when you and Kim were making sweet music."

"She doesn't need me complicating her life."

"Still, you have a soft spot for her. Then again, who doesn't? By the way, I've ordered us a fifteen-year-old Glenfiddich. Made with water from the Robby Dhu springs—"

The steward came by with the drinks and a small carafe of water.

Thomas glanced toward the crowded dance floor. "I noticed Nicole doesn't seem any the

worse for your left hook. And look who she's dancing with now."

"Petrie."

"You got it. *Spook* or not, I can't get a handle on that guy. The jaw's too square, the teeth too white. God knows how many languages he speaks…or women he's bedded."

"Are you talking unqualified admiration or total disdain?"

"A little of both. I have a built-in aversion to guys who seem too perfect." They clinked glasses, prompting Thomas to say, "To more urgent matters: I talked to the librarian. Not only is he a Nobel Prize winner, but someone the Russians treat as a home-grown hero. To consider he's in trouble while on board is serious stuff—to say nothing of you, almost being deep-sixed in your own cabin."

"Along with that, I've discovered a flaw in your earlier theory about the hit man making it look like I'd drowned in the bathtub. Medical staff would realize I didn't die that way from an obvious lack of water in my lungs."

"On the contrary. Medics on board don't have the equipment or authority to perform an autopsy. The ship's hospital would note it as a possible accidental death. By maritime law, you'd be kept in a cool place on board with an obligatory autopsy performed at the first port of call."

"You know that for sure?"

"I had a cousin die at sea. The paperwork alone took many days to file. In your case, it would be handled by the London/Tilbury Port Authority. Not listed, I'm sure, as one of their priorities, when the death is deemed accidental. They'd line up a local coroner who's undoubtedly underpaid and overworked."

"It would at least confirm I'd been murdered."

"It would too late by then."

"Too late for what?"

"You tell me. Writers store away stuff they read, hear, overhear, or things they shouldn't hear or overhear. Two simple words kick-start the imagination. 'What if...?'

"What if what?"

"*What if* Harmon C. Page wasn't drunk, as the cops decided, when he ended up in the ocean off New England? *What if* a Nobel Prize scientist *is* in real danger aboard the *Casimir III*?"

"Where do you go from there?"

"Me? To the ship's library where I stumbled on a news item in the latest *Maclean's* magazine. A Russian scientist's pacemaker malfunctioned, killing him outright.

His name was Boris Yevtushenko. He was into your type of research. Ring a bell?"

"I can't put a face to him."

"What got me thinking was he'd died the same Saturday night you ended up in the ocean." Thomas leaned forward. "Think of it. Two scientists. One in the U.S., the other in Russia. Both hit on the same night. Coincidence? I don't think so."

"The *same* Saturday night?"

"Indeed. I told myself not to get involved. Me? I observe. Make notes, write stories. That's what I do. Then my conscience got the better of me. I like this guy, Harmon Page. He's honest, good humored, but way out of his depth."

"I know what you're going to say. So, forget it."

"Why? We writers salivate over stuff like this. Besides, you need someone to watch your backside. Funnily enough, I don't see any volunteers lining up to help, except me."

Harm thought about it. about it. "Okay. On one condition. Should things turn nasty, you'll back off."

"Deal," Thomas said with a grin and a handshake. "What's our first move?"

It came moments later when knocking on Nicole's stateroom door.

"Hi," they said in unison when it opened. "We—"

Victor appeared behind her, his black bow tie untied.

"Your little friends want you to come out to play, Nicky." He kissed her on the bare neck and eased by them. "Don't forget, kiddies, Ms. Hagen needs her beauty sleep."

Nicole rolled her eyes and stepped aside. "This better be good."

Both noticed an open bottle of Teacher's Highland Cream on the nightstand, along with two glasses.

"A Russian scientist died while eating in a Moscow restaurant," said Harm. "We're curious how it happened."

Nicole glanced at Thomas. "Did Page talk you into this?"

Thomas shook his head. "I volunteered."

Harm said, "Contact Ted, your boss at Langley…"

"… For your benefit, Nicole," chimed in Thomas, "if not ours."

Nicole stared from one to the other. "You think whoever this Russian is—"

"Boris Yevtushenko," Thomas said. "It had something to do with his pacemaker."

Harm added, "Tell Ted that the dead Russian might have a connection to Leszek." He paused. "Then again, what if your boss knew already, and didn't tell you?"

"And you expect me to bother him at two in the morning?"

"Or whatever time it is back there, yes," Harm said. "Leszek's life might depend on it."

Nicole eased them out into the corridor. "Where did you hear this?"

"We have our sources," said Thomas as the door closed behind them.

"*We have our sources,*" said Harm, imitating Thomas' gravelly voice as they walked back to his stateroom. "Thanks to *Time* magazine."

"*MacLean's,*" Thomas corrected him. "Do you think she'll brush us off?"

"Not if she's curious enough."

Once back in the cabin, they left the door ajar and were ordering a large pizza, all dressed, and a bottle of Italian *Chianti,* when Nicole stormed in barefoot and hot-tempered.

"I want answers, you *low life*. How did you know the Russian scientist was dead?"

"We're more interested in *how* he died," said Harm, admiring her flashing, angry eyes.

"Officially? From a faulty pacemaker."

"*Un*officially," said Thomas.

"The pacemaker…might've been tampered with."

"It either was or it wasn't tampered with," Harm said.

"It was *tampered* with, if that makes you both feel any better."

"That's murder," said Thomas.

"Who confirmed it?" Harm asked.

"Ted Grosvenor," she paused. "Why are you two so smug?"

"Thomas has a warped notion we're caught up in a conspiracy."

"It's the first I've heard of it," she said.

Harm thought of the plastic bag pulled down over his head. "That's comforting."

There was a knock at the door. Nicole eyed them both.

"It's the room steward," said Thomas, "with our order of pizza supreme."

"With the works. Anchovies included." Harm thought of inviting her. After all, she hadn't let them down.

"Join us," he said, surprising the hell out of Thomas.

Nicole had had enough for one night. Yet…

She leaned against the dresser. "Only if there's a bottle of wine to go with it."

CHAPTER TWENTY-THREE
Sunday, October 9, 7:02 AM

Harm slept through the ship's early morning announcements to be awakened by a knock on the cabin door. He forced himself out of bed, pulled on a bathrobe, and opened it.

A server entered, pushing a large breakfast trolley. "Dzien dobry, Pan Page."

Nicole swept in behind him in a wool skirt, a crewneck sweater, and sandals.

"Don't blame me," she challenged his frown. "It was Doctor Poplawski's idea."

The server removed the white covering over the trolley to show an array of juice glasses, coffee cups, and sterling silver plate warmers. Piled high were buns and croissants peeking out from the folds of a warm linen towel.

"I thought you'd like an early start," she said.

She sounded almost civilized to Harm, as she slipped the server American dollars on his way out.

Leszek arrived in a suit, a sports shirt, which was loose at the neck, and a nervous smile.

"Dzien dobry," he said, shaking hands with Harm and turning to speak to Nicole in Polish.

"I'm sure he's asking how I've taken it so far," said Harm.

Nicole reached for the coffee carafe. "I told him you didn't throw a tantrum."

Leszek was smiling. "I am happy you are not angry Harmon," he said in English. "I am excited about working together, though I am lost in remembering where we finished off."

"How sound waves affect the brain," said Nicole, adding cream to her coffee. "I went off after that because you both were reviewing some material."

"She's right," Harm said to him. "I had asked what you thought of these waves entering the human ear and setting off a chain reaction of impulses. Besides—"

"First, we enjoy breakfast," Nicole announced. "Not forgetting Peter Lount is giving his first lecture later this morning in the Little Lounge. We shouldn't miss it."

"I hope he doesn't drag it out," said Harm, realizing he was still in his bathrobe.

Thomas and Hugh were at the stern of the Promenade, waiting while a burly seaman reloaded the large black metal trapshooting device. Crooked under their arms were Remington Trap 12-gauge pump-action shotguns.

Hugh shoved his out from the body at an angle and barked, "PULL!"

A sudden clank broke the silence as the trap's spring-loaded arm catapulted the bright orange clay pigeon high over the water. The Englishman's shotgun roared, giving Thomas barely time to see the spinning disk before it exploded into fragments.

"Where did you learn to shoot like that?" muttered Thomas, not having hit one, with Hugh never missing.

"The British Army, my boy. Mind, I was better hitting targets than the enemy." Hugh leaned against the railing. "I must say, Harmon Page remains a bit of a mystery to me. Friendly enough, yet there's something about him that baffles me. Do you know much about him?"

"You'll have to ask him," said Thomas, wary that the remark seemed oddly out of place.

The final slide showed a sketchy, sepia-colored photo of a five-mast schooner battling waves as high as itself, its rails packed with glum-faced immigrants.

"No stabilizers back then," said Peter, holding the mic, "to keep the ship from rocking and rolling." His monotone delivery inspired little enthusiasm among those in the Little Lounge.

"Atlantic travel some one hundred and seventy years ago meant many passengers would not survive the trip. Especially those crowded into the dirty, dank conditions below deck. These sea voyages, lasting some thirteen weeks, were pure unadulterated hell of suffering beyond belief."

He waited while Entertainment Officer Filip Sotek translated this into Polish, as he had done during the past two hours.

"Thanks for your undivided attention," said Peter, when Filip had finished. "The next lecture will be held on Tuesday, same time, same place. We'll trace the sinking of the White Star liner *Titanic* which sunk on Sunday, April 14, 1912."

There was clapping, shuffling feet, and scraping chairs as many passengers, including Nicole, Gwen and Kim, crowded around Peter.

Leszek, glancing their way, broke into a smile.

"Madame Hagen is reminding me of the wife of a colleague," he said to Harm and Thomas. "A younger…" His voice trailed off as they stood up.

"A younger version," said Thomas.

"Yes. Of Anna Karlovna. Wife of Boris, my assistant and very close friend."

"Boris Yevtushenko?" Harm asked, catching them both by surprise.

"When did you see him last?" said Thomas.

"They invited me for dinner at their favorite restaurant, before I am leaving on this voyage. My old friend had everyone laughing with his antics, his singing. I am trying several times to reach him since, by *telefonu*." He glanced at the two somber faces. "Something is wrong, then?"

"The news of your old friend is not good," said Harm, trying to soften what knew must be told. "Boris is dead, Leszek, Thomas and I are both so sorry."

The old man sank down on the chair. "My friend is dead?"

"When his pacemaker failed him," Harm replied.

"This cannot be," Leszek wheezed, his breath coming in short bursts.

"I'll fetch a doctor," Thomas said.

"No, *lekarza, prosze*." The old man gripped him by the arm. "Madame Hagen will tell me in my own language what has happened to my good friend."

Nicole, stepping away from those surrounding Peter, was shocked to see tears flowing down Leszek's face. She hurried over, staring at Harm and Thomas in disbelief as she knelt beside him.

She took his hands in hers. "What is it, Leszek?"

"Explain to me, please, Madame," his voice barely audible, "how Boris is dead."

Nicole glanced up at Harm. "Surely you could have—"

Thomas cut her off. "We had no choice."

"No *choice*?"

"Better from us," said Harm, "than some faceless bureaucrat telling him over the phone."

Leszek squeezed her hand. "Do not be critical, Madame Hagen. I only wish to understand in my own language what caused Boris to die."

"We told him his friend's pacemaker had problems," Harm explained. "Nothing more."

Nicole looked relieved, telling Leszek how his friend had been dining with his wife when the accident happened. Satisfied, the old man got slowly to his feet.

They reached out to steady him, but he brushed them aside.

"I am not ill but grieving for a dear old friend." Leszek glanced at Harm with obvious affection, while speaking directly to Nicole in Polish.

She said, "He wants to thank you both for explaining in such kind words."

Harm and Thomas insisted on walking him to his cabin, with no ifs, ands or buts, as Thomas put it—an expression that sailed right over Leszek Poplawski's head.

Chief Officer Pawel Klimek's first break over the Montréal defections came unexpectedly. It was his habit of dropping by the crew's canteen to make himself available for questions or complaints; a practice the seamen on board felt encroached on their personal time.

It had paid off when he overheard idle talk about a young member of the kitchen staff who'd been crying himself to sleep since his lover had jumped ship in Montréal.

Pawel had made a mental note of the kid's name.

It was mid-afternoon in the ship's kitchen; that brief, quiet period between the end of one meal and busy preparation of the next. The only activity was the dishwasher cleaning up.

Unease came over Chief Officer Klimek, as he entered from the dining room where he always felt as being an outsider. He noticed the *chef de cuisine* was in his glassed-in office, busy correcting what would be the dinner menu proofs.

A smallish man appeared from behind a row of chrome ovens, clutching freshly folded kitchen whites. On seeing the officer, he said, "You are looking for him, Mister Klimek," he whispered, nodding over his shoulder. "Benedykt, the pot washer."

The *sous-chef* hurried off. To be known as a Klimek informant was not good.

The plump young man in soiled whites had hung up a large metal pot when he was startled by the sudden appearance of the senior officer.

"Come," said Pawel in Polish, walking on between the pots suspended on hooks.

The kid glanced down at his hands. The flesh was puffy and swollen from constant immersion in hot, soapy water. He wiped his damp face on a towel tucked in a pocket, and followed the officer, having no idea what he had done wrong.

Passing behind a several large dishwashers, Pawel grabbed him by the sweat-soaked shirt, ramming him up against the closest unit's ribbed metal side.

"It was your lover, Benedykt," Pawel hissed in his ear, "who jumped ship in Montréal."

"Yes…sir." Benedykt stammered.

"Officer Szalinski was also among them," he breathed in the young man's face. "Who else knew of this?"

The pot washer closed his eyes.

Pawel drove a knee up into pot washer's groin, a blow that doubled him over. Pawel wrenched him upright. "The *name,* or you'll be scooping your gonads up off the kitchen floor."

"Officer…Olecki, s…sir."

Pawel stepped back. "Lie to me, and your nights aboard will be tormented ones."

Thomas, in his tuxedo, was the first of the group to arrive in the Boat Deck Bar for the cocktail hour.

Nicole joined him moments later in a simple black dress held in place by two thin spaghetti straps. An added touch was the fancy gold earrings matching the pendant hanging from a chain around her neck. They sat at the bar, nursing dry vodka martinis.

"You and Page were right," she said, "not telling Leszek that his friend was murdered."

"Leszek is also aware of your connection with the CIA."

"*Page* told him?"

"Yes. Harm, by the way, almost drowned in a car crash two weeks ago. The details will have to come from him." Thomas sipped his martini. "There's more…"

"Tell me he's ready to admit to stealing my Walther."

"It's nothing to do with the handgun. It's personal…"

"Give me a hint," Nicole persisted. "It can't be all that bad."

Harm was shaving when there was a hefty knock at the door.

"It's unlocked, *prosze*." he called out, expecting the steward bringing fresh ice.

Nicole loomed large in the open bathroom doorway.

"You told me *nothing* about it, damn it!"

Harm rinsed his safety razor in the sink. "Nothing about what?"

"I forced Thomas into tell me that someone tried to kill you. Here, on the ship. I was stunned. You *know* who I am. What I do for a living."

"What could you do about it? You don't trust me, for some reason." He carried on shaving. "You didn't like me. Right from the start."

"I never said that."

"Your body language gives you away."

"Admit you stole my handgun," she said, "and I'd feel better."

"Why would I steal it?"

"To protect yourself after nearly being killed. A second time." Why, she wondered, did he annoy her so easily, without him even trying?

"You must've dragged it out of Thomas. As for your Walther, it was long gone before I got whacked."

"Is that so?" she said, annoyed he might be right.

Harm caught her reflection in the mirror, the dark hair tied up in a loose ponytail, the silky cocktail dress offering a hint of cleavage before slipping down over her hips.

"You're staring," she simmered.

"I find you mildly attractive, in an odd sort of way."

"*Odd* sort of way?"

"It's a figure of speech, Nicole. If you'd been up front with me about your day job, things might've been different. I also know what's bugging you, and you're taking it out on me."

"What's bugging me?"

"If I was hit with so little trouble, anyone on board is an easy target."

Nicole blushed at his logic. "Thomas said you were lucky to survive."

"To say nothing of you putting yourself in danger with no backup. Except, perhaps, for Victor. Isn't that why he's here?"

"God, you're irritating."

"That was supposed to be a compliment."

Harm drew the razor down his cheek. "Let's call a truce so we can talk—"

He heard the cabin door slam shut.

"Then again," he said to himself, "maybe later."

The first storm of the crossing hit the *Casimir* northeast of Newfoundland shortly after midnight. For those in the Grand Lounge, it began with a slight list to port, then starboard.

With no better time to broach Nicole about a truce, Harm asked her to dance.

"Relax," he said, feeling her stiffen in his arms, "and quit thinking you're about to throw up. Besides, you took the Dramamine—" Nicole looked away. "You have them with you."

"In my cabin."

"Let's go," he said, "before you upchuck on yourself, the dance floor, and all over the captain when he's hungry for a bit of female companionship."

She forced herself not to smile. It didn't work.

The Dramamine was where Nicole left it, on the bathroom basin. She swallowed two pills and stretched out on the bed.

"It isn't working," she said, moments later.

"Instant gratification isn't how it works. Give it time. Barf them up now, and they won't have dissolved through your system."

"What would you have me do?" she grumbled. "March around my cabin in single file?"

He smiled, it not being the sense of humor he expected from her.

"Better we get you some fresh air. Change into something warm—"

"And go outside? Are you insane? It's cold and stormy."

"All the better. Five minutes. If you're still lying down, you're on your own."

Feeling she'd bring up at any moment, Nicole knocked off an email to Gerry about the attempt on Harmon Page's life. She mentioned connecting with Victor...

Harm had swapped his tux for jeans, a sweatshirt, runners, and a comfy zippered Lands' End squall jacket. Certain that Nicole Hagen might abort the plan, he headed out of his cabin, ready to pound on her door.

He was surprised to find her waiting in the corridor, wrapped in a tan raincoat over a hoodie and wearing jeans and runners.

"I'll be pissed off," she told him as he marched her along the hallway, "if these pills don't kick in soon."

"They will. Besides, nothing gained, nothing lost..."

"Except possibly my dinner," Nicole said.

The storm hit them on the open portion of the Promenade Deck.

"This is crazy," she shouted, sure she'd barf any moment.

"Relax," he yelled, guiding her by deck chairs that were stacked under canvas and lashed to the railing.

Nicole struggled to stay upright. "Relax? I'll bet you say that to every woman."

"Only the obstinate ones."

Buffeted by the wind and driving rain, they stopped to hold on to the open railing beyond the mesh-covered pool. Nicole forced herself to glance back over her shoulder, and down the entire length of the ship.

Heavily shrouded in mist, they watched the vessel slice into the mounting swells topped with billowing whitecaps. The stern moved upward taking Nicole's stomach with it.

"Surely the boat has those wing things that jut out into the water," she called out.

"Stabilizers. To keep a rocking motion in check. Not so much the up and down." Harm looked at her. "Are you okay?"

Nicole felt physically, wonderfully challenged. Despite the rain pounding her face and running off her chin. In her eyes.

Harm, working himself between her and the railing, wrapped an arm around her waist.

"What are you doing?"

"Turning you round to face the bow," he shouted as the stern began to drop. "Let me know when you've had enough."

"When I'm just getting the hang of it?"

"Fine. It'll cost you a truce."

"A truce?"

"Working together to keep Leszek alive, until we reach London/Tilbury."

"Can't help you there," she said. "You've caused us too much grief."

"It was probably *you* people who ran me off the road up in New England."

"Why would we do that?"

"Ask your boss."

"I'll think about it."

"He'll deny it. A truce. Yes, or no?"

"Partial."

"How *partial*?"

"We'll work it out," she said, knowing she shouldn't be enjoying herself so much.

Not with Page.

CHAPTER TWENTY-FOUR
Monday, October 10, 8:15 AM (Moscow)

Vladimir Lyubimov was hanging up his raincoat, when he realized his assistant was asleep at his desk, her head resting on her arms.

He slipped out, returning from the commissary with two strong coffees, one black for her and the other with brown sugar added. He was putting them down, when she stepped, bright-eyed, from his private washroom.

"Good morning, sir," she said, dressed in jeans and a light blue cable knit sweater.

He handed her the coffee. "How long have you been here?"

"Since midnight. I couldn't sleep." Olga twisted her hair, tying it back with a plain elastic band. "What kept me awake was the thought of Tobias reaching the *Casimir*."

Vladimir pried the lid off his coffee. "It bothers you that we had no proof?"

"That's why I came here," she replied, "picking up where I left off on Friday. I began by listing his aliases against the seven hundred passengers emailed to us from the shipping lines."

"Meaning you remembered my portion of the list as well as your own."

"I'm sure you did the same." Olga picked up her coffee. "None of those names showed up. Not even 'Gritsenko'. Tobias could only have reached Montréal by air, in time for the ship's departure."

"You might consider there are dozens of other foreign carriers arriving in Montréal—"

"With only *one* Canada Customs. I phoned Ottawa and was connected to a night supervisor. I identified myself, having no reason not to, and learned she was from the Ukraine. When she heard I was from the Carpathian region, it broke the ice."

Vladimir knew his assistant would drag this out for the best affect, not that it mattered.

"I was candid in explaining I needed the name of a particular passenger on a flight from Moscow to Montréal. Because of the timing, she and I narrowed it down to an Aeroflot from Sheremetyevo to New York's John F. Kennedy Airport last Tuesday evening. It arrived too late for passengers to connect with a flight to Montréal."

Olga sipped her coffee. "They boarded a United Airline morning flight, bringing them to Pierre Trudeau International Airport. My contact gave me a list of those passing through Canada Customs. One of them was Alexey Gritsenko."

Vladimir shook his large, shaggy head. "Tobias. He's been on board since Montréal."

"The ship's passenger list does not include Gritsenko."

"He's using a new alias." Vladimir sighed. "Men like Tobias, Ms. Tuseva, carry with them a certain, profound arrogance. They thrive living on the edge, tempting fate yet getting away with it."

"I'll contact Mister Grosvenor at Central Intelligence…"

"Not directly this time," said Vladimir, pleased with what his assistant had accomplished.

Kim, in black tights and a long-sleeved T-shirt to hide the worst of the bruising, gripped the horizontal bar with one leg raised behind her. Breathing in deep, she pushed her upper body forward, and held it.

She bent lower, surprised at the effort it took. Once, she could have touched her knee with her nose. She was forcing herself lower, when her hamstring cramped in the unbent leg.

"Damn it," she murmured, limping around to work out the tightness in her leg. She blamed it on having turned thirty-eight. Only *two years from forty*.

She had noticed little lines around her eyes, finding more with each glance in the mirror. She brought the latest anti-aging creams and lotions away with her these days, touted to make the face and body youthful again. Worse was discovering gray hairs appearing in her crotch, forcing her to tweeze them out one at a time.

The door opened behind her, and she saw Angus reflected in the mirrored wall, still in his tux.

Kim leaned back against the horizontal bar. "You must be tired, honey."

He came over to kiss her wet cheek. "I did well, though it took all night."

"You think I wouldn't notice?"

"I hit the jackpot, Kim." He gave her a big, sappy grin. "You wouldn't believe the money floating around this barge, despite not having a casino."

She massaged the upper leg to release the tension. "Drop by the purser's office; have them put it in the safe."

"I have already." He paused, admiring how good she looked in tights, the fabric accentuating her soft curves. He reached out…

She ducked under his outstretched arms and shoved him toward the door.

"G'night." he said, with genuine affection.

Kim stretched down slowly to touch her toes. "Sweet dreams, Gus."

For Kim, keeping fit had become an obsession for the eternally youthful body. Yoga fusion blending in pilates, sculpting and the other fancy movements too numerous to name. She was after the perfect *abs, buns and thigh,* even at her age.

The door opened a second time.

"Go to bed, darling," she said.

Arms encircling her from behind, she knew, didn't belong to her husband.

"Is that an invitation?" said Victor, trailing his lips down the back of her neck.

Kim stretched upward. "You must've noticed Angus."

"I waited for him to leave." Victor took her gently by the shoulders and eased her back against the wooden bars on the wall behind them. "I'll say this much: he plays one hell of a game of poker. I left around three, and he was still at it."

Kim looked Victor over, top to bottom—a pleasant diversion she knew most women enjoyed but would never admit it.

"Not getting enough these days, Mrs. Stockwell?" he said, bringing his body against hers. "Do you fantasize about others when Angus is making love to you?"

Kim felt a tension growing within her own body.

"What we do is none of your business."

She fantasized, of course. Didn't most women? It was the only way she could get through making love to Angus, not that she didn't love him. Yet, without fantasizing, it was difficult trying not to fake it. Her favorite…humping Gus while other couples were watching…

Victor pushing against her brought Kim back to reality. She could feel him stiffen through his sweats. She watched as he walked over to lock the door, returning with two skipping ropes that were hanging from hooks on the wall.

"You take your exercising seriously," he said, tying her wrists along the horizontal bar. "Which is a good thing. You've kept your youthful appearance, yet you have that aura of sensuality that most women your age, even younger, no longer possess."

"And you're kinky." She tipped her head to run her lips down his neck to the edge of his damp sweatshirt collar. "Untie me, Vic."

"Be patient." He kneaded her crotch through her tights with the palm of his hand.

"How can I, when—oh!"

"You saw Nicole and me together the other night, while you were servicing those randy seamen. You must've heard us."

"Yes," she said feeling aroused, which wasn't her intention. She took a wiser, direct approach. "Nicole was angry with you."

"At what?"

"How should I know? Untie me, Vic, please."

"Not until you tell me what you heard."

"Only that Nicole seemed upset at whoever sent you on board…the ship."

"Who did she say sent me?"

Kim closed her eyes, feeling a dampness between her thighs.

"I didn't hear…who or why."

"Who else have you talked to about this?"

"No one."

"Page, maybe? You two seem chummy enough."

"What would I tell him? That I heard you and Nicole arguing?"

Kim felt vulnerable, ashamed at losing her self-control. "Besides, I had my hands full."

"You certainly did." Victor untied the ropes. "I want you to forget that you saw Nicole and I together."

"Fine," she whispered.

Their mouths became a tangle of lips and tongues as she worked his sweatpants and jock strap down over his knees. Off came her tights and she shivered, naked to his touch. Seizing the bars above her head, she pulled herself up, locking her bare legs tight around his neck. Victor reached down, ready to thrust himself inside her.

"Let me do it," she whispered.

A wild flurry of thrusts drove them to the point of no return. They came in unison, each lost in their own, singular pleasure.

Gerry stared at Ted Grosvenor's computer screen, while his boss poured his first coffee of the morning.

"Who's it from?" Ted asked him.

"Vladimir Lyubimov...or Olga. Filed through Ghana. He's confirming Tobias has been on the *Casimir III* since leaving the Port of Montréal."

"Shit!" Ted came across the room, bringing his coffee with him. "Confirmed?"

"According to our intrepid duo, there's no doubt. He passed through Canada Customs at Pierre Trudeau International Airport using the name 'Alexey Gritsenko'..."

Ted joined him, swearing under his breath. "Contact the shipping agency."

"Olga insists we won't find the same name on the passenger manifest. And quite truthfully, I believe her."

"I'm beginning to feel the same, Gerry."

The computer signaled the arrival of another email.

Nicole Hagen's coded file appeared, then the text.

Waiting for your reply RE: Page attacked here. Confirming possible prior hit on subject. He suggests we ran him off road in New England.

"Tell her affirmative on Page's car. Assure her it wasn't us."

Gerry added it. *Need more. Page survived hit aboard ship?*

Yes. Details sketchy and unconfirmed. Page & Poplawski heavily into related research. Problems with translating, so I am added to mix. Petrie has yet to confirm his connect to Pentagon. We're still on schedule, docking in London/Tilbury late Friday/early Saturday morning.

Ted leaned over his assistant to hit the keys. *Grosvenor here. A report has a Russian on board codenamed Tobias. We are working on ID. Visual. Boris Yevtushenko's murder confirmed. Status of Poplawski's safe passage pivotal.*

Nicole: *Add to this my missing Walther. Convinced Page stole it to protect himself from another attempt on his life. He denies it. Also run ID on SLATER, Thomas E. Seems privy to whatever going on. Do I seek Petrie's help should situation turn sour?*

Affirmative. Pentagon denies Petrie link. We confirm otherwise. Good luck.

She signed off and went looking for the one person she might have to depend on.

Victor Petrie was dozing under a blanket on one of the open decks when Nicole found.

"Hi, Vic," she said, sitting on the empty deck chair beside him.

He opened one eye. "Hi, yourself. What's up?"

"I hear you're with the Pentagon. Not us."

"It took you long enough to figure that out."

"It took longer to figure out why you didn't come clean in the first place."

"Because I follow orders. Like you do."

"Does the codename 'Tobias' mean anything to you?"

Victor stretched, raising his arms above his head. "It's a codename tied to Russian Military Intelligence. Small-time."

"Interesting, when Grosvenor puts him up there as a sanctioned assassin."

"Ted exaggerates whatever suits him. When he doesn't get his way, he'll throw a heavyweight into the mix to back him up."

"Tell me about it. I didn't like this assignment and turned it down. Grosvenor had someone in reserve who changed my mind."

"The President's so-called chief liaison officer?"

"Willy Novak." Nicole all but laughed out loud. "You *know* him?"

"It's Grosvenor's pet name for someone who doesn't exist. He uses it to get his way." Victor grinned. "You were conned, Nicky."

Nicole drew in a deep breath. *That lying sonofabitch…*

"Hit a nerve, did I?"

Nicole blushed. "I came to ask for help, should things screw up."

"You're expecting trouble?"

"No, other than ensuring Leszek has a safe crossing."

"He's a tough old bird. Watch him in the Polish Bar, drinking with his cronies, or dancing the night away with us."

"Throw in the countless hours he spends with Page," she added.

"Discussing what?"

"The workings of the brain."

"Do you ever listen in?"

"I translate for them when language gets in the way. I should be with them now. First, I need an answer about you helping me out."

"If any shit hits the fan, I'll be with you, taking whatever flak the Pentagon brass throws at me."

She leaned over to kiss him on the lips before getting up.

CHAPTER TWENTY-FIVE
Monday, October 10, 2:20 PM

Nicole sat cross-legged on Harm's bed, concentrating on such terms as *neurological* cells and cell membrane potential. A *synapse*, if she recalled from the previous day, was a conjunction between two neurons. She closed her eyes, remembering impulses traveling from the dendrite, to cell body, and along the axon. *Or was it the other way around?*

"Hold on," said Harm, catching up on his notes.

This, to Nicole, slowed everything to a crawl. She had suggested they'd save time if she took over the notes.

"I don't have to know what every bloody word *means*," she snapped at him. "If I can't spell it, I'll ask."

The sudden outburst caught Harm by surprise. "Do you take shorthand?"

"No, but watching you, I could write upside down and still be faster."

Leszek did his best not to smile. "Is it not worth trying, Harmon?" he asked.

"And if she misses something? It's lost. Gone forever."

"*Lost and gone forever*," Nicole deadpanned. "That's an original thought." She spoke to Leszek in rapid Polish.

Harm cut in. "I'd appreciate a translation."

"It sounds better in Polish," she fired back.

The argument would have continued had not the last call for second sitting lunch boomed from the corridor.

"… And this evening in the Grand Lounge, you will be royally entertained by an extravaganza of dance and music put on by talented members drawn from our very own crew."

Nicole put the laptop down and headed for the door. "Deal with me typing the notes after lunch, Harmon C. Page, or you're on your own. Period. Full stop."

Harm turned to the old man as her footsteps faded down the corridor.

"What's bugging her?" he said.

"It means you, Harmon, and Madame Hagen are at last...on the same...hmm…"

"On the same *page*?" Harm replied. "Don't kid yourself, Leszek."

CHAPTER TWENTY-SIX
Monday, October 10, 10:35 PM

Costumed in brightly embroidered blouses and long skirts, hand-decorated vests and billowing pants, the male and female Polish dancers brought the evening's tribute to their country's past to a toe-tapping, table-thumping finish.

The audience packing the Grand Lounge was on their feet, applauding the two-hour performance. The forty breathless dancers joined hands to serpentine between the tables, their faces wreathed in smiles and perspiration.

At a reserved table next to the dance floor, tears ran down Leszek's flushed cheeks.

"How it is...*piekny*, Madame Ashcroft," he sniffed. "Many of the dances tonight come from the Carpathian Mountains where I am born. It makes me feel home... hmm."

"Homesick, Doctor Poplawski," Gwen sympathized with him. "I, too, am looking forward to returning to England." She slipped him a tissue, which he accepted shyly and wiped his eyes.

"To you, Leszek Poplawski, and to Poland." Harm raised his glass. "Na zdrowie."

"Na zdrowie," echoed the others.

Nicole's black dress with bare shoulders offered a sharp contrast to Kim's slinky one-piece, gold-sequined sheath. Gwen repeated the flowery dress she wore on board the second night, hoping no one would notice. Had her husband given fair warning of this sudden inspired transatlantic voyage, she wouldn't have been caught in such a dilemma. Still, returning by sea was reward enough.

The band struck up a slow song from the fifties. With it came Captain Jablonski to whisk Nicole onto the dance floor. Gwen and Victor were next, then Thomas and Kimberly, her husband having already disappeared.

Peter Lount, a minor celebrity among a clutch of history buffs, was dragged off to another table to give a preamble of his next lecture. Which left the two scientists on their own.

"You mentioned Nicole taking over the notes this afternoon, Leszek," Harm said. "I have to admit, she proved me wrong."

The old man beamed. "It is best you tell her so, my friend."

"It means dragging her away from the captain."

"She is merely flattered by such attention. It is my understanding women need constant reminding that they, hmm…"

"Still got it."

"*Still got it,*" repeated Leszek. "It is some feeling others share in different ways. As one grows older, Harmon, it becomes more of a burden to think of one's own failures than successes. I often wonder why the Russians had such faith in my work. Early failures still haunt me."

"I've my share of screw ups," said Harm. He mentioned how he had worked on a compound he hoped would put a new spin on the elusive neurotrop.

"The results were a disaster, Leszek. I separated two rats from a dozen mates, and injected them with an untested serum before putting them back with the others."

Leszek leaned forward to catch every word.

"I couldn't recall why I'd left the room, when I heard squeals from my lab. I rushed back to find the two were slaughtering their companions. Eating them. Tearing them apart. With teeth, claws."

"These rats—" Leszek was drowned out by Entertainment Officer Filip Sotek's voice booming through the lounge.

"The next dance, a Gentlemen's Choice. You must choose someone you do not know. Ignore this, and it's twenty laps around the Promenade Deck."

Gwen, caught up in the fun, made her way off the dance floor to reach Leszek.

"I am aware it is gentlemen's choice, Doctor Poplawski. However, if I waited for you to ask me to dance…"

Leszek stood up to take her hand. "It is my pleasure, Madame."

"As for Mister Page," came the entertainment officer's voice again, "sitting there like a bump on the proverbial log. On your feet! Find someone to dance with or it will be an automatic *fifty* laps for you…at a gallop."

Harm added to the fun by exaggerating his search which settled on a young woman in uniform talking to a fellow officer.

"Mister Page is on the move, ladies and gentlemen, approaching…wait for it…approaching, yes, our gorgeous Officer Helena Witka. Will she turn him down…?"

Harm's face was wrapped in a wide grin as he reached her.

"You know why I'm here, I hope…"

Helena gave him an infectious smile. "I have *no* intention of turning you down."

"You may not remember me," he said, as they stepped out on the dance floor, "but we've already met."

"You lost below deck. I'm Helena Witka."

"An officer in charge of what?" he asked.

"Dispensing seasick pills, mostly, and helping those suffering from hangovers."

Ladies' Choice came later when she asked him, in return, to dance.

"My companions berated me," he said, "for referring to you as the ship's charming nurse. When, indeed, you're the ship's charming surgeon."

"The *junior* surgeon," she said, smiling. "It's my first voyage, and I'm desperately fearful of being seasick."

"Try Dramamine—"

"Change partners," came Filip, spoiling their fun. "And still Ladies' Choice."

"Does it work?" Helena teased, stepping away.

Harm had only a chance to nod, when a voice behind him asked if he cared to dance. He turned to find Nicole, with her black dress and bare shoulders, beside him.

"We missed you for the usual drinks before dinner," he said, as she slipped an arm loose around his shoulder.

"Only because I had trouble deciphering your godawful handwritten notes into my laptop."

"I have trouble deciphering them myself." Harm swung her around, establishing who was leading this parade. "I owe you an apology. You were right about you taking notes. I was wrong."

Nicole eased her cheek against his, an unconscious move that surprised even her.

"And I was wrong," she said, "about not needing help keeping an eye on Leszek. I'm aware someone might target him while on board."

"Maybe the same guy who took a run at me."

Nicole pulled her cheek away. "If this particular hit man was targeting you, you'd already be dead, from what I hear."

Harm didn't like the sound of it. "That came from your boss, Grosvenor?"

"Yes. His team is working on an ID." She paused. "You understand, now, why I need my Walther back."

"If I had it—"

"Change partners."

Peter Lount moved in beside them. "You heard the entertainment officer, Mister Page."

"Get lost," Harm said.

Peter glanced woefully at Nicole, hoping for a favorable second opinion. It didn't happen. He turned away as the music began again.

Her cheek was back against his. "No one but you had the opportunity to steal my PPK."

"Someone has it, Nicole. And if it isn't me—"

Filip Sotek's voice boomed once again for a change of partners. Peter showed up once more, showing off a boyish grin.

Not far off, a wobbly Kim cornered young Officer Olecki.

"Hello," She said. "Want to dance?"

"You bet," he said, with a wide grin.

"It was sexier when you spoke Polish," she murmured, pressing herself against his clean white uniform. "Besides, you're cute."

"And you're…"

"Drunk."

"…a good dancer, Mrs. Stockwell."

"Yes, pissed." Kim wrapped both arms around his neck. "Strange things are going on, Officer Olecki, right under your nose." She hiccupped. "Have you any idea that a devious plot involves our beloved scientists? They're in deep shit." She stopped dancing. "What's the time?"

"Shortly after two in the morning."

"Shit." Kim kissed him on the lips and disappeared.

Thomas Slater was nursing a Courvoisier, when Harm sat down beside him.

"I saw you dancing with Nicole. What's this, a peace pact?"

"You might call it that." Harm noticed her dancing now with the captain. "Have you seen Kim?"

"She's with Officer Olecki, rubbing his buns."

"Not at the moment. He's dancing with someone else."

"She's probably in the ladies' room. With all the drink our Kimberly packs away…" Harm pictured her dancing in the Disco. "Angus is playing poker. She's loaded and lonely. You know what that combination adds up to."

"Trouble," said Thomas.

"If she bumps into those yahoos again? She's vulnerable, under all that wackiness."

Thomas put down his unfinished drink. "We'll visit the Disco, first. Witness that frenzied, undisciplined display of human emotions translated into the uninhibited gyrations of the seventies."

Harm grinned. "Only you could express it that way."

"They were wild times," said Thomas. "Something I couldn't do then any more than I could now."

It took several wrong turns before Harm and Thomas found the Disco, but not Kim. They split up and met thirty minutes later in the Boat Deck Bar. Neither had found any trace of her.

Harm suggested they check the one place he hoped not to find her.

Armed with a flashlight borrowed from Feliks the bartender, they ventured out on the Promenade Deck to find the cool night air cutting through the thin fabric of their tuxedos.

They reached the small pool with Thomas sweeping the beam of light across the heavy mesh cover. It picked up a far corner where the mesh had pulled aside. They moved on, removing the chain with its CREW ONLY sign before taking the steps down to the next level.

They stood on the partially open, dimly lit deck housing the large capstan and chest-high coils of heavy rope.

Thomas shone the light on garbage bags piled to the ceiling. "The Twenty-First century and we're still tossing waste overboard. We're killing the oceans with our garbage."

Harm agreed as he looked about him, feeling the steady throbbing of the twin screws beneath his feet. "It's illegal, isn't it?"

"It should be, but out here authorities are stumped because there's no legislation to stop them. All in aid of wealthy goddamn conglomerate ship owners not bothering to bring it ashore." He let the beam of light linger on the darkness beyond the ship. "Do you need the flashlight? If not, I'll check out something the next level up."

Harm shook his head and wandered over to a steel door. He glanced through its small, dirt-stained window at the kitchen where a lone seaman was mopping the tile floors.

Giving the cramped space a last look, he climbed back up to the open deck.

Thomas was on the pool's far side, shining the flashlight on the loose section of the mesh.

"Maybe it's nothing," he called to Harm, waving him over. "Yet, why has this corner of the mesh been pulled free?"

Together, they unhooked more of the mesh clipped on the underside of the pool's edge and pulled it aside. Thomas shone the flashlight into the darkness and shook his head.

"Nothing here but discarded newspapers, empty boxes, broken bottles…the stink of—Jesus Christ!"

Harm leaned in as the beam pinpointed a body lying face down amid the debris.

Thomas thrust the flashlight at him. "I'll get help."

Harm sat on the edge of the pool, working his legs through the opening in the mesh. He twisted around onto his stomach and lowered himself. He was hanging by his outstretched arms, when he barely heard a voice break the silence.

"*Jesien basen…Jesien basen…*"

He closed his eyes and let go.
"*Jesien basen…Jesien basen…*"

CHAPTER TWENTY-SEVEN
Tuesday, October 11, 1:25 AM

Doctor Helena Witka, in slacks and an unbuttoned raincoat, crouched by Kim's body on the swimming pool floor. Most of the heavy mesh webbing had been removed. An aluminum ladder leaned against the inside wall, a blanket slung over one of the rungs.

Harm had trouble holding the flashlight steady as she finished her preliminary examination. He felt empty inside, his mind numbed by what he and Thomas had discovered.

"The neck is broken," Helena said quietly. "I take it you knew her, Mister Page."

"She's Kimberly Stockwell. Her husband, Angus, is on board."

He stared down at Kimberly's soiled white, one-piece outfit, her face streaked with a patchy mixture of dirt and blood. He stepped aside, bent over, and brought up his dinner.

"Mrs. Stockwell wouldn't have suffered," Helena said aloud, her voice drifting upward. "I'll know more once the body is taken to Sick Bay."

From above came an audible murmur of response from those ringing the pool. Among them was Thomas, a uniformed nurse, and a handful of the crew.

A bright light burst on them from above, as seamen rigged up portable lights. Helena tightened the belt of her raincoat against the chill.

"There's nothing more I can do," she said to Harm. "Permission to remove the body must come from Doctor Dudek, the ship's senior medical officer."

Harm unfolded the blanket, tucking it around Kim in a futile gesture to keep her warm.

The young doctor touched his arm, and she held on before turning away, crunching back through the broken glass to the ladder.

They reached the deck, where the ship's chief surgeon pushed through the small crowd.

Doctor Ludwik Dudek stopped beside his junior medical officer, his hands thrust deep into the pockets of his hooded Gloverall.

"Where's the body?" he asked, his loose jowls reddened by drink and the raw wind.

"At the bottom of the empty pool," Helena replied, without indulging him with anything more.

Pushing her aside, the chief surgeon gazed over the edge.

"The particulars?" he asked, ensuring those around would know who was in charge.

"It appears to be an acute transection of the spinal cord," said Helena.

Ludwik Dudek licked his lips, the flaccid, dry tongue removing small amounts of white Maalox deposited in the corners of his mouth.

"Go on."

"I will confirm it with a more detailed examination in Sick Bay."

The chief surgeon scolded her with a single glance. "Must I remind you, Doctor Witka, the *Casimir* is not equipped to perform any fancy procedure you might have in mind?"

"We *are* capable of preliminary procedures, doctor. As it is, the body reeks of alcohol. There is a broken champagne bottle, among other things, down there, that might have some bearing on—"

"Is there a husband on board?" he asked, cutting her off.

Helena nodded.

"Have the body removed to Sick Bay, Doctor Witka, and inform the husband of his tragic loss."

Helena suggested the news should come directly from him, as the ship's senior physician.

"Must I remind you," he snapped at her, "that *you* are the medical officer on call?"

Dudek walked off, avoiding what Helena knew was any further challenge to his authority.

Harm moved in beside her. "To make it easier for you, Doctor Witka, Thomas Slater and I will come along. We know her husband, which might help."

"I owe you both a big favor," she said, turning to ask a seaman to bring a Gurney.

Helena cleared the Boat Deck Bar, asking Feliks, the bartender to stay, should she need his help. Thomas and Harm had already brought Angus from his card game and sat him in a chair. He was visibly annoyed at losing a poker hand to come with them.

"Has someone complained I've been cheating at cards?" he muttered.

"No, Angus," Harm said. "It's about Kimberly. She's had an accident."

Angus shrugged it off. "What did she do? Drown herself in a dirty martini?"

"Kimberly is dead, Angus," Thomas added, not wanting to drag it out.

Angus stared at the faces around him, trying to make sense of it all.

"What do you mean, *dead*?"

"Kim was out on deck, Angus," Harm replied. "She, unfortunately, fell into the empty pool."

Helena spoke up. "And I'm Doctor Witka. What we're telling you, Mister Stockwell, is true. I'm sorry for your loss."

Angus stared at them, his anger growing as he grasped what they were saying.

"Is this some fucking kind of joke? Where is she?"

"In our ship's hospital," Helena replied.

As reality set in, Angus sprang to his feet. "Kimberly!"

Hands grabbed him, as his legs gave way under him.

Thomas wandered around Harm's stateroom, clutching a whisky. "You know as well as I do, Kim was drunk well before she left the lounge."

He took a good swallow of the scotch and went on.

"What if she had a sudden, stupid urge for a midnight dip? Off comes the corner of the mesh, in she goes."

Harm held back a yawn. "You think? In her sheath cocktail dress?"

"She's pissed and leans over the pool clutching the bottle of Mumm's. The ship shifts. She loses her balance and—" Thomas stopped to listen. "Did I hear someone knock?"

Harm, halfway to the door, opened it. A grim-faced Hugh Ashcroft, in a paisley robe and slippers, nodded and stepped past Harm.

"I'm sorry to trouble you, chaps, but this rumor about Kimberly…"

"She's dead, Hugh," said Harm, fixing him a scotch.

"How in God's name did that happen?"

Thomas said, "She somehow ended up in the bottom of the empty pool."

Hugh nodded his thanks and took the glass.

"When Gwen and I found ourselves wide awake, we called our night steward to bring us some tea. He mentioned a woman dying on board. He thought the name was Stockwell. And Angus, the poor chap?"

"In Sick Bay, with her." Harm stared out the window at the darkness. Something didn't fit, but he didn't know what.

Thomas caught Harm's puzzled reflection in the window. "What is it?"

"I can't get my head around it…"

"Maybe I could offer a fresh perspective," Hugh said. "I'd have to see the pool, along with you both, before it's crawling with inquisitive passengers." He finished his drink. "If you lads will give me a moment to change…"

Thomas left for his cabin for something warm, leaving Harm to cross the corridor to rap on Nicole's door.

It took several knocks before it opened.

One look at him, and she sagged against the door frame.

"Leszek," she whispered, pulling the red silk robe tight around her.

Harm fought back his emotion. "It's Kim, Nicole. She's dead, after tumbling into the empty pool. The fall broke her neck."

"Oh, God. And Angus?"

"He's with the body down in the ship's hospital."

"Somebody should be with him." She touched Harm's hand, held it, and let go. "I'll drop by."

The pre-dawn light spreading across the horizon outlined three figures by the pool. It softened their edges and bathed them in a faint orange glow.

With heads bowed, they looked like silent mourners from some Easter pageant. That they weren't praying did not detract from the solemn moment.

A breeze angled across the vessel's stern, bringing with it a damp chill the men ignored.

"Such a waste," Hugh said, his frame rocking with the slight motion of the ship.

Thomas shone the flashlight along the mesh, which had been pulled back and tethered to hooks on the underside of the pool's lip.

Harm took the flashlight from him and walked over to crouch where Kim had tumbled in.

"What is it, son?" asked Hugh.

"Something's screwed up here," he said, waving them over. He asked Thomas to bend down and pull the mesh free.

It took his friend several good pulls before he loosened it.

"It's obvious Kim couldn't have pulled back the mesh on her own," said Harm. He glanced at Thomas. "Even you had trouble freeing it."

"Meaning she wasn't alone," Thomas replied. "Even if she were, at the very least, she would've broken her fingernails."

"We must know this for certain," Hugh said.

"Angus is with her," Harm said. "We'll have to let it go for now."

They returned to the Boat Deck Bar, ordering to find something hot to ward off a chill they all felt.

Having stayed up all night, Harm and Thomas tracked Filip Sotek to the Little Lounge. They cornered him while he was supervising the building of the horseracing set. They mentioned dropping by Sick Bay, earlier, to pay their respects to Kimberly.

"We were turned away," said Thomas, "by the cranky duty nurse. She told us the body wasn't there."

"Blonde. Early forties?" said Filip. "That would be Nurse Szyller, and she's right. The body's been transferred to an unspecified location." He glanced at them and shrugged. "We lack the facilities found on more modern cruise liners, with their temperature-controlled morgues."

Harm asked where they might find her.

"It's not something we publicize," Filip replied, adding, "Give me a minute."

Preparations for lunch were well underway when Filip paraded two passengers, Thomas and Harm, through a kitchen alive with shouts and banging pots and pans.

The tantalizing smell of herbs and sauces filled the room as sous-chefs moved among the cooks, exacting perfection for a meal soon to be served.

They found the *chef de cuisine* sampling a steamy bouillabaisse.

"Of all the times to bring us visitors, Officer Sotek," Chef Samek chided him. "Anyone but you, and I would quickly show them the door."

""They are relatives of the deceased," Filip said, "wishing to pay their respects."

Handing the spoon to an assistant, the chef led them by the cooking area, passing several chrome refrigerators to stop by a thick, wood door. He left them on their own.

They found the fridge filled with shelves of cold cuts packaged in bulk, along with other meats and seafood. Filip guided Harm and Thomas through to another door and into a self-contained unit.

Harm breathed in a strange combination of a cool, dry metallic and refrigerated odor and what he could only imagine was an indescribable, overpowering scent of death.

A single bulb showed empty shelves surrounding a sturdy wood table. On it was a black nylon bag dusted with a thin film of frost.

Harm paused, then began sliding the zipper down the body bag, a task made difficult with its folds stiffened by the cold air. He had only started when Kimberly's nose protruded through the opening, as the blonde hair, freed from the confines of the bag, dropped down around her bare, alabaster shoulders.

Both Harm and Thomas noticed color draining from Filip's face, his hands bunched into fists. It was Thomas who suggested he and Harm would handle it if the entertainment officer had other pressing matters.

Filip nodded, with obvious appreciation, and closed the heavy wood door behind him.

Thomas eased Harm aside, squeezing the fastener between thumb and forefinger and running it down the length of the zipper.

Kim's naked body was stretched out before them, her skin a sheen of white translucent marble. Blood, turned a mottled bluish color, had pooled along the one side of the body. Yet her face was serene, even childlike, Harm decided, as if a vestige of youth had returned to her in death.

A deep pain reflected in their faces as they checked her fingernails. Wasting little time in zipping the bag closed, they bowed their heads in a silent, final goodbye.

Hugh Ashcroft, seated in the Boat Deck Bar, watched as Thomas and Harm sit down opposite him, their facial expressions telling him nothing. Their similar body language was another matter.; a certain lack of tension.

"I take it her nails were perfectly intact, chums," he said to them.

"None was chipped or broken," said Harm, keeping his emotions in check.

"Which means," said Thomas, "Kimberly wasn't alone when she died. And if so..."

"It's not wise, jumping conclusions," Hugh said. "Not before Doctor Witka gives us her opinion. Now, I'd best find Gwen before she sends the Emergency Task Force looking for me."

"I was hoping you'd mention the seamen who raped her," said Thomas as Hugh left.

"Kim wouldn't have gone anywhere near them, believe me. You'd understand, had you seen what they did to her. And Hugh's right, waiting to find what Helena comes up with."

Harm looked away, struck by an agonizing, deep loss for someone he had known for such a short time.

Nicole balanced the laptop on her outstretched legs as she leaned back against the bed's headboard.

Wiping away the tears, she picked up where she had stopped moments ago.

There is a curious situation here, Gerry. A female friend in our group died in the early hours this morning. A twelve-foot fall into the ship's empty swimming pool. Unrelated but sad. Would appreciate you ID the Russian soont. I don't want to be caught with my unmentionables down around my ankles.

She was signing off when a muffled voice echoed through her cabin door.

"Hi. It's Harm."

Nicole, wanting to say go away, surprised herself.

"The door's unlocked," she sniffed.

He poked his head in. "Are you up for a drink before second sitting lunch?" He noticed the tears. "Hold on," he said and disappeared.

Nicole closed her eyes, picturing how Kim's smile brightened a room. How men and women were drawn not only to her physical presence, but to her easy laughter and self-confidence.

This made everyone, Nicole knew, feel they'd known her for a lifetime. Yet for all her worldliness, Kimberly had displayed a naiveté, which, to Nicole, was less understood.

A light knock and Harm came in with a tall, frosted glass.

"Feliks the bartender's specialty. When I mentioned you needed cheering up, he made you a frozen Daiquiri."

"You didn't bring one for yourself?" she asked, not wanting to sound disappointed.

"Mine's waiting for me at the bar." He sat down on the bed. "You shouldn't be alone, you know. Kim's death is a real shock. We're all feeling it."

Nicole nodded and shifted her legs around to sit beside him.

"When I took on this assignment, it was nothing more than shepherding an old man across the Atlantic. And here I am, sipping a daiquiri with the one person I've been warned to avoid."

"No one will hear it from me. Leszek wonders if the three of us might get together after lunch, if you're up to it."

Nicole raised the glass to her lips, enjoying its cold and sharp, yet sweetened taste.

"I'm up for it," she said.

He looked to see if she meant it and stood up. "When you're finished, join us in the bar."

"Thanks," she said, wishing, strange even to her, that he wouldn't leave.

"…and the neuron is polarized, meaning it has a negative electrical charge…." Harm noticed Nicole was distracted. He glanced at his watch. "It's quitting time."

Leszek had fallen asleep on Harm's bed, his back against the headboard. They had been working since lunch, with a room service dinner thrown in. They had continued until now, close to midnight.

She watched Harm spread an extra blanket over the old man.

"I'll back up what I've got on my flash drive," she said, tucking her laptop under her arm.

"Care to join me for a nightcap?" Harm asked.

"I'm off to bed."

"Sweet dreams," he said, as she disappeared into the hallway.

Harm dropped by the Grand Lounge to find Thomas on his own. He sat down beside him.

"Kim's death has dampened everyone's enthusiasm," said Thomas. "I'd have done the same, if not for the dreaded ICS."

"What's that?"

"Inside Cabin Syndrome. No porthole. No natural light. Stay too long, and you soon won't know if it's day or night."

"From what I hear," said Harm, "those behemoth cruise liners solved it by having virtual 'windows' installed inside cabins. They show what you'd see outside in real time."

Harm ordered two Courvoisier's from one of the stewards. "You could at least have had a cabin with a porthole."

"I have a habit of booking late." Thomas stretched out his legs, crossing one over the other. "This may sound piss poor of me, but I miss our Kimberly sexing things up."

"A free spirit." Harm nodded toward the officers' table where Helena Witka, in a crisp white pantsuit uniform, was with several other officers.

"Our good doctor looks bored. Ask her to dance. Mention Kim's untouched nails."

Thomas got slowly to his feet. "I'm lousy at talking and dancing at the same time."

Harm was delighted to see him waltz Helena around the floor, followed by an old-time jive that had them clearing the dance floor. The music ended with loud applause.

Thomas dropped breathless into a chair. "God knows when I ever danced like that."

"You both did yourselves proud. You told her about Kim?"

"Yes, but there's a problem. The senior surgeon took her body away before she could examine it. I told her about the freezer. We're to give her ten minutes and meet her in the foyer."

They arrived in the ship's kitchen, greeted by a young seaman. Harm remembered seeing him through the window in the kitchen when he and Thomas were searching for Kim.

"Dobry wiecvzor, doktor," he said to Helena, looking at the other two with little interest.

"Dobry wiecvzor," Helena replied, continuing in Polish. "And your name?"

"Ivan Josef Jurek. Night kitchen staff."

"We've come to view the deceased."

Josef Jurek blushed. "I wish I could help, but the refrigerators are locked at night."

"Could you not find the keys?"

Ivan spoke rapidly, making Helena smile.

"He tells not only are the fridges locked up, but the *keys* as well. For fear the 'night kitchen staff' would help themselves to the food." She added, "Despite Josef being the only one on the nightshift."

Helena promised them she would examine the body in the morning.

It was customary for the band to continue playing in the Grand Lounge late into the night or early morning, provided passengers were still around. Entertainment Officer Sotek was guiding one of the older matrons in a slow waltz, while his assistant, Jerzy Olecki, relaxed in a large couch when the sound system missed the bass notes.

Jerzy glanced over his shoulder to see an older, heavy seaman fiddling with the controls on the system's amp. Jerzy wandered over.

"What's your problem?" Jerzy asked as he realigned the bass.

"You're to come with me," he said, and turned back toward the foyer.

Jerzy saw Filip was busy showing the matron new steps. If nothing but curious, the young officer caught up to the seaman.

Neither talked as they set out along the empty Promenade Deck. It surprised him when Chief Officer Klimek stepped out of the shadows along with two broad-shouldered seamen.

"Good evening, Mister Olecki. Come with us."

The group crossed the open portion and dropped down the steps by the mesh-topped swimming pool. A seaman removed the chain with the CREW ONLY sign, and they trooped after the senior officer to the lower level.

Jerzy knew this area well, having complained to Filip Sotek how much of the ship's refuse went overboard in the early hours of the mornings. Filip brought it up with Senior Officer Klimek, who did nothing about it.

Here was proof, with plastic garbage bags piled to the ceiling.

Jerzy glanced at the senior office, feeling the vibration of the steel floor and hearing the continuous thump-thumping of the vessel's twin screws.

Light from the bulb in the ceiling shone behind Pawel, making his face barely visible.

"I need answers, Mister Olecki, about those of the crew who left the ship in Montréal. Among them, Officer Szalinski."

Jerzy shook his head. "I know nothing of it, sir."

"Then let me refresh your memory. You and Officer Szalinski were good friends. You must've known of his plans of jumping ship. You didn't report it. Failure could result in serious charges against you."

"I wasn't party to—"

"There was yet a third officer involved," Pawel persisted, "who, unlike Mister Szalinski, failed to make it off the ship. His name, please…"

Despite the cool night, Jerzy felt sweat soaking the fabric of his white cotton uniform.

"He wanted me to go with them," he said in a low voice. "I refused. Rumors spread that *I* was the other officer leaving the ship. I denied it. I still do."

"Why would anyone seek asylum in Canada? Arriving legally can't be difficult. There must be another explanation. Another purpose. I want to know why."

Jerzy stared tight-lipped, unblinking.

"I know nothing of it, sir. Other rumors persist. Like our two scientists on board." Jerzy began repeating what Mrs. Stockwell had told him. "There's a serious plot against them going on right under our noses."

Pawel planted himself next to the waist-high, extended opening in the steel hull. "As they say in America, Officer Olecki, you are talking bullshit." The wind caught Pawel's face, crinkling his skin as he gazed down at the frothy, dark water below. He nodded to his three men.

They grabbed the young officer, dumping him spread-eagled on the grimy steel floor. Another nod, and they used the lighter ropes from the hawsers to lash the plastic garbage bags around the young man's wrists and ankles.

They hoisted him up, balancing him on the steel railing, the excess rope trailing on the steel floor.

"Provided sharks don't get you first, or the ship's twin propellers don't tear you apart—"

"Air in these garbage bags," Pawel shouted at Jerzy, "will keep you afloat for a while."

Pawel had concocted the ruse to frighten the young officer, should everything else fail. Nothing had worked, so here they were. He pushed his face up close to the young man. "The officer's name!"

Petrified, Jerzy lashed out with both feet. The unexpected outburst broke him loose, and he toppled over the side.

"You fucking idiots," Pawel screamed as the seamen scrambled to grab the loose ropes snapping along the floor.

Jerzy felt the numbing impact of the frigid water, the sudden taste of salt. His body was smacking against the ship's hull while bouncing along the surface of the water.

"Yank him up," he heard the officer's angry voice floating out into the darkness. Then came the sound of the liner's propellers sucking him under...

Jerzy sensed he was lying motionless, with sea water dripping between his clenched teeth. Someone was crouched beside him, their fingers pressed against the base of his neck. He fought to stay with it.

"There's a pulse," said Pawel Klimek. "Cut the ropes. Toss the plastic bags overboard."

"There's a small piece of the rope clenched in his fist," mumbled one of the seamen, "I can't—"

"Leave it," Pawel snarled

Jerzy felt the officer's breath on his face. "Who was the other officer, Mister Olecki, or over you go. For good."

Jerzy forced his lips move, not knowing if the words even left his mouth...

The rattling of a heavy steel door brought heads swiveling back to the kitchen entrance.

Night staffer Ivan Josef Jurek had stepped out, ready to dump the garbage overboard. As his eyes adjusted to the semi-darkness, he saw shadows shifting back toward the far steps.

A figure in white stood up beside of the garbage. More curious than scared, Ivan backed up against the steel door, watching the white uniform join the others.

"Stop!" Ivan yelled, praying to God they wouldn't.

Nicole logged into her laptop. Finding no messages, she sent her own.

Can't sleep, Gerry. I could use a buck-me-up note in the AM.

A sudden reply surprised her.

I am pulling an overnighter. No problem with Stockwells. Sorry to hear passenger died. Thomas E. Slater. Clean. Travels on a Canadian passport. Author of numerous books. Nothing more on Russian. Do your best with Poplawski.

Ivan was throwing the plastic bags overboard when he heard a groan from under what remained of the garbage. He cocked his head and heard it again. Tossing several bags aside, he found himself staring down at someone in a torn, soiled officer's uniform.

Young Ivan Jurek stood, dumbfounded and agonizing over what do next.

CHAPTER TWENTY-EIGHT
Wednesday, October 12, 1:45 AM

Dr. Helena Witka kept her finger on the button marked 'B Deck'. She knew, from experience, the contrary little elevator might stop anywhere of its own accord. She noticed Filip, beside her, clenching and unclenching his fists.

"Who found him, Filip?"

"A couple strolling on the stern of the Promenade Deck. They all but tripped over him."

The obstinate elevator suddenly clanked to a stop. Helena struck the DOWN button several times before it began moving again.

Filip pushed his fingers back through his dark, unruly hair.

"Last time I saw Jerzy, we were together in the lounge. The next moment, he was gone. God knows what got into him."

Helena puzzled over the two incidents within the past twenty-four hours. Kimberly Stockwell's death, and now this. She thought it better to keep this unlikely coincidence to herself.

"Suppose," said Filip, "it's as simple as Jerzy losing his balance, hitting his head."

"No obvious contusions or abrasions on his scalp rules that out."

The elevator jerked to a stop, and the single metal door jerked open.

"Something set him off," she said, hurrying toward Sick Bay.

Filip kept up to her. "What if I talk to Jerzy."

"You won't have much luck. The nurse and I had to use restraints to keep him from throwing himself off the bed. Even so, he went berserk. I thought he might injure himself, so I gave him enough sedative to knock out a horse."

"How did Doctor Dudek handle it?"

"He hasn't shown up. Not that it matters."

"Ludwik is the chief surgeon. Surely—"

"Jerzy is *my* patient, Filip. *My* responsibility." She pointed down the corridor. "First room past surgery."

Chief Officer Pawel Klimek stopped pacing in his cramped private quarters, as he repeated over and over the single word young Olecki had whispered to him.

Jablonski.

Pawel would never have believed it. The ship's captain had planned to defect in Montreal? Why? What stopped him?

For Pawel, Captain Jablonski as a potential defector was too good to be true. But why would the fleet's most prestigious senior master contemplate such a thing? Yet, with him gone, Pawel knew he had the opportunity to become a ship's master. To say nothing of the new vessel replacing the *TSS Casimir lll*.

Following in his father's footsteps as a captain with the Polish Shipping Lines was a dream Pawel had nurtured since his teens. There was no question in his mind that Stanislaw Jablonski deserved whatever got him into trouble. Hadn't the sonofabitch replaced his father as senior officer of the fleet?

There had been controversy that Pawel had never understood, other than that it left his father as an embittered, angry man until his death five years ago. Pawel relished getting back at the captain for his father's sake, if for no other reason.

If Jablonski had intended to desert the ship in Montréal, he thought to himself, what would stop the bastard from trying again at the first port of call?

Pawel promised himself he'd have every exit covered.

In the glow from the overhead night light, Filip Sotek made out the figure of his assistant stretched out on the bed, the arms by his side, his eyes closed.

"His breathing has improved," said Helena, taking his wrist to check his pulse. "It's his lack of response to stimuli that bothers me. Verbal or visual. He was dripping wet, as if he'd been in a shower with his clothes on. But that's not where he was found."

Filip looked down at his young assistant. "You don't often see him this peaceful."

"It's the Lorazepam," she said. "I'm worried about the low pulse, but not dangerously so." She tucked Jerzy's arm back under the single sheet, opened the drawer in the small metal table nearby and took a small piece of rope, passing it to him.

Filip rolled the rope between his fingers, noticing a gritty, salty dampness to it.

"Jerzy was clutching it when we brought him to Sick Bay. Nor could we pry it loose until the sedative took effect."

He was putting it back when he noticed the drawer was empty except for Jerzy's ring of keys.

"No watch," he asked, puzzled. "No wallet along with the keys?"

"That's all he had on him, Filip. Otherwise, I would've told you. He was in shock. His uniform dirty, wet, soiled. He has scratches on his face, neck, arms, legs. No shoes."

"Will he remember what happened?"

"I have no idea."

Filip looked around. "Where's his uniform?"

"We double-bagged it, with socks, shirt, underwear. The stench was overpowering."

"Where are they now?" Filip asked.

"In the ER." Helena leaned over Jerzy to fluff up his pillow. "Unless the duty nurse sent them down to the ship's laundry."

"Christ," Filip groaned and charged from the room.

The deafening roar from the industrial washers struck Filip like a body blow.

"Mister Witold?" he called out.

A bare head poked out from between two enormous clothes dryers.

"Mister Sotek, as I live and breathe," bellowed the lusty custodian of the laundry's night shift. Then came the rest of Aristide Witold, short, barrel-chested, and in a sweat-soaked tank top, soiled jeans, and rubber boots. A lump of

Copenhagen chewing tobacco protruded from under his lower lip.

"Lost your fancy boxers, have we?"

Filip felt the intense humidity already soaking through his white shirt.

"I'm looking for a uniform—"

"Belonging to Officer Olecki, yes?" Aristide wiped his broad forehead with a wrinkled cotton cloth. "Brought here by a shapely nurse, who I wouldn't mind stretching out on the—"

"Where are his clothes?" Filip interrupted. He was in no mood for such banter.

The laundryman pointed to a large washer running under full throttle.

Filip raised his arms in a hopeless gesture. "Where can we talk and hear one another?"

"Never seen anything worse done to the uniform," said Aristide, ducking under massive overhead pipes. "Ripped, covered with grease, dirt, grime." He stopped to aim a stream of tobacco at a drain in the floor. He hit it square on. "Young Olecki had shit himself," he said, stepping into an office no larger than a closet.

Filip remained in the doorway. "Nothing more?"

"Isn't that enough?" Aristide chewed thoughtfully. "Why were his clothes soaked in brine…?"

It was a question the officer couldn't answer.

CHAPTER TWENTY-NINE
Wednesday, October 12, 7:30 AM

Nothing distressed Stanislaw Jablonski more than a member of his crew suffering a misadventure. An officer or ordinary seaman, it made no difference.

"There must be some explanation," he said to his entertainment officer while eating breakfast in his private quarters. It doubly worried him, as it had followed so close the accidental death of the woman passenger.

"No idea, sir." Bleary-eyed Filip Sotek had been up all night and now stood by the small table set with breakfast for two. "We'll know more when the sedative wears off."

Stanislaw nodded to the empty chair. "Have something to eat, Mister Sotek."

Filip sat down, unwrapping the knife and fork from the folded linen napkin. He stared empty-eyed at the plate of eggs and bacon.

Stanislaw watched his officer pick up his fork and stab the egg. The yolk broke, spreading a yellow stain across the plate.

"If eating is the last thing on your mind, son, go now. Catch up on your sleep."

Filip nodded his thanks and got up from the table.

Sleep turned out to be the last thing on Filip Sotek's mind. A message from Helena directed him to Sick Bay. She was waiting for him in her white lab coat.

"Doctor Dudek is with Jerzy," she said, hurrying him along the corridor, "We were hoping he might wake up clear headed. It didn't work. Yet his vital signs are stable."

"Meaning?"

"Mentally, he's buried away where we can't reach him."

"It sounds like PTSD."

"Some form of psychosis. He stares directly at us as if we weren't there. Whatever he's gone through, Filip, it has disconnected him from reality."

"You expect him to snap out of it, I hope."

"With total rest and quiet, he could, as if nothing had happened. Doctor Dudek isn't so sure." She stopped at a closed door. "He and I agreed a familiar face might make a difference."

"I'll do what I can."

"Don't be fazed by the bruises and abrasions to his face and upper body," she said, easing the door open. "More puzzling are deep cuts on both legs that needed stitches." She paused. "I'll stay here by the door."

Filip entered, waiting a moment while his eyes adjusted to the semi-darkness.

He was shocked to see Jerzy crouched on the bed, his knees drawn up against his chest, the striped hospital gown pulled up leaving the rest of him exposed.

Filip stopped next to the doctor.

The senior surgeon kept his voice low. "Thank you for coming, Mister Sotek. The patient must recognize you first. I'll tell you when to speak to him."

It took several minutes before the doctor nodded.

"It's me, Jerzy," Filip said, his voice hushed.

The young man's eyes searched the room and locked on Filip. With it came a haunting moan from deep within him.

Helena stiffened. "Back away, Filip. *Now*!!"

He stepped closer to the bed. "I only want to tell you how sorry—"

A scream shattered the silence as Jerzy lashed out with both feet. He caught Filip on the chest, driving him backward into the wheeled night table and down hard on the floor.

Helena raced across the room, throwing herself on Jerzy's flailing legs. He in turn reached forward, wrapping his arms around her neck.

Filip had staggered to his feet. Sucking lost air into his lungs, he grabbed Jerzy, squeezing him in a headlock.

"Let her go," he breathed in Jerzy's ear, "or I'll break your fucking neck."

Jerzy was slow to do so, with them both struggling to pin him to the bed.

Aware they were alone with him, Helena glanced over her shoulder to see the senior surgeon staring at them in shocked silence.

"God damn it, Ludwik." she screamed. "The restraints!"

Dudek snapped out of it and hurried from the room. He returned red-faced with the webbed belts. With Jerzy swearing a mixture of Polish and English, the men held him down while Helena cinched the young officer's wrists and ankles to the bed frame.

With this done, she turned to Filip, asking him to have the duty nurse bring the Haldol.

"And you, Officer Sotek," the breathless senior surgeon shouted as Filip left the room, "keep away from my Sick Bay! You've caused enough damage."

Filip was coming down the corridor, when Nurse Schyler charged from the dispensary.

"I heard it all," she murmured, waving a syringe as she passed him and disappeared into the room.

Helena joined a bone-weary Filip in her office, her hair in tangles, the sleeve of her blouse torn loose at the shoulder.

"Doctor Dudek had no right to speak to you like that, Filip. We both asked you to come to Sick Bay. Nor did we have any expectation of what might happen. Trust me," she said, dabbing at her bloodied lip with a damp surgical towel, "it's not your fault. Yet look at you…"

"Look at *me*?" said Filip, feeling sore all over. "What about you? And how's Jerzy?"

"Getting the Haldol into him wasn't easy. I'd have gone for the thigh, where it's less intrusive. Then again, I wasn't in charge." She took his hand in hers. "As for Doctor Dudek, he has a penchant for voicing what seems to be the obvious, when it never is."

"Let's face it, Helena, Jerzy took one look at me and went berserk. As if I were his worst enemy."

"God only knows why." She squeezed his hand go. "He kept repeating the captain's name after you'd gone. And shouting how our two scientists on board were in danger."

"I'll handle it," he said, kissing her on the lips. "Don't forget the skipper's formal reception in his quarters. For Harm Page. Tonight. Before second sitting."

Helena promised she wouldn't miss it.

Doctor Ludwik Dudek stared down at the still form of Jerzy Olecki, the physician's gray eyes reflecting his own troubled soul. His hope that this would be an uneventful round trip, had been shattered the day before the *TSS Casimir III* was sailing home from Montréal.

It began mid-afternoon when he left Doctor Witka on duty, giving him time to visit his favorite haunt. It was in nearby Old Town, with its ancient structures and cobblestone streets. Of special interest to him was Boulevard St. Laurent, *the Main*, though most of its exotic clubs on the strip had disappeared, since he first came here, to make the area more respectable.

A few remained, among them the Red Orchid with its flashing lights, its raw music, and its strippers gyrating naked on stage. He enjoyed the lap dancers most of all.

Ludwik had ordered a spicy Bloody Mary, when a stranger sat down opposite him at the small table. The doctor took in the wore jeans and plain white T-shirt, the eyes lost beneath the wide rim of a *Canadiens'* hockey cap.

Ludwik, wanting to be alone, was ready to complain to the server, when the uninvited guest shoved an unsealed brown envelope across the table. He noticed it was addressed to Mrs. L. H. Dudek, Zeglarzy Street, Puck, Poland. Curious, he opened it.

He was shocked to see explicit photographs of himself making love to a nubile young woman he recognized from an earlier crossing. Like himself, she was naked, and stretched out on an examining table in the *Casimir's* Sick Bay.

The color photos left nothing to the imagination. The ship's senior surgeon mounting her from behind. His face buried in her hairless crotch. Other photos showed his arms and legs lashed to the bedposts in his private quarters with her mouthing his erect penis.

Ludwik, mesmerized by what he saw, barely heard the stranger tell him the envelope and its contents would not reach Poland, nor a similar batch delivered to the ship's captain. Provided he followed instructions to be given to him during this return trip.

As a parting gesture, the man in the *Canadiens'* hockey cap paid a satin-skinned stripper to sit astride the doctor's thighs, shifting to the beat of the club's loud music. By then, Ludwik Dudek's heart wasn't in it.

Jerzy Olecki's moans snapped the chief surgeon back from his unpleasant reverie. He removed the stethoscope from around his neck to check the young officer's heart rate, when Nurse Schyler appeared at the door.

"A passenger insists on seeing you, doctor," she said, "regarding certain photographs."

"Have him wait in my office," he said.

Having no idea what would happen next, Ludwik removed a silver flask from his hip pocket, and drained what was left.

Filip dropped by Harm's stateroom to find Leszek and Nicole with him. He remained in the corridor, telling Harm of his assistant's mishap and erratic behavior. Jerzy, he said, had repeated over and over to Doctor Witka how both Harm and Leszek Poplawski were in grave danger.

"She wanted you to know this at once," he said.

Harm's silence prompted Filip to add, "If there's anything you want, or need, don't hesitate to ask."

Harm thanked him and stepped back into the cabin.

CHAPTER THIRTY
Wednesday, October 12, 7:00 PM

Nicole arrived while Harm was in the bathroom concentrating on tying his black bow tie. He noticed her yellow, strapless sheath of a cocktail dress held up by…he could only imagine. Her dark hair was pulled back and knotted loose with a wide red ribbon. He admired the matching earrings and brooch.

She had planted herself in the bathroom doorway, arms folded.

"I'm under strict orders to bring you to the Captain's Reception," she said. "Should you decide to give it a pass."

"Don't worry," he said. "I'll find my way."

"Who'll they blame if the guest of honor doesn't show? Me." She watched him fumble with lining up the bows. "I hope you're not leaving your tie like that."

"Why not?"

"The ends are uneven. My late husband always…Never mind."

Harm turned out the bathroom light and started to ease by her, not unaware of those bluest of blue eyes scowling at him.

She stepped in his way, reaching up to give one end a pull. The tie fell apart.

"Why did you do that?"

"Because the knot looks messy." Needing a distraction while working on the tie, she settled on mentioning his daughter.

"I know so little about Samantha…"

"When you Agency types know all about us? Like Sam wanting to come back home."

"Could she really give up L.A.? To live with you in the middle of nowhere."

"It seems so. Her mom went ballistic. Me, challenging the status quo. Sabotaging the precious mother/daughter relationship."

"You showed up in a Los Angeles court…" Nicole took the ends and lapped one over the other. "… and caused the judge a great deal of trouble."

"Only because I took exception to my ex-wife's legals going after Sam, insisting she let me badger her into coming back east." Harm looked down at the tie. Nicole bumped his chin out of the way with her forearm.

"The judge set a temporary injunction, keeping you away and from contacting your daughter." Nicole whipped the ends into two bows. "Leaving you to return home…"

"What else could I do?" Harm wished she'd get the bow-tying over with. "Sit out there, fiddling my thumbs?"

"True. The court date is scheduled for late the *next* week. Friday, the nineteenth. You won't even be back in the States by then."

"I didn't realize the trip would take longer than expected." Harm took a softer approach. "Show some heart. Use your connections to have the court date extended."

Nicole lined up the ends with the bows and pulled tight. "We're the CIA, not a charitable organization." She stepped back to admire her handiwork. "Nor do we make the rules."

"You don't look like someone who goes by the rules," said Harm, picking his tuxedo jacket up off the bed.

The Captain's quarters hummed with the conversations of small groups of invited guests, including the ship's senior officers. Mixed in with it were strains of Bach's *Goldberg Variations* played on a small electronic keyboard by a member of the ship's quartet.

The captain's desk displayed a tantalizing array of hors d'oeuvres and canapés, as several seamen moving through the gathering with glasses of champagne.

The captain was talking with Hugh Ashcroft, when Harm and Nicole appeared at the open doorway.

"For what it's worth," Nicole whispered to Harm, "I'll pass on your request about changing the date of the court case in Los Angeles. Don't expect anyone to give a damn."

"Ladies and gentlemen," announced the captain, "please welcome Harmon Page and Ms. Nicole Hagen, who was delegated to ensure our guest of honor wouldn't duck out on us."

The remark was met with smiles.

"It is indeed an honor to welcome you, Mister Page," said Stanislaw, coming over to shake his hand.

Thomas slipped in beside Nicole, handing her a glass of champagne. They listened as the captain praised Page for his single act of bravery in rescuing a young woman during her descent down the side of the ship at Québec.

Harm's modest reply mentioned how the outcome would've been different had not Officer Filip Sotek shouted tough orders from above, having taken him for a member of the tugboat's crew. It was met with a round of cheers from the officers, applause from the guests.

A blushing, grinning Filip cornered Harm, thanking him for sharing that moment and how a grateful captain had ordered a chilled bottle of *Moet & Chandon* from his private stock to be sent on to Harm's stateroom.

Helena Witka and Thomas eased Harm over to a quiet corner. She explained how her unauthorized and too short an examination of Kimberly Stockwell's body had turned up unexpected results.

"I noticed injuries to the back of the head," she said, "when I first examined her at the bottom of the pool. I had decided these bruises could be the result of the fall into the empty pool."

"And now?" Harm asked.

"I'm convinced her neck was broken *before* she ended up in the pool. Those deep bruises were deliberately caused by the snapping of her vertebrae in one quick, fatal stroke."

"You're telling us it was a professional hit?" said Thomas.

Helena hesitated. "I can see it no other way."

"Done by someone skilled enough," Thomas said, "to know what they were doing. "

"Yet I can't prove it."

"You've seen this before," said Harm, "during your stint in London?"

Helena nodded. "This may seem strange coming from me, but could there be a connection between Mrs. Stockwell's death and what happened to Officer Olecki?"

"What about him?" Thomas asked.

"He was in an accident and brought, badly beaten, to Sick Bay. He went into total, uncontrolled rage when Filip Sotek dropped by to see him. Two incidents happening so close together."

"I doubt if there's any connection," said Harm. "It's strange to me that he'd turn on someone who, I'm sure, he trusted."

Thomas agreed. "What if it was Filip's body language that put Officer Olecki off—"

The lights in the room dimmed, and the young doctor sighed.

"This is Captain Jablonski's not too subtle approach, telling us the party's over."

They looked to see him already at the door, shaking hands with his departing guests.

Nicole sat on one of Harm's twin beds with the laptop. They both had changed into jeans and sweaters after Second Sitting. Leszek had gone off on his own while they reviewed notes taken during the day.

"You both decided to start off tomorrow," she said, reading her notes, "with Wernicke's area of the left temporal lobe."

"Essential to understanding language." Harm glanced at the time.

"That's a wrap," he said, coming away from the window.

"I hope you won't think of something else." she said, ready to close her laptop.

"Nope. Shut it down, I'm taking you on a Magical Mystery Tour."

"When?"

"Now."

Nicole looked at him sideways. "What's involved?"

"If I told you, it wouldn't be a mystery. There's one condition. We have at least one drink at each stop."

"And when I want to go to bed? No argument?"

"Not from me," he said, opening the door.

It was past midnight when they reached the Grand Lounge, the lights dim, the music soft and slow.

"We can't go in," Nicole warned him. "Not in jeans."

Harm dragged her in and onto the crowded dance floor.

Closing her eyes, she let her body relax against him. "Tell me, did you…never mind."

"No, I didn't."

"You don't know what I'm thinking."

"That I made love to Kimberly."

She touched his cheek with hers. "That isn't it," she fibbed.

"I helped her out of an embarrassing situation."

"Boy Scout to the rescue," Nicole said. "There's something else…"

"Nor did I steal your Walther PPK."

Nicole pulled her cheek away from his. "You remembered the make."

"How many times have you badgered me about…Uh-oh. Our friend Officer Klimek is looking our way. Scowling."

"I'm more interested in my missing handgun."

"What will convince you I didn't steal it?"

"By giving it back."

"You must've driven your parents wacky, Agent Hagen. Contrary. Headstrong…ah."

"*Ah* what?"

"The first officer's coming our way."

"Let's blow this pop stand." Nicole hiccupped. "Lordy, I haven't said that since I was a gangly sixteen."

"Nice gangles," Harm murmured, as they danced off the floor.

"I *feel* like a teenager tonight," she said, reaching the foyer. "Out long after curfew, to say nothing of being slightly pissed."

"Good, because the MMT continues."

Nicole surprised herself by not objecting.

The Disco, one stop among many, was packed with undulating bodies, raucous music, and wall-to-wall noise. Harm and Nicole drank whisky sours and danced until their legs turned to rubber. They finally sought refuge in the Boat Deck Bar, where they found Thomas nursing a cognac.

Nicole wriggled onto the stool beside him. "What's up, handsome?"

"Nothing much," he said, surprised she was tipsy.

Harm rested his elbows on the counter. "Agent Hagen's been leading me astray."

"Bullshit," she said.

"It was you, Nicky, who insisted we change into in our jeans and cavort among the tuxedos and cocktail dresses in the Grand Lounge."

"He plied me with drinks, Thomas." Nicole hiccupped. "Danced me breathless in the Disco. And took advantage of my good nature by insisting we go on with his Magical Mystery Tour."

"Ah, The *Beatles,*" Thomas said. "Abbey Lane. Good stuff."

"Come with us," said Harm. "Help me keep this beautiful woman from getting sloshed."

"You *think?*" She stole Thomas's glass and finished off his cognac. "I could drink you both under the table." She smothered another hiccup. "I'm taking over."

Harm felt none too sober himself. "What did you have in mind?"

"We'll bundle up, crawl into a lifeboat, and see who's first to pick out the Big Dipper." She noticed their lack of enthusiasm. "Guys, show a little spirit. Or I'll do it alone."

Harm warmed to the idea. "We'll need a blanket. Along with the bottle of the chilled bottle of *Moet & Chandon* champagne left in my cabin. Courtesy of the captain."

"Champagne?" said Thomas. "Three's definitely a crowd."

"Come with us," Nicole pleaded. "We'll sing silly songs, tell dirty jokes."

Thomas thought it over. "No embarrassing wailing and gnashing of teeth when I decide to pack it in?"

Neither Nicole or Harm objected.

They sat in the open lifeboat Number 12, their backs against the gunwale. They shared a heavy Melton blanket and took turns drinking bubbly from the bottle. They told jokes and sang songs with questionable lyrics, learned at summer camp.

In a competition to tell the dirtiest joke, Nicole Hagan won hands down. Three votes in favor, none opposed.

While giving a heartfelt rendition of the classic, "*Bonsoir, mes amis, bonsoir,*" Thomas kissed Nicole on both cheeks and disappeared down onto the deck.

"I'm glad he came with us," said Nicole, closing her eyes. They popped open when Harm moved closer to her. Not, she knew, that she couldn't handle him on her own.

"He's become a good friend," said Harm, passing her the champagne. "Tell me, what makes a good spook?"

"Feeling comfortable in a new identity," Nicole said, drinking from the bottle. "Looking and feeling the part. I was recruited directly from Harvard. Central Intelligence came to me. I thought it was a joke but signed up anyway."

"What made you do it?"

"It was different from anything I expected to do with my life. Reality hit when I was at the training compound, learning to defend myself with a paring knife."

Nicole took another swig, feeling it wise to keep up a conversation. "Climbing telephone poles without a ladder, lessons in unarmed combat, surveillance techniques and handling weapons, to name a few…"

She knew she shouldn't be feeling this good. "I remember being blindfolded and dumped off alone in the middle of nowhere, wearing what I had on at the time. I had to rely on locals, without telling them who I was or what I was doing." Nicole decided it was wise to change the subject. Away from her.

"Tell me more about your daughter," she said.

"You have a close relationship. Something went wrong when she was late returning to California after visiting you."

"You know everything about it by now. And me. We had the stipulated two weeks together. Sam arrived from Los Angeles, insisting we go camping, like we did when she was a kid. We compromised. We'd do it if she didn't take her cell phone."

"That's pretty scary."

"She agreed, which surprised me. We picked up new equipment at L.L Bean in Freeport, Maine. While I gassed up the car, she wandered into a nearby second-hand bookstore and came out waving a tattered copy of *The Edible Wild.*"

"Don't tell me—"

"Yes. Sam decided we'd feed ourselves solely by the recipes in the book. Which meant frying grasshoppers and milkweed shoots. Dandelion salad with dried bacon bits we had with us. Snails, Freshwater crayfish sautéed in butter and garlic."

"I'd have fit right in," Nicole said, drinking more before handing back the bottle.

"I bet you would. Unfortunately, we stayed longer than we should have."

"Because you stopped off at Cape Porpoise on the way home, to help an old friend set out his lobster traps."

"You've read the report. Sam returned late to California. Her mother filed a grievance with the Los Angeles county court system. She claimed I'd ignored conditions in the Child custody agreement. You know the rest. Sam's recent phone call…"

Nicole took back the bottle. "I'd like to meet her someday."

"We'll take you camping." Harm leaned over and kissed her.

She pulled away. "Don't...complicate things."

"Fair enough," he said, kissing her again.

Nicole blamed the evening on an alignment of the stars, an ocean voyage, the seductive *Moet & Chandon*, or, worse, a feeling that she wanted more.

"Inhibitions have a way of being forgotten at sea," he was saying. "Fantasies fulfilled."

She eased her head back against the gunwale. "I'm not so sure."

"No? What wild and wacky urges make you break out in goose bumps?"

"Can't tell you."

"Fair enough."

"The possibility of being caught..." She couldn't believe what she was saying. Here in the middle of the Atlantic... "while making love in public."

"Ah, serendipity. The element of chance. Something to do with the Three Princes of Serendip." He took the bottle and drank from it. "We'll ask Thomas about them tomorrow. He's a walking, talking encyclopedia. And you, that's one of your fantasies? Getting caught or getting away with it?"

She felt a warm, fuzzy feeling right down to her toes. "Getting away with it works for me."

Harm held out the bottle. "Think of it as a one-night stand."

"Excuse me?" Nicole polished off the last of the champagne. "A *one-night* stand?"

"Here in the middle of nowhere. No regrets. No prolonged feeling of guilt afterward."

She loosened the ponytail and let her dark hair fall loose about her shoulders.

"We keep this strictly between ourselves, Harm."

"That's fine with me," he said, putting the empty bottle down beside them.

Nicole suddenly swung a leg up and over to sit astride his thighs. "Promise?"

"I promise."

She bent down, kissing him on the mouth.

"Cross your heart."

Harm did as he was told.

Having made their way along the sheltered portion of the Promenade Deck, they stopped in partial shadow at the outside entrance to the Little Lounge. Harm eased her back against the wall and wrapped the blanket around their shoulders.

"I'll be really upset if no one shows," she whispered.

"Be patient," he said, slipping a hand under her sweater.

Admitting to herself that this *wasn't* the Nicole Hagen she knew, she closed her eyes as his tongue aroused her nipples.

Every fiber in Harm's body seemed on fire in this moment, he knew, which never should have been. Yet she was here, pressing against him, working her jeans down over her bare hips. He bent lower, conscious of a delightful ache in his groin.

She tried to stifle a cry as his tongue worked magic between her thighs.

"Oh my God—"

Several young couples appeared further along the deck. Arms linked, singing, legs kicking high in their version of the French can-can.

Nicole pulled Harm up by his shoulders, tightening her arms around his neck.

The couples, having reached the entrance, stopped to stare at them wrapped in a blanket.

"Hi," said Nicole, holding him close. "Nice night for…well, whatever."

"I'd settle for *whatever*," said one of the guys as they laughed and ducked inside.

"You have such a way with words," he said, picking up where he left off.

Harm leaned against the wall outside Nicole's stateroom, the heavy blanket draped over his shoulder.

"It was all very naughty," she said, opening the door. "Goodnight."

He reached in to hang out the Polish version of the DO NOT DISTURB sign.

"*G'night?*" he said, following her in. "You're not aware that one-night stands officially end at daybreak?"

She tried to find some hidden meaning. "Really?"

"Like me, waking up next to you in the morning."

Nicole kicked off her runners. "Waking up next to me in the morning."

"That's the general idea."

She turned on a small desk lamp and disappeared into the bathroom. She came back wearing a sweatshirt with *I love Paris* on it. Harm was sure there was nothing under it.

"Nobody has ever said that to me," she said.

"Said what?"

"How they wanted to wake up next to me. And you, the *one* person I should avoid. The *one* person I shouldn't go to bed with, let alone make love to." She came over to stop in front of him. "I've sobered up enough to know this night should end. Here. Now." She hesitated. "I expect, at the very least, you keep what happens as a blip on the radar."

Harm grinned. "A *blip on the radar?*"

Nicole went all soft and quiet. "I feel vulnerable, Harm. I'm not used to letting myself go. Physically. Mentally. Emotionally. All of me. And what's worse, I'm enjoying it."

"That's only the *pâté* before the entrée."

She put her arms around his neck. "I'm still horny, but don't expect much. I'm…out of practice."

"It's like climbing back on a bicycle…"

She moved a hand down between them to caress her own crotch through her jeans.

"I have more unfulfilled fantasies," she whispered.

"I have a few of my own," Harm said, reaching down to take her hand.

CHAPTER THIRTY-ONE
Thursday, October 13, 8:15 AM

Fresh dew still clung to the lush green grass at the Pines Golf & Country Club in Alexandria across the Potomac. On the sixth tee, Ted Grosvenor rattled a shot off a tall white pine.

"Did you see where it went?" he asked his partner, Irwin Rasky, secretary of state.

"Not after hitting the tree." Rasky yawned, having yet to shake off jet lag after last night's flight from Israel. "It could be in the rough."

Nathan Edgars admitted to not seeing it. Nor did the fourth club member sharing his golf cart.

Ted sat brooding in the passenger seat. How had he developed such a slice? Something goddam new to haunt him.

He watched Irwin waggle his big-headed Callaway at the ball, bring the club back slow and easy, and swinging through. *Thwack*!

The ball climbed, its flight path taking it straight down the middle of the fairway.

"It's a game of concentration, Ted," Rasky chirped, climbing back in the driver's seat. He jammed his expensive golf shoe down hard on the accelerator, and the cart took off. "That's what's totally lacking in your game."

"My concentration would be one helluva lot better, Irwin," Ted shouted over the high-pitched whine of the cart's electric motor, "if you'd pressure the Pentagon into admitting why they have a sudden interest in Leszek Poplawski."

"You can't push 'em," Irwin replied, far from admitting his lack of clout with the Pentagon. "You know it. I know it."

"There are innocent people on board the *Casimir III,* along with a hit man. He'd ice 'em faster than you could knock off a Moscow Mule."

"A Moscow what?"

"It's a *cocktail,* for Christ sake."

"Don't tie yourself in knots," Irwin replied, hitting the brakes to send the cart slithering sideways through the tall wet grass. "Your ball landed somewhere here."

"I don't give a damn about my ball. It's those on board I'm worried about."

The secretary of state shook it off. "I'm golfing with the president next week. Or is it the week after? I'll have my girl check my schedule and get back to you."

"A lot of fucking good that'll do," Ted grumbled. "The ship docks at London/Tilbury in less than forty-eight hours."

Irwin leaned over to poke the toe of his shoe down into the grass. He bent down, picked up a ball, and turned it between his thumb and forefinger.

"Was yours a Maxfli 3?"

Ted shook his head, resisting the urge to strangle the little jerk right there in the rough.

Thomas Slater watched Harm and Nicole enter the ship's Dining Room just in time for a late breakfast. Something about them, he knew, had changed.

Small things. The slight brushing of their shoulders, the inadvertent touching of hands while their eyes looked elsewhere. Coming down the aisle, they parted without a word, as if, Thomas decided, none was needed.

"Good morning," she said cheerily, avoiding eye contact as she sat down next to him. She ruffled her hair and glanced at the two empty chairs. "Where's everyone?"

"Leszek and Peter are long gone," he said, finishing his coffee. "I enjoyed last night..."

"Me too." She glanced at the menu. "You'll have to teach me that song about the three old ladies stuck in the john."

"You mean the four old ladies locked a lavatory?"

She put the menu aside. "Yes. Talking about numbers, what do you know about the *three* princes of Serendip?"

Thomas couldn't figure out where this had come from. "Author Horace Walpole wrote about the princes making major discoveries by coincidence. By chance. With them having no control over the circumstances. Maybe you saw the film *Serendipity*. Where this girl and guy living at opposite ends of the country—"

Thomas could see from her expression her mind was elsewhere.

"Never mind," he said.

Helena Witka checked off the nurse's night report. It listed a handful of passengers dropping by Sick Bay in the past twelve hours, complaining of seasickness.

She knew how they felt, the definite unsettling movement of the ship, the slight dizziness leading to queasiness in the pit of the stomach. Faced with the same dilemma, Helena put on a brave face with nothing but sheer determination.

Harm appeared. "Got a moment?"

Helena waved him in. "Seasick? Hangover? Both?"

"None of the above," he claimed, leaning against the open door. It's about our conversation at the captain's reception. You described Officer Olecki going off the deep end. When Filip came into the hospital room. I said no one switches so dramatically against someone they trust. And I think Thomas hit it right on, Helena, suggesting something distracted young Olecki. That's where the conversation ended."

"If you have anything to add, I'd appreciate hearing it."

Harm came over to sit on the corner of her desk. "What were you wearing at the time?"

Helena gave him an odd look. "My lab coat."

"And the chief surgeon?"

"The same."

"Filip Sotek?"

"A white uniform." Helena put down the report. "Why is this important?"

"Thomas thought Filip might've distracted Officer Olecki. Take it another step. Nothing had disturbed the young officer until Filip arrived. Then all hell broke loose.

Now, suppose young Olecki was not reacting to Filip, but rather to—"

A young nurse poked her head in the door without knocking.

"The call bell just sounded, Doctor. From Room Three." Helena came around the desk.

"I'm fascinated. We'll talk later?"

"Of course," said Harm, musing over whether he and Thomas had any other bright ideas.

Filip Sotek, dressed in black pants with the sleeves of his white shirt rolled up, was enjoying a relaxed coffee in the Grand Lounge, when his name broke over the speaker system. He was needed in Sick Bay. He hurried off.

Helena whisked him down the hospital corridor to stop outside Jerzy's room. Filip took a deep breath and stepped inside.

Jerzy was sitting up in the hospital bed, covered by a light sheet.

"Hey, boss, what kind of friend are you? Not coming to see how I'm doing." His twinkling eyes settled on Helena. "And what do I have to do to scrounge up a meal?"

In gathering material for his report on those jumping ship in Montréal, Pawel Klimek had summoned the ship's officers one at a time to his quarters. He had kept Chief Engineer Niski until last.

"You're saying you heard nothing of the defections, Mister Niski?"

"Not until much later."

"Yet your crew has a dubious reputation for knowing everything that goes on almost before it happens."

"They have that distinction. As their senior officer, they don't share hearsay with me."

The chief engineer knew this was far from the truth. His engine room crew prided themselves on keeping him alerted to every and all gossip.

Pawel planted himself before the older man. "What do you know of a *second* officer planning to defect in Montréal, but never accomplished it?"

"I was unaware of it until we left port." Henryk had heard as much from his crew. "No name was mentioned."

The chief officer pushed his face up close to Henryk's. "And what do you think this *same* senior officer is planning when we reach London/Tilbury?"

Henryk's weathered face remained impassive. "I have no idea."

"And you, the one sonofabitch who should know." Pawel shook his head. "You're dismissed."

Chief Engineer Henryk Niski paced before his crew within minutes of leaving the chief officer's quarters.

They were lined up beside the mammoth steam turbines, whose racket thundered in their ears.

"Something is going on," Henryk barked, "and I will not ask again."

His men stood uncomfortably erect, like reluctant schoolboys summoned before the principal. Getting no response, Henryk stomped off.

He had no sooner entered his small office, when Rafal, the largest of his crew, filled the narrow doorway, his dark face flushed beneath his thick black beard.

"We have kept something from you, Mister Niski," he said, making an awkward gesture with his large calloused hands. Only because what we heard was not worth repeating."

"Let me be the judge of that, Rafal."

The big man stood silent, finally speaking barely above a whisper. "It seems Captain Jablonski intended on leaving the *Casimir* in Montréal."

Henryk waved it off. "If it were so, I'd be the first to know."

"Maybe not," Rafal replied, turning away to leave a baffled chief engineer alone in his office.

Jerzy Olecki's hairy legs dangled down the side of the bed as he polished off a large portion of pancakes, bacon and eggs. He looked up a Helena and Filip.

"How come I'm stuck here in Sick Bay, Doc?"

"You've had a mishap, Jerzy," Helena said, pressing her fingers against his wrist while checking his pulse. "Do you remember what happened?"

"I lost my balance. In the shower. And couldn't get up. Funny, though. I remember the salty taste. The smell of it—"

Helena frowned when Filip started to speak; a warning for him to stay out of it.

"Salt water in the shower?" she asked.

The young officer closed his eyes. He began swaying, clasping and unclasping his hands.

"Salt water was all around me, Doctor Witka. I was... drowning... hitting my head..."

"Hitting it on what?"

"I... can't remember."

"Were you pushed?"

Jerzy opened his eyes, tears spilling down his cheeks. "We were dancing, and she told me the two scientists were in danger..."

"Who is *she*?"

"Mrs. Stockwell. She wouldn't stop talking about Doctors Page and Poplawski. How...they were in deep trouble...with no one to help them."

Filip came close to the bed. "When was this, Jerzy?"

Helena pushed Filip aside, swung Jerzy's legs back onto the bed, and eased his head down on the pillow.

"Try to sleep," she said, taking Filip by the arm and guiding him out into the corridor.

"You pushed him too damn far, Helena," he muttered.

"There was too much riding on this, Filip. You must understand, it was *my* call. Had I known you couldn't keep quiet, I would've left you in the hallway."

Filip backed off. "You're right. I'm sorry. I had visions of him going off the deep end again."

"I understand," she said, squeezing his hand, and letting go. "I had to know how deep the amnesia had affected him."

"What about him tasting salt water in the ship's shower?"

Helena stopped short of the reception area. "When his subconscious couldn't cope with the trauma of what really happened, his brain substituted a less stressful alternative."

"You mean the shower. But how do you explain the salt water?"

"I can't, for the life of me. Yet the shower meets the necessary parameters. It's a safer place, in his case, for him to get wet."

"And should what happened come back to haunt him?"

"I will say this once, Filip. Jerzy has convinced himself about being in the shower. This may never change."

"And if it does?"

Helena shoved her hands deep in the pockets of her lab coat as they walked on.

"Should it be triggered by the simplest of everyday events, a bright, self-reliant individual like Jerzy Olecki would work it out, his way."

"It was no accident, Helena. I'm sure of that. Can you keep him in Sick Bay until we find who's behind it?"

Helena stepped into her office, despaired at being asked a second time to put off doing her job. First, Harm Page about keeping Kimberly Stockwell's death unrecorded. Now this.

"Doctor Dudek will more than likely check him over and send him back on duty." Filip's look of despair didn't help. "All right. I'll mark it on the chart that he's suffering from an acute concussion and needs constant care. Pray the senior surgeon takes my word for it. Not that he ever has."

Filip took her hand, squeezed it, saying nothing more.

From his elevated captain's chair, Stanislaw nodded at Henryk coming into the wheelhouse.

"Chief Engineer," he said aloud, watching him head directly for the port flying bridge. "Perhaps you can settle a dispute for us. I say our Loran C navigation system was installed in—"

"I must speak to you in private, Captain."

Henryk's remark left no doubt something was amiss. He removed his hooded coat from the rack nearby. "As you were, gentlemen," he said to the others.

A blast of cool air greeted him, as he rounded the enclosed auxiliary navigational equipment and stopped by the railing next to his chief engineer.

"You're still upset," he said, "over those undelivered hydraulic parts."

"It has nothing to do with the parts," Henryk replied, taking a deep breath. "It's the rumor you came close to deserting us in Montréal."

Stanislaw leaned against the railing beside him. "You heard it from that damnable crew of yours?"

"It's Officer Klimek you should be cursing, after his verbal assault on every officer aboard. He's determined to uncover the second one who failed to leave the ship in Montréal. He questioned me, stopping barely short of accusing you…"

"With good reason, my old friend. I *was* that officer."

Henryk felt a sudden tightening in his throat. "Have you lost your mind, Stanislaw? You, the most reputable, experienced master of the fleet."

"I'm aware of it." He glanced down at the bow of the ship slicing through the waves.

"Do you recall, Henryk, what happened shortly before we sailed from Gdynia?"

"Yes, if it means you going before members of the advisory committee. It was to confirm your conducting the sea trials for the new vessel before taking over the ship on a permanent basis."

"It was assumed that's what would happen. But those bloated bastards told me with three years left until my retirement, it would be counter-productive to have me handle the sea trials for the *Casimir IV*."

"Are they out of their minds, Stanislaw?"

One would think so. "I'm to be replaced by a younger officer needing only to do a reasonable job with the trials to earn his commission as master of the new vessel."

"Why didn't you tell me?"

"I felt angry," Stanislaw murmured, "betrayed."

"They must have other plans for you, surely. A member of the advisory committee at the very least. Your knowledge alone is invaluable."

"*Me* at head office? Carping over what a terrible job they're doing? On the contrary, Henryk, I am to be reassigned to one of the fleet's smaller ocean freighters. Either that or accept early retirement the moment we dock the *Casimir III*."

Henryk watched a thick, dark mass of cloud sweep over them as the ship's bow cut deep into the white-capped waves.

"It's grossly unfair."

"Moments before leaving the Gdynia harbor," Stanislaw went on, "I received a hand-delivered, sealed confidential memorandum to be opened once at sea. It would confirm the officer taking over the new vessel and the sea trials."

"There can't be many on the list."

There's one. Our own chief officer."

"*Pawel Klimek*? My crew will throw the bastard overboard when they hear it. Or jump ship—" The chief engineer's eyes narrowed. "Those who left us in Montréal *knew* of your plan?"

"It seems Officer Szalinski caught wind of it from a contact at head office. He came to me. I told him, unwisely so, that I planned to leave the ship, warning him if anyone left the *Casimir*, I would not." Stanislaw choked back his emotions. "Six disobeyed me."

Henryk wiped his tears away with the sleeve of his jacket. "It is so difficult to believe."

"I wanted nothing more than to embarrass those idiots back in Gdynia. When I was summoned from the farewell party the night before the departure, it was to learn Officer Szalinski and the others had already left the ship. I tried to reach them. All but Officer Szalinski had given themselves up to Canadian immigration authorities. I saw him before we sailed."

"I remember when I joined you, you were staring at someone in a baseball cap on the building opposite. It covered much of his face."

"That was Officer Szalinski. He had waved goodbye."

Henryk shook his head. "As for Pawel Klimek, Stanislaw, he is nothing short of a disaster. Born with an innate distrust of everyone, not unlike his damnable father. You have told him of his promotion?"

"I've been told the official notification will come when we dock at Gdynia. Besides, I wouldn't give him the satisfaction of hearing it from me."

"I can only imagine the uproar you caused at headquarters before we sailed."

"I told them a few things that bothered me. It was just as well they didn't tell me an incompetent would take over the sea trials until we were already out at sea. I'd have skinned them alive.

Later, I didn't know how to make my protest known effectively."

"Until you settled for jumping ship. Which didn't happen." Henryk looked directly at Stanislaw. "I can only hope you will not be foolish enough—"

"To leave the ship at London/Tilbury? I plan to."

"Then you fail to understand what drives your chief officer, Stanislaw. It's his unswerving ambition. Believe me, Pawel will screw up, if left to his own devices. Besides, he's out of his depth in handling sea trials of such magnitude. They will be forced to change their minds. Keeping you on for both the sea trials and commander of the new ship."

"A slim chance, Henryk, but I'm determined to go through with it."

"Then I will be at your side on the London/Tilbury pier. Along with members of my crew, who wouldn't have it any other way."

"I will not allow it, Chief Engineer."

His friend smiled. "Try and stop us, Captain."

CHAPTER THIRTY-TWO
Thursday, October 13, 1:55 PM

Work had gone well for Harm, Leszek, and Nicole after many hours of concentrated talk in Harm's cabin. The slight heaving of the ship did little to disrupt Nicole, her attention absorbed by transcribing notes into her laptop. She blushed, from time to time, when visions of the night with Harm interfered.

She was in her usual spot, leaning back against the bed's headboard with the laptop on her legs. Leszek was wandering about, mumbling to himself.

Harm stared out the window, having no success in putting aside the smallest of details of the evening with Nicole. He began again where he hoped he'd left off a moment ago.

"Key to this is the high sodium concentration—"

The loudspeaker interrupted, announcing the final call for second sitting.

Nicole put the laptop aside and slipped off the bed. "Lunch," she said, easing her bare feet into her runners. "*Now,* you two."

Leszek talked directly to Nicole in rapid Polish.

"*Rats,*" she replied to Leszek in English. "Like mice, only bigger." She turned to Harm. "Leszek insists we get back to the rats. I don't remember talking about them."

"You were off on your own yesterday, while Leszek and I consoled each other over individual experiments we'd screwed up over time. Mine involved rats."

"I have thought of little since, Harmon," said Leszek, his eyes twinkling. "How, I ask myself, could such a thing like this occur? And you said there was…hmm."

"A feeding frenzy. They began slaughtering their own kind in one long bloodbath—"

"Don't spoil my lunch with that," said Nicole. "It's a buffet. I want to enjoy it."

"The pair doing the slaughter, Leszek," Harm said as they followed her into the corridor, "was carried out with patience, precision. Vicious little buggers. A terrifying yet awesome sight."

"You must have, hmm…"

"Triggered a killer instinct."

Nicole had reached the small elevator. "Come on, or it's back to room service. Again."

Victor Petrie, catching up to Nicole as she was leaving the dining room after lunch, eased her away from the others. He had decided, as if amused by his decision, to break his silence.

"You've told me you work for the Pentagon. What more is there to say?"

"It's about the illicit sale of government information to a foreign power, Nicky. Involving your friend Page and the Russians."

She stopped short of the staircase to the Promenade level. "I don't see the connection."

"It's classified material. Financed under the jurisdiction of Washington's Department of Science & Technology. It was stolen out from under their noses."

"You're implying Harm is selling his research to the Russians?"

"And his old friend Leszek Poplawski is involved in no small way."

Nicole continued up the steps. "Harm had no clue Leszek was in America, which means he wouldn't have had—"

"Once he found out," Victor interrupted, "Grosvenor's little band of incompetents couldn't stop Page from reaching Montréal and the *Casimir,* even though they'd pulled out all the stops."

Having reached the foyer, Victor guided her out onto the open deck.

"Surely you have proof, Victor, of what he's up to."

"There are some missing pieces, such as where he's leaving the ship."

"At London/Tilbury."

"He told you this?"

Nicole glanced down at the rolling blue water and nodded.

"It's *my* guess Page is booked on to Gdynia," Victor said. "A short hop across to Mother Russia."

Nicole conjured up more images of her and the same Harmon Page making love.

"I can't believe it," she whispered.

Victor leaned back against the railing. "Do me a favor, Nicky. Flag anything Page could trade off with the Russians. Whatever it is, it's bugging him that he can't solve a problem alone. He's counting on Leszek's help."

"I'm over my head as it is…"

"It would be something specific. A possible war drug."

"A *war drug!* Nothing could be farther from their research."

"No?"

"They specialize on the workings of the brain."

"Page is way out of control. Can't you see that? S&T canned Page for taking his research that they endorsed in the wrong direction, apart from screwing up an experiment that cost them a bundle. They had no idea the experiments involved rodents."

"As in *rats*?" she said.

"Rodents, rats. What's the difference?"

"Nothing. Other than Harm and Leszek made a passing reference to them."

"Jesus suffering Christ. This could be the key. And you, telling me as if it isn't important!"

"How in hell should I to know? I was bullied into this goddamned assignment…"

"Tough luck. When you're working from now on with those two guys, make notes. On every little detail, no matter how trivial it seems."

"I have been from the start."

"Good. Better still, look for hidden meanings. Especially from Page. He's sure to let something slip. Now go, do it."

"Do you ever say *please*?" she said, her stomach churning as she left him.

Stunned by Victor's allegations, Nicole arrived in Harm's cabin numbed. He was circling the room, while Leszek sat on the bed beaming with delight.

"And then there's..." Harm stopped in mid-sentence to glance her way. "Hey, you don't seem your old feisty self."

"I'm fine," she said, picking up her laptop and sitting on the nearest chair.

The old man broke into Polish, the words tumbling from him.

Harm leaned against the wall by the window. "What's he so excited about?"

"He's telling me..." Nicole was having trouble getting the words out. "how he ... might have a solution to your failure with the rats. But his poor English gets in the way."

Harm came over to her. "I tried telling him he was on the right track. It's what I needed... Forget the rats—"

"No, no," Nicole burst out, almost knocking the laptop off her knees.

"You've got a thing for rats?"

Leszek spoke up. "Harmon is correct, Madame Hagen. It is more important to understand, how you say in English...?"

"It's more important how stress affects our lives," said Harm. "Brought about by we humans who rely on anti-depressants and tranquilizers to control it these days. Opioids work on the nervous system to relieve pain. Percocet. Tylox, Demerol, among others."

Nicole buried her head in her typing, giving Leszek a verbal running translation at the same time.

"We ignore the side-effects," Harm went on. "Drowsiness, listlessness. Bringing on low blood pressure, postural hypotension. Chronic lower back pain, to overstate the obvious."

Harm let her catch up. "You can see why scientists in the private sector work overtime to develop new drugs that are side-effect free. Ones which won't dullen our mental abilities, like a non-deleting neurotrop—"

"Translating something like a *non-deleting neurotrop*," she said, trying her best to keep calm, "is far beyond me. Typing at the same time doesn't make it any easier."

"You've been doing well so far."

"You think? I should have some idea of what a non-deleting neurotrop is."

"They're chemical compounds, working directly on the brain's nerve pathways to control stress. Done without screwing up our mental functions."

"Unfortunately, Madame Hagen," Leszek cut in, "the non-deleting neurotrop can do too good a job…"

"Leszek is right. Under certain circumstances, it can produce a side effect that's troubling, which brings us back to our not-so-friendly rats."

"Why not so friendly?" she asked, not sure she wanted to know.

"Put it this way. Imagine what excruciating anxieties soldiers face in modern warfare. In occupied territories. Afghanistan. Iraq. Many come home with post-traumatic stress disorder. PTSD… Are you with me?"

"I'm doing my very best," she replied.

"Right. Some are diagnosed, some not, despite their lives being in tatters. Now, what if soldiers are treated *before* a firefight with some variation of a non-deleting neurotrop? Doing away with the emotive side of combat."

"Give me a second," she said, her fingers flying across the keys.

Harm went on when she was ready.

"Take my two rats, in an experiment. I inadvertently turned them into killing machines. No feelings. No post remorse. A non-deleting neurotrop which could potentially become—"

Nicole stopped typing. "You think it's a good thing?"

"I'm trying to establish the possibility. If you'd listen—"

"You're talking about a war drug."

"I didn't say that."

"You *implied* it."

"What the hell's the matter with you, Nicole?"

Leszek broke in to avoid disaster. "I am arguing with Harmon, Madame, how research on a non-deleting neurotrop is far from new. It is that nobody considered it…hmm…"

"Important," said Harm.

"How do you know that?" Nicole shot back.

"Because it's one thing to have it exist theoretically, another to literally produce such a drug. Not that it hasn't been tried."

"You know this for certain?"

"No question."

Nicole looked up from her laptop. "It leaves me wondering if you really know what you're talking about."

Harm, caught by her sudden, annoying attitude, tried not to let it get to him.

"Scientists, backed by funding from the Pentagon, have been working on such a drug."

"How do you know if that's true?"

"Is personal experience good enough?"

"Try me."

"Our friendly US military snooped around when I was under contract initially to S&T, which also has close ties to the military. I couldn't understand why I seemed so important to them. Where would I fit in? They went so far as to suggest I break the contract with S&T and work exclusively with them. They'd take care of the fallout." He stopped again. "Are you okay with this?"

"I'm listening, aren't I? Go on."

"Nathan Edgars went ballistic when he caught wind of what the military was trying to pull off. But the gutless wonder didn't have the balls to make the indiscretion public. He relied on me not jumping ship, failing to realize the military is the last bunch I'd work with."

"Why?"

"Integrity works both ways, Nicole. I don't trust how the Pentagon operates."

"What's this to do with you and Leszek?"

"We've agreed to poke around. Find out what the military brass was up to while we're together on board. We decided it must have something to do with the rats. I told him about my screwup with the rat experiment. And Leszek suggested it might have something to do with them."

She stared at her screen. "Give me a moment. I'm behind in my notes."

Nicole took the better part of an hour to type into her laptop the full story of the rats and everything else that went with it.

When done, she insisted on backing it up on a flash drive she'd left in her cabin. She went off, taking the laptop with her.

Leszek hobbled around, working the circulation back in his legs.

"I sense the mention of a war drug worries you, Harmon."

"You have only to look at the US federal government, Leszek. It can't stop hash, cocaine, heroin, or opioids from being smuggled into the country. What if the wrong people got their hands on our research? Extolling it as the drug of choice? In one form or—"

Harm knew Nicole should have returned by then. "Wait here. I'll be right back."

Getting no response to his knock on her cabin door, he carried on to the Boat Deck Bar.

He saw her there having a drink with Victor Petrie. Thinking he and Leszek had expected too much from her, and she could use a moment away from them, he returned to his cabin.

He found a note left by Leszek, of two or three words, explaining he had gone to his cabin to rest before dinner.

Harm decided the old man deserved some quiet time alone.

Nicole lifted her glass, distracted enough to jiggle it and make the ice clink against it.

"Harm told me the Pentagon had offered him a research assignment," she said, "only if he broke whatever contract with S&T. They'd handle the fallout."

Victor took his time sipping his beer. "Page makes any situation sound convincing. Even if it didn't happen that way."

Nicole put the drink down, untouched. "Come again?"

"Page is screwing with you, Nicky, admitting he took his S&T research project in a new direction. The truth is, they refused to go along with it. He turned to the brass at the Pentagon next, asking if they were interested. S&T heard about this and terminated his contract, blaming him for taking the project way over budget. They literally tossed him out on his ear."

"And the Pentagon?"

"Not wanting any part of it, they told Harmon Page to bugger off. Rumor has it, he tried the Russians after that. They sent Leszek to America to see if Page had the right stuff. Next thing we know, he's on board the *TSS Casimir III*. Now you're telling me his destination is London /Tilbury. Are you sure about that?"

"I'm positive. He's getting off there, while Thomas is carrying on to Gdynia."

Victor put his half empty glass down on the table. "Let's find out if he was bullshitting you."

Nothing ventured, nothing gained she decided, following Victor out of the bar.

No one was taking advantage of the ship's Computer Room, when Nicole and Victor arrived. Of the many computers, most were idle, except for a few on standby.

"Passengers demand such distractions as this on board," said Victor, sitting down at one of them. "Then promptly forget about it. Or like you, they find it more convenient to rig up their own laptops in their cabins."

Nicole looked around the room. "Which doesn't explain why we're here."

He pushed a key at random to bring the PC back to life.

"It's to prove one way or another where Page will exit the ship." He hit more keys in rapid succession. "For that, we need the *Casimir's* passenger list."

Nicole leaned over Victor's shoulder to look at the screen. "I suppose snooping has its rewards."

Harm was on the move. First stop: to the cubby-hole where the duty steward was arranging folded bed sheets. He had forgotten his key card in his cabin, and could he borrow the master card? The steward slipped the cord from his neck and handed it over.

Harm went directly to Nicole's stateroom, left the door slightly ajar, returned the card, and came back to her cabin.

'Ports of Call' appeared on the screen. Victor punched up LONDON DEST. and scrolled down to the letter P. PAGE wasn't listed among them.

"Maybe he's out of alphabetical order," Nicole said, hoping she was right. "He picked up a last-minute cancellation, missed boarding the *Casimir* in Montréal, and caught it off Québec City."

They had no better luck with Rotterdam, the next port of call, and moved on to Gdynia.

Nicole's pulse quickened as the screen flashed up FARROWS, HAYNES, followed by JANKOWSKA, MAKAR, and ORLOF. After OSTROWSKA came PAGE, Harmon C.

"The sonofabitch," Nicole swore under her breath.

Harm had returned Nicole's laptop to the dresser, when he heard familiar voices coming from the corridor. He started for the bathroom, changed his mind and ducked into the closet.

"Don't come onto me, Vic," came Nicole's frustrated voice as the door opened. "I'm not in the mood."

"I appreciate you're upset being lied to," he heard Victor say. "I should remind you how vital it is that there's no connection between the two us. With no mention of Page's real destination."

"Obviously not. I'll see you for cocktails."

Real destination? Harm peered through the small slit between the two louvered doors. Nicole was alone. His curiosity got the better of him when he noticed she took gum from a dresser drawer and popped several flat pieces into her mouth. She began chewing, much to his delight.

What next? he wondered, when Nicole took a flash drive from the pocket from her jeans and pressed it into the softened gum. He knew it could only be the flash drive used in keeping a spare copy of his conversations with Leszek.

He watched, fascinated, as she slipped a hand behind the dresser, pressing the flash drive there for what he guessed was safekeeping.

Harm smiled to himself. He was learning something new about Nicole Hagen.

She was a woman who would *never go for the obvious*. A Central Intelligence Agency trait, perhaps?

His smile vanished when he noticed her rounding the bed and heading his way. He eased himself behind the hanging clothes, hoping she wouldn't open both sections at once.

One opened. A bare arm appeared. The hand flipped along the line of clothes on hangers before stopping at a green strapless dress close to his face. It disappeared off the hanger. He listened to her footsteps pad back across the cabin and heard the bathroom door close, the shower turned on.

It was time, he told himself, to set things straight.

With this accomplished not long after, he returned to his cabin, stretched out on the bed, relaxed, and closed his eyes.

CHAPTER THIRTY-THREE
Thursday, October 13, 7:55 PM

The main course dishes were being cleared away when Harm, having dozed off, arrived late for second sitting. Thomas intercepted him well before he reached his table.

"Leszek's missing," he said, steering him back into the foyer. "Nicole's on the warpath."

They saw her coming from the Polish Bar and straight for them.

"What did you do with him?" she snapped at Harm.

"Leszek?"

"Who else? You were with him last."

"He left my cabin to snooze before dinner. Anything else?"

"I'll think of something," she said, turning toward the elevator.

"How 'lost' can you be," Thomas muttered, "when you're on board a ship?"

They split up, with Thomas heading for the Boat Deck Bar and Harm dropping by Leszek's cabin. They agreed to meet in the ship's hospital.

The poker-faced nurse studied Harm from behind the Sick Bay reception desk. He had asked if Doctor Poplawski was here. She told him she wasn't at liberty to say.

Harm dug deep to be pleasant. "Then I'll speak to Doctor Witka."

"Our *junior* surgeon is at dinner."

Harm glanced at her name tag. "Who's in charge besides you, Nurse Szyller?" he asked, when Thomas appeared.

She eyed them both and set off down the corridor, her white nursing shoes squeaking on the shiny linoleum tile.

"Leszek is here," said Harm, "but Nurse 'Frosty' won't admit it."

The senior surgeon arrived, in a lab coat over his white uniform, along with the nurse.

"Nurse Szyller tells me you asked about Leszek Poplawski. To clear up any misunderstanding, he is with us. He is in stable condition and resting comfortably."

"Comfortably from what?" Harm asked.

"I can only say we are presently running tests—"

"Why?" said Thomas.

"If you'd let me finish. He was found comatose on the floor of his cabin. It is my opinion he suffered heart failure. If not a full-blown heart attack. We are disadvantaged, of course, at having no access to his medical history."

"Which means it was an emergency." Harm said.

"We received the call from his steward. A medical team handled it."

Thomas again. "What time was this?"

"Seventeen hundred hours to seventeen hundred-fifteen. Five to five-fifteen."

Harm tied it in with Leszek returning to his cabin for a rest.

"We dispatched them at once to his cabin," the nurse said.

"Dispatched how, Nurse Szyller?" Thomas asked.

"We don't divulge medical procedures," the doctor interrupted. "Especially in case of an emergencies. Now if you will excuse us…"

Harm blocked his way. "We'd appreciate seeing him. Now. However brief."

Doctor Dudek, stepping around him, started down the corridor. Nurse Szyller mouthed what both men took for *gotcha* in Polish and followed the surgeon.

"The lying sonofabitch," said Thomas on leaving Sick Bay.

"Lying about what?" Harm asked.

"When there's a medical emergency anywhere on board, it's relayed at once over a ship's communication system."

"The same as in hospitals?"

"The same protocol. Hospitals, in general, use a 'Code Seven', or 'Code Blue' with medical staff sent *STAT* to the location. It's done on the quiet, so not to panic patients or visitors. The actual codes differ aboard ship. The QE 2 used *Starlight* at one time."

"And the *Casimir*?"

"You heard it after we found Kim's body. I went for help. The code, *Jesien Basen,* meaning *Emergency swimming pool,* hit the loudspeaker system throughout the ship."

"You said Doctor Dudek was lying. About what?"

"There was *no* such emergency code sent out for Leszek, Harm. I promise you. Once you're aware of those codes, on land or sea, anywhere, bells will go off in your head."

Harm wasn't convinced. "I'd feel better with a second opinion. From Helena."

Thomas nodded. "Let's find her."

The elevator clanked to a stop a level above them, only to start back down again.

They opted for the neighboring stairs.

Helena Witka was leaving the Dining Room with Chief Engineer Niski, when she noticed Thomas and Harm feigning interest in the display of shipboard photos of passengers. She excused herself and joined them.

"You've heard about Doctor Poplawski?" she said. "I knew nothing until I noticed his name on the admission sheet." She paused. "It seems he suffered a heart attack."

"He was found lying on his cabin floor," said Harm. "Thomas insists there was no emergency code sent out at the time."

"The code would have been the first response, no question." She touched Harm's arm and disappeared into the dining room. She returned moments later, her lips pinched together.

"I reached the ship's Communications system," she said. "There was no such call recorded there, which means there was no code sent out. I'll report it at once—"

Harm asked her to leave it. For now. Thomas agreed.

Helena decided to trust their judgment.

Nicole's search for Leszek sidelined, when she detoured by her cabin to find an email from Gerry Smith.

Our Moscow contact is hoping soon to put a name Tobias might use while on board.

We are working on photo ID. Keep Poplawski under tight surveillance.

Nicole replied: *Affirmative. Be aware the passenger list shows Harmon C. Page disembarking at Gdynia. NOT London/Tilbury. The lying bastard is surely Russia-bound.*

He's full of surprises. Bring Victor Petrie on side should the situation worsen.

There was a knock at the door.

"Hold on," she called out, typing: *Later.*

Nicole expected Victor. She faced instead the somber duo of Page & Slater.

"We've found Leszek," said Thomas.

"In Sick Bay," Harm said, "suffering an apparent heart attack."

Nicole stared at them. "Who confirmed it?"

Harm said, "Doctor Dudek. The chief surgeon."

"How serious?"

"Stable," Thomas replied.

"Doctor Dudek ruled out any chance of us seeing Leszek," Harm added. "Doctor Witka will look in on him, giving us a better idea of what happened."

Nicole bit her lip. "I'll go to him."

"Good luck with that," said Harm.

CHAPTER THIRTY-FOUR
Thursday, October 13, 9:42 PM

Thomas and Hugh were ordering another round in the Boat Deck Bar during the usual group gathered for after-dinner drinks.

"Where, may I ask, is the elusive Mister Page?" asked Gwen.

A somber Nicole nodded toward the exit.

Harm appeared in the doorway, arguing with a disheveled Angus Stockwell.

"Jolly good," Gwen said, "persuading the poor man to join us. No mean task, I'm sure."

The two came toward them, Angus, unshaven, shirt wrinkled, and his eyes ringed with dark circles. He sat down next to Gwen, while the other two men handed out the drinks.

"Harm dragged me here," he said shyly, "by the scruff of the neck." His casual aside gave the others a moment to relax.

"Best thing for you, my lad," said Hugh. "A drink, perhaps?"

Angus worked on a smile. "A soda, maybe. Canada Dry."

Harm settled for a cognac.

Gwen asked if it were true that Leszek had suffered a heart attack.

"It seems so," said Harm. "The ship's senior surgeon told us he's in stable condition, yet he insists on no visitors."

Harm, wondering if Nicole had had any better luck, glanced in her direction. She turned her head away.

"If indeed he is stable," Hugh argued, "our old friend could use a visitor or two."

"It's good having you all here for me," Angus said.

Gweneth suggested someone arrange to have a card table and four chairs in a corner of the bar. Hugh and Victor volunteered.

Ivan Jurek of the night kitchen staff paced the foyer outside the Grand Lounge. This area of the ship was totally foreign to him. He had come wearing clean jeans and a white shirt. Now, knowing there was no turning back, the young seaman stepped inside.

He glanced past the crowded dance floor toward the bandstand, his eyes all but popping out of his head. There was Janusz, assistant to the assistant fry chef, on drums.

Keeping well clear of the officers' table, Ivan worked around the bandstand as the set ended and the dance floor emptied.

"Hey, Jurek," whispered Janusz, "what you doin' here?"

"I could ask you the same thing," Ivan whispered. "Do you know what the entertainment officer looks like?"

"*Looks* like? Sure. We're a team. He's off somewhere." Janusz did a little drum roll. "What d'you want with him anyways?"

"An... uh, audition."

"Cool. For what?"

"Singer. Will he be long?"

"No." The drummer leaned sideways across his snare drum. "Can you really sing, kid?"

"Like a bird," said the sober night kitchen staffer.

Filip Sotek, returning from Sick Bay, found a cautious pair of eyes watching him as he reached the bandstand.

"Are you lost, son?" he asked the young man in Polish.

"Are you…Officer Sotek?"

"Yes. How can I help you?"

"How…is Officer Olecki?"

"He's on the mend. Do you know him?"

Ivan said nothing.

"And your name?"

"Ivan… Jurek, sir. Night kitchen staff."

Aware the young seaman seemed overcome by his surroundings, Filip guided him to a quiet spot behind the sound equipment. He asked if he knew what happened to Officer Olecki.

The young kitchen staffer nodded. "I saw them…beating him…"

"*Beating* Officer Olecki?" said Filip, the quiet words catching him off-guard. "Who did it?"

"They were seamen outside the kitchen, where I throw garbage overboard."

"Would you recognize them?"

Ivan stared down at his dirty runners. "No, sir. But one wore a uniform."

Filip, not wanting to scare him off, offered him a beer.

Ivan blushed. "A *Zywiec*. Please," he said.

* * * *

Angus apologized when he folded after one hand of poker. Nor did he object when Thomas, ready for an early night himself, suggested he walk him to his cabin.

Nicole left without saying good night to anyone. Harm, noticing she didn't seem herself, caught up to her in the hallway. He asked if she remembered the lifeboat, sharing the bottle of champagne, a sky full of stars…

She walked on, saying nothing.

He tagged along. "What's bugging you?"

"Nothing."

"You're annoyed. Why? Because Doctor Dudek wouldn't let you visit Leszek?"

Nicole reached her stateroom, slipped in the key card, opened the door, and went inside. He heard the lock snap into place.

Harm wandered back to his cabin, wondering why when a woman says 'nothing' it means she's pissed off at something.

The Entertainment Officer rested his elbows on the arms of a Grand Lounge chair. Seated beside him was young Ivan, drinking the beer from the bottle. Filip knew the question he was about to ask might well end the conversation. He took that chance.

"Was it you, Ivan, who carried Officer Olecki up to the Promenade Deck and left him there?"

Ivan picked at the bottle's label with his bitten fingernails. "Yes… sir. I waited… not far off …for someone to find him. Should I admit bringing him there… I'd be accused of beating him."

Filip's heart went out to this young man. "I wouldn't have let that happen."

"Strange things go on, sir, when you're the night kitchen staff." Ivan went silent, then added, "Officer Olecki was stinking too. I had to scrub my clothes afterwards."

"You were in the kitchen when it happened?"

"I had stepped out to deal with the garbage."

"What did the officer look like?"

"I couldn't tell. It was dark. He was tall. He left with the others. I almost stepped on Officer Olecki buried in garbage."

Filip saw the haunted eyes, the fingers probing the bottle with no label left to pick off.

Ivan brightened. "I met Officer Olecki first when he dropped by to check if the garbage was thrown overboard. He came back inside, shook my hand, and sat on a counter. We talked while I scrubbed the floors. It was like we were friends. He drops by every now and then. I came here to find out how he was doing."

Filip was touched by the young man's honesty. "He's recovering, Ivan. It will take time."

"I don't know what they did to him, or why, sir. I only know whatever it was…"

Ivan's voice trailed off.

Filip said, "Would you come back here tomorrow night? You might notice…"

Ivan stiffened, sending a silent message Filip understood.

"Then again, son, you've done enough for us already."

Ivan looked down at his hands. "If Janusz, the drummer, asks about me," he said, finishing his beer. "Will you tell him my audition with you didn't go so well?"

Filip assured him it would be no problem.

Ivan stood up, his face reflecting the wonder of the bright lights, of the band playing, of the dressed-up, dancing couples.

Filip watched him walk off, aware it took an act of raw courage for young Ivan Jurek to come up here, despite being the sole night staffer in the ship's kitchen.

CHAPTER THIRTY-FIVE
Friday, October 14, 7:10 AM

"...and at the farewell dinner and dance this evening," came the daily announcements over the vessel's loudspeakers, "formal apparel would be appreciated. Clocks will *not* be set back. The time is ten minutes past seven. Thank you."

Harm Page stretched and climbed out of bed. "You're welcome," he said, ready for his morning shave and shower.

He had gone to sleep after Nicole had stormed down the corridor and into her cabin. He had wakened moments ago, still wondering what he'd done to upset her.

He appeared in Sick Bay shortly before eight o'clock to find Helena alone in her office.

"At least you brighten my day," she said. "When I suggested to Doctor Dudek that I check on Leszek, he turned me down. Add to this, young Officer Olecki is buried in a trauma so deep, it's frightening."

She came out from behind her desk in her light blue scrubs. "I had considered sending him ashore on the tender that drops off the pilot."

"What changed your mind?"

"Keeping him in familiar surroundings is better than sending him away." A smile replaced the frown. "Fresh coffee? I have it brewing in the next room."

"Please. Milk only."

Left on his own, Harm took in the framed medical degrees on the wall from both Krakow's Jagiellonian University and the Royal College of Surgeons. He was impressed and curious why, with such high credentials, she'd be a junior surgeon on a transatlantic liner.

Helena returned with two steaming coffees in Styrofoam cups.

Harm pointed to the Royal College parchment. "How long were you in London?" he asked, taking the proffered coffee.

"Six years. Post graduate," she said, sitting on edge of the desk.

"Yet here you are, a junior surgeon aboard a ship bound for the scrapyard."

Helena sipped her coffee. "It must sound strange. I moved to London to specialize in internal medicine. And learn English. After that, I wanted a year doing nothing more than getting away from it all."

"And here you are. Aboard the *Casimir III*."

She smiled. "Yes, here I am. I took the job sight unseen, only to discover it presents a whole new set of complications. Like Mrs. Stockwell's untimely death, or Ludwik Dudek's refusal to let me examine Doctor Poplawski. When I'm a specialist in internal medicine."

"Your senior surgeon is hiding something, Helena. Why would he lie about how Leszek ended up in Sick Bay?"

"I'm more concerned about his apparent heart attack. My every attempt to see him has been blocked. I'm not giving up."

"Watch what you get yourself into," Harm said, not wanting to spoil her day.

With Angus Stockwell's lack of appearance at breakfast and the Ashcrofts having come and gone, Harm sat alone finishing off a plate of sausages and eggs. Suddenly, he noticed Nicole joining Peter Lount, who was eating by himself.

Harm hoped she'd look his way. When she didn't, he shrugged and left the dining room.

Shortly after 800 hours, the Officer of the Watch sighted the lighthouse perched on a spit not much larger than the structure itself.

"Bishop's Rock," he called out, his voice rising above the dead calm of the bridge. "Six degrees' longitude, fifty degrees' latitude."

The captain knew he could've easily dozed off, had the announcement not aroused him.

"Much obliged, Mister Polanski."

The location put the *TSS Casimir III* close to the Scilly Isles off the southwest coast of England. The lighthouse also showed up on the electronic equipment, though Officer Polanski knew the skipper insisted visual clarification still had its place in modern-day navigation.

A second officer cradled a phone. "A message from the purser's office, sir. Passenger Harmon Page wants a word with you."

Stanislaw stretched and straightened his black tie. "Show him directly to my quarters."

Chief Purser Marzel tapped his fingers on the counter and smiled benevolently.

"You are indeed more than fortunate, Mister Page. Seldom does the ship's master interrupt his morning schedule to accommodate the wishes of a passenger." He called to a member of his staff, "Mister Bibrych, I have a job for you."

Harm and the young officer had barely left the purser's office, when Victor wandered by. He waved Rysard Marzel over to the counter.

"Tell me, Mister Marzel, where is Harmon Page off to now?"

"He wished to talk with the captain, Mister…"

"Petrie. He's obviously forgotten we were having coffee in the lounge. Have you any idea why he'd speak to the captain?"

"I can only imagine it is of great importance, Mister Petrie."

"Maybe he has more complaints," Victor replied, with a wink.

The chief purser leaned forward, his voice low. "You must've heard how he behaved the first night on board. And me, only extending our gratitude for helping the young woman—"

"It takes all kinds," Victor said, walking away.

Harm and Officer Bibrych were waiting outside the Captain's Quarters, when Stanislaw Jablonski came along. He shook his guest's hand and guided him inside.

"The chief purser tells me you have something on your mind, Mister Page. As one favor deserves another, how may I help?"

"It's Doctor Poplawski," said Harm, using the same direct approach, "and his apparent heart attack. We're worried about him."

"As we all are," the captain replied. "Let me relieve any doubts. I have it on good authority that Leszek Poplawski has greatly improved over the past twelve hours."

"The authority being Doctor Dudek."

"My senior surgeon, yes."

"I'd appreciate a second opinion."

Stanislaw's eyebrows went up. "A second opinion would have to come from my *junior* surgeon."

"You have only to appreciate Doctor Witka's qualifications."

"I am quite aware of it," the captain replied, with a hint of frustration. "I brought her aboard. Besides, such a request would put my chief surgeon in an untenable position. A junior officer questioning her superior's decision…"

"I am merely asking for her *opinion*," said Harm. "If it's not possible, what about having Doctor Poplawski transferred to the Folkestone pilot tender? From what I understand, it's coming out soon to drop off the pilot to guide the *Casimir* up the Thames."

"Helping a healthy young woman off the ship at Quebec City is child's play, Mister Page. Maneuvering a sick old man down to a bobbing tender in open water is quite another. Especially when approaching the English Channel, an unpredictable, challenging stretch of water. If there is nothing more—"

"Another matter," said Harm. "If Leszek Poplawski's condition has so greatly improved, why are we kept away from visiting him? If for no other reason than giving him moral support."

"Leave it with me. Now if you don't mind—"

"And while you're at it, Captain, could you explain why no emergency code was given when Doctor Poplawski was found lying helpless on his cabin floor?"

The unexpected remark brought the captain up short. "I assure you," he said, put off by Page's quiet persistence, "there is a logical explanation."

"I can't wait to hear it."

Stanislaw drew in a deep breath. "You, Mister Page, have the annoying habit of getting under one's skin."

Harm broke into a smile. "I have to admit, Captain Jablonski, it's not one of my endearing qualities."

The self-deprecating remark caught the captain unprepared.

"Then again, I recognize in you someone not acting out of impartiality or mischief. I will find out why our patient is not allowed visitors. And why, if you are correct, no emergency call was given at the time."

Stanislaw walked Harm out into the corridor, where Officer Bibrych was waiting.

"Should I slip up, giving your name to any officer will be sufficient."

Harm and the young officer started off when the captain called after them.

"It might amuse you, Mister Page, that a member of my crew found an empty bottle of *Moët & Chandon* in Lifeboat Twelve. I trust the evening had its own reward."

Harm acknowledged it by a friendly wave over his shoulder.

Stanislaw returned to sit at his desk, reflecting on the latest turn of events before calling his senior physician. He asked for an update on Leszek Poplawski. And if so, was it necessary, or even wise, to keep the old man from having visitors?

"To be blunt, captain," the surgeon's voice echoed over the line, "by *visitors,* you're referring to passengers Page and Slater. I have done so, because they've been nothing more than a persistent irritant to us in Sick Bay."

"How so, Doctor Dudek?"

"By pestered my nursing staff to the point of rudeness. Demanding to know the patient's condition, what tests he has undergone. They also insist on visiting him."

"It also seems no emergency code alerted the medical staff to the patient's sudden illness."

"As it happened, our medical team was carrying out a routine drill not far from Doctor Poplawski's cabin on C Deck. They were summoned at once by his on-duty steward. The team assessed the situation and brought him directly to Sick Bay."

"And if I ask for a second opinion from Doctor Witka about his condition?"

"She knows nothing of my patient, Captain, nor did she express the slightest interest in his progress. I make decisions, not by relying on someone I have yet to give my full confidence."

Stanislaw bristled at this off-handed remark. Helena Witka was someone he considered every bit as competent as her senior counterpart, if not more so.

"Medically speaking, Doctor, would there be a complication should the patient be taken ashore on board the tender at Folkestone later this afternoon and removed to a hospital there?"

"Complication?" Doctor Dudek's voice rattled in his ear. "It would assuredly *kill* him. Besides, jurisdiction over such matters is my responsibility. I would not only strenuously object, I would not permit it."

"You're forgetting, Doctor, this is *my* ship—"

A loud *click* came over the line.

Stanislaw slammed down the phone, annoyed that his senior surgeon had hung up on him.

Feeling relaxed in jeans and a sky-blue turtleneck, Nicole had made herself comfortable in the ship's library, when Victor dropped into the chair beside her.

"I've been looking all over for you."

Nicole kept reading her magazine. "Then you should've looked here first."

"Your humor is misplaced."

Nicole glanced up. "What's got you so riled up that you're taking it out on me?"

Victor leaned forward in the chair. "Page is with Captain Jablonski. I want to know why."

"I'm more concerned about Leszek. The poor old dear has been isolated in Sick Bay. And we can't even visit him. If there's something else—"

Victor softened. "I need a favor, Nicky. The Pentagon wants a transcript of your notes made with Page and Poplawski."

"No problem. Submit a formal request to Langley—"

"It's me, remember? I only want a copy of what Langley didn't expect in the first place."

Nicole tossed the magazine aside and stood up. "Then we negotiate."

"We don't negotiate."

"Come," she said, "to my cabin."

Victor snapped off a grin. "I thought you'd never ask."

Nicole stood with the laptop open on the dresser, Victor beside her.

"I'll show you what we have," she said, moving the cursor down the list of documents, "so you'll know what you're missing." She selected one, double clicking it. "Expect nothing until I clear it with Langley."

Victor leaned in close. "The screen's blank."

"A glitch." Nicole tried again. She clicked *doc.backup* with no better results. "There's a flash drive stuck behind this mirror. "Reach in and pull it out."

"The purser's safe," he said, shifting the dresser away from the wall, "is a better place."

"I can't run down there every time I need it." She watched him slip his hand in and feel around. "Besides…"

"There's nothing here."

Nicole pushed him aside and felt around. The flash drive was gone.

"Who's been here?" Victor shook his head. "Surely to God you haven't been screwing around with Page."

Nicole blushed and turned away.

Victor shifted the dresser back against the wall.

"You trusted that lying bastard? He told you about disembarking at London, when he's traveling on to Gdynia."

Nicole held his gaze, knowing there was nothing she could say.

"This stolen flash drive is his handiwork, Nicky, like him marching off with your Walther PPK. It fits the pattern. Page caused enough shit when he worked for S&T. Over-budget, doing things his way..." He watched her cross the room. "Where are you going?"

"To find out why Page met the captain. Isn't that what you wanted?" She opened the door and glanced back. "If all else fails, Vic, Harmon Page is all yours."

Thomas was at the Boat Deck Bar, nursing a draft, when Harm sat down on the stool beside him.

"You're on a beer kick?" said Harm, slipping an envelope along the counter toward him.

"A pleasant change from the hard stuff I've been ingesting." Thomas picked up the envelope folded and wrapped in transparent tape. "What's this in aid of?"

"Something I found stuck in an odd place."

"And what am I to do with it?"

"Keep it safe."

"Will it get me in trouble?"

"It could get you killed."

Thomas grinned. "I like living dangerously. And if anyone asks about it, before they kill me?"

"Tell them you know nothing about it."

"That won't be difficult," said Thomas. "I *know* nothing about it."

"If the worst comes to the worst, you'll know what to do."

Thomas shoved it in one of his baggy cords pocket. "I'll keep that in mind."

Gerry Smith was at his desk, munching on a toasted Danish, when the phone rang. He tongued the sugary topping off his fingers before answering.

"Hi," he said, taking another bite.

"Put down whatever you're stuffing in your mouth," came Ted Grovenor's voice, "and listen up. Have you reached Irwin Rasky?"

"Yes and no. His sexy, bodacious female assistant tells me he's done sweet dick-all about the *Casimir III*. It might've been prudent, she told me, had you not beaten the piss out of the secretary of state at golf the other morning. Her words not mine, 'Specially on the back nine."

"The miserable little prick deserved to lose."

"By *that* wide a score? Where are you?"

"Stuck in Finance. I'm having trouble convincing them that you're not stashing your excessive travel expenses in an off-shore account. Do me a favor. Book me an overnight flight to London's Heathrow. First Class, Where the seats morph into beds."

"Not through the usual government travel protocol?"

"It's a lousy time to pinch pennies, Gerry. Besides, it would take them too long to set it up. I'm leaving tonight. Have a decent vehicle waiting at the other end. Not one of those little English puddle jumpers. I'll drive myself."

"Drive yourself where?"

"To Tilbury. I'll arrive there early tomorrow morning, *English* time. Hopefully before the *Casimir* docks. By the way, I'll need a handgun."

"The Brits dislike parting with their weaponry, boss. Besides, you'll have to file a zillion release forms that'll tie you up for days."

"Who knows better than you how to get around the goddam system? Make sure it's left in the vehicle's glove compartment. And remind them I'm partial to a nine-millimeter Smith & Wesson."

"Model 39, eight-shot clip." Gerry punched AIRINFO into his computer. "You'd be amazed how popular updated S & W models are these days."

"Get on with it."

Gerry bit off another chunk of the bun. "I am, already."

Nicole called the purser's office, giving her name and asking to speak to the captain. She was transferred to the bridge to be told he would contact her as soon as possible.

Stanislaw reached her within minutes. She asked if there would be a problem meeting with him privately. He promised to dispatch an officer to her stateroom at once.

He was working at his desk, when she arrived. His freshly starched white uniform made her feel woefully under-dressed in her muted tartan skirt and V-neck sweater.

"This is indeed an honor, Ms. Hagen," he said, holding her hand too long before letting go. "However, I find it difficult to persuade myself this is purely a social visit. Which means it invariably involves our mutual friend Doctor Poplawski."

Nicole's cheeks reddened at his frankness. "We worry about him, Captain. Mister Page reached you earlier, upset, I can only imagine, at how the senior surgeon ruled out visitations."

"I assured Mister Page that your old friend is well looked after. He is in stable condition. How I promised to keep him posted of any change. I extend the same courtesy to you."

Stanislaw offered her a drink, uncertain what game Ms. Hagen was up to. He decided to play it by ear.

Victor moved aside, making room for Nicole to take a sweater from the top drawer.

"You drank from the captain's private stock discussing what? The fucking weather?"

"You wanted to know more about his meeting with Page. He told me how worried he was about Leszek, as we all are, and assured me the patient was in stable condition."

"That's what they tell you when a patient is half dead. No unofficial chatter?"

Nicole tossed the sweater on the bed. "*None.* Take it or leave it."

"You're way out of your depth, honey. Which begs the question: what did Grosvenor get in return for adding you to his team?"

Nicole's fist came out of nowhere. It caught Victor on the jaw, snapping his head back as spittle flew from his open mouth.

"Asshole," she murmured, watching him wipe his dampened cheeks with the back of his hand.

Victor took a moment to collect himself. "Never try that again, Nicky."

"Then don't tempt me," she said, watching him disappear out the door.

Nicole rubbed her knuckles, surprised she had instinctively tucked the thumb away before hitting him. Something she had been taught at The Farm some years ago.

At four in the afternoon, the tender from Folkestone appeared out of a fog. Harm and Helena were on the Boat Deck as it pulled alongside.

"If only I can find proof that Leszek Poplawski suffered a heart attack or stroke," she said, "or, quite possibly, neither."

Harm pulled his eyes away from the pilot scrambling up the rope ladder.

"Why would you say that?"

"I was making a daily update of our meds when something struck me as odd. All our bags of intravenous were accounted for. Nor were any of the IV poles in use."

"You're telling me had Leszek suffered a heart attack or stroke, he would've been hooked up to an IV the moment he reached Sick Bay. If not sooner."

"Exactly. I'm worried about him, Harm. I need to see him, to prove to myself what's going on is genuine."

"How long do you need?"

"Five minutes."

They watched in silence as the tender pulled away to disappear between the swells.

"When is Dudek on call next?" Harm asked.

"Tonight, from six o'clock. A twelve-hour shift."

"Any social events scheduled for the captain?"

"This evening? Nothing, other than a private reception for the Polish ambassador between first and second sittings. He's returning from duty in South America. He's a pompous, demanding old pro, who complains to us incessantly about being seasick. As if it were *our* fault."

"Where's the reception?"

"The same place as yours: the captain's quarters."

"Are the usual suspects invited?"

"Senior officers and whoever the ambassador adds to the guest list."

"And Dudek?"

"He'll be there. It means free booze."

"Despite him being on call."

"I take his place the odd time, when he's had too many scotch-on-the-rocks."

"You'll be there?"

"*Me*? Captain Jablonski likes to show he's liberated enough to have a female doc on board. Albeit in a junior role." She squeezed his hand. "I have to go."

"We'll get you your five minutes, Helena."

She glanced back from the foyer entrance. "How will you arrange that, Harmon Page?"

"I have friends in high places."

"High enough?" she asked, disappearing inside.

Harm grinned at her reply as he looked down at the water below. It had turned from the deep blue of the crossing to the gloomy, greenish-brown of the English Channel.

It left him wondering what chance he had delivering those precious five minutes Helena deserved. What she'd learn from it, Harm knew well enough, could mean the difference between life and death for his old friend.

Harm cheered up on finding Thomas and Hugh in a corner of the Boat Deck Bar. They were drinking and munching from a bowl of peanuts.

Harm picked up a Kronenbourg from Feliks and joined them.

"Good timing, my boy," said Hugh. "I've been asking Thomas if he'd heard of some cock-up going on aboard."

"*Cock-up*?" Harm replied. "As in *screw-up*? Not that I know. Other than we've been trying to visit Leszek in Sick Bay with no success."

Thomas took a handful of peanuts and began shelling them. "Even Doctor Witka has had no luck."

Hugh did the same to the peanuts in his hand. "Which begs the question, lads: do either of you see a connection between Mrs. Stockwell's death and Doctor Poplawski's apparent illness?"

"There he goes," said Thomas, "asking questions and wanting to know more about *you*, Harm. All the while having his wife believe those binoculars are for birdwatching."

Harm took a drink from the bottle. "There's too much for the British to sit idly by while the Yanks and who knows, the Russians, are mixing it up."

"And who'd look innocent enough to watch the action than a Brit bird fancier."

"He's right in the thick of it, Thomas. British Intelligence. MI5, disguised as a tourist…?"

"You're barking up the wrong tree, chums," said Hugh. "It happens to be the Foreign Service. MI6."

Harm grinned, "Nicole must've been on to you all along."

"She has no idea who I am, other than a stuffy, doddering, old Englishman."

"What better persona to hide behind?" said Thomas.

Hugh picked up his scotch. "Retired. Does that satisfy your insatiable curiosities?"

"Retired yet back on MI6 payroll, I'll bet," said Harm. "'Fess up, Hugh, or we'll take Gwen aside…"

Hugh eyed them over the rim of his glass. "Gweneth and I were in New York, when my old contacts tracked me down. There were whispers both the Russians and Americans were concerned for the safety of an old scientist sailing out of Montréal."

Hugh reached for more peanuts. "They asked if I would trade in our British Airways flight for a sea voyage home. To keep an eye on whatever developed."

"And the rest of it, Agent Ashcroft?" Thomas said.

"Of equal interest, chaps, was a connection between the US government and the illicit transfer of classified material to a foreign power. I was to pay close attention to you, Harmon C. Page. No reason given. I was to identify Agent Nicole Hagen, not letting her know of my connection. I recognized her early on, in the departure area before we sailed."

"Did MI6 link the classified material to me?"

"If there was any inference to you, lad, I can't say. The briefing lacked detail. I was left with the impression that I was to observe and do nothing more."

Thomas said, "Harm's been targeted *twice* by a hitman, Hugh. Once along the New England coast, and again on board."

"I'm terribly sorry," said Hugh, visibly troubled. "I can only help, if you lads fill me in on every detail, including how you plan having Doctor Witka free to examine our old friend."

"Thomas and I have tossed several possibilities around. We'll pick which works best and let you know."

Thomas glanced at Harm. *Pick which works best?*

It was news to him.

CHAPTER THIRTY-SIX
Friday, October 14, 7:14 PM

Doctor Helena Witka slipped away from the ambassador's reception unnoticed. She bumped into Harm, Thomas, and Hugh in a corner of the crowded Boat Deck Bar. She refused a drink, saying she had to return before the captain discovered her missing.

"Doctor Dudek is there now," she told them.

"Who's left in Sick Bay?" Harm asked.

"Nurse Szyller." Helena fixed the three men with her soft brown eyes. "Whatever your plan, it must be foolproof. The captain will surely cut the reception short, as he often does."

"Whatever happens, Helena," said Harm, "it's vital that Doctor Dudek handles what will be an emergency, here, in the Bar. You'll also have to deal with Nurse Szyller in Sick Bay."

She gave them one last glance, and hurried off.

"Whatever *we've* dreamed up," Thomas said to Harm, "it better be good. And soon."

"You best tell me how this works," said Hugh.

"Shy of having a Trojan horse to fall back on," Harm said, "we're about to create a diversion. I'll trip over a chair. Hit my head on the corner of the bar. Out cold. Thomas, you set up a *Jesien Boat Deck Bar* through the speaker system."

"With what intended result?" Hugh asked.

"Doctor Dudek is on call. He'll come down from the captain's reception to cover *my* emergency. This frees Helena up to examine Leszek."

"That's poppycock, my dear boy," said Hugh. "The chief surgeon will check your pulse, your heart rate. He will shine a light in your eyes to see if your pupils are dilated. He'll know at once you're *faking it*, as they say."

"Have we a Plan B?" Thomas asked Harm. "It must be—"

"To make it *work*, gentlemen," Hugh cut in, "Harmon must execute something truly convincing. A heart attack would about cover it."

"If you think I'd know how to…" Harm's eyes narrowed. "No way in hell, Hugh."

"Look here, lads, everyone expects old fogies like me to keel over at any given moment. My wife notwithstanding." He thrust his empty glass at Thomas. "Time's up," he announced and marched off.

Harm thought it insane.

Thomas thought it brilliant.

Peter Lount was describing the doomed Titanic's last dinner in First Class to Gwen, when Hugh appeared at her elbow. He frowned at her empty glass.

"Let me freshen your drink, my dear," he said, reproaching Peter with a raised eyebrow.

"A refill, yes," Peter stammered, embarrassed at the oversight.

"Good thinking. A gin and tonic for Madame, scotch for me. No ghastly ice."

"How deplorable of you, Hugh," Gwen said as Peter hurried off. "He was kind enough to bring me a drink at all."

"When I've been supplying that scallywag with enough booze to sink a lifeboat?" Hugh dropped his voice. "Don't be alarmed, dearest, but I must initiate a slight shortness of breath."

Gwen glanced at him sideways "Have you gone completely bonkers?"

He coughed into his open hand. "For reasons which must remain unexplained...I intend bluffing, as it were, a heart attack."

Gwen sucked in her breath. "I should've twigged to you and Sir Oliver back in New York, sensing that you old dinosaurs were up to no good."

"My dear—"

"Tell me you're back on MI6 payroll, Ashcroft," she said, leaning in close, "and you'll have reason enough to be short of breath."

"Gwen, darling—"

"Don't *Gwen darling* me," she snapped as Hugh grabbed his chest and sank to his knees.

Doctor Ludwik Dudek, looking presentable in a black, double-breasted tuxedo, was in a lively discussion with the Polish ambassador's robust wife. It was about David Hume's *Inquiry Concerning the Principles of Morals*.

"I must correct your assumption, Madame, that Hume gave little thought to this same treatise. He considered *Morals* one of his best works and..."

His voice trailed off on hearing a low-pitched *Jesien Boat Deck Bar* coming from the quarter's loudspeaker. The doctor glanced around the room, to discover Helena not far away.

"A medical emergency, Doctor Witka," he said, brushing her off with the wave of his hand. "You handle it."

"Must I remind you, Doctor, you are the one on call. Your medical bag is by the door, not mine."

It delighted her to see a pained expression cross Ludwik's podgy face. "I'll return to Sick Bay and send Nurse Szyller up with whatever you need."

The senior surgeon nodded a mute apology to the ambassador's wife and headed off, followed by his bemused junior surgeon.

Hugh sat on a straight-backed chair, the black bow tie hanging loose about his neck, the pleated dress shirt unbuttoned to the waist. A stone-faced Gwen stood beside him.

Gathered around were patrons of the Boat Deck Bar, their attention focused on the chief surgeon. He was probing the mass of curly gray hair on the Englishman's chest with his stethoscope.

"Again," mumbled Ludwik Dudek.

Hugh drew in a deep breath and exhaled, shivering at the coolness of the stethoscope's flattened metal plate on his skin.

Dangling the scope round his neck, the doctor examined the base of Hugh's finger nails. To confirm, or not, a lack of oxygen in the patient's circulatory system. There was no such telltale bluish tinge to worry about.

"Any discomfort?" the surgeon asked, playing to his audience.

"No, Doctor. Not being able to catch my breath brought on a momentary panic. Fortunately, it has passed."

"Perhaps so. However, you will be removed from here to the ship's infirmary until you are stabilized, Mister..."

"Hugh C. Ashcroft," said Gwen, aware of a nurse arriving with a portable oxygen tank.

"To be on the safe side," the surgeon went on, "we will run a few tests. Extensive blood work…"

Nurse Szyller placed a brownish capsule in the doctor's upturned palm.

"Open your mouth, Mister Ashcroft. Wider." He slipped the capsule under Hugh's tongue. "I am giving you nitroglycerine. A vasodilator to improve your circulation."

Hugh tried to spit it out, but Gwen gave him a short, sharp poke in the ribs.

"My circulation," Hugh protested, "does not warrant a—" The words caught in his throat as he saw a steward pushing a wheelchair through the crowd toward them. When he tried to stand in protest, Gwen pinned him to the chair with both hands.

"Serves you right, you old fart," she said, bending down to whisper in his ear. "Besides, I've seen a better performance from the South Devon Ladies' Auxiliary Dramatic Club."

The ship's dining room was alive with clinking glasses and popping champagne corks for this, the farewell dinner. Servers bustled between the tables in their black trousers, short, white formal jackets and black bow ties, their oval metal trays held aloft.

Over the hubbub came the strains of the classical quartet playing the first movement from a Mozart symphony.

With Angus Stockwell insisting to eat alone in his cabin and Hugh hospitalized, Gwen invited Nicole, Thomas, and Peter to join Harm and herself.

Nicole, in a figure-hugging white dress with a high front and low back, showed her displeasure by ignoring Harm with an aloofness no one missed.

"We must make the best of it," Gwen said, looking younger in her new red dress from the ship's clothing shop. "It being our final evening together."

Thomas caught Harm's attention, nodding toward the captain's table. Helena was whispering to the captain and setting off toward the main doors. Harm excused himself and headed in the same direction. He found her waiting in the foyer.

I was hoping you'd see me leave," she said, easing Harm away from the entrance. "Mister Ashcroft fooled Doctor Dudek completely. It gave me enough time to examine your old friend. First, I found nothing to show Leszek suffered a heart attack or a stroke."

"Thank God for that," said Harm. "And second?"

"There are signs that disturbs me. I believe he's been injected with curare."

Harm gave a soft whistle. "*Curare?*"

"It brings on muscular paralysis that someone, especially of Doctor Poplawski's age, might not tolerate. Its latent effects on him are identical. Heavy eyelids, weak jaw and constricted throat muscles, to name a few."

"You've obviously had experience with the drug."

"Yes. I was part of a team operating at the Royal Hospital in London. It was used very sparingly under strict conditions to sedate patients with extreme heart failure. The operating room had been equipped with a special ventilator system, a tracheal intubation equipment."

"How is Leszek?"

"Conscious, but the poor old dear is unable to raise his head, arms, or legs. Or even move any part of his body. He stares at seemingly nothing. Too high a dosage could kill him, Harm. Curare is no longer commercially available, yet this batch came from somewhere."

"I can only imagine your senior surgeon brought it aboard."

"Why would he take such an appalling risk," she relied, "to keep Leszek isolated, immobile? A patient can overdose no matter how careful curare is handled."

"Surely Dudek would have an antidote."

"It's for me to find it," said Helena. "At Doctor Poplawski's advanced age, it could easily damage his respiratory system. Even cause cardiac arrest. Still, I've no proof it's curare."

Harm took both her hands in his, "Despite second-guessing yourself, you wouldn't have told me, or anyone, unless you were certain."

The young doctor blushed and glanced toward the dining room. She gave him an unexpected hug. "That makes me feel better."

Harm waited until she had disappeared inside the dining room before heading down the nearby stairs.

* * * *

Nurse Szyller, perched on a stool at the Sick Bay Reception desk, was filing her nails when she realized Harm Page was in the doorway.

"Hi," he said pleasantly. "I'm here to see Hugh Ashcroft."

She returned to her nails. "No visitors."

"I'm his attorney," he said, continuing down the corridor. "If I find any Sick Bay irregularities, you will be first on my list to get nailed."

"*Pokoju osiem*," her voice echoed after him. "Room Eight. You have two minutes before I cause you considerable trouble."

Hugh, wrapped in a hospital gown, was eating sparingly from a tray on a wheeled trolley. The plastic oxygen nasal prongs lay untouched beside him on the pillow.

"Top of the morning, Agent Ashcroft," Harm said, glancing at the wheelchair.

"It's evening," Hugh corrected him. "And don't tell me how much you're enjoying the food in the dining room. Everything here is boiled, mashed or stewed beyond recognition."

"You volunteered, thank you very much." Harm leaned on the iron frame at the end of the bed.

"Doctor Witka was pleased how you conned the chief surgeon. Ever considered acting as a second career?"

"That is *not* how my wife saw it," the Englishman snorted. "Of more importance, tell me Doctor Witka had time enough to examine Leszek."

"Yes, and found no sign of a heart attack or stroke. Except her diagnosis targets Leszek as having been injected with curare."

"*Curare*? Good Lord, someone is playing with fire."

"The likely suspect is Doctor Dudek."

Hugh poked at his food. "Has our young doctor friend any idea why?"

"She thinks it's to keep Leszek isolated, immobile. Beyond that, she can't do anything until there's proof that curare is the culprit. I trust her judgment."

"She's bright, articulate. Not one to make a rash decision."

Harm knew his two minutes were up. "Got to go. Nurse Szyller is on the warpath."

"Then you'll miss what I've learned from snooping around."

"Snooping?"

"We agents do that, from time to time. Only when that blasted nurse finally found something better to do than plague the life out of me."

"We should've had her shackle you to the bed."

A smile lit up Hugh's face.

"I must say, I enjoy your American sense of humor. As it is, I tiptoed down the corridor after hearing young Olecki was in Sick Bay. I like the lad. He took my wife and I from the departure lineup, when she mistakenly thought I was about to collapse."

"Helena's worried about the young officer."

"He seemed jolly fine to me. Well enough to slip out of bed when he heard commotion from the corridor. He saw our old friend wheeled on a stretcher by Doctor Dudek and two attendants. He told me Leszek was soaked in perspiration and very still, yet with his eyes wide open. Now, you tell me about curare. Very, very worrisome. It seems they left him in the far room on the left." Hugh made a face and put the knife and fork aside.

"Victor Petrie was with them," Hugh went on. "I could only imagine he was there to ensure Leszek was being well looked after."

"If Helena is right about the curare, why would Petrie be involved? Either way, it means we must get Leszek out of Sick Bay."

"Then what?"

"Off the ship."

Hugh pushed his trolley aside, his dinner unfinished. "The likelihood of that is dreaming the impossible, lad."

"We have no choice, Hugh. Any idea where the *Casimir* might be now?"

"My guess, entering the Straits of Dover, or close to it."

Harm turned toward the door. "And from there?"

"We cut across to the Estuary of the Thames."

"How long before that?"

"From four to eight hours, depending on weather conditions, prevailing winds." Hugh picked up the oxygen prongs beside him. "Getting Leszek off the ship would be futile."

"What's the alternative?"

"What if Victor Petrie is confining our old friend, merely to protect him from dangers we are unaware of? Where does that leave us?"

"What if Leszek is being injected with curare for other reasons? They're taking one hell of a chance as it is."

Hugh clamped the twin prongs in his nostrils, breathing a continuing stream of oxygen into his lungs. "Go, before that blasted nurse turfs you out."

Harm returned to the dining room, where a small band played for those dancing between courses. Nicole, Victor, Peter, and Gwen had taken advantage of it.

"From your look," said Thomas, sipping wine, "Helena's verdict isn't good."

"There's no evidence Leszek had a heart attack or stroke. The problem is, she believes he's been injected with curare."

"*Curare?*"

"Hugh suggests Victor might've brought Leszek to Sick Bay in the old man's best interest. Except—"

"Except, if Leszek has been drugged with curare, it's too goddam lethal."

"The symptoms are all too familiar to Helena. I trust her judgment. Which means finding some way to get Leszek off the ship, once we reach the Thames." Harm caught the server's eye and asked a favor.

Hugh was drifting off to sleep, when he heard noises from the corridor. He picked out Doctor Dudek's guttural speech and Nurse Szyller's squeaky shoes as they passed by his door.

The footsteps returned not long after to stop outside his room. Hugh closed his eyes, letting his head nod to one side. The door opened.

He felt the doctor lift his arm. For one terrifying moment he envisioned being injected with curare himself, only to relax when the physician's fingertips pressed against the inside of his wrist.

"His pulse is good," said the doctor, "for an old fart."

The door closed. The voices faded.

"For an old fart?" Hugh snorted, removing the nasal prongs. He clambered out of bed to feel the slight shifting of the floor. Not bothered by it, he picked up his wastebasket, found the corridor empty, and walked barefoot down to the last door on the left.

Once inside, he noticed Leszek in the dull light, lying motionless on the bed, his arms tucked close to his body. The old man's eyes were open, unblinking, the pale skin and bloodless lips. Spittle soaked the beard where the hair was darker than the rest.

Hugh came closer, sensing Leszek was awake and watching him from behind the vacant stare.

"We'll soon have you off the ship, old chap," Hugh whispered. "You have my word."

He exchanged the plastic-lined wastebasket with his own and stepped into the corridor.

The floor was shifting even more when Hugh reached his hospital room. He placed a towel on the floor and dumped the contents of the wastebasket on it. He began searching through the discarded blue wipes, gauze, tissue and used cotton swabs.

He was spurred on by soft creak-creaking of Nurse Szyller's shoes. He found what he was looking for, jammed the towel and its contents into his metal locker. He climbed back into bed, pushed the nasal prongs into place, and feigned sleep.

He heard the door open, sensing her putting a pitcher of ice water by the bedside and leave.

Hugh Ashcroft smiled to himself. Mission accomplished.

Stanislaw Jablonski took the moment before dessert to rise from his chair at the captain's table. Both music and chatter faded away.

He launched into his farewell address, in Polish, of his passion for life at sea. Of the hardships and accomplishments at this, the *TSS Casimir III's* final voyage. He switched in the same breath to English.

His heart-felt message to the passengers had ended when the dining room went dark.

The silence was shattered by a wave of servers bursting from the kitchen with trays of baked Alaska held above their heads, the flames of blue and orange dancing in the darkness.

Applause filled the room as the band struck up a medley of spirited polkas. The servers circled the tables, placing down the desserts before the flames died away.

The lights had no sooner come on than both Harm and Thomas saw a junior officer whispering to the captain.

The exchange ended with Stanislaw leaving the dining room.

"That looked serious," said Thomas. "Is he abandoning ship?"

Harm grinned. "I'll be pissed off if he is."

Among those present on the darkened bridge was the baggy-suited ship's river pilot. He was caught in the subdued glow from the surrounding instruments, when Stanislaw arrived and spoke directly to him.

"I understand we are in trouble, Mister Jenkins."

"Yes, Captain. Our weather report shows the wind is steady out of the north-northwest."

Stanislaw gazed out at the bank of dark clouds boiling on the horizon. "You've contacted the weather center?"

"They are aware of it, yes, and the heavy overcast. They tell me it will swing away from us. I beg to differ."

To Stanislaw, the contrary opinion came from a man who had spent a lifetime working this portion of the English coastline.

"I trust your judgment, Mister Jenkins."

"I can almost *taste* it in the air, feel the weight of it pressing down. The roll of the ship is increasing despite the activated stabilizers. Nor have I felt as certain of this weather pattern since the last time the Center made a major cock-up. October, '87. They predicted moderate wind and rain. And what did we get? A bleeding tornado hit us and swept across Europe."

Master of another liner at the time, Stanislaw, remembered the powerful storm, though his vessel was well clear of the English coast when it struck.

He recalled the power of it had been unequalled in more than a century, devastating the coastal regions to sweep along the northwest coast of France and down into Portugal and Spain.

"With all the Center's fancy instruments they have at their disposal," Stanislaw mused, "they expect us to take their word for it."

"God help us, captain, if this is a repeat performance."

Stanislaw stared into the shifting grayness. "How far are we from the Thames?"

"We're approaching the Isle of Sheppey. It should place us within the influence of the estuary at 2300 hours. Don't count on it offering much protection. The river comes with its own hazards. The shipping channel is relatively narrow, and should the storm catch us broadside—"

"Are you suggesting we delay our approach?"

"No. I wanted you to be aware of it. Being where we are now, we should continue."

Stanislaw turned to one of senior men. "The usual precautionary details, Officer Bryla. Cabin hatches secured, safety ropes affixed to the stairways. You know the drill. Without undue stress to our passengers."

Pilot Jenkins breathed easier. "I must warn you, Captain, I have the rather dubious reputation of being a constant worrier."

"In your job," Stanislaw assured him, "I find it nothing less than refreshing."

Nurse Szyller was confronted with her own Sick Bay Catch-22. It was the arrival of passenger Page, for a second time. He was balancing a loaded tray, resting on one hand and his shoulder against the roll of the ship. He walked by, saying nothing.

"You want trouble?" he heard her exclaim as he entered Hugh Ashcroft's room.

The patient pulled himself upright on the bed.

"You're a sight for sore eyes, lad."

"Happy to hear it," said Harm, placing the tray on the mobile trolley. He wheeled it over Hugh's outstretched legs.

"For your eating pleasure, Agent Ashcroft, we offer you shrimp salad *frascati*, cream of turtle soup and *Tournedos Victor Hugo*." He pointed to a carafe of chilled white wine. "Eat up before Nurse Szyller bursts in and confiscate it."

"Over my dead body." Hugh lifted the warming lid off the *tournedos*. He was breathing in the steamy aroma, when Thomas appeared in the doorway.

"How did you get by the Iron Maiden," Harm asked, "without her threatening you with all kinds of abuse?"

Thomas closed the door. "If you're referring to Nurse Szyller, I softened her up with a bottle of Bordeaux red, compliments of the three of us. I also promised we wouldn't be rowdy. Helena's on her way here."

Hugh said, "By the by, chums, I have—"

Helena hurried in, a lab coat pulled over her cocktail dress. She held up an unopened vial.

"I found the antidote," she said, "tucked away in the chief surgeon's office refrigerator, along with several more."

Hugh shoved a hand under his pillow. "I have something for you too, Doctor," he said, pulling out a used vial and explaining where he'd found it.

She read the label, *Tubocurarine chloride*.

"It's a powerful curare derivative," she explained. "The accumulated effect would force the surgeon to inject smaller, more frequent dosages to keep him immobile. A full dose would kill him." She hesitated. "Count on him returning soon to give him another shot."

"We're checking Leszek out of Sick Bay," Thomas said. "On the sly."

Helena told them she needed time to inject him with the antidote.

"It works extremely fast," she warned. "And don't expect him to be much help. He'll suffer from poor motor functions. Slurred speech, apart from being a dead weight. It will also difficult for him to concentrate."

She backed toward the door. "Wherever you hide him, keep him moving. It will speed up recovery." She gave them a cautionary nod before leaving the room.

Hugh took little time in pushing the trolley and untouched meal away, swinging his feet down onto the floor. He shed his hospital gown on his way to the metal locker.

"And where are you off to?" Harm asked.

"No time to lose, lads." Hugh reached inside for his tuxedo pants. "Our immediate problem is removing Leszek from here." He pulled them on. "Then off the ship."

"And *you*," said Harm, "insisting earlier it was a Mission Impossible."

Hugh's shirt came next. "Then we *do* the impossible." He slipped his arms through his suspenders, looping the loose ends of the bow tie around his neck. "I promised the dear old boy we'd do as much for him."

Taking his jacket from the locker, he pointed at his wheelchair. "Use it."

"Nurse Szyller will be pissed off," said Thomas, "to see us wheeling Leszek out of here."

Hugh stuffed his socks in his pocket. "Leave her to me." He slipped his bare feet into the patent leather shoes.

"She'll eat you alive," Harm said.

Hugh steadied himself against the increasing roll of the ship. "I will simply overwhelm her with kindness," he said, stepping into the corridor. "Wait for my signal, gentlemen."

"*Nurse*," he bellowed, the 'overwhelming kindness' already a passing whim.

Nurse Szyller stuck her head out the office door. "*You!*" she stammered as Hugh steamed toward her.

He eased her inside and shut the door. "I am discharging myself forthwith."

She locked her long arms cross her ample chest, trying her best to stare him down. "I won't permit it."

"Why not?"

"Not without proper authorization."

"Horse puckies, Nurse Szyller. Have me sign the release, or I'll hold you legally accountable for letting me walk out of Sick Bay."

"But you can't…" Unnerved, she rummaged through the counter drawers for documents she'd never laid eyes on.

The last evening aboard the *Casimir III* accounted for standing room only in the Grand Lounge festooned with balloons and paper streamers. The dance floor was packed, the noise level aided by laughter and the constant popping of Champagne corks. The roll of the ship was treated good-naturedly with a chorus of *ohhs* and *ahhs*.

Peter Lount, seated alone, barely raised his head when Nicole appeared behind his chair.

"Under the weather, Pete?" she said, looking down at the pale, drawn face. "Have you seen Page?"

Peter shook his head.

Gwen was next, hoping to stir a little life into him. "A fox trot would do you a world of good, Peter dear. It will shake up your—"

Victor joined them. "Will I do, Mrs. Ashcroft?"

Handing the bleary-eyed Peter his half-empty glass of champagne, he waltzed Gwen out onto the dance floor.

"I hope your husband is feeling better. Shortness of breath, was it? A few tests and he'll be good as new." Victor looked her over. "Red becomes you. It brings out a certain… naughtiness."

"I take that as a compliment," she said, enjoying the repartee. "I can only hope my husband's impression of the dress will be as delightful as yours."

"Meaning he won't like it?"

"He has yet to see me wearing it. As it is, I have no idea what he's up to down in Sick Bay. Trust Hugh to find something to distract him—"

Gwen froze.

Victor's dark eyes penetrated deep into hers, searching, she could only imagine, for a hidden meaning…

"Christ," he murmured, taking off across the crowded dance floor.

Harm and Thomas had worked Leszek's unresponsive body into his clothes. After loading him into the wheelchair, they waited by the open door for Hugh's signal.

It came with his muffled voice filling the hallway. "Damn it, Nurse Szyller, I can sign nothing without a pen."

In the stillness of the nursing station, Hugh heard the squish-squish of a wheelchair's rubber wheels rolling down the corridor, and he fumbled in his jacket pocket.

"I seem to have misplaced my reading glasses," he said aloud, hoping to cover any sound from the corridor.

Nurse Szyller took a pen, striking a large "X" at the bottom of the form. She was handing it to him, when the phone rang. She picked it up, barked her name, and thrust the phone at him.

Gwen's voice exploded in his ear.

"I said something to Victor that I shouldn't have, dearest."

Hugh glanced at the nurse with a faint smile. "Don't worry. All's well."

"Whatever I said startled him. I'm certain he's on his way down to Sick Bay."

"Cabin, then." He handed back the phone, signing the release *P.T. Barnum*.

CHAPTER THIRTY-EIGHT
Friday, October 14, 11 PM

Harm parked Leszek and the wheelchair next to the small passenger elevator. He was pushing the UP button when Thomas joined him.

"There's a problem," Thomas said, breathless from running to catch up. "I waited outside Sick Bay for Hugh to make a safe exit. He told me about a call from Gwen. Victor was on the warpath. She thinks he's coming here—"

The empty elevator arrived with a bump and a groan.

"What triggered it?" Harm asked as they maneuvered the wheelchair into the elevator.

"I don't know…Shit."

The large wheels had jammed against the elevator's narrow steel door frame. Unable to wedge it inside, they plucked Leszek's limp body from the wheelchair, carried the half-conscious old man in, and eased him down onto the floor.

Harm stepped out, gave the wheelchair a push down the corridor, and came back inside.

The door rattled closed, and Harm pressed the UP button. "What did Hugh tell her to do?"

"Go to their stateroom, bolt herself in. He'd meet her there. Meanwhile, he'll take what he called a 'recce' to find the best place for moving Leszek off the ship."

The elevator hadn't moved, and Harm pressed the button again. "Then we'll have to—"

Feet pounded on the landing above them. Harm let the button go, counting on the stubborn elevator not moving.

Thomas shifted himself to peer out the elevator's small window as the feet plunged by.

"Was that Victor?" Harm asked.

"Yes, with Nicole."

Harm pressed the button again, holding it there. The elevator came alive with a short, mechanical grunt before making its slow upward climb.

"We'll have Hugh meet us at my cabin."

Thomas made a face. "First place Petrie will look."

"Let's hope not," Harm replied, counting that the elevator wouldn't stop until they reached the Boat Deck level.

Victor stared at the rumpled, empty hospital bed. Nicole, tight-lipped, clutched the door frame as the floor rolled under her. Nurse Szyller stood silent, waiting for Victor's next outburst.

"How could you lose a patient? You *saw* nothing? *Heard* nothing?"

"I was eating my dinner brought from the kitchen." A touch of redness appeared on her cheeks. "I closed the door to have a quiet moment to myself."

"If you're lying—" Victor looked around. Nicole was gone.

The small elevator slowed and shuddered to a stop. The door rattled open onto an empty Boat Deck corridor.

The two men stepped out to stretch Leszek on the carpeted floor.

"Check his pulse, Thomas," said Harm. "I'll be right back."

He joined them, wheeling a laundry hamper half-filled with folded bedsheets.

"Pulse fairly good," said Thomas. "And the hamper?"

Harm glanced down at the old man's ashen face, his haunted, staring eyes.

"Compliments of my steward," he said as they lowered him down among the sheets.

"Should we bump into anyone from the Boat Deck Bar," Thomas said, pushing the hamper along the corridor, "we'll have a lot of explaining to do."

Victor caught up to Nicole, leaning against the wall halfway down the corridor.

"I know Page is behind this, Nicky. He should've known that taking the old man out of Sick Bay could kill him."

Nicole fought to keep from throwing up. "I'm sure Thomas was with him."

"How far can they go? The dead weight alone—"

Nicole nodded to the abandoned wheelchair ahead of them.

Nurse Szyller watched from the Sick Bay entrance as they broke into a run. That bastard Englishman, she knew well enough, had distracted her while the others spirited the old man away. She should report it! Then what?

The problem settled, she went into reception and closed the door. Uncorking the red Bordeaux, she took a drag from the bottle with the pleasant thought of sharing it with no one.

Having returned the hamper, Harm was helping Thomas ease Leszek's arms into a life vest, when Hugh appeared in the doorway. He was dripping wet, his gray hair matted to his scalp.

"The self-inflatable life rafts are scattered on deck in off-white fiberglass containers. Our best bet: the stern, port side." He shook his head, spraying water in every direction. "There must be an alternative to this madness, lads. Gain the captain's confidence—"

Harm shook his head. "With Petrie wagging his credentials under the captain's nose?"

"Swearing we'd kidnapped Leszek," Thomas added, "and put his life in danger."

Harm tossed Thomas a spare vest from the closet. "To saying nothing of Nicole admitting she's with the CIA and backing Petrie up with whatever he tells the captain."

Hugh caught their drift.

Harm moved in close to Leszek. The old man's lower lip hung loose, saliva bubbling at the corners of his mouth. He told him to hold on. He wouldn't have to suffer much longer.

They started along the empty corridor, clutching Leszek's sagging body between them.

The storm caused a concern in the *Casimir's* engine room. "One of the hydraulic units has packed it in, Captain,"

Chief Engineer Niski shouted into the phone, his hands, clothing, and face streaked with grease. "My men are endangering their lives trying to repair the damage."

In the darkened bridge, its windows under assault from the storm, Stanislaw listened with a calmness befitting him.

"I've putting you in an untenable position, Mister Niski. Yet, without more power, we're in danger of running aground. Tugboats are coming, though God knows when they'll reach us."

He had barely hung up when the large ship shuddered. He told his officers to prepare to drop anchors fore and aft, should the ship not have power enough to keep moving.

The vessel's sudden shift caught the three men easing Leszek down with his back against the open railing. Harm and Thomas set off at once to track down a life raft container.

Victor slapped a key card into Harm's stateroom door slot and pushed it open.

The cabin was empty.

"The bastards could've stashed the old guy anywhere, Nicole."

She suggested Thomas's out-of-the-way inside cabin for a start.

Thomas and Harm returned to drop a heavy, bundled inflatable raft on the deck near Hugh and Leszek. They began fumbling with the multitude of clips and straps.

"Steady on," Hugh called out, doing his best to shield the old man from the storm. "Those self-inflatables have a nasty habit of—"

From inside the inflatable's heavy folds came a flurry of loose, rubberized canvas. The two men leapt on the ballooning sides to pin it down. They were not match for the driving force of the wind as it tilted the raft up on end, knocking them down onto the deck.

They watched the full-blown inflatable take flight, veering close to Hugh and Leszek, before slamming into the railing above their heads, and disappearing over the side.

The ship's list to port had little effect on the quiet sobriety of the bridge. Stanislaw sat on his high stool, quiet and concerned, waiting for Officer Bryla to give him what he wanted to hear.

The young officer hung up the phone. "The tugs' ETA is within two hours, Captain. They're finding it difficult to make progress. They want to know if we'd already gone aground. I told them we were holding our own, even after losing an anchor and having a partially-crippled engine."

The phone rang again. Officer Bryla listened and handed it over. "Chief engineer, sir."

"Tell us," he said, "that you've worked miracles, Mister Niski."

"Temporary repairs have been made, Captain, though full power might be a problem."

"Do what you can. And thank your crew." Stanislaw hung up, relieved not all was lost.

Gweneth Ashcroft feared the worst on hearing the knock on the cabin door. "Who is it?" she whispered.

"It's us," came a muffled voice of her husband.

Relieved, Gwen unlocked the door and stepped back. She was shocked as the bedraggled men struggled inside. Harm and Thomas were supporting a semi-conscious Leszek between them.

"Gwen and I will slip him into dry clothes of mine," Hugh said, as they settled him in a chair by the window. "You do the same, lads. Before you catch pneumonia."

They stepped into the corridor, waited to hear the lock click into place, and walked on.

"Me, insisting we'd get Leszek off the ship," Harm muttered. "It was truly insane."

"Don't be so hard on yourself—"

They heard Hugh call out to them from his cabin doorway.

"The antidote is working. Our old friend is mumbling what Gwen and I take for the name *Baranov*."

Harm thought back to several previous conferences, one in Paris and the latest in Copenhagen.

"Leopold Baranov? He's with the Russian Academy of Sciences. A humorless sort, Hugh, but with good intentions."

"I'll have MI6 contact him once we reach Tilbury," said Hugh, closing the door.

Harm shucked off his wet life vest, dropping it in the corridor as they passed his cabin.

"You're not changing?" said Thomas.

"Not until I track down Nicole."

"And then?"

"Talk some sense into her."

"You know she won't listen, Harm. You'll end up with Petrie pushing you around."

"I'll take that risk," he replied, as they reached the small elevator.

"You'll need backup. I'll change into some dry clothes."

They settled on meeting in the Grand Lounge.

Harm eased through the crowded lounge, when a voice confronted him from behind.

"What have you done with Leszek, you despicable sonofabitch?"

He turned to face Nicole. "He was in Sick Bay, the last I heard."

"Bullshit." She looked Harm over. "You're soaked through. What have you been up to?"

"Looking for you—"

"Wait for it," broke in the entertainment officer's voice. "Here by popular demand, it's Men's Choice. Let me see no woman left unattended."

An owl-faced passenger stopped next to Nicole. "A dance, Madame?"

"Bugger off," she said, steering Harm out onto the dance floor.

"I liked you better," Harm said, "when you told us you were with Compdata."

"I liked you better when I'd never heard of you."

The band started with a slow number. She rested a hand on his shoulder, keeping him as far away from her as possible. "You disgust me, by spiriting a sick, dying old man from Sick Bay. Top that with your defecting."

"I'm doing what?"

"Defecting. Taking classified material with you, which includes research on a *war* drug."

"Hey, hold on—"

"You couldn't fully develop it without Leszek's help, isn't that it? Add that to a litany of charges against you. I could hardly believe it when Victor told me."

"I'm sure Petrie is paid handsomely to make up nasty things to say about me."

Nicole stopped, with the music playing on. "You stole unauthorized research material and were supposed to develop exclusively for the Pentagon."

Harm wondered how this could go so terribly wrong. "And you believe that?"

"Why not? You've been lying to me ever since I met you."

"Everyone lies to you, Nicole. You suck it up like a Dyson vacuum." He watched her eyes go dull; a sure sign she was tuning him out.

"You," she said, "turning the war drug application over to the Russians."

Thomas was right. *She wouldn't listen.*

"How would I do that?"

"Lying to me that you're leaving the ship at Tilbury, when you're really sailing on to Gdynia. With Russia a step away."

"Petrie told you that too?"

"He *showed* me the passenger list with those disembarking at Gdynia. Your name was right there, among others."

"Petrie will go to any length to have you on his side. It's called divide and conquer."

"Why would he do that?"

"Because he needs you."

Nicole's face reddened. "That's not true."

"Come to my cabin. I'll show you my ticket marked Destination: London/Tilbury."

"I went to your cabin once, and you nearly broke my jaw."

"For Christ sake, what is it with you...?"

The music faded into another slow tune. Neither moved.

"As for Petrie," he said, "what your buddy wants, your buddy gets."

"Tell him yourself," she said, holding him by the arms.

Harm looked back to see Victor weaving his way through the dancers, his face devoid of expression.

"You've been conned, Nicole," he said as Victor approached. "Worse than conned. You've been drawn into something you tried to avoid from the beginning. When you should've relied on your instincts, your wits. I've seen that in you. Others came along and you broke a bond with yourself. Who? Grosvenor? Your buddy Victor? Too bad, you let yourself down—"

He felt Victor jab something hard into the soft flesh below his rib cage.

"And you, Page, have been busy. Abducting a dying man from Sick Bay, pilfering a flash drive that doesn't belong to you." Victor eased him off the dance floor. "You're soaking wet. Outside, were you? Doing what? Not that it matters. You and I have business to settle."

Nicole trailed close behind. "If Leszek dies, Page…"

"Victor won't let that happen," said Harm. "Nor will he tell you how you've been set up."

Victor nudged him forward. "Wait here, Nicky. I won't be long."

"*Et tu, Brutus*," Harm murmured to her, as Victor pushed him out into the foyer.

CHAPTER THIRTY-EIGHT
Saturday, October 15, 1:11 AM

Victor's handgun was jammed against Harm's ribs, as the little elevator clambered upward. It jerked to a stop at the Boat Deck level.

"I take it that's Nicole's Walther," said Harm, breaking the silence.

"It's my SIG Sauer." He nudged Harm out into the corridor. "Swiss design, German made."

Victor scooped up the life vest he'd passed by earlier and brought it with him. "The mag's loaded with jacketed hollow points. Those slugs rip into a body, exploding into fragments when they hit something solid. Like bone. Very, very messy."

"And here I thought your types stuck to things American. Smith & Wesson. Colt."

"This is my weapon of choice."

They reached Harm's cabin, where the open door was swinging back and forth with the motion of the ship. Victor pushed him inside.

It seemed to Harm like the stateroom had been hit by a hurricane. Mattresses from the twin beds had been slashed to pieces, the foam from it lying in clumps all over the floor. The dresser drawers dumped. Clothes strewn everywhere. Framed prints were torn from walls, and the luggage tossed aside, the lining in shreds.

Harm took a closer look. "It seems the Russians beat you to it, Vic."

Standing behind him, Victor reversed the SIG Sauer and raised it above his head.

"I *am* the Russian," he said, bringing the handgun's grip down hard, angling it between Harm's neck and shoulder.

The blow spun Harm around. He hit the wall and slid down onto the floor, his legs spread out in front of him. Pain surged through his body, his ears ringing. He felt the back of his neck.

"Victor Petrie. The Russian," he said, his fingers coming away covered in blood. "Who'd believe it?"

"I'm Colonel Yury Nikolayev Petrovich. GRU. Military Intelligence. Codename, Tobias. Your American intelligence wanted me dead during the Cold War, but they never quite managed it."

"With the same killer instinct, then. As now."

"Something like that."

Victor picked up the life vest he'd brought with him from the corridor. He sat down on the nearest messed-up bed. "When the Cold War ended on both sides, Russian and American put their differences behind them. I became Victor Petrie, contracted to the Pentagon and other agencies."

"A double agent."

"This project is a US/Russia joint operation."

"Does the CIA know about this combined force?"

Victor shook his head.

"And Nicole?"

"I used her to get at you."

"This is about the war drug."

"What else? Both the GRU and Pentagon had been keeping what you were working on to themselves." He pulled out a Swiss Army knife. "Until you and Poplawski screwed it up by separately researching a similar version of the drug."

"Our research is for peaceful purposes."

"It might've remained that way, had you and your rats not changed everything. The feeding frenzy."

Harm's ears were no longer buzzing as loud. "How did it change everything?"

"You'd invaded the Pentagon and Russian Military Intelligence's turf. They knew you'd discover what they were after, sooner or later." Victor opened one of its blades and poked at the life vest. "Unfortunately, the reality of a war drug makes you and Poplawski expendable."

"Meaning we're 'collateral damage,' along with Boris Yevtushenko, and beautiful, innocent Kimberly Stockwell."

Victor sliced through the canvas and pulled out a handful of foam stuffing.

"What can I say? Curiosity can fuck things up."

"From the look of my cabin, you're still looking for what I expect is the flash drive." He watched Victor pull out another handful. Wouldn't it be easier beating it out of me?"

"That was my intention," Victor looked through what he'd pulled out and dropped it on the floor, "until I found this wet life vest left in the corridor. I thought nothing of it, until I found you in the Grand Lounge with Nicole. Your tuxedo was wet, like the vest. It dawned on me there must a connection…"

"And the penny dropped."

"You could say that." Victor pulled out more stuffing and, with it, came the flash.

Victor held it up. "What a surprise."

Harm noticed traces of gum sticking to it.

Thomas appeared in the Grand Lounge in rumpled cords and a heavy-knit sweater. It caused little concern from those crowding the dance floor. Spotting Nicole dancing with the entertainment office, he joined them and nodded at Filip.

"Where's Harm?" he asked Nicole.

She continued dancing. "How should I know?"

"You just missed him," said Filip, ignoring Thomas's outfit. "He and Victor Petrie left the lounge a few moments ago."

"Together?"

"The two of them, yes." Filip excused himself, knowing it was for the best.

Thomas studied the taut lines of her jaw, the angry eyes, and steered her toward the foyer.

"Where were they headed?"

"Harm's cabin. Victor promised to return something Page stole from me."

"Not the goddamned Walther PPK."

"No. It's…a flash drive."

Victor pulled a burnished blue pistol from the back of his waistband.

"Nicole's Walther," said Harm. "I might've known you stole it."

"I needed a fall guy. You." Victor checked the chamber. "Agent Hagen wouldn't use it anyway. She's way out of practice."

"I'd say once you learn something, you've got it for life. Like getting back on a bicycle."

"Hardly. Killing takes an innate instinct to go for the jugular." He emptied the magazine, shoving the shells into his pocket. "With no second thought, let alone a first one," he said, snapping it back into place. "Our Nicky lacks the mindset. If she ever had it."

"Unlike you, Victor or Yury Nikolayev, if that's what you're called, it's obvious you made a career of wasting people."

"It has its ups and downs. Near misses. When both agencies realized Poplawski was boarding the *Casimir lll* for the return trip home, a cabin was reserved for me."

Harm focused on staying alive. A distraction would help. The briefest of seconds was all he could hope for.

Victor left the Walther on the dresser. "You, showing up, displeased just about everyone. Central Intelligence included." Stepping over the debris, he leaned down to jam the SIG Sauer's barrel against Harm's cheek and dragged him to his feet.

"It's time for you to disembark, Page. Somewhat earlier than expected."

Nicole's mouth formed a bitter, straight line as she and Thomas reached the foyer.

"Harm stole that disk," she said, "after deleting everything from my hard drive."

"To save it from ending up God knows where."

"What the hell does that mean?"

"It means he gave it to me."

Nicole grabbed him by the arm. "Gave you what?"

A flash drive. The one with everything on it."

"Have you checked it? What if it's blank?"

Thomas eased her hand away. "Harm staked his life on that disk, Nicole. He trusted me to deliver it to Langley." He remembered Harm's words. *Should I not leave the ship alive.*

Nicole felt her muscle tighten across her chest. "Delivered to…?"

"Some guy called Grosvenor."

"Fuck," said Nicole, bolting for the staircase.

CHAPTER THIRTY-NINE
Saturday, October 15, 1:32 AM

Nicole slumped against Harm's cabin door, her eyes fixed on the streak of blood down the wall.

"That sonofabitch," she whispered.

Thomas picked the handgun off the dresser and tossed it to her. She caught it. "And don't go into complete denial. You know Harm didn't steal it."

Nicole checked the Walther with a deliberate, effortless motion. The magazine was empty; the chamber as well.

"I had no idea Victor would take it this far."

"Only because you listened to him, and not to Harm who tried to tell you..." Thomas shrugged it off. "We'd better look for them. The stern. Easiest place to dump a body."

Nicole reacted by grabbing a heavy wool shirt from among the scattered clothes and charging from the cabin.

Victor prodded Harm across the slippery Promenade Deck, dodging strewn loose folding chairs driven by the pounding wind.

"Once you're rid of me," Harm shouted, "what happens to Leszek?"

"Overboard, before Rotterdam. The old man leans on the railing to watch the sunset—"

A seaman, wrapped in a yellow slicker and armed with a flashlight, appeared beneath the line of motorized lifeboats on the far side of the deck. Victor pressed the handgun's barrel against Harm's cheek, forcing him back against the flapping tarp covering what remained of the stacked chairs.

They watched the seaman, his body bent against the force of the wind, circled the pool, and dropped down the steps to the lower level.

"With you off the radar," Victor went on, "Nicole has no choice than to back up your defection, despite Moscow denying it."

"Where does that leave The Pentagon?"

"They'll write it off as 'mission accomplished'…"

The seaman returned, fighting his way back across the deck and disappearing inside.

"And you go on your merry way," Harm shouted over the storm, "until you bump off the next poor bastard. Days from now? A week?"

"It depends on the traffic. Besides, I'm only a figment of your imagination, Page. 'Victor Petrie' doesn't exist. Or won't much longer after I scratch you and Leszek from my hit list."

Victor pushed him across the deck, stopping at an open railing opposite the small pool.

"Climb up," he yelled, raising the automatic. "Jump, before I get trigger happy."

"I'm dead one way or the other." Holding onto the upper railing, Harm planted both feet on a lower one. He glanced back at Victor.

"I'm counting on you missing me from there, Petrie."

Victor stepped closer, balancing himself against the roll of the ship.

"I never miss," he yelled, taking the weapon's first pressure.

Wind, buffeting his outstretched arms, pushed the handgun slightly off-target.

Harm hurled himself off the railing, striking Victor chest-high as the handgun went off. Torn free by the impact, it hit the deck and bounced into the dark.

Both men, clutching at each other, stumbled back, tripping over the built-up edge of the swimming pool. They landed on the mesh in a tangle of arms and legs.

Thomas and Nicole reached the Sports Deck. Having heard the gunshot from below, he charged over to the railing, unaware Nicole was no longer with him.

She had hurried down the stairway to the steel door and the Promenade Deck. Putting all her strength behind it, she forced it open enough to wedge her head and shoulders through, and the rest of her before the storm battered the heavy door shut.

On reaching the rain-swept open deck, Nicole kicked off her high heels as she dodged the folded chairs blown helter-skelter along the deck. An errant chair caught her at the ankles, whipping her feet out from under her. She hit the deck, landing on something that jammed against her thigh.

Thomas peered down on what he could see of the deck below. He picked out two shadowy figures trying to free themselves from the pool mesh. One of them had made it, leaving the other struggling while he disappeared under the line of overhead lifeboats cantilevered over the open water.

Thomas moved over to the outer railing where he found the first guy hooking his arms on the gunwale of a lifeboat directly below him. He was struggling to drag himself up, before tumbling down into the lifeboat.

"*Harm?*" Thomas yelled.

He took the second guy for Victor, who appeared out of the mist on the opposite end of the lifeboat. He had lowered himself down on the ribbed flooring and came toward Harm, arms out to keep his balance.

"This is a lousy place to hide, Page," Victor yelled.

Thomas had a leg over the Sports Deck railing, when Victor spotted him.

"I wouldn't do that, Slater," he shouted.

Harm twisted around enough to see Thomas shift his other leg over the railing.

"Petrie's right," Harm yelled. "Don't—"

Thomas jumped, his knees buckling on impact with the lifeboat engine's raised cowling. He toppled out of sight.

"So much for Slater coming to your rescue," said Victor, reaching Harm. He pulled his tuxedo jacket open, nodding at the formal white shirt stained a deep red.

Victor took Harm under the shoulders, dragging him across to the outer side of the lifeboat.

"I told you, I never miss."

He dropped him face down on the narrow gunwale.

"As I've already told you, Page," he said, "it's time for you to disembark—"

Thomas's head appeared above the lifeboat's cowling.

"I wouldn't do that, Petrie."

"Who's to stop me, Slater?"

"I will, Victor," a voice broke over the storm.

Clutching the SIG Sauer in both hands, Nicole rested her elbows on the lifeboat's gunwale while balancing barefoot on the ship's railing below.

"That's my handgun."

"I thought you'd left it for me," she said, strands of loose, wet hair clinging to her scalp and rain splashing against her face.

Harm hooked his good arm on the underside of the gunwale, aware the slightest move would topple him overboard.

Nicole motioned with the handgun. "Step away from him, Vic."

"And if I don't? What will you do? Shoot me?"

"Try me, only if you think you know me well enough."

"It's not in your DNA, Nicky. Or genes. Whatever. Besides, the Pentagon would go ballistic. Your boss would say he'd never again send another woman to do a man's job."

Nicole tightened the grip on the handgun. "That's the crap I'd expect from you. Move away from Harm." She spoke to Thomas without taking her eyes off Victor.

"Free the land line at the stern. Roll it up and toss it to Victor. Stay where you are."

Thomas gathered it up, throwing it to land close to Victor's feet.

"Tie your hands together, Vic. Tight. I'm sure that's no great stretch for you."

"Sorry, Nicky, I can't do it. My Pentagon contract says nothing about tying my hands together. Nor does it have anything to do with the CIA. Or you."

"It has everything to do with the Agency. And me."

Harm fought off a sudden sensation he might pass out. "Petrie's right, Nicole. He has…*executive status* with the Pentagon. To say nothing…of his connection with Russian Military Intelligence."

"Page would say any goddam thing," Victor shot back, bending down to pick up the rope, "to save his sorry ass."

"Such as me telling Nicole your *real* name?" said Harm.

"It's classified, asshole."

"Then I'll *un*-classify it. Colonel Yury Nikolayev Petrovich. Russian Military Intelligence. He's on a joint operation involving the Pentagon. Codename is Tobias."

"*Tobias*? Special Ops would have ID'd him by now."

"Don't tell me Grosvenor never kept anything from you? When he never mentioned how the Russian scientist died. Not at least until Thomas and I badgered you into asking him."

Ignoring him, Nicole shifted her body to ease the pressure on her bare feet.

"It's not about you, anyway," Harm went on, "or Petrie. It's about the Pentagon and Russian Military Intelligence keeping *the war drug* under wraps. They intend to—"

"That's bullshit." Victor cut in. "Give me back my big, nasty automatic, Nicky, before someone gets hurt."

"Do that," Thomas yelled, "and we're dead."

Harm wondered what Victor was up to? Waiting for Nicole to change her mind? Compromise? Lose her concentration? Her footing?

He decided to push Victor. Rattle him.

"Pissed off, are you, Vic?" he said, holding off a wave of nausea. "Because the odds are against you? Nicole holds your handgun. What if she's forced to squeeze the trigger? Thomas and I would testify she had no other choice."

"I won't tell you again, Victor," Nicole shouted. "Move back."

Harm ratcheted it up a notch. "Tell her why you killed Kimberly…"

Thomas picked up the pace. "You broke her neck to make it look like an accident. Then dumped her into an empty swimming pool, you sonofabitch. Among the garbage, rats, and broken glass. In her white cocktail dress, for Christ's sake."

"That's bullshit." Victor took a step toward Nicole. "These bastards are making it up as they go along."

Nicole blinked at the rain. "Stay where you are, Victor!"

"With me dumped overboard," said Harm, "what happens to Leszek? How'd you put it, Vic? The old man leans on the ship's railing, admiring the sunset on the way to Rotterdam—"

Harm gaped in stunned silence as Nicole unconsciously lifted a hand to wipe rain from her eyes.

Victor lunged.

A bluish glow spurted from the handgun's muzzle as twin, ear-piercing explosions erupted in rapid succession.

The slugs tore into Victor Petrie's upper body driving him back, wide-eyed, arms dangling at his side. He dropped down on the gunwale next to Harm.

He stared at his chest, a burgeoning messy red patchwork of torn skin, shattered bone, and strands of fabric.

Without a functioning heart, Victor was aware that blood still in the brain would supply enough oxygen to keep him alive. For what? Another ten seconds?

Nine, eight, seven...

Having dragged herself into the lifeboat, Nicole stood erect, legs apart, silent, the SIG Sauer held in both hands, still aimed at the target.

Six, five, four...

Victor's watery eyes settled on her. The beginning of a smile touched his bloodied lips, sealing some mystical absolution between himself and the woman who had ended his life.

Three, two, one...

With a tilt backward, Victor's feet lifted off the lifeboat floor. He disappeared as the darkness beyond the lifeboat swallowed him up.

Nicole stood motionless, clutching the handgun, her rain-soaked face twisted in agony. With a sudden groan rising from deep within her, she hurled it out over the turbulent, frothy waters of the Thames.

Thomas, having scrambled over to Harm, eased his friend down onto the floor ribbing. He peeled back the tuxedo jacket, worrying over the obvious loss of blood.

A tearful Nicole joined him, slipping a comforting arm under Harm's head.

"The shot we heard earlier, Thomas..." she sniffed.

"Compliments of the late departed. It must've missed a vital organ, or our buddy here would be—"

"I heard that," Harm murmured, his eyes closed.

Thomas got to his feet. "I'll get Helena."

Nicole leaned over, shielding Harm as best she could from the storm.

"I know you're not all right," she whispered. "But please tell me you're okay."

"Just groggy," he said, working on a smile as he drifted off.

CHAPTER FORTY
Saturday, October 15, 2 AM

"The slug passed through the shoulder. Clean, yet causing excessive trauma to the surrounding area. It left a half-moon shaped exit wound…"

Harm, lying in what he took for Sick Bay, recognized Helena's voice. Then Nicole's, asking if he had suffered much.

"Think of being stabbed with a red-hot poker, Ms. Hagen. Yet faced with such unimaginable pain that most of us wouldn't realize we'd been shot."

He heard Thomas next. "How, then, would we react, Helena, when hit like that?"

"Emotion is high, with an intense focus. I'm sure Mister Page experienced it. Pulling himself up into the lifeboat would've been a struggle, with his strength greatly compromised."

Harm wanted to open his eyes, but his body wouldn't cooperate.

"Although Mister Page is stable, there can be residual effects. Sudden headaches. Mood swings over almost losing one's life. As for now, there is nothing more than total bed rest."

Nicole's voice was fading. "That's asking a lot, Doctor Witka…"

Taking someone's life, Harm imagined, couldn't be routine, even for someone like Nicole, who was trained to do it.

How was she dealing with her own emotions? He wanted nothing more than hold her.

But damned if he wasn't…drifting…off again....

CHAPTER FORTY-ONE
Saturday, October 15, 7:45 AM

From the flying bridge of the *TSS Casimir III*, Chief Officer Pawel Klimek surveyed the empty dock of the London Port Authority's Tilbury terminal. Stretched out along the vessel's starboard, the dock itself was connected to the mainland by concrete pass overs leading to several large windowless buildings beyond.

What concerned Officer Pawel Klimek was the lack of activity. It should have been bustling well before now with tractors, trucks, and disembarking passengers.

"No change, Mister Klimek?" said Stanislaw, coming up beside him.

"None, Captain. No gangway, no longshoreman. They must be inside the main building. Or on strike."

"God forbid," said Stanislaw. The ship had broken through the storm not so many hours earlier. He had been relieved when several tugs had come out of the dark to toss them towing lines and help guide the ship upstream to the Tilbury docks.

On the brighter side, the bad weather had moved off, unfortunately, to cause havoc along the Brittany coast.

What followed had been a phone call to him from a Port Authority spokesman. He apologized for the unfortunate delay in disembarking the England-bound passengers. He asked for the captain's indulgence in providing them with a little more time.

No explanation was forthcoming.

Stanislaw turned back toward the bridge. "Let me know when the matter is settled."

"Where will you be, sir?"

"At breakfast, as usual," Stanislaw assured him.

Once in his quarters, the captain called Officer Sotek, asking of Junior Officer Jerzy Olecki's welfare.

"According to Doctor Witka, Captain," was Filip's reply, "he is almost his old self. She wanted him out on deck within the hour for some fresh air."

"And Leszek Poplawski?"

"He suffered from a misdiagnosis, luckily picked up by Doctor Witka."

"That's good news. Have you eaten, son?"

"Not yet. I have a few problems to iron out."

"Nothing serious?"

"Nothing, sir."

"Come up to my quarters when you can. I have far more breakfast than I can handle."

Stanislaw cradled the phone and lowered himself down in the plush leather chair behind his desk. He didn't relish eating alone.

Not this morning.

Ted Grosvenor's mood was glacial at best, having flown into Heathrow in a storm severe enough that later flights had been diverted to Manchester.

What followed was a long, miserable drive down to Tilbury on what Ted deemed was the wrong side of the road, as the English practiced it.

By North American time, *his* time, it was still the middle of the night. After identifying himself to Port

Authority officials, he was left alone in a cramped custom's cubbyhole with a window view of the *TSS Casimir III* berthed not a stone's throw away.

Nor did the room do much to lift his spirits, with its old oak desk, straight-backed chair, and what passed for a British telephone. Following frustrating attempts to master it, Ted was finally put through to Hagen's stateroom.

"Agent Hagen?" he barked into it.

"Mister Grosvenor, of all people. I have a call waiting on your office phone."

"I'm not in my office. I'm here. At the Tilbury docks."

"I had no idea you were coming. In that case, you won't want to miss what's going on soon in the Port Authority terminal building."

"I'm *in* the terminal building."

"That's even better."

Ted could see she was the same headstrong female field operative he'd first laid eyes on during their disruptive initial meeting.

"Assure me, Ms. Hagen, that Doctor Poplawski is none the worse for his transatlantic crossing."

"None, Mister Grosvenor. He's recovered beautifully. Better than expected—"

"Recovered? From what?"

"Take it from me, sir, he's fine. And don't worry about security. British Intelligence has gone to great lengths to have it covered."

"*MI6*, for Christ's sake?" Ted paced the small room, as far as the phone cord would allow. "Only the Russians are supposedly involved. Now the Brits?"

"It's a long story."

"I bet it is."

"Of importance is a flash drive that I guarantee will please you. Oops, duty calls."

The line went dead.

Ted wasn't ready for that. Nor was he happy about being left with no idea what was going on. Cradling the phone, he opened the door to face a youngish man in a navy-blue suit, crisp white shirt, and striped tie. He was slim, athletic. Not a strand of sandy hair out of place.

"Good morning, Mister Grosvenor. I'm Sitwell. MI6. I'm here to ensure you won't find yourself at odds with your surroundings."

"I'm already at odds with my surroundings," Ted grumbled. "You can make amends by getting me on board the *Casimir*."

Agent Sitwell's brown eyes held steady. "Not possible, I'm afraid. And I must add insult to injury by asking you for your Smith & Wesson. 9 mm. For verification only. Issued, from what we gather, by security attached to the American Embassy in London. It's one of those bothersome regulations that haunts us all."

Ted reached inside his jacket, removed the handgun from its clip and handed it over.

Sitwell, packing it away under his belt, led Ted through an adjoining door and down a long, empty corridor.

"You'll be surprised at what's been arranged, Mister Grosvenor."

"I'm counting on it," Ted assured him.

Hugh Ashcroft, in a tweed suit, open Oxford shirt and paisley ascot, was alone in his stateroom. He was staring at the cordless phone, willing it to ring.

Well before the *Casimir* docked, he had reached British Intelligence, explaining, briefly, the outcome of the assignment, along with what he expected from them. He had also dealt with Doctor Witka, who insisted any activity on Mister Page's part could cause undue stress.

"It would also have dire consequences for his all-round recovery," she had told him.

Therefore, he would not be available to take part in the morning media conference. This, Hugh knew, would play havoc with how to deal with the media in less than an hour.

The phone rang at last. Hugh picked it up.

"I expect security to be exceptionally tight down here—" He heard a knock at the door. "Unfortunately, there is change of plans," he said, walking over to open it. "Key personnel handling the bulk of it—"

Harm stood in the corridor in jeans, sport shirt, leather jacket, and his right arm in a sling.

"In actual fact, we are back to full strength," said Hugh, waving him in. "I want it thoroughly understood those involved have put their lives at risk. No telling who might disrupt this media event."

He listened, satisfied. "Full complement? A tactical force as well? Splendid. There will be six personnel. Vetted. Inform the ship's master why the delay, excluding the sordid details."

Hugh hung up, shaking his head. "Who in blazes let you out of Sick Bay?"

"I followed your example," said Harm, adjusting his sling, "by signing myself out."

"And you, pale as a ghost. Doctor Witka must've thrown a fit."

"That will come when she discovers I'm missing. Where's everyone?"

"In Nicole's stateroom. Gweneth, Leszek, Thomas." Hugh paused. "You're feeling up to it, lad?"

Harm managed a grin. "I wouldn't miss it for anything, Hugh."

With British Agent Sitwell at his side, the CIA's head of Special Operations walked into the large barn-like structure echoing with loud shouts and screeching airbrakes. From black SUVs poured men sporting short hair, dark suits, and tan raincoats.

They looked every inch secret service personnel to Ted, in their infinite variety of muted striped ties and telltale earplugs with curly cords disappearing down the back between neck and collar. They were linked, he knew, to a central mobile command post parked nearby.

He was watching a flood of cars and trucks disgorging television types hauling out cameras, myriads of cable, and other equipment. In their wake were camouflaged transports, filled with helmeted soldiers in full battle gear.

"What kind of odd-ball circus is this?" Ted asked.

"A hastily-organized media conference, sir."

Agent Sitwell would say nothing more.

Gathering up his toiletries, Stanislaw brought them over to the open briefcase on his desk. It already contained various files and papers, along with a change of civilian clothes.

His hands were shaking as he packed in his toothbrush, toothpaste, shaving brush, and safety razor. He was adding his dead wife Hildy's framed photo, when his eyes filled with tears.

Torn by anger and frustration, he removed the photo, picked up the briefcase, and flung it across the room. It was still in flight when the phone rang.

Hugh's arrival with Harm in tow was greeted with shocked silence. Nicole was the first to find the words.

"What the hell are you doing here?"

Harm wasn't sure how to answer.

"You should be recuperating in Sick Bay," she said, set to boil over. "But no, you endanger your life, while others here are perfectly capable of handling every little detail…"

Her outburst faded away with Doctor Helena Witka's appearance. She was pushing an empty wheelchair.

Helena was on fire. Had a sudden mood swing driven him from Sick Bay? Was he suffering from a severe headache?

Nicole cut in, suggesting his stubbornness knew no bounds. They both would've gone on, had not Harm ended it with a few sharp comments of his own.

"Get this straight. Poplawski and Page are a team." He nodded at a beaming Leszek. "He and I have gone this far together, and nothing will get in our way." He glanced at Helena. "Admittedly, I could be in better shape—"

"*Better shape*? You're fortunate we didn't have to bury you at sea."

Harm started to speak, but she cut him off.

"There is much more to be done. Checking your vitals. Monitoring for possible infection. Evidence of fatigue. Dizziness. Trauma, high on the list. What if you're still in shock, but unaware of it?"

"I'm fine, Helena."

She looked him over, up and down, side to side, her anger changing to concern.

"I know you're in pain. I'm a doctor, remember? Right now, you feel light-headed, a slight lack of balance or even incoherent thought." She turned to Thomas and Hugh. "Watch for any of these odd behaviors." She paused. "I also insist he use the wheelchair."

"Helena…"

She glared Harm. "You heard me."

CHAPTER FORTY-TWO
Saturday, October 15, 9:15 AM

Helena Witka walked beside him, her unsmiling presence in lab coat and slacks showed her lack of enthusiasm for this parade. What made her feel even worse was a *Casimir* seaman pushing the empty wheelchair behind them.

She was overcome by all the attention: curious passengers swarming the ship's decks; the spectacle of British Special Forces in battle fatigues, helmets and heavy trappings lining the pier.

"If you were *sitting* in the damned wheelchair," she murmured to Harm, "I'd feel better. At the very least, put your arm back in the sling."

In doing so, Harm glanced behind him. Hugh, Nicole, and Leszek were coming down the gangway under military escort.

"And must I remind you," Helena went on, "the assorted pills in the small bottle are color-coded. Pink for nausea. Blue, light-headedness. Yellow, fatigue. They are best taken with water."

Harm stifled a yawn. She had the *fatigue* part right.

"Promise me," she said, "you will have complete bed rest when this is over."

His slight nod did little to assure her that they were on the same page.

They reached the terminal where he gave her a warm, one-armed hug.

"Take care, Helena," he called out as she walked back toward the ship.

Journalists and camera crews packed the room close to a bank of microphones.

Harm and Leszek appeared with Agent Hugh Ashcroft, MI6, retired, who introduced them to the hushed crowd.

Harm's opening remark told of a 'mind-altering drug' based on research he and Doctor Poplawski had been developing separately over the past few years, for peaceful purposes.

"There's no question, certain military liaisons within both the United States and Russia have covered up the existence of this war-drug-in-the-making. And why? I can only imagine it was to keep it solely to themselves. Which meant Doctor Poplawski and I were deemed collateral damage. That and—"

A journalist interrupted. "Are you saying attempts were made on both your lives while crossing the Atlantic?"

"That's why we've called this press conference," said Harm. "To explain the overpowering potential behind what went on. How something of such magnitude could be sidetracked and intended for other than peaceful purposes."

A reporter asked if they were in such danger aboard the liner, were they not now risking their lives by making such news public?

"We've brought to light what we sincerely felt was wrong," Harm replied. "By talking to the media, we are making a concerted effort to save our own skins. Besides, we've only pointed out the collective shortcomings of our respective governments."

"From what you've told us so far, Mister Page," said an American television newswoman, "can we expect you to name names?"

A hum went through the large terminal.

Harm chose his words carefully. "A killer, codename Tobias, who contracted jointly to both the US Pentagon and Russian Military Intelligence, took innocent lives. Including a Russian scientist and a beautiful young wife who, unfortunately, was in the wrong place at the wrong time."

Another reporter asked, "Can you give us a time frame for this incident?".

"Two weeks ago. Saturday, October 1st. The Russian scientist died in a Moscow restaurant, ostensibly from a 'faulty' pacemaker. When, in fact, he was murdered by someone who manipulated his pacemaker."

Chatter broke out among the crowd, giving Harm a moment to catch his breath.

"The same night," he went on, "I was run off the road while driving along the New England coast. I wasn't supposed to survive."

Harm was aware of the increased tension in the room. With it came a feeling his legs might give out under him. Nicole, sensing this, moved in, her arm wrapping round his waist.

"Do you want to call it off?" she whispered.

Harm shook his head. "Any more questions?"

"Can you name the victim in the Moscow restaurant, Mister Page?"

Leszek's voice rose above the hum. "If I may answer. His name was Doctor Boris Fyodorovich Yevtushenko. He was my assistant connected to the Russian Academy of Sciences. A dear, close friend. We can only...hmm," he listened as Nicole whispering in his ear ... "*imagine* he died for knowing too much."

Caught up emotionally in the moment, Leszek went on in hesitant English. "I am honoring his memory...with Doctor Page's help, by continuing...the important research we share...in common."

The press conference ended with both men urging that the United Nations convene a symposium of the world's scientific community, as soon as possible. It would constrict future advances, they said, done in the name of military preparedness.

As Harm and Leszek stepped away from the microphones, an applause echoed through the building.

A smile of approval came from the CIA's head of Special Ops.

"You both better watch your backsides," Ted murmured to himself.

With the official portion of the news conference wrapping up, disembarkation of the two-hundred-odd passengers from the *TSS Casimir III* at Tilbury had begun.

The scientists were delayed by one-on-one interviews; Leszek was taken aside by a small group of Polish journalists based in London.

Harm looked for Nicole and found her coming through the crowd of reporters and camera personnel.

"My boss is here, Harm," she shouted over the racket. "Be kind to him. He's jet-lagged and grumpy. Meaning he hasn't slept in the past 24 hours."

He gave her a lopsided grin. "Grosvenor?"

"He flew in last night." She pointed to him. "The tall guy heading toward us."

"Is that sour look meant for you or me?"

"Who's knows?" she sighed as Ted reached them.

He glanced at Harm while saying to Nicole, "You're full of surprises, Agent Hagen."

"It comes with the territory," she said, introducing him to Harm.

Ted eyed the sling. "I'm amazed you're still alive," he said, looking back at Nicole. "You've piqued my curiosity about a certain flash drive."

"It's safe, sir—"

"Safe with me," Harm cut in.

"It depends who owns such property in the first place," Ted replied.

"Possession is in the hands of the holder," Harm countered, spoken more with humor than fact. "Doctor Poplawski and I are not opposed to cooperating with the authorities, once the US Department of Science & Technology and the Russia's Academy of Sciences get their acts together."

"Which brings up your relationship with the Pentagon, Mister Page. They have a penchant for making life miserable for those who've burned them. They'll be doubly upset when they discover the full impact of what you told the media. It puts them in a shockingly bad light."

"I expected nothing less."

"Not that the bastards don't deserve it," Ted added. "There is a downside. They'll hound you by passing on misinformation. Discredit your research. Not that we can't run a little interference for you."

"I appreciate your change of heart, Mister Grosvenor." Harm grinned. "From the last time, you and I had a difference of opinion."

Ted enjoyed this short exchange. "The circumstances were quite different, but you have a point. We also want you healthy for your revised court date three weeks from now in Los Angeles."

Harm's stray glance at Nicole was returned with an innocent shrug.

"Contact my assistant at Langley. Gerry Smith will set you up with the schedule. Court times, flight accommodation. Per Diem on us. And *win* it. From what I hear, your daughter, Samantha, deserves as much."

"I didn't expect this kind of cooperation."

"No? If it hadn't been for—"

An American newsman interrupted, saying *The New York Times* wanted a photo of him with Leszek. Harm nodded, glanced at Nicole, and disappeared into the crowd.

"Page has balls, I'll say that much for him," Ted said, guiding Nicole to one side. "Gerry sent me a text from Langley, telling me to query rumors Victor Petrie died onboard the *Casimir III*. Set the record straight, Agent Hagen."

"Let's say, sir, there'll be no need for an autopsy."

Ted raised an eyebrow. "A coroner's report will surely—"

"Not if the body has been lost at sea."

"And you expect me to believe that?"

"Probably not. You might change your mind, when I tell you Petrie's codename. Tobias."

"Christ almighty," Ted muttered.

"He was Colonel Yury Nikolayev Petrovich. Russian Military Intelligence, though I wouldn't be surprised that was his cover, his day job. He had many aliases, including *Victor Petrie*. He worked on this mission for both the Pentagon and Russian Military Intel. If not on other occasions as well."

"Who killed him?" Ted asked, thankful that someone ended the sonofabitch's life.

"I can't say, sir."

"I shouldn't have to remind you that all the dirty little secrets come out at such debriefings. Including what the tight-lipped Harmon Page will say. Under oath. They'll rattle both your cages to get at the truth."

"I have no problem with that, Mister Grosvenor, "though I can't speak for Page."

Ted glanced at her. "What is it with you two? Stubborn. Self-willed. Both with an uncanny knack for getting under peoples' skins."

"Me? Not so. Page? I had the same reaction to him. In part because he didn't trust anyone on board. Except Thomas Slater."

"The author."

"Yes, and whatever you might think, sir, Page put his life on the line. Had he not made it off the ship alive, he was depending on Thomas to hand-deliver the flash-drive to Langley. To you, personally. A blank drive ended up in Tobias's pocket."

"About the 'war drug'."

"The flash drive was important enough for Page to keep the Pentagon and Russian Military from getting their greedy little hands on it."

"And keep the drug to themselves, as Page said." Ted covered up a yawn. "God knows who you can trust these days. Which doesn't explain why he wouldn't turn it over to you. He must've known your connection to us sooner or later."

Nicole took a moment to answer. "It was an alternative, which never materialized."

"How so?"

"I… had little faith in him. Particularly after hearing what you'd said about Page during our initial meeting. It sounded something like, ''Cuff him, throw the sonofabitch in the trunk...' "

"You've taken me out of context, Ms. Hagen," Ted replied. "Now, it seems, MI6 has made the arrangements for you and Page to stay overnight in London. You'll fly stateside tomorrow morning. Sunday. The extended debriefing is already scheduled for early Monday morning."

It brought a frown from Nicole. "Has Page been told?"

"Not yet."

"And if he won't cooperate?"

"Let him try wriggling out of a federal subpoena."

"Who's going to tell him? After all he's been through."

"I'm leaving it up to you to break the news to him."

"But sir…"

"You probably know him better than anyone. Suites are booked for you and Page on arrival in Washington. At the Madison."

"It won't work, Mister Grosvenor."

Ted, looking for some clue in her body language, found none. "Why not?"

"We had…unpleasant issues on board."

"Like what?"

"His aversion to doing whatever I asked of him."

Ted shook his head, muttering how *that* was a lame excuse.

Nicole countered with, "Consider the lack of success you had with Page. You couldn't keep him from reaching Montréal, let alone boarding the *Casimir III* in Québec."

Ted shook it off. "Things happen. And should he cause the same sort of problem, drag him home in handcuffs, or a straitjacket, if need be. You've got the authority. Use it."

"But surely—" Nicole saw the 'don't-tread-there' look on Ted's face and gave up.

"You should know, Ms. Hagen, I've put through a directive keeping you attached to our department. Permanently. My assistant is drawing up the transfer papers…"

"I'll think it over."

"No option."

"If I turn you down?"

"Not possible because I'll—"

"Because you'll complain to Willy Novak. The President's chief liaison officer. I've been that route. Besides, he doesn't exist."

Ted's unshaven face broke into a grin. "Who tipped you off?"

"I have my sources."

"I don't doubt it. Now, the debriefing. I want it understood…"

Ted's voice trailed off, distracted by someone smiling not far off and waving in their direction. He noticed the brown suit with a tan overcoat hanging loose over the shoulders. Add the thick, curly hair. To Ted, he seemed vaguely familiar.

"What am I to understand, Mister Grosvenor?"

"The CIA brass will be attending en masse. Along with those connected to the White House. S&T. Reps from all over. Most curious to look at Page in the flesh…"

Ted was preoccupied even more by the attractive woman with him. She wore a snug-fitting suede outfit and a smile that lit up her tanned face.

"…Page's testimony is vital, Agent Hagen, as is yours…" Ted watched the man pass a cell phone to the woman.

Both Nicole and Ted heard a cell phone ringing and pulled out theirs. Nicole pocketed hers. Ted listened, nodded, and shoved it back in his pocket.

"Knowing how you handle things," Nicole quipped, "that's Gerry Smith, your assistant. Assuring you I've already been signed, sealed, and all but delivered to Special Ops."

"You're wrong. It came from Vladimir Lyubimov, Russian FSB. The same big guy with the fuzzy hair coming our way."

"And the woman with him?" she asked.

"It would be his assistant, Olga Tuseva. Will wonders never cease?"

"They're both smiling," said Nicole. "Ms. Tuseva as much as her boss."

"You'll understand why once you meet her. As for the debriefing, I want you and Page in the Bubble on Monday morning. 8 AM. And no fucking excuses."

Nicole, watching him hurry off, was unaware Harm had slipped in beside her.

"Who's the big lug about to wrap Grosvenor in a bear hug?"

"Vladimir Lyubimov of the FSB," she said, pleased to have him with her. "Russian Federal Security."

"And the woman? Stunning, like you."

Nicole smiled. "Something's cropped up, Harm, that needs—"

"No problem, after we say goodbye to the Ashcroft."

They caught up to them waiting in line for a taxi at the main terminal entrance.

"Mark my words," Hugh told Harm over the commotion around them. "After what's happened today, I foresee the United Nations convening a conference on the dangers of war drugs within the year. It will involve both you and Doctor Poplawski. I have connections—"

"Connections," Gwen cut in, "are what lures my husband into trouble." Giving both Harm and Nicole big, warm, teary hugs, she stood back. "You make a gorgeous couple."

Nicole hid her embarrassment by asking about Thomas's whereabouts, as a black London taxicab pulled up beside them.

"He went back on board," said Hugh, "muttering about shedding a writer's block. Cheers," he added as they climbed in.

The Captain Jablonski gazed down from the flying bridge at the unloading of passengers and cargo.

"The tide concerns me, Mister Malek," he said to the officer beside him. "The sooner…"

Something below caught his eye, and, without a word, he hurried back to the bridge.

Harm and Nicole moved through the crowd on the pier, to the echo of the mixed sounds of cranes, the whining of electric move-alls, and the shouts from the longshoremen.

Angus Stockwell, spotting them from the gangway, reached them at once.

"I was thinking something had gone wrong," he shouted, "only to have the authorities admit what I already knew. Kim. Drunk. Diving headfirst into the empty pool."

"She's someone to remember," said Nicole, holding back tears. "For all of us."

Angus clasped Harm's good hand. "The night she turned to you for help…You never let her down." Wiping away his own tears, Angus walked on.

"That Boy Scout yarn you told me about Kim was true, then," Nicole said.

"She was a good person." Harm thought back, stung by what had happened. "How will the authorities handle her murder?"

"Tag it as accidental. They'll find a way to compensate Angus."

"'Compensate' will hardly make up for it. And Petrie's grisly end?"

"Filed under 'death by misadventure'." For Nicole, it was over. Mistakes made. Lessons learned. The debriefing would be the last big hurdle.

"I missed saying goodbye to Thomas," she said. "We still have time to bring our luggage ashore."

"If we can pry him away from his laptop," Harm replied. "I'll bet he's writing a version of what happened aboard the *TSS Casimir III*. The war drug. The Pentagon. Russian Military Intelligence. Fiction based on fact. His specialty."

Harm paused. "Another bestseller. Look, your friend, the captain, is coming our way. I'll leave him to you," he said, wandering off.

Chief Officer Pawel Klimek was called to the purser's office to settle a dispute when passengers on board were clamoring for upgraded cabins.

"Has anyone seen the captain?" he called out, when returning to the bridge.

"I was just with him," replied Officer Malek from the chartroom, "when he hurried off."

Pawel, knowing what the captain was up to, left the bridge at a dead run, arriving at the Promenade Deck. Glancing over the railing, he saw Vladimir hurrying down the gangway packed with disembarking passengers. Taking two seamen with him, Pawel took the same route.

Stanislaw and Nicole heard screams break out behind them. The chief officer was coming their way, his face twisted with rage.

"*Seize him,*" he yelled at the seamen who stared at Officer Klimek in disbelief.

Stanislaw raised his hands, bringing the three up short.

"You are making a fool of yourself, Mister Klimek," he said with quiet concern. To Nicole, "Let Mister Page know, I must apologize personally for what happened during the crossing. Especially after what I've learned from British Intelligence."

He kissed Nicole on both cheeks and guided his chief officer away.

"You are one very stupid individual, Pawel," he muttered, propelling him toward the gangway. "And with such a promising future, you wouldn't want to put it in jeopardy."

"You planned to jump ship," Pawel shot back. "I know that much."

"I couldn't have Madame Hagen leave without saying goodbye."

Above, Chief Engineer Niski watched the two officers walk back toward the ship, the captain gripping his chief officer by the forearm. Henryk was overjoyed, witnessing Stanislaw who, if ever, had changed his mind about deserting the ship.

Junior Officer Jerzy Olecki stood by the Sport Deck, soaking up the bright, warm sunshine. He was watching the vessel's main crane lowering an oblong box onto the pier below, when Doctor Witka found him.

"I'm so pleased with your progress, Jerzy," she said in Polish, leaning against the railing beside him. "The color is back in your cheeks. You walked up from Sick Bay on your own?"

"With breath to spare," he replied, pointing to the wooden box. "That must be Mrs. Stockwell's casket. She was such a good person. Fun. Lively."

This surprised Helena. "You knew her, then?"

"She always had time to talk to me…" Jerzy suddenly stiffened. He moaned and thumped his forehead on the railing. "Oh, God! It's him."

"Who, Jerzy?" she said, wrapping her arms tight around his shoulders.

"He had them…tie my arms, my legs. Garbage bags. They lifted me up. I fought back…and I went overboard. I tasted salt water in my mouth, Doctor Witka, my nose. The propellers…so loud."

Helena fought off her growing anger. "Who did this to you, Jerzy?"

He was whispering now. "The officer… gangway."

Helena peered down to pick out two white uniforms moving up against the flow of disembarking passengers.

"The captain…?"

"The other…"

"*Officer Klimek*? He did this to you?"

Jerzy nodded and pushed his face against her starched white uniform.

"Mother of God, Jerzy. Would you testify to this?"

Jerzy looked up, muttering in English what she took for, "You bet."

Nicole caught up to Harm in the crowd. "The captain was sorry he didn't have a chance to say goodbye." She tucked her hand in beside the elbow of his good arm. "We'd better fetch our luggage before the *TSS Casimir III* sails away with it."

"Didn't I tell you?"

"Tell me what?"

"I'm staying on board."

Nicole, stopping dead, jerked her arm free.

"You're sailing on to Gdynia!"

"No. I'm getting off at the next port-of-call."

"Rotterdam."

"To catch the express train to Paris. A little R&R in the City of Lights. Filip Sotek was kind enough to make the arrangements."

Nicole conjured up the head of Special Ops, who would be waiting early on Monday to debrief them.

She stood back, hands pressed against her hips. "You *can't!*"

"I can't what?"

"Go to Paris."

"Why not? You heard Doctor Witka. I need complete bed rest. No undo stress. She said I might still be in shock, and I don't realize it. The pressure alone…"

"She didn't say that much…"

"Close enough. Where was I? Stay on the Left Bank. Soak up the Louvre, Jeu de Paume." She wasn't listening, and he carried on anyway. "Dine on the *Bateaux Mouches* while cruising the Seine. Quaff a *pression*—"

"It won't happen," she said, louder.

"Montmartre. Pigalle and the Moulin Rouge. The Lolita Club across the boulevard. Very French. Very, very naughty. *Escargots* sautéed in garlic at Café Départ, Place St. Michel…"

"No way, goddammit."

"A relaxing guided tour of the Paris sewers…" He glanced at her fiery eyes. "What am I missing?"

"Grosvenor has set up a crucial debriefing for *this* Monday morning. At Langley. Me *and* you. Any trouble, and I'm to drag you stateside in handcuffs. A straitjacket. Or both."

"A *straitjacket*?" Harm grinned. "You've got yourself in a real bind, Hagen."

"Don't 'Hagen' me, Page. I have the authority to do it. You have no choice."

"No? When we already have reservations on the Left Bank?"

"There's no way in hell—" Nicole glanced at him sideways. "What's with this '*we*'?"

"You and me. At the Hotel Dauphine Saint-Germain." Harm slipped his sling-less arm around her shoulder. "Paris wouldn't be the same without you."

"I…can't," she said, finding herself caught between the proverbial rock and a hard place.

"And what if I'm still traumatized and didn't know it, to quote Doctor Witka. Or worse, I get whacked in a dark alley in Montmartre by some freelance operative contracted by the Pentagon? Just because I pissed all over their parade."

"Now you're saying it's *my* fault."

"No, I'm saying Grosvenor will blame *you* for not following your instincts, something he's been relying on all along. By coming with me to Paris and saving my life."

For Nicole, it was one disaster after another.

"You have no idea, Harmon C. Page, how much shit will hit the fan."

"We'll text him from there. 'Due to circumstances beyond our control…'"

Nicole made a face. "I'll want my old cabin back."

Harm eased her toward the gangway. "It's long gone. Upgrades are a hot commodity, even for the last part of the voyage. Then again, you can always bunk in with me."

"Grosvenor would love that."

"We'll promise him you'll sleep in the other twin bed."

That, she decided, was what she loved about Harmon Page.

His humor, his odd way of looking at life.

They waited at the gangway for the last of the passengers coming ashore. In pulling her close, he felt something solid bump against his hip.

"What's that?"

"Nothing to worry about."

Harm slipped a hand down between them. "We're not taking your Walther PPK with us."

"How else could I protect you?" She took a moment to enjoy how his hand circled her waist and pulled her close. "Besides, you can't have everything your way."

"I can live with that," he said, squeezing her tight with his good arm.

CPSIA information can be obtained
at www.ICGtesting.com
Printed in the USA
LVHW090810200819
628229LV00001B/30/P

9 781949 472783